Three Women and a Boat

'Life-affirming and funny'
Good Housekeeping

'A joy to read'
Culturefly

'Hugely tender'
Yours magazine

'This gentle meander down England's waterways has
a bittersweet meditative charm'
Mail on Sunday

'A tender story of friendship amidst the challenges and
glory of canal-boat life'
Woman's Weekly

'Gentle and charming. A chance to think about
what really matters'
Reader's Digest

A Complicated Matter

'A tender, often wry novel, rendered with
impressive period authenticity'
Mail on Sunday

'Skilful, understated. Comes compellingly to life'
Harper's Bazaar

'Note-perfect. Like a forgotten classic republished by
Persephone Books or Virago'
East Riding magazine

'A touching story full of love and humanity'
Yours magazine

'A beautiful story of love and belonging'
Woman's Weekly

'An absolute delight'
Saga

A COMPLICATED MATTER

Anne Youngson

PENGUIN BOOKS

TRANSWORLD PUBLISHERS
Penguin Random House, One Embassy Gardens,
8 Viaduct Gardens, London SW11 7BW
www.penguin.co.uk

Transworld is part of the Penguin Random House group of companies
whose addresses can be found at global.penguinrandomhouse.com

First published in Great Britain in 2023 by Doubleday
an imprint of Transworld Publishers
Penguin paperback edition published 2024

A CIP catalogue record for this book
is available from the British Library.

ISBN
9781804991862

Typeset in Adobe Garamond Pro by Jouve (UK), Milton Keynes.
Printed and bound in Great Britain by Clays Ltd, Elcograf S.p.A.

The authorized representative in the EEA is Penguin Random House Ireland,
Morrison Chambers, 32 Nassau Street, Dublin D02 YH68.

Penguin Random House is committed to a sustainable
future for our business, our readers and our planet. This book
is made from Forest Stewardship Council® certified paper.

For Paul

The organisation for the transfer of more than 10,000 people is a complicated matter and His Majesty's Government feel certain that you will do your best to assist the authorities and to comply with the instructions which will be issued to you from time to time.

Extract from a notice to Gibraltarian evacuees in London, September 1940

Part One

Gibraltar and Morocco

1

At Home

At first there was the Rock; nothing else. Only the Rock and the sea beyond it, which was like the sky in the place I am now as I write: vast, changeable, terrifying to contemplate and so easy to ignore. It is where I once began and so it is where I will begin this story that you have asked me to set down for you. Even though you cannot read what I am writing. I will put as much of myself on the page as I can, so you will know and understand me, when it is finished and I share it with you. This is what you have told me you want, but it will not be easy for me to do. I am unused to speaking about myself, and I have to be sure I can avoid exaggeration, pettiness and self-righteousness, which would all disgust you. I do not know if I can do it to my own satisfaction, without disgusting myself. But if it will please you, it is worth trying to do, and do well. And I will be able, as I write, to record the ordinary, extraordinary woman who was my mother. So I will start, and then it will be done. With the Rock.

I was born in Gibraltar, in the building where I lived until May 1940 when I was twenty-three years old. I was my mother's seventh child but only the second who lived. She christened me Milagros, which means 'miracle' in Spanish, the language she spoke most often and most fluently. It is not an unusual name, in Spanish. My father spoke English most often and most fluently. If he could have managed it, he would have cultivated a Scottish accent because his surname was Dunbar. He was Duncan Dunbar, and proud of it. My name on my birth certificate might have been Milagros Dunbar, but he called me Rose, and Rose is what I have always called myself. There are few roses growing on the Rock and I did not think to wonder whether I deserved to be linked in this way with a flower that inspires thoughts of beauty and fragrance. I was Rose Dunbar from MacPhail's Passage. A category of one, defined by the family to which I belonged.

My mother never walked again after my birth. She could stand, take a few steps, hobble from one chair to another, but nothing that could truly be called walking was possible, afterwards. The arthritis that gripped and crippled her was not brought on by giving birth to me. It was present in her joints from the time she was the age I was when this story starts. But I was a big baby and dislocated her pelvis as she pushed – and Maria the midwife pulled – me into the world. I was what sent her over the edge from being a woman in pain who managed, despite it, to keep her house and tend to her husband and son, into a woman so severely limited in her movements that my earliest memories are all of my father, giving me my bath, cooking my food, dressing me, hugging me.

By the time I was a teenager I was doing everything that Ma needed doing to keep her clean, tidy, fed. All these being things she could not do for herself. My brother, Jamie, did much of the work in the house with my father's help. We were a household of two women, two men, but the two men did what might usually be described as women's work and the two women were reduced to one unit, like a cart and horse. The cart (Ma) only being able to be of any use with the help of the horse (me). We were not usual. But we fitted in. There was a Dunbar-shaped piece in the jigsaw of life in the back streets of Gibraltar that interlocked with all the other pieces. We were part of the picture, however odd.

My mother was Mercedes Dunbar, and she had a reputation. 'Never a good word to say for anyone', as the women on the street or on the staircases and landings said, talking about their neighbours. If they had known I could hear them, I think it would have made no difference. And of course they were right. There was no softness to Ma, no tolerance. She did not, as I suspect the staircase gossips thought she did, hold herself to be superior to them. It was just that she fought, every day of her life, with pain and the indignities of being dependent on others, and she used all the mental and physical strength she had to keep herself from falling into despair, to avoid letting herself slip into sloth and dirt and self-pity. She could not tolerate those who would not make the effort, small in comparison to hers, to set themselves standards. She had expectations of other people that, if met, were rarely exceeded, and for this reason she did not pay compliments. The most that could be hoped for was that she did not point out the ways in which you had fallen short. The mothers of my friends would often suggest she did not demonstrate any gratitude to me or Jamie or my father, but this was to wish my mother a different person, and I would never have wished that. She was thankful that we were there and able to care for her. If she had told us so, each time we helped her, or even randomly, on occasion, she would have had to be the sort of person who thinks it is important to say only what others want to hear. Ma was not that sort of person. I loved her, which was, I know, a mystery to many. Though loving her did not prevent me from resenting that her distorted limbs had similarly misshaped my life.

My father worked on the docks. Every morning men would come out of the houses and walk down Castle Steps to Main Street to meet a truck with flapping canvas over hoops covering wooden benches. They would climb into the back, grabbing hold of one another's shoulders to pull themselves up, hanging on to the hoops or the edge of the canvas to steady themselves as the truck drove away. My father and the other men in the back of the truck wore overalls that were clean on each morning, filthy by nightfall when the truck rattled back and emptied the men into the street.

'When will you be old enough to go on the truck?' I asked my brother. He might have been eleven or twelve, so I would have been seven.

'I'm never going on it,' he said. 'I mean to have more control over my life.'

Until then, I had thought climbing on to the truck was the pinnacle of achievement, something only men could aspire to, and only the best men. There were others who had jobs in the town, but I assumed these were the ones left behind, like the women, because they were not rated highly enough to be given space on the benches. They worked in shops or on market stalls or in the hotels.

As we talked, I would have been cobbling together the edges of the rips in my father's overalls, or unpicking the hems of my brother's trousers or my skirts to find an extra inch of length to keep the outgrown garments in use for a few months more. We would have been sitting in the alleyway behind the building where we lived. I picture us with our legs crossed and backs against the wall under Mrs Echado's window, me with my wiry curls bent over a piece of cloth and Jamie with his much shorter, sleeker hair bent over his homework.

'How are you going to do that?' I asked, having no idea what he meant.

'Studying,' he said. 'Passing exams.'

I was still thinking of control as a physical thing; I had a notion that it was the unsteadiness of the men in the back of the moving truck that he had in mind.

'How does that help?' I asked, not able to see how reading a book would keep you from falling.

'It means I can get a job where I don't have to wear overalls,' he said.

'What would you wear, then?'

He turned his head from his book to look at my legs crossed under a thin covering of faded, once flowery, cotton frock.

'A suit.'

Almost all the men I saw in Gibraltar wore working clothes or uniforms. Or clothes that announced their religion, or their background.

'No one wears a suit,' I said.

'Teachers do.'

'Are you going to be a teacher, then?'

'No,' he said. 'Because I don't like children.' We would both have laughed at this. Because he loved me, and he knew I never doubted that. I began to doubt my father, though. I was less sure he was the hero I had always thought him.

When Jamie left school he went to work for Mr Mifsud, who had a tailor's shop. It was a clean job. Which was a good thing, since water was scarce and washing clothes was hard. He wasn't a tailor but sat in a back room and did all the paperwork for Mr Mifsud, who was old and wanted to protect his remaining eyesight for the business of cutting and sewing cloth. Jamie was good with figures. But he was not where he wanted to be; he had ambitions for more. For the authority and the respect he knew he could never hope to have. The chance to challenge and to change what seemed to him badly arranged.

The families in the streets around spilled out of their houses and walked up and down, arm in arm, in the evening time, chattering. Out of this crowd first one girl then another would make herself agreeable to Jamie, who had a good job, was good-looking and had a reputation for being safe and solid. When he was twenty-one, he allowed Conchita Macombo to claim him for herself with the sanction of society and the Church. I don't know why he chose her. She was beautiful but restless, and no good at all for anyone's peace of mind. She was like him in that she wanted her future to be better than her past, but in unimaginable, impossible ways. Out of anyone's reach.

I think Jamie decided to marry her for a number of what seem like small reasons which all occurred at the same time – and isn't it often so, that big decisions don't arise from serious contemplation and weighty concerns? A couple of rooms became available. I turned sixteen, left school and had more time to look after Ma; he wanted to be able to sleep with a woman without subterfuge or inconvenience. And Conchita was the girl who was just then holding his arm.

I have considered the sort of girl I was, before May 1940, and how little I thought then about what my life was like and what it might become. Up to a certain age, I believed the world had been created for me; every stone and grain of sand, every sunrise and sunset, every crumb of cake or crust of fresh bread made for me by God, who was more than an idea in our lives. He was a man who lived in the church but just out of sight, behind a curtain, obscured by the bulk of the priest's body, in a dusty nook over our heads. We knew what he looked like, though. He looked like a European, which was not how all the children in my class at school or the men and women in the streets looked, though this did not occur to me at the time. As I grew older, I lost the certainty that God had created a world around me. More than that, I began to think of myself as something tacked on to the edge.

My best friend was Sonia Gutierrez, who lived in the same building. The whole Gutierrez family, all nine of them, were my best friends when Sonia and I were toddling about on the stairs and in and out of each other's rooms, but when we started to go to school together, we became a unit that was separate from either of our families. We remained a unit, even when we were mocked by the other children, who could only see how different we were in appearance. She was small, sleek, agile, quick in everything physical – quick on her feet, to smile, to speak and speak quickly. I was tall and wiry, my light, curly hair a perfect reflection of my body, as Sonia's straight, smooth, glossy black hair was of hers. I was only quick where she was slow, at learning. I would have traded my ability to do equations and read *Great Expectations* without difficulty, just to have Sonia's hair.

It was important to us to remain friends because we were like two halves of a bridge between two shores; each of us could only see the far bank with the help of the other. By listening to me talk, she had a glimpse of the places I knew about from reading.

'How can you bear to read?' she would say. 'Read a word. Then the next word. And so on to the end of the page, then there are more words on the next page and more pages after that, on and on.'

She, on the other hand, knew everything about how to be a real girl in the real streets of Gibraltar. She understood how to have relationships with boys, and with which boys it was safe to have relationships. She understood how to have fun. When I went up and down the streets with her, she would see something happening, or learn of something about to happen, and join in. I would hang back. Sometimes Sonia would let me do this. Sometimes she would not.

'Picnic tonight,' in a whisper. 'In the Alameda Gardens. After your mother's gone to bed. There's a gap in the fence on Europa Road. Don't say you won't.'

It was warm and dark in the gardens, the lights of Algeciras below us, the lit-up windows of the Rock Hotel above. The picnic came from the hotel, leftover food slipped into pockets and bags by the kitchen workers. We spread ourselves out in the calm and beauty of the garden, couples embracing in the shadow of palm trees and clusters of friends speaking in whispers. We might have been part of the vegetation. Had we been caught, our names could have featured in the police court reports in the *Gibraltar Chronicle*, alongside the drunks from Irish Town or the unlicensed cab drivers, but we owned the Alameda Gardens that night.

I was a clever girl. Ursula Gonzalez and I were the clever ones. We won prizes and had our names read out first when students were ranked in order of achievement. I treasured my cleverness because, by this time, I knew I wanted a job, as my brother had, where I would be able to use my brain, not my hands. A job that did not require overalls. But being clever was not enough: I needed to be able to type, so I took a part-time job in Povedano's greengrocery to pay for a course. If I had thought this was what I would do for my whole life, I would have despaired, but it was not a hard job. Every morning, early, I went down to set out boxes of tomatoes and peaches and onions at the front of the store, and every Saturday I served the customers, who were more of a problem to me than the vegetables and fruit because they always wanted to chat, or to complain. I liked Mr Povedano, and his son, Peter, was the most persistent of the young men who had attached themselves to me, out of the group that Sonia gathered around herself. I was not in love with Peter Povedano, but my indifference did not deter him as it had others. He came to be more than a friend to me as none of the others had. He was a sturdy young man, barely as tall as I was, with a round face and a quiet voice and muscles he had built up, working in his father's business, hidden under the shabby, badly fitting clothes he wore.

When I finished the course, I applied for a post in the Garrison Library. It was not a place where I should have felt comfortable; it was somewhere for the men from the garrison to go and read books or play cards or do whatever men do when they are alone together. But I did. This was partly because of the books. The way they covered the walls as if this was a building built with books instead of bricks. Apart from the books I had read at school, my only source had been the Exchange and Commercial Library, which I had been able to join for a subscription of four shillings a quarter, and before I started working I made sure of having the money for it. I was in charge of shopping for the family food and I had learned how to make savings by waiting until the end of the day to buy the fish and meat and vegetables. I knew where there were traders who sold things just a penny or two cheaper, and if this meant I had to walk further, and carry my shopping back up long, hot streets and steep, dusty stairs, then so be it. Jamie did the household accounts and whenever we spent less than we had expected to spend in a month, a share of the savings came to me, most of which went on paying this subscription.

My teacher wrote a reference and showed it to me. I was conscientious, attentive to detail and reliable, she said. In comparison to my classmates, this was true. I was more serious, and the rest of it, than they were. But was this enough? I went to the interview convinced I would not be offered the post, but equally certain that I deserved to be given it. Ma did not believe in false modesty, or in birthright.

'You may not be offered it,' she told me, 'but you deserve to be given the chance. Remember that, and look them in the eye.'

I was interviewed by Mrs Mason-Fletcher, who would be my supervisor, and Major Vereker, who was part of the committee running the library. He wore a uniform and so did she. His indicated his rank in the army, hers confirmed her status in society. It was an effort for me, in my best cotton frock, to lift my eyes above his brass and her pearl buttons, but I wanted this job with a fierceness that had not possessed me before, so I looked at their faces and told them why I was the person they needed. They gave me the job.

Mrs Mason-Fletcher, who was a kindly woman, pointed out to me that, although it was not my job to read the books, it was nevertheless not forbidden to do so, as long as the work was done satisfactorily. I was not allowed to take books home, so I read in my breaks, and added ten minutes to the beginning of my working day and ten minutes to the end. I could not afford the time for more, having still to look after Ma and do my share of the cooking and cleaning and laundry.

With my hours full of tasks and my head full of the stories I was reading in those few minutes when I was not required to do anything else, I was not as conscious of what was happening around me as I perhaps should have been. I relied on Sonia to keep me in touch with life on the streets. She had a job looking after the children of Captain Thrupp, a naval officer who lived in the sort of house Sonia would have liked to live in, so I suppose she had also chosen a career where the setting in which she worked was the embodiment of all her dreams, but was nevertheless not hers to feel part of, only hers to serve.

If I sound bitter it is not because it is in my nature to be bitter; it is because I am my mother's daughter. I do not want to pretend that what is wrong is right. But when I started work in the library, I was not preoccupied with who won and who lost in the hierarchies that kept us in an inferior position. I was too happy to have found myself a job I loved to pay attention to the war that was taking place over the border in Spain, or the rumours of a war in which Britain might fight.

Before I left for work, I would settle Ma by the window that let in the most light, with a drawing board and pencils, charcoal, pen and ink within reach. This was the way she filled the time she had alone with her pain. She drew birds. There was almost no sky visible from our window and it was rare for her to catch sight of a bird, but my father took photographs, and in the spring, when flocks of birds migrated across the Rock, we would hire a cart to take us up to the top and we would sit all day, while she looked and looked and maybe drew a little, but mostly just looked. Then for the rest of the year she would draw from memory and beyond memory, so not all the drawings she did were birds you might recognize. They were all, though, bird-related. When I was a child I had been frightened of the pictures she drew. I could imagine the wicked eye and the evil beak taking flight from the page and perching at the turn of the stairs, half hidden in the darkness. But her drawing was not something she wanted to share and I was able to avoid looking until I became old enough to appreciate the skilled draughtsmanship and to see that the eye, the beak, the wing, the claws were expressions of her own pain.

2

Living with Uncertainty

When war was declared in September 1939, we all held our breath. Then we let it out again as nothing happened. In the history books there will be pages on the preparations made, but this was not taking place at our level, in MacPhail's Passage. We talked, for a week or two, about this new threat to our way of life, but we had no idea what we were talking about and our way of life changed not at all. So while we may have remembered, from time to time, to look up at the sky and imagine a squadron of planes arriving to drop bombs on us, in fact we carried on doing what we always had. I would prepare my mother for the day ahead, go to the library, come home and cook and clean and prepare my mother for the night. I might find time to go out and walk around the streets or to visit a bar with Sonia or with Peter Povedano.

While the war had only been in prospect, Jamie had been made restless by the idea of it. His life in the back room of a tailor's shop, which had never felt like the life he had wanted, was made even more burdensome by the idea of conflict. He wanted to join the army, or the navy, and to go off to fight. Conchita reacted badly to this ambition.

'Why would you do this? Why would you leave me? Is it so

hard to be my husband, to be the father of two beautiful babies, that you want to run off and be killed? What have I done to deserve this!'

My mother was blunt.

'You have responsibilities here. If we are attacked, then you must fight. Until then, you must do what you have committed to do.'

So by the time war was declared, Jamie had stopped talking about going to meet it. He was like the rest of us, leading the life he had led before. But, unlike the rest of us, he was hoping that the war would change everything. And of course, in the end, it did.

'You know, Rose,' Mrs Mason-Fletcher said to me one day, a month or two after the beginning of 1940, 'this work you do won't be classed as essential.'

I thought she was speaking in general, was letting me know that cuts were to be made and the job I felt so privileged to have had been found to be no job at all.

'I'll have to leave, then?' I asked, meaning 'leave the library'.

'Not if you can transfer to essential work,' she said. 'In the hospital, for example. You're a clever girl, you should be thinking about training to be a nurse.'

I could see no connection between working in the library and nursing, but I did not ask her to explain. I did not find it easy to talk to Mrs Mason-Fletcher, even though she was kind, because she wore corsets and make-up and had her hair in a rigid permanent wave and I could not imagine what she saw when she looked at me. So it was only when I took this conversation home and repeated it that my father explained to me that there were plans to evacuate the civilian population. The women, and the children, and such of the men as could be of no use to the garrison.

'Mrs Mason-Fletcher is right,' he said. 'If you applied to do nursing training, you would probably be allowed to stay.'

'Is it real, then?' I said. 'Can they do that? Make us leave? Where would we go?'

'They will tell us,' said Ma. 'They will say that we will not be safe on the Rock. That the Germans will drop bombs and there will be nowhere for us to shelter. They will say it is for our own sake that we have to go wherever they choose to send us.'

'Perhaps they are right, Mercedes,' said my father.

I realized this topic had been discussed between the two of them and I had been oblivious, thinking only of the book I was reading or some idea triggered by the book I had just finished.

'It may not happen,' my father said to me.

'It will,' said Ma.

As the rumours spread, the subject began to dominate conversation. Conchita and Jamie had two sons – Alf was five and Freddo three – and she was three months pregnant with the third.

'How can I be sent goodness knows where?' she said. 'I'm about to have a baby. I need to stay here.'

'That's why you will be top of the list to go,' said Ma. 'The doctors and the hospital will be needed to patch up wounded men, not deliver babies.'

'Well, in that case, anyone who isn't completely fit should be on the list, too.' Conchita lacked the courage to add, as Ma would have done in her place, 'You're a cripple, they won't want you.'

'It might not happen,' said my father.

17

'Perhaps,' said Jamie, 'you might be sent somewhere you could be more comfortable than you are here.' He knew his own wife; if it was going to be better, she would fight to be first on the boat.

'If Ma has to go,' said Conchita, 'Rose will have to go with her.' Everyone looked at me.

'I think so, too,' I said.

'It's a sacrifice you can choose to make. You don't have to make it,' said Ma. 'You could apply to be a nurse. You have had practice.'

'If you have to go, I'll go with you,' I said. I endured the nursing care I gave my mother because she was dear to me; I did not want to do the same for strangers.

The rumours persisted, became more coherent and consistent until we all knew to expect that we would have to leave. I was comforted by knowing that, when it happened, Sonia would go with me. Her mother had died just before the outbreak of war; her elder sister was married to a Spanish man from Algeciras and, though it seemed to Sonia and to me a risky choice to make, they were going back to his home town to 'wait it out', as, Sonia said, her sister had described it to her. We didn't know what Spain would do. Become another enemy trying to kill us, stay out of it altogether or (and this the papers and Sonia's employers deemed unlikely) join in on our side. If we didn't feel safe on the Rock, I would have felt even less safe, as a Gibraltarian, in Spain.

Sonia's brothers and her father had what now turned out to be 'essential' jobs, on the docks or, in the case of her father, Luis, in the kitchen of the Rock Hotel, where there were plenty of people needing to be fed. The Thrupps, Sonia's employers, were due to return to England and nothing had been said about taking her with them. So she would come with me. Then, at the last minute, they told her they could not manage without her. I was devastated, but I have seldom seen her more excited. Like me, she had evaded marriage, even though her family urged her to it, as mine did not. My own failure to chase up the possibilities that presented themselves was to do with an incoherent expectation that this was not my destiny. Sonia's was to do with fun. There was more fun to be had, she told me, reporting yet another proposal rejected, and now was not the time to walk away from it. Now, her fun horizon had just been extended beyond her dreams. She left before we did, and hugged me for so long I had little bruises on my shoulder blades.

On 20 May 1940, the first evacuation notice was posted, requiring all women with children under the age of fourteen to be available for transportation to French Morocco. On 1 June, Conchita, Alf, Freddo, Ma and I boarded the *Mohammed Ali el-Kebir* as the first step of our journey.

3

Leaving the Rock

The rail was wet and after I lifted my hand to my face to wipe away the spray, I could taste salt on my lips. The ship that had seemed the size of a street full of houses was being thrown about by the waves as if it were no bigger than the empty bottles washed up in the surf at high tide. Beside me, my mother sat, as still as the boat was skittish, wearing, as I was, a dress over a blouse and skirt and a coat over the top. So the suitcases on which she sat could have room for a few more of the things we knew we would miss if we didn't bring them with us. She was holding a roll of blankets to her chest and looking to her right, away from, not towards, the Rock. Which neither she nor I had ever left before, except to cross the *campo* into La Línea.

I bent my head and put my face against the chilly, salty rail.

'What are you doing?' Ma asked.

'I don't know,' I said, standing upright again.

'Keep hold of yourself,' she said. 'Look at them' – she made a motion with her head to indicate the people around us on the deck – 'and what do you see? I will tell you. All manner of weakness. I do not expect you to be weak.'

It was true that many of the women on deck were crying,

and making a great deal of noise. Others just looked frightened, held their children and their belongings close. I did not feel like crying and I did not feel frightened; at least, such fear as I felt was not for now, and the future was too unknown for the fear of it to have a shape.

'I won't be,' I said. 'Weak.'

She shut her eyes, briefly. Then opened them again. I turned back to watch the Rock growing smaller. Darkness fell before we lost sight of it.

Ma and I sat side by side on the suitcases, wrapped in the blankets we had brought. Conchita and the boys, all three unnaturally quiet, had created their own island of belongings behind us. The wind was chill, even through our layers of clothing, and there was dampness in the air, spray or rain, it did not matter which. We had to endure it. There were not cabins enough for us all. At some time in the night I fell asleep and woke to the feel of my mother's body pressed against mine, and the sound of the wind and the waves striking the ship, and the smell of vomit.

Ma was awake. I could see the glint of her eyes in the reflection of the ship's lights on the polished metal rails. I had the strange sensation that she was looking after me as a mother might be expected to, but as mine had never been able to do.

'I need the lavatory,' she said. At once we were back in the relationship with which we were familiar.

When we reached Casablanca, we were among the last to disembark. Conchita and the boys had gone ahead, but I waited until there was no risk Ma would be jostled on the way down. I carried the suitcases and dragged the roll of bedding along behind me while my mother walked step by painful step, leaning on the rails, down the gangway. There was chaos in the shed where we, the landed cargo, were being processed. Women behind counters handed out cups of tea while men behind desks tried to sort out where we were to go next. I could feel from the weight of her that my mother was close to exhaustion, nearly at the point of collapse, looking down at the surface beneath her feet as if she knew that, any moment, she might have to slide off the support of my arm and arrange herself as best she could on the stones. Someone – a woman so like Mrs Mason-Fletcher from the Garrison Library that I nearly greeted her by name – found a chair. When a weary while later we were directed to a bus, this same woman said:

'I hope you find somewhere comfortable to live.'

'I'm not expecting comfort,' Ma said.

I was, though, I realized, when we reached the end of our journey and comfort was not what we found. The reports on the first evacuations had made me think we would be going to a hotel, that we would be taken to rooms that were bigger, brighter, better furnished than our own rooms at home. And we would not have to clean them ourselves, or cook our own food. I didn't expect this to last, but I didn't expect the whole strange situation to last. It was temporary.

In the seat behind me on the bus was a woman called Eugenia who had been at school with me. She had married, by now, as so many of my schoolmates had done, and was sitting with a baby on her lap and a toddler leaning against her shoulder. Both the children were asleep, and Eugenia's face was so empty of emotion that I wondered if she, too, had fallen asleep but forgotten to shut her eyes. The front of her dress was stained and damp where her breasts had leaked milk.

'Eugenia,' I said, quietly, 'do you know where we're going?'

She hoisted the baby further up her lap and shook her head.

'Will we ever see Gibraltar again?' she whispered.

'Of course,' I said at once, because I was revolted by her expression of defeat, and because it had not occurred to me that this was anything but a rude interruption of normal life which we ought all to be enduring, if we were not capable of making the most of it, until it was over. Eugenia shook her head again, not looking at me but staring out of the window at the dusty landscape. I turned back to face forwards.

'So you believe that, do you?' said Ma.

'Why?' I said. 'Don't you?'

'No,' she said. 'I'm not sure I will ever see the Rock again. But I'm being realistic. She' – with a jerk of the head towards Eugenia – 'is being emotional. She'll forget to be miserable, soon enough. Whether she goes home or not.'

'And what about me? Am I being stupidly naive?'

'No, you're being optimistic. Optimists are frequently stupid and naive, but as long as there is some basis, however small, for the optimism, you are lucky to be one.'

The bus stopped outside a building that was not a hotel. That piece of optimism was misplaced. There again, we did not have to cook for ourselves. We could not have done so even had we been eager to, for this was not a house of any sort, with the usual facilities for preparing food. It was a dance hall. A rectangle of space with nothing in it but a network of wires over which sheets of cloth had been hung to curtain off cubicles. One cubicle per family, or such was the idea. Into our cubicle we fitted Ma and me, Conchita and the two boys, and Eugenia, following us in a daze of misery, with her baby and her toddler.

It was hot and noisy. There were mattresses on the floor and nothing else. Eugenia sank down, unbuttoned her dress and fed her baby. Conchita's two boys started playing with the sheet walls, rolling back and forth underneath them, lifting and letting them fall. Conchita sat on a mattress and began to unpack her suitcase, looking for something that would make her feel better about the situation she was in – a mirror, I imagine, a lipstick, a jar of face cream. I settled Ma as best I could and went to see where everything we needed could be found – food, lavatories, water.

Food was being prepared in an annexe on the side of the building. The cooks and the people serving it were all locals, but the food smelled good, familiar, and the line of evacuees waiting to receive it was long. I found a row of lavatories in the main building; queues had already formed here, too. There were no showers; mothers were stripping the clothes off their children and standing them in the sinks to sponge them down, then unbuttoning their own dresses to wipe themselves clean. The smell was already close to unbearable. I went back and joined the queue for food, which was being dished up on to metal plates. There was a woman standing beside the serving hatch saying, again and again, that the plates must be brought back. The plates must be brought back. She spoke in French, which I doubt many of those who heard her understood. I carried two plates and a jug of water back to our cubicle; it was all I could manage. Conchita came back with me for more food, and I stood in line while she wandered along the queue talking to those of her acquaintance she could see. Even after a night on a boat, still wearing the same clothes, with the dirt of the journey on her face, she managed to look so much better than the mass of us that she might have been a visiting dignitary come to cheer us as we waited. I think this was the role she was playing, as she walked up and down, barefoot because she had left her shoes in the cubicle, skirt swaying with the swing of her hips, because the people she paused beside and spoke to looked brighter, while she stood in front of them. For a moment, they could have been any crowd at a dance hall, come out to fetch refreshments, about to go back to where the music was playing, ready to dance.

After we had all eaten, I took the plates back and joined the queue for the lavatory. I had no idea what time it was; the day was passing in a curious mixture of urgency and boredom. There was so much to do and yet everything took so long to achieve, and could only be achieved by standing still. There was a Gibraltarian man in our cubicle when I returned. He was shiny with sweat and looked as if he would like to lie down on a mattress and go to sleep and never have to talk to or listen to anyone again. Especially not women like us. He was trying to explain, to Conchita, Eugenia and Ma, that it was up to us to find ourselves better, more permanent accommodation in Casablanca. That there would be help provided to enable us to do this, over the next few days, and also help with claiming the money we needed to live on from the government. Eugenia had obviously only listened to his first few words – 'It's up to you to find accommodation . . .' – and was rocking back and forth repeating all the reasons why, for her, this was impossible. She was exhausted; she didn't know the town; she couldn't speak French; she had a baby to look after. She wanted to stay here, where she felt safe. From time to time the official managed to repeat that help would be available, but Eugenia had found a corner that was not moving, and was therefore better than a ship, and where food was available, and for the moment this was enough. It represented happiness.

Conchita was stroking the mound of her pregnant belly and pouting. Couldn't he find us somewhere, she said, stretching her legs out in front of her, not adjusting her skirt to cover herself. I don't believe the official even looked at her. He had been going from cubicle to cubicle all day; he was beyond blandishment.

'When will the help you suggest is coming arrive?' asked my mother.

'They will be here tomorrow morning, but I must ask you to be patient. We cannot sort out everyone's problems in one day.'

'Obviously,' said Ma. 'You have told us all we need to know.'

He drew himself up a little straighter and looked as if he was remembering that he was an official, and therefore in control.

4

Madame Goncourt

We stayed in the dance hall for three days. It was three days of queuing up and feeling helpless. Inside the hall, the heat, noise and smell were close to unbearable on the first day, but by the third day these had come to feel like just the way it was, and there was no point even thinking about it. Outside the hall was hot and there was nothing to do, no queues to join, so we stayed inside, where it felt safer. By the fourth day, I had been supplied with a list of possible addresses. A young man, so young his upper lip was filmed with a few dark hairs he did not yet have the years to cultivate into a moustache, had circled one of these for me.

'I'd go there, if I was you,' he said, dropping his voice, though it was hardly necessary as the volume of voices around us was so great he could have shouted and been heard by no one but me. 'I think it might suit you.' He gave me a map, marking with a cross where the bus that would be coming to take us into town would drop us off, and the address he thought I should visit first.

The next morning I got up early and washed before the queue had formed. I unpacked a dress I had not worn since I folded it away in Gibraltar and which still smelled of home. Conchita lay on her mattress watching me dress.

'You shouldn't wear patterned frocks,' she said. 'You're too tall. All that fabric – it looks as if you've wrapped yourself in a curtain.' She sat up and ran her hand round her belly. As if she was loving the fact of being pregnant. But I didn't think she was. I thought she only made the gesture for my benefit, to point out to me just one of the many ways in which she was a woman and I wasn't.

I looked round at Ma. I had taken her to the lavatory, helped her wash, dressed her, fetched her some breakfast from the kitchen, and now she was sitting up in the chair I had fashioned from suitcases and blankets.

'She may be right,' Ma said. I had been thinking the same. Conchita was no longer paying us any attention. She had been talking to be spiteful, but that didn't mean she was wrong. She had good judgement, in respect of how to make the most of her appearance.

Alf and Freddo were playing with Eugenia. She was covering her face and pretending she couldn't see them, then jumping in mock fright when they crept up and touched her. Her daughter, whose name was Anna – I had had to ask, as Eugenia only addressed her with a string of diminutive endearments – was sitting on her mother's lap, giggling. As I sat on the bus, I thought how both Eugenia and Conchita had begun to find reasons to be pleased with life. Eugenia in playing with the children, Conchita in having nothing to do that required her to make an effort. Not even looking after her own children. Whereas I had been oppressed by the neediness of my mother, without the comfort of even ten minutes alone with a book. But now my spirits had begun to lift with the thought of a task to be done, something to be accomplished. In the end, we will all find ways of being happy.

As we travelled through Casablanca, I was already chastising myself for having been so oppressed by fears and false expectations on the journey from the ship that I had not taken more note of the town. It was somewhere to marvel over, for someone like me who had spent her entire life going up and down the same streets. This time I noticed the people going about their business for the day, the market stalls, the square, white buildings. When the bus stopped and I stepped out on to the pavement, the very smell of the place was different. I could not have described how Gibraltar smelled, but Casablanca had a scent that was unfamiliar: rich, redolent of strong flavours.

I was not used to maps, and although the address I had been given was only a mile or so away from where the bus stopped, it took me an hour to find it. I did not mind. It was like solving a puzzle that at first sight looks impenetrable, but teasing away at it makes first the overall pattern then the solution plain to see. I enjoyed the challenge, and the feeling of victory in arriving at last at 40 rue de Tangier. There was a massive wooden door in a wall with no windows on the ground floor and I expected the rooms available to be small and dark and mean, but I had not been hopeful, for all the young man's hints that this was somewhere special, for anything except as much space as we had at home, and that would not be difficult to achieve.

I had set my expectations, in this case, too low. 40 rue de Tangier was a beautiful house, owned by a beautiful woman called Madame Goncourt. The other side of the great door was a courtyard shaded by galleries on to which opened the rooms up above. Mme Goncourt invited me to sit with her, on benches covered in embroidered cushions, in the shade, and gave me a glass of mint tea. She spoke to me as if she knew and understood who I was, and had decided before I turned up that she would like me. She began at once to tell me her story, which was short enough, and sad enough. We spoke English; once or twice, lacking a word, she used French, but I had been taught enough of the language by a French nun in the school in Gibraltar to be able to guess at a translation.

Sylvie Goncourt had been born in rural France into a big family and had expected to create, in time, her own big family within which she could live out her days. She had married Jean Goncourt when she was still very young. She chose him because she loved him, even though (or partly because) he was twenty years older than she was. He was a diplomat. Her expectations of a large family house in Franche-Comté were compromised from the beginning. They had travelled. His final posting had been here, to French Morocco, and he had died here a few years since. They had had only one child; the houseful was never to arrive. She brought out a photo of the boy to show me; a teenager promising to become an elegant and handsome man. Only he never did; he was still a teenager when he died in an accident on the quayside, where he had gone with friends to watch a cruise ship depart. A cable had snapped on a crane loading crates. A matter of seconds, which was all the time it would have taken him to walk past, between safety and certain death.

He was buried in the cemetery, as her husband was, in Casablanca. It was impossible for her to leave, now, because all the family she had was here, not living but nevertheless present, as they would not be if she returned to France. She cared little for what went on outside the walls of the house, but she had once spent some time in Gibraltar with Jean, and when she had heard that accommodation was needed for the evacuees, she had thought she should do something.

It was so peaceful in the courtyard, listening to Sylvie Goncourt's precise English, I caught myself thinking I must come back some day when I had time to enjoy the place, as if I was only there for a few days. When, for all I knew, this would turn out to be the place I lived from now on, until I died, an old woman, to be buried in the local cemetery alongside Jean Goncourt and his son.

She showed me the rooms we could use. And there were so many of them that I asked if Eugenia could come too, with her children, knowing she had made no move to find herself anywhere to live. Mme Goncourt actually laughed with delight.

'Of course, of course!' she said.

I arranged a taxi for the following day to take us all to 40 rue de Tangier. The preparations we needed to make were few, but the time was almost not long enough for Eugenia to make a decision on whether to come with us or not. On the one hand, she felt safe where she was, and she and her children were being provided with food. On the other, she would miss Alf and Freddo, and if we went, and another ship arrived, she might have to share a cubicle with someone she did not know. None of the three of us was sympathetic, or helpful. Ma said: 'Just make your mind up,' and no more. Conchita wanted her to come with us as Eugenia had fallen into the role of nurse-maid and that suited Conchita. But the effort of sustaining the conversation was beyond her. Having said, 'You must come,' and 'We would miss you,' two or three times, she had exhausted both her persuasive repertoire and her patience. The same could be said of me. I pointed out the advantages, and repeated them once, then gave up and let Eugenia run up and down the scale of her emotions unchecked. I had decided that she would, whatever we said, come with us, but I might have had the humanity to listen and respond.

She came. We had to take two taxis, the three adult Dunbars in one, Eugenia and all the children in another. The drivers chose different routes which meant we arrived second, and I was worried that Eugenia's English would not be good enough to enable her to communicate with Mme Goncourt, but verbal communication had not been necessary. Mme Goncourt was so excited about the children and Eugenia was so thrilled with the house that they had not progressed beyond exclamations of pleasure, which hardly need knowledge of language to be interpreted.

That first night, we sat at a long table set up in the middle of the courtyard and ate food prepared by Asmae, an Arab cook who lived in the house with Mme Goncourt. She was large and sleepy-looking and spoke French with an accent too strange for me to understand. Conchita's boys, having spent the day running round the house and being spoiled by both Mme Goncourt and Asmae, were tired and badly behaved, expressing disgust at the unfamiliar food and then grabbing the sweet cakes Asmae brought out without waiting to be given one. Asmae, as beguiled by this invasion of high voices and chubby arms and legs as Mme Goncourt, cleared up the food they had thrown to the floor, righted the salt cellar they had knocked over and swept up the salt, put a cloth over the water they had spilled to soak it up.

'You should clear up after your children,' Ma said to Conchita. 'You shouldn't expect others to do it for you.'

She spoke in English, out of courtesy to Mme Goncourt, but Conchita answered in Spanish.

'Can't you see how she's loving it?' she said, nodding towards Asmae. 'The poor cow probably never had children of her own.' Asmae's facial expressions rarely changed but it was true, what Conchita said; she was enjoying herself. 'Anyway, she's paid to do it.'

'But not by you,' said Ma, in Spanish.

'Tonight,' said Mme Goncourt, 'we will be indulgent. We will let our youngest guests eat what they want and we will not chastise them. Tomorrow, we will find out how to live together peacefully.' She looked around at us, smiling slightly, and I thought if anyone could bring harmony to our flawed and fragile group, it would be her.

She had what Ma had never managed to achieve: the ability to make those around her lift their standards in order not to let themselves down in her eyes. Maybe if Ma had not had the pain to cope with, had had the opportunities to travel, and the education, that Mme Goncourt had had, she would have developed the tolerance that would have allowed her to behave as Sylvie Goncourt did, pleasantly, while setting an example by what she said and how she acted that meant those around her thought more carefully about how they presented themselves. Ma commanded respect, but not admiration; Mme Goncourt did both.

I was alert to how everyone involved in this household behaved because I felt responsible to everyone in it for having brought them together: to Mme Goncourt for having deposited these imperfect and often irritating strangers on her; to my mother, Conchita and Eugenia for having introduced them into this environment where they could not feel natural or behave naturally. I was generally alert, at this time. If I kept my attention, all of it, on what was going on around me, I was able to avoid thinking ahead. The future was no more certain now than when we boarded the *Mohammed Ali el-Kebir* in Gibraltar.

Conchita was alert, too, but only to our hostess. She watched Mme Goncourt and copied her. The way she did her hair; the way she used her hands when talking; the way she modulated her voice so that everything she said sounded calm, however sharp (and she could be sharp) the comment. I even thought I could begin to detect a hint of a French accent in Conchita's English.

'She is trying to be like you,' Ma said to Sylvie Goncourt when we were sitting, as Ma did every day, in the shade of the overhanging balconies, drinking the mint tea that had seemed strange at first but now was so much a part of this life we were leading under the Moroccan sun.

'I hope you are not suggesting she is worse because of that?' Mme Goncourt said.

'It is only the outside she copies,' said Ma. 'It changes nothing.'

'It's a start,' said Mme Goncourt.

'She should not allow Eugenia to do all the work while she sits idle,' said Ma.

I felt the same. It had been decided, the first day after our arrival, that Asmae could not be expected to cook for us all and the maid who came in every day to do the other chores around the house should not also be expected to clean up after us. Conchita, Eugenia and I would have to pick up a share of the tasks. As the only one who spoke any French, I had taken on the business of food, going with Asmae, to begin with, then on my own to the market, helping her prepare and serve the meals. I enjoyed doing this; I liked the clamour and bustle of the marketplace, which made me feel, as long as I was in it, that I was part of it. I liked watching Asmae prepare the dishes and learning from her how she did this, and though the food I had cooked at home had been plainer, less spicy, still she wanted to learn from me what dishes would please a Gibraltarian palate. We communicated with the simplest words, without verbs or grammatical formulae, which I would in any case have been unable to manage. Her face was always expressionless and her voice monotonous. Yet I began to understand when she was pleased, when she was uneasy, when she was unhappy. I never saw her cross, or irritated. Even without the barrier of language, I would have found her unknowable.

Eugenia took charge of the children and everything to do with them, their clothes, their cleanliness, their lessons, for Alf should have been at school and Freddo, the brighter of the two boys, was quite capable of learning if it was made interesting, and in this Eugenia showed unexpected abilities. Conchita had agreed to keep the rooms we lived in clean. But her tolerance for dirt, as long as it did not touch her person, was much greater than Eugenia's, or mine, and the truth was that she did almost nothing, but left it to us to sweep and dust when we noticed, as we were bound to do, that it needed doing. The maid, a woman small enough to be a child though her face was wrinkled, also set herself higher standards than Conchita and would hurry through her usual tasks in order to have time to wipe down the stairs up to Conchita's and Eugenia's rooms.

I was not interested in taking Conchita to task over this. She would never, I thought, be any use to have in a house and telling her so had no effect. It did not even make her unhappy to know I thought her useless; she had no interest in my opinion and set no value on usefulness. Ma did not believe in letting what was wrong go unremarked and did tell her she was letting us down, and, because she had the habit of obeying Ma, she would respond by sweeping the dust under the bed before going back to arranging flowers for Mme Goncourt. She was better at arranging flowers, it has to be said, than Ma or I would have been.

Now Mme Goncourt said: 'She is expecting a baby, Mrs Dunbar. Whatever her faults, that is a wonderful thing to contemplate and we should be careful for her health.'

At that moment Conchita came out of the kitchen carrying Anna, Eugenia's daughter, and the sun picked up the gold in her hair, the little girl's legs across her hips accentuated the bulge of her stomach; she was laughing at the child and Anna was smiling back at her. It was a picture of beauty and happiness. I wished I did not know how hollow it was.

Mme Goncourt had the deepest reserves of compassion and humanity, and these had been left untapped following the death of her son and then her husband. She had closed the doors and let no one but Asmae and the little maid in, and while she cared for them, looked out for any treat she could give them, still her tendency to kindness had been stifled. We unlocked it. And we were easy to please because she had something she could give each of us that would bring the greatest pleasure we could imagine. For me, it was books. She had an extensive library and while much of it was in French, she had some works written in English, in the original language. I did not keep a list of what I read, but I have only to remember reading certain books to bring back to me the smell of 40 rue de Tangier, the quality of the light, the domestic sounds, even the feel of the wickerwork chair on which I sat pressing into my thighs. I read *The Great Gatsby*, *The Scarlet Letter*, *Anna of the Five Towns*, *The Romany Rye*. With the help of a French–English dictionary, I managed to read, understand and, finally, appreciate *Le Père Goriot*. That the books I read in Morocco will stay with me is partly thanks to Mme Goncourt, who not only directed my choice but talked to me afterwards about what I had read, deepening and fixing the impression the books had created.

To my mother she gave paints. She had tried her hand at watercolours, she said, and found she had little skill, or at least not skill enough to realize the idea in her mind. Ma had resisted using colour in her drawings before, but when Mme Goncourt demonstrated how watercolours could be used from the palest hint to a rich, layer-on-layer depth of colour, Ma began to experiment. The colours she used were not those that birds would have in nature. But I think they took her to another level of interpretation of the state of mind of Mercedes Dunbar, which is what all her drawings were about.

With Ma, Mme Goncourt made her only mistake. She arranged for a bird in a cage to be delivered, thinking this would be the greatest thrill for Ma; a subject held in front of her for hour after hour, a bird she could observe and reproduce exactly. It was a beautiful thing, the bird. The cage was exquisite, too. White filigree with decorative scrolls around the top and the bottom. Mme Goncourt placed it carefully on the table in front of Ma, smiling in anticipation of her delight.

'That's monstrous,' Ma said. 'I can't bear to look at it.' And she turned her head to avoid seeing the caged creature swaying on its perch.

Mme Goncourt stopped smiling and pulled the cage back towards her as if to protect it, or herself, from Ma's fury.

'You should be grateful for a lovely present,' said Conchita, placing a finger on the bars. 'I'm sure if I reacted like that you would be the first to tell me off.'

'That is true,' Ma said. 'I was impolite, Madame Goncourt, and I apologize. But I cannot bear to see something that has the right to be free denied that freedom.'

'Please,' said Mme Goncourt, 'do not apologize to me. I like it that you are honest and I realize I have made a mistake. I thought you would be pleased to have a bird you could draw from life, but of course you do not need that.'

'It isn't life,' said Ma, taking a quick glance at the bird.

'I will remove it.' Later, Mme Goncourt spent some time looking over the drawings and paintings Ma had done. 'I see now,' she said, 'you are drawing the nature of birds, not the anatomy.'

For Conchita, the gift Mme Goncourt gave was, firstly, attention, but also the loan of make-up, clothes and advice. Mme Goncourt was more stylish than Conchita and she was prepared to share her tips. Given time and access to the same amount of money, Conchita could have ended up the more stylish of the two of them; I don't know if that would have mattered to Mme Goncourt. I admit to feeling it diminished Mme Goncourt a little to be pandering to Conchita's vanity in this way. Perhaps she should have had more discrimination.

But what am I suggesting, by saying that? That kindness should only be shown to those I think worthy of it?

With Eugenia, there was no need for Mme Goncourt to do anything but join her in loving and playing with the children. I thought Mme Goncourt was pretending to kindness she may not have felt naturally in her dealings with Conchita; I could not swear that the same did not apply to the acts of care and friendship towards myself and my mother. But with the children, no artifice, no carefulness, no possibility of a role adopted for the purposes of experiencing pleasure through giving pleasure to others could be supposed. Eugenia, with her slightly plump, round face and untidy clothing, and Mme Goncourt, in her slender elegance, were alike enthralled by each child, from the assertive Alf, to the quiet Freddo, the giggly, clinging Anna and the alternately adorable and wailing baby.

I had never been away on holiday – I still haven't, though so much else has changed for me since then – but I imagine it must be like the weeks we spent at 40 rue de Tangier. I never imagined it would last and yet, at the time, it felt permanent and out of the reach of the war. Mme Goncourt had a wireless, but if she listened to the bulletins, it was when we were out of earshot. All we heard from it was music. She would turn up the sound to fill the courtyard when there was dance music playing, and she and Eugenia, Conchita, the children and I would dance, while Ma sat watching us.

Jamie wrote to Conchita, my father wrote to Ma, and Eugenia's husband, Humbert, wrote to her, with news from Gibraltar. All of them were now working for the garrison in one way or another, but in what way, they none of them said. Their letters were about what they had been eating, the friends they had met, the incidents in the street they had witnessed or heard about, like a stray dog frightening a horse or a cart colliding with an army truck. 'All is well', they were telling us, 'all is as it has always been', even though it wasn't.

If we were not keeping up with news of the war, the citizens of Casablanca were. I noticed that stall keepers who used to smile at me and serve me willingly were becoming surly and grudging, and I thought they must have troubles of their own that were making them miserable because I had not understood that I was an alien. Even though I felt myself to be displaced, to be somewhere I did not belong, I assumed that my significance to them was too small to register. I had not understood the power of an individual to represent a nation and to be hated for this and no other reason.

When a rotten orange struck my shoulder as I left the market, I mentioned it to Mme Goncourt; I had no idea if it had been thrown deliberately and, if so, whether I had been the intended target, but I was shocked enough to tell her of it, and, after that, Asmae went to the market in my place.

'They no longer know who is an enemy and who is a friend,' she told us. 'You must know that France has been occupied by the Germans and a new government is in power. One that supports the Germans. So now the officials here do not know which way to look and the people hear rumours that it is the British who have abandoned them and the Germans who will protect them.'

'We're not British,' said Eugenia.

Mme Goncourt looked uneasy. She turned towards Ma, who nodded.

'We are British,' she said. 'In this family' – she stretched out her hands to indicate Conchita and me – 'we are British.'

'That is what the locals think,' said Mme Goncourt.

This must have been towards the end of June; we had been living in the house for nearly a month and we none of us wanted to believe that there were troubles still to be overcome. I had begun to think that with the journey to Casablanca and the days in the dance hall, the worst was over. As if we would be allowed to stay where we were, in this beautiful building, for months, or it might even be a year, to cement our friendship with Mme Goncourt, before the Germans were defeated and we could sail back, waving our farewells again from the deck, only this time to Mme Goncourt and Asmae and the maid. And Gibraltar would be waiting to welcome us with a few more tunnels dug, a few more buildings put up, but the same, beyond that, as it had always been.

Then, at the beginning of July, the British attacked the French fleet near Oran, round the coast from us in North Africa. Shelled it as if the French were their enemies instead of their allies. More than a thousand French sailors were killed, Sylvie Goncourt told us with tears in her eyes. The ground shifted at that moment. Before, we had been sure of who we were and who our friends were; now this was uncertain, even within the cooling, sheltering walls of 40 rue de Tangier. If we were British, did we therefore support this aggressive action against the French, in which case, could we call Mme Goncourt – French, not Moroccan – our friend? And if we sided with her, then where could we put our feet in the future in the sure knowledge that they had a right to be on the soil on which they stood?

But Mme Goncourt was a diplomat's widow and had spent many years understanding the difference between the citizen and the nation; she knew as we did not how subtle were the judgements made by governments, and that this made the outcomes of those judgements impossible for the people governed to understand and, lacking understanding, to judge in their turn. So she wiped her eyes and told us she had been thinking of the sailors trapped on the ships that had been sunk, of their mothers and sisters and sweethearts left behind in France; that what had been done was beyond us to rule on as right or wrong, and what mattered now was how to keep ourselves safe.

Mme Goncourt may not have been alone in thinking like this, but her view was not widely shared. The French population blamed us. So small a pronoun. So hard to understand who this meant. Not from their point of view. It meant the British, and they had no difficulty in including the Gibraltarians in that category. Despite how little English we spoke, our Spanish names, our total ignorance of the British Isles, which we understood from books and plays and films but not from first-hand experience. But from our point of view, they, the British who directed our lives in almost every way, were 'them'. We were part of 'them' insofar as we were not Spanish. We had observed the chaos of the war in Spain, and taken sides, and been kind to the refugees (never thinking to become one), all the time grateful that we were British and so protected by all the pomp and uniforms and men who spoke with authority in accents we could not emulate.

I know that the British authorities in Gibraltar thought of us, the Gibraltarians, like the monkeys on the Rock, as native fauna. Our right to live there was contingent on us being largely helpful, or at least not an inconvenience. As soon as we became an inconvenience, they removed us. Yet having been born on the Rock and never having lived anywhere else, we did not feel our right to call the place home was contingent on anything. It was ours, although we made no push to take over the running of it, but it did not necessarily occur to us – to people like my father and brother – that we could.

Now, in Casablanca, in July 1940, we were being told we were British, that being Gibraltarian was just some figment of our imagination that had no substance in reality. Now we were having our identity reallocated. I can't say I thought all this at the time, only I was tripped up by those pronouns, 'us' and 'them', and by the realization I no longer understood what they meant.

I am giving my own view here, as I have understood it, in retrospect. It is hard, at the distance of enough years that I am closer to thirty now than to twenty, to be sure if I thought so clearly before I had the chance to know so many people who were not like me. Who made me see and understand what I had not understood before. Before I knew you, and it became important to consider where I belonged.

We had a visit from an official telling us we should make ourselves ready to evacuate Morocco at short notice. That night, under the stars, round the table in the courtyard, there were tears and a circular, aimless discussion. Much like the discussions in MacPhail's Passage before we accepted as inevitable our evacuation from Gibraltar. We had less information now than we had had then. The official had been unable to tell us where we would be going next. Not back to Gibraltar; somewhere else would be found for us where, he was certain, we would be happy and provided with everything we needed.

'We're happy here,' said Conchita. 'We have everything we need.'

'It is likely to become impossible for you to stay,' said the official, glancing sideways at Mme Goncourt. He had tried to position himself at an angle that excluded her from the conversation, even though he spoke in Spanish, which she did not understand.

In the to-and-fro of the conversation that night, we were free with expressing both hope and fear, but we had no confidence that either was real. Mme Goncourt proposed that Eugenia and the children stayed; she would be able to pretend they were her niece and her niece's children, from the Basque region, where Spanish might be spoken. This silenced us, for a moment. I thought, how she loves the children; they are what is important to her. Conchita, who might have been angry at the suggestion she separate herself from her two sons, had a thoughtful look on her beautiful face. Eugenia put her hand over her mouth and shook her head. Ma was the one who spoke.

'Eugenia and Conchita and their children must be ready to return to Gibraltar as soon as they are able to do so,' she said. 'They have husbands who would expect their families to stay under the protection of the Gibraltarian authorities, to go where they are sent.'

'Yes,' said Eugenia. 'I must go back to my husband.'

'Of course.' Mme Goncourt watched the children with such yearning I felt sorry for her, though she was the one with the lovely house, was not being bundled from country to country like a cargo of rotting fruit. 'Perhaps I should have suggested you stay, Mrs Dunbar. And Rose, if she wishes.'

'Rose must leave when she is ordered to do so,' said Ma. 'She cannot stay here, idle. And I will not be parted from her.'

I felt tears come into my eyes – and I do not cry easily – at this so rare acknowledgement that Ma was not just forced by disability to keep me by her side, but wanted to be with me. I saw Conchita and Eugenia looking at me, expecting me to pay a compliment of my own in response to what Ma had said. But I knew better than that. It would have devalued her words to load more words on top.

5

Deportation

We were told to go down to the docks the next morning, a hot, hot morning in July, with our luggage. Asmae went out to find us a man with a taxi or a cart we could hire to take us there, but when they understood the purpose of the journey, none was willing. The little maid went next and came back with a relative, a dark, scowling man with no teeth, and a cart and donkey. We put Ma into it and set out to walk alongside. Mme Goncourt wanted to walk with us, but Asmae, who understood the mood on the street better than she did, talked her out of it. Our farewells were taken in a hurry, with the donkey shifting restlessly in the shafts and the driver, whose name, like the little maid's, I never knew, urging us to move; at least that seemed to be his intention, I don't know what language he was speaking. We turned often, on the walk to the first corner, to catch a last glimpse of Asmae's solidness and Mme Goncourt's elegance, and it was only when we were out of sight of them and looked forwards again that we realized the little maid had slipped out and joined us, and was walking in front of the cart.

As we came closer to the quay, there were other Gibraltarian families dragging their children and belongings, helping the elderly as best they could. The locals passing or standing on the side of the road shouted abuse at us, and we were still some distance from the port when the owner of the donkey cart became frightened of the hostility and the ever-increasing crush of refugees, and refused to go further. We stood, afraid and uncertain, while the little maid argued with him, or so we thought, but it turned out she was negotiating, with all the force and shrillness of an argument. At last he stepped back to the edge of the road, where he could be safely taken for a local seeing off the sailor-murdering British, and the little maid took the donkey's bridle and began to lead it onwards.

When we were close enough to the port for her to walk the rest of the way, Ma stepped down from the cart and asked Conchita to give her the earrings she was wearing. They were only cheap – I knew where Conchita had bought them, in one of the Indian shops on Main Street – but if anyone other than Ma had asked her to give them up, she would have refused. Because it was Ma asking, she handed them over, sulkily, and Ma gave them to the little maid. The maid's young/old face lit up with pleasure and it was to Conchita she turned with her thanks, squeezing out the only English we had ever heard her use.

'Beautiful lady,' she said, 'beautiful lady,' pronouncing the first syllable in the French way and swallowing the end of the first word and the 'y' at the end of the second. It was enough, though, to put Conchita in a good mood, for a short while, at least.

When we reached the port, the contrast with the last time we had been there, on arrival, left no doubt, if we had still had any, that we were no longer considered worthy of any kindness. There were no women offering help and a cup of tea, no tables with officials to check our documents and advise us where to go. The only people on the dock, apart from thousands of our fellow countrymen, were Moroccan soldiers armed with guns which they were using as clubs to force us into a single group penned up against the fence. We were wearing fewer clothes now than we had been on arrival, but still we were too hot, and the longer we stayed there, with nothing to do, nothing to see but other people in the same state as ourselves and the dusty ground, the metal fence, the blue, blue sky, the harder it became to bear.

We could see the funnels of ships beyond the dock gates, and squadrons of scruffy-looking men in French uniforms were brought out and marched past at intervals. They looked at once dangerous and defeated. The tension and hostility were so strong I folded my arms round little Anna, who I was holding on to while Eugenia fed the baby, as if she needed sheltering from the atmosphere as much as from the sun. We waited. And waited.

At last, the gates leading out on to the quayside were opened and there was a surge towards them. We could hear the people ahead of us making a sound between a gasp and a sigh as they stepped on to the quayside, but it was only when we had made sure that the four of us, the four children and all the baggage were still safely together that we had time to look up and see what it was that they had seen. The harbour was full of ships. British ships. The collective sound was one of relief. We were being rescued. Only a day before, we, the Dunbars and Eugenia, had not thought we needed rescuing, but already the events of the morning, the hostility, the rush, the discomfort, had shown us that we did. That Morocco did not want us, and it is dangerous to stay where you are not wanted.

We waited again.

We had fruit and bread and water that Asmae had insisted we fit in, somehow, to our bundles, and were therefore better off than many of the people around us who had expected to be taken straight on board a ship and transported – where? Everyone had formulated a theory, based on rumour and hope, and all their expectations were optimistic; I know this because we fell into conversation with those around us, many of whom I knew, by sight if not by name. Next to us, on the hard, hot stone, was a woman with three small children who lived in MacPhail's Passage and whose shopping I had carried up the steps for her when I met her on the way back from market. Nearby was the mother of a boy I had briefly imagined myself in love with, when I was still at school. I had visited her house, which was immaculate and smelled of cinnamon. Now she was crouching in a heap of badly tied parcels with her two daughters, looking like a refugee. We shared our water among those around us who had none; the adults moistened their lips so the children could each swallow a mouthful. An old woman close to us fainted and more of our scant stock of water was used to revive her. Night fell and we were still there.

Mme Goncourt had given me a copy of *The Adventures of Huckleberry Finn* as we left and I had tucked it into the waistband of my skirt, where it dug into my ribs with every step I took through the town. But when the next day arrived and had to be lived through, it saved me from the boredom that was almost as much of a torture as the hunger, thirst and heat. As I turned the curled, sweat-stained pages, I was able to lift myself off the hard stone of the quay to a boat on the Mississippi, from a nightmare to an adventure. It helped me control the hatred for the indifferent, uncaring soldiers keeping us

penned up like cattle waiting for slaughter, and whatever mas-
ters they obeyed, which might otherwise have overwhelmed
me. As I watched the men patrolling, I remembered seeing a
woman whose husband had been arrested running after the
guardsmen marching him down the streets, tugging at their
clothing, beating them with her fists, cursing and crying and,
as many of the bystanders said to each other, 'making a spectacle of herself'. I had thought her foolish at the time, because
what point was there, when nothing she did or said could
make a difference? But now I understood that it was impossible for her not to behave as she did. I did not run mad and
beat at the soldiers guarding us, because I had Huckleberry
Finn and Ma, who would have told me it was demeaning. But
I understood it might have been possible.

When at last the negotiations were over and the ships were
ready, we were not quick enough, moving up the gangplanks,
to satisfy the Moroccan soldiers. We would not have been fast
enough even if we had not had the children, the bags, the
bundles, and if Ma had been able to walk at a normal pace.
The soldiers who were shoving and striking us needed no
excuse; we were an abomination and they wanted rid of us.
We reached the deck of SS *Dromore Castle*, which was
crowded, but what did we care for crowds, now? There were
seamen moving among us, bringing water and, just as welcome, smiles and kind words. One of them stopped and tried
to comfort Alf, who had gone beyond fretfulness to exhaustion during the wait on the quayside, but had now recovered
enough to be hysterical. The young man's kind attention may
have meant nothing to Alf, but I could see Conchita lifting
herself up to meet it, refreshed by it as much as by the drink
of water. We were all on deck because the holds were

contaminated by the filth of a thousand French soldiers who had been transported in these ships from England. The soldiers we had seen being marched away at the beginning of the ordeal. The stench coming up the companionways was appalling. Only ladders gave access to the area below so, in any case, Ma would not have been able to attempt it.

Towards the end of the day, all the ships had been loaded. The quay we had begun to believe we would never leave was empty. As the convoy sailed out of the harbour, word spread around the deck that we were going home. Back to Gibraltar.

'Don't believe everything you hear,' Ma told Conchita as she announced this as a fact. 'Be cautious.'

But in this case, the voice of rumour was correct. Every face was turned, as daylight came, in the direction of the Rock. Every one of us yearning for the moment when we would first catch sight of its solid, jagged, familiar shape on the horizon. Until there it was. Emotion spread throughout the crowd, audible as a sigh and a muted sound of weeping. We were home.

Soon enough, the news reached us that, though we could see our country, could see our loved ones among the crowd on the dock, could even, in some cases, see the roofs and windows of the houses where we lived, we were not being allowed to land.

We spent two days on the deck, which were two days of much less physical discomfort than those we had spent on the dock at Casablanca. Food was delivered, and it was the food of home. But I found it hard to bear, and I cannot have been alone in this. This time spent waiting to be allowed ashore was like the point at which, having broken my leg jumping off a wall as a child, I was able to leave aside the plaster cast. The day before, I had been a girl with a broken leg; the next day, I imagined I would be normal. I was astonished to find it was not so; I was still weak. The incident of the broken leg was not definitively over, as if it had never been, when the cast came off. I thought of that incident, during the hours within the clasp of the harbour at Gibraltar but out of reach of the land. The shock of the evacuation, the journey, the uncertainty, the breathtaking new experiences had carried me along and, though the future was too opaque to be open to scrutiny, I had always imagined, as I had done when I broke my leg, that when this was over, everything would go back to what had previously been normal. On one day, nothing was as usual, and then on the next day, it would be.

We sat on deck looking towards our houses and nothing happened to suggest I was wrong to hold on to such a hope. What I recognized, though, in those hours, was that the past I had dreamed of going back to was based on a false belief. I believed I had a right to be in Gibraltar. No one better. I certainly had no right to be anywhere else; I think I had known that even before our recent experience in Morocco. Now I knew that this right was granted to me by people who had the power to withdraw it. And if I did not belong here, where did I belong? Who was I? If it does not sound presumptuous for a poor young woman with no position in the world to be asking that question. Although some of them may have been thinking as I was, there were plenty of other people on the deck who did not see that this refusal to allow us to disembark was calling our rights and identity into question. Certainly the mood was one of outrage. 'How dare they?' was the phrase I heard again and again.

'I don't know why everyone keeps saying that,' I said to Ma. 'Of course they dare. What are the consequences for them?'

She nodded. 'The consequences of letting us back in are obviously more serious, for them.'

'When we arrived in Morocco,' I said, 'you told me you did not expect to see the Rock again. Yet here we are. Within sight of it.'

'An unexpected pleasure,' said Ma, with a rare smile. 'But I don't imagine you are fool enough to believe we have returned, never to leave again.'

When they finally let us down the gangplanks, it was, we learned, in response to demonstrations and strikes by the men whose families were being kept away from them, although so close. It was only, we were told, to allow time for the ships that had brought us from Morocco to be made ready to take us somewhere else. For security reasons, we could not be told where this mysterious place might be. If indeed the authorities knew themselves. Whether they did or not, we were told that we would be leaving for it in a matter of days.

Jamie was waiting at the foot of the gangplank when Conchita and the boys came down it. He looked bigger, more hairy than I remembered. He looked like a man when in my head I had him fixed as a young boy. All three of them – Conchita, Alf and Freddo – wanted his attention and I saw that the trick of satisfying any one of the three without upsetting the others would always be beyond him.

My father was there, too. He kissed me and Ma and managed to take from me the burden of much of the luggage as well as the weight of her from my arm.

'You have neglected yourself,' she told him. His clothes

were not clean, and could not have been clean that morning; the hem of his jacket sleeve was hanging down and he needed a shave.

'I have missed you,' he said. 'I've started to sag without you.'

'I hope we'll be here long enough to jack you back up,' she said.

Eugenia's Humbert was a little late in arriving, fighting his way through the crowd to greet her, breathless and excited, as she was, the two of them hugging and kissing each other as if they could never stop, the baby trapped between them, Anna clinging to her mother's legs and the stream of weary, anxious, but, for the moment, happy people flowing round them, smiling.

6

Return Home

I was taking scraps from our meal down to Mrs Echado's dog in the basement, our first night home, when I met Peter Povedano on the stairs. It was dark and I didn't know at once who it was. If there had been more light, I might still have had to pause for a moment to bring him into focus, because he was wearing a uniform. His usual silhouette was defined by the shabby bagginess of the canvas trousers and jacket he wore. Trimmed up in khaki, he was, for an instant, unrecognizable, until he said my name. He came up to the stair where I was standing above him and put his arms round me, kissed my lips. We had gone little further than this in our intimacies before I left for Morocco. I had often felt a sinking sense of emptiness and frustration when he stopped, just as I was wanting him to go on. I might not have stopped him, if he had been bolder, but nor was I capable of encouraging him. We were both restrained, in this as in so many other ways.

'Will you come for a walk with me?' he said.

'Yes,' I said. 'Just let me deliver these scraps.'

I left the empty bowl on the step up to the doorway of the building and we walked down in the direction of Casemates Square. The streets were busy but, despite the disembarkation of the ships, there were many, many more men than women. A solid mass of uniformed bodies, young, pulsing with energy. I kept my hand tucked under Peter's arm and walked close beside him.

'You've joined the forces,' I said.

'Yes. There's no way to be in Gibraltar, now, unless you are part of the forces. Men like your father, who are older, who have skills that are useful to the garrison, they can carry on as they did before. But I began to feel as if I was clinging to a ledge over a steep drop. I don't know if you understand.'

'I'm beginning to think we were always clinging to a ledge, only we never looked down so we didn't realize it.'

'No, no, I don't think so. We belonged here. It was only when you all went, all the women and children, that there wasn't a choice any more. To be a civilian.'

'Will you have to go away and fight?'

'I don't think so. They need men here, to do the work. To make the Rock secure. To fight to defend it, if we need to. Those of us whose home this is, we have somewhere to live. We're easy to keep.'

I strained to hear a note of bitterness in his voice, but he spoke as if explaining a situation it had not occurred to him to judge. But then, I knew the extent of his self-control; he was never one to let his opinions and emotions show.

We had walked as far as Main Street when the sirens sounded. We had had air-raid drills before war was even declared, in the expectation of bombs falling on us, and I assumed this was, still, just a practice, until people around us began to move quickly in the same direction and Peter took my hand and pulled me after him, back up to Willis's Road. It was only when we reached the mouth of the shelter dug into the hillside that I realized the noise I was hearing over the sirens was the sound of aircraft approaching. Then I tried to free my hand.

'I should go home,' I said.

'You should not.'

He kept hold of me and forced me into the dark, noisy interior, where people were jostling for a place on the benches or, failing that, a foot or two of floor space where they could wait out whatever was about to happen. The noise outside increased, the rattle of anti-aircraft guns followed by the deep boom of explosions. Inside, noise dropped away as the squabbles and the speculation were silenced by the realization of real danger. Peter and I stayed standing, quite still, in the middle of the press of bodies.

The guns kept firing and the sounds of planes faded, grew, faded, but there were no more explosions and the collective breath inside the shelter was let out, whispered conversations started, children began to cry and voices called out to soothe or reprimand them.

'I don't know if Ma will have made it to a shelter,' I said.

'No,' said Peter, 'but you wouldn't have made any difference, if you had gone back to help.'

Around us, people we could hardly make out in the light of a few bulbs strung across the roof shifted and settled, and there was space enough for us to be able to sit. The air was cold after the warmth of the evening outside, and I shivered. Peter took off his khaki jacket and wrapped it round me. I leaned against him. There was nothing else for me to lean on.

'Rose,' he whispered in my ear, though the chatter had grown so loud he might have spoken normally and not been overheard, 'I want to ask you something.'

I lifted a hand to my mouth and wiped away a thread or a strand of hair.

'Go on,' I said.

'Will you marry me? Before you leave?'

The shock was so great I jerked away from him and jolted the shoulder of a woman sitting behind us. I turned to apologize and we recognized each other from the deck of SS *Dromore Castle*.

'They were right to send us away,' she said. 'This is what they wanted to protect us from. I hope they get us out soon because until then, I can tell you, I'm not leaving this shelter. Here I am and here I stay. At least it's safe. They were right, weren't they?'

'I don't know,' I said. 'Perhaps.' I was closer to Peter than I was to her, and I was speaking softly.

'Perhaps?' he said, pulling me back towards him.

'Oh, Peter. No. Why are you asking me? I hadn't expected it.'

He took a breath and exhaled slowly; I could feel it brushing my cheek. He picked up my hand and drew his thumb from the tip to the base of each finger in turn.

'Nothing in the future is certain,' he said. 'I mean, it never is, but now, it's as if we're crossing a desert and we know there should be an oasis on the other side, but we can't be sure it's there, and we can't be sure we will live to see it, even if it is.'

'I understand that,' I said. 'But why does that make you think you want to marry me all of a sudden?'

'I've always wanted to marry you,' he said. 'I just didn't think there was any hurry. But now. I feel we need to make a pledge, to believe in the oasis, and to stay alive, so we can reach it.'

'Peter,' I said, catching his restless thumb and holding it, 'I haven't always thought we would marry. I never thought we would.'

I could sense rather than see his eyes peering closely into my face, probing for more information than my words were giving him.

'What then?' he said, his voice low and almost aggressive, in contrast to his normal tones. 'You don't want to marry, or you don't want to marry me?'

Of all the times and places to be having this conversation, there in the chill near-darkness of a tunnel cut into a hillside, with hundreds of people around us and bombs falling outside, might seem the most ill-chosen. Yet it wasn't. In daylight, in a familiar situation, I might have been unable to think through both the implications of what Peter was asking and my own response. But the fact that I could hardly see him, and our situation was so far from normal, brought a sort of clarity to my thoughts.

I knew, all at once, that I had been failing to face the future even before the declaration of war and everything that followed on from it. I had understood my brother Jamie's frustration at the narrow compass of his life, but had thought myself exempt from longing for something beyond what it was reasonable to expect. I was a woman, after all, and my expectations must be lower than his. Yet I had not reconciled myself to the narrow limits of the life of a woman such as me. I had not accepted them as applying, in my case. I had not sought out chances to follow the path to marriage and motherhood, which was the only one open to me. On the contrary. I had avoided it, always resisting intimacy. The very reason I was sitting here now, wearing Peter's jacket, with his arm round my shoulders, was because he had seemed the man least likely to confront me with the precise decision he was now asking me to make: will you be a wife?

I found, in the shelter that night, that I did not know what other future I wanted to fulfil. If I answered his last question honestly, and told him that I would not be rejecting him but the institution of marriage, then what was it that I intended for myself? Because I would be turning my back on good things. Children. Loving intimacy, including sex (which I knew I could have, and had thought of having, without a marriage to sanction it). And for what?

I turned to Peter and leaned my head on his shoulder, the coarse fabric of his shirt with its scent of soap and tobacco pressed against my cheek. I chose to answer only the first question he had asked.

'I haven't made a decision to marry anyone,' I said.

'We have no time,' he said, still speaking with more ferocity and force in his voice than was usual. 'You will go again in a few days. I will lose you.'

'Why should you?' I said, sitting up.

'You will go beyond my reach. I know you too well. You have . . .' he made a gesture of frustration, looking for the words '. . . the ability to see and understand, and wherever you go, you'll be' – another gesture – 'enlarged.'

'Peter,' I whispered, 'Peter, Peter. These experiences might, for all you know, diminish me. Things will happen to me and things, different things, will happen to you, and if we meet in the oasis, after all this, we will not be the people we are now.'

He was silent for a while. And when he spoke again, his words were drowned out by the sound of the all-clear. At once there was a stampede to be out in the open, to be among the first to know where the bombs had fallen. We waited until the clatter had died down. I asked Peter to repeat what he had said.

'I want to be sure of you,' he said. 'I love you. If you won't marry me before you leave, will you promise to marry me when you come back?'

I felt this was a mean thing to ask, pressing me to a promise that I had no idea whether I would want to keep in the impossibly distant future when whatever lay ahead of us was behind us, but I understood his desperation. I was the precious object he wanted to hang on to in the flight from the burning building. I did not blame him for asking.

'I won't marry you before I leave,' I said. 'I will think about the other question.' I knew the answer was no, but I also felt I would need to explain why, and now was not the time.

We walked back to MacPhail's Passage. Everyone from the building had gone down to Mrs Echado's basement and huddled together in her one room. The huddle was breaking up when we arrived, and I helped Ma back up the stairs to our rooms above.

'Peter asked me to marry him,' I said, as I prepared her for bed.

'What did you say?'

'No. At least, not yet.'

'You were right,' she said. So many evenings, as we went through this ritual, she looked weary beyond bearing. But that night she seemed brighter. 'There are paths for you to explore before you decide,' she said.

We were home for two weeks. I went to two weddings, neither of them mine. The brides were both girls I knew from school, and they were rushing into matrimony now for different reasons. Or so I thought, knowing them and watching them as they went through the ceremony, and afterwards, drinking and dancing with their family and friends at the wedding feast, or as close as their parents could come to a wedding feast in those peculiar times.

Amanda was short and plump and apparently cheerful but (I had known her a long time) actually anxious and uncertain. She was marrying a widower, some years older than she was, and watching them together I thought they were giving each other what Peter had been looking for when he proposed to me. Some certainty for the future; some hope that, when it came, their lives after the war would be better and therefore something to look forward to. Amanda cried, intermittently, throughout the ritual, and her new husband, whose name I forget, looked like the image Peter had put into my head of a man clinging to a ledge, only slowly becoming aware that a rope was being lowered to him, and that it was within his reach. I believed in this marriage. It might have been brought about by weakness, but it was a mutual weakness and I had confidence in their ability to be stronger together.

Ma came to this wedding with me, and was critical of Amanda, of her silliness, the shallowness of her emotions and the way she displayed these through excesses of tears and laughter. But I liked Amanda and offered up the goodness that was in her as a shield to Ma's criticisms. Though justified in what she said, I told her, she was wrong in condemning Amanda for being less solid and profound than she was herself.

'You should keep an eye on your tendency towards compassion,' Ma answered me. 'It can lead to excusing the inexcusable.'

'There is nothing inexcusable about Amanda,' I said. Ma's mouth turned down at the corners as she watched the bride struggling to control the unfortunate abundance of her white lace frock.

'Maybe nothing serious,' said Ma.

The other bride was Ursula, my clever classmate, who was marrying Eligio Montez. He had been the focus of many daydreams when we were younger, a representation of the ideal young man, good-looking, confident, a star on the football field. Even I, who did not cherish the same ambitions as my classmates, had wasted a few idle moments wondering what it would be like to walk through doors with his arm around my waist. His status among us was raised even higher when he went to an English university, coming back with the patina of glory he had had before now polished to an even more dazzling brightness by a job in a government office. Soon after his return, he had abandoned all his other flirtatious connections in favour of Ursula. They had been sweeping into rooms together for a year or more before the evacuation to Morocco, which she had avoided or evaded, and she would avoid it again, as Eligio had procured her a job in the foothills of the garrison. I did not know why she was choosing to marry him now. While Amanda, despite her tears, and her husband had both seemed relieved and comforted to be committing themselves in this way, Ursula looked as if she did not care greatly whether she went through with it or not, and Eligio was strangely casual. He had a smile on his lips throughout the ceremony, but it gave the impression of self-satisfaction rather than happiness. He was – and who can blame him? – pleased with himself at all times, but on his wedding day he was like a man holding a set of cards which would be sure to win him the game, when he revealed them. I had not presumed to judge him when we were younger, but since his return from England I had been closer within his orbit, because Ursula was my friend, and I had found him to be too much aware of his own magnificence to be likeable.

I was busy, in those two weeks. I had to do all the jobs in the house that my father had neglected, or been unable, to do, which included cleaning the cooker and the pans, but also mending his clothes, something I could do sitting on the step in the sunshine. Jamie came to sit by me one afternoon. He talked about the job he had in the stores at the docks, and the sort of people he worked among, a mixture of servicemen and some women, the wives or daughters of the rich or well-connected who had chosen to stay on the Rock. He made me laugh, talking about these people, the tensions between the men and the women. The men knew about rank; they expected anyone less senior to do as they were told, and also accepted that they would obey anyone of a rank above. The women didn't have cap badges and braid, but they did have socially acceptable ways of behaving that they understood perfectly. Now these two sets of expectations had come together like waves breaking on the shore, both forces indestructible but each having to change shape under the impact of the other.

'What about you?' I said. 'Where do you fit?'

'You know what they call us,' he said. 'Rock Scorpions. Poisonous little creatures who cling on to the surface. Nobody thinks I am due any respect.'

I put down my sewing. 'You know they're wrong,' I said, 'even if that's true. They may not see you the way you think they do.'

'They hardly see me at all, Rose. I know what you're saying; you're advising me not to become so bitter I begin to believe everyone I meet is treating me with contempt. But just being ignored is diminishing. You know that, officially, you and I are useless mouths?'

'I didn't know that.'

'It's true. That's the way they discuss the Gibraltarians who don't serve any of their purposes. Useless mouths. Like unwanted kittens in a litter.'

I picked up my sewing again and placed a few stitches.

'Nevertheless,' I said, 'they haven't drowned us.'

'No. That would be a step too far.'

'Or perhaps they know we can swim?'

He laughed. 'I think that's the point, actually,' he said. 'We need to have a bit more control over our own lives. Over our own country. Not carry on letting ourselves be tossed about. Look what happened when they said you couldn't disembark from the ships that brought you back from Morocco. We stood up, for once, and said we wouldn't accept the decision, and they backed down. We need to organize ourselves better, speak more clearly, lay out an agenda for what we want to happen.'

'You could be part of that,' I said.

He nodded. 'I intend to be.'

Then Conchita came up the street with the boys, and he stood up to take the shopping bag she carried and hoist Freddo on to his shoulders for the short walk back to their home.

Peter came with me to Ursula's wedding and afterwards we climbed up Queen's Road and sat on a wall looking out across the sea, the sun striking shafts of light off the ripples on the surface almost strong enough to blind us, even at this distance. I had prepared what I would say when this moment of quiet solitude arrived, but I waited to see if he would speak first. The breeze lifted my skirt and he put a hand on it, pinning it to the stones of the wall.

'I'm sorry,' he said, 'about the other night. I shouldn't have said what I did. It was the wrong time. I see that now. It is still the wrong time. It wouldn't be fair to make you promise to marry me when, for all we know, I may be a cripple, after the war. Even if I'm still alive. I've seen the life you lead looking after your mother. You could be promising to take on another such burden.'

I had planned to say, if he had not spoken first, that I would not make a promise to marry at a point in the uncertain future. I was fond of Peter. He was a decent man, not dangerous but not dull. On the way up the hill I had been wondering whether there might be worse fates than marriage to someone who I liked and respected and who would in turn treat me with respect. Until he spoke, I had thought to soften my refusal, not rule out that he could ask me again. His speech, though, filled me with horror. I wasted little time on regretting the way Ma's illness had shaped my life. Where was the point? But when Peter forced me to contemplate a future in which he was the invalid, needing my attention, taking up my time, drawing his energy from my energy and leaving me with none to spare, I knew I could never do it. I knew that, if I ever did commit to marriage, it would have to be to someone I could contemplate serving in this way without bitterness, as I did Ma. Peter Povedano was not that person.

'You mean,' I said, 'that if we pledge ourselves now, we will make ourselves responsible for each other.'

'Yes,' he said.

He stood up and chased away one of the circling apes that was reaching for the strap of the bag at my side. When he sat down again, he said: 'I would like to be responsible for you, one day. I love you.'

I could think of nothing to say in reply, because I could not repeat the words back to him.

'You were going to say no, weren't you?' he said.

'It is "no", Peter. I can't be sure what I want, but I don't want to commit to marriage. Not yet. It would feel like the end of the story. Of my story.'

'That's not how most girls feel.'

'It's how I feel.'

I was sorry for the distance between us as we walked back to the town. I did not want to hurt him, but I was my mother's daughter and I was incapable of saying what I did not mean, just to soothe his feelings. When we parted, he held me for a while and kissed me, and asked me to write to him, with no edge of bitterness. Which meant he had reconciled himself to the conversation in some way, accepting it with stoicism, or convincing himself there was still hope. I did not ask how he felt.

Part Two

London

7

Leaving, Again

When the day came to leave the Rock for the second time, the doors of houses along the street opened and we became, as we stepped out, evacuees again, grouped together with our bedding, plates, mugs, knives and forks at the rendezvous point, surrounded by those who were staying, forbidden to follow us to the port, giving last-minute embraces or instructions or words of encouragement. We had been advised to travel in family groups. Ours was small: Ma and me, Conchita and the boys. Conchita had a mother living, and several younger siblings who would all be in the convoy, but Conchita, a child accidentally conceived while her mother was still at school, had chosen to separate herself, on her marriage, from a family of which she had never felt herself to be a member.

At Waterport, we were loaded on to lighters and taken out to the cargo ships that had brought us from Morocco. Although some secrecy had surrounded our destination, it was understood by the time we set sail that we were going to London. This was enough to cheer Conchita, who had visions of shops such as she had read about in magazines, though how she thought she would be able to afford to shop in them, even if the war had not depleted their stock, I did not know. Her enthusiasm was enough to convince the boys that treats unimaginable lay in store, and they were excited and difficult to control. I was looking forward to seeing the city that features in so many of Dickens's novels, though I did not expect to find the streets and buildings exactly as he described them.

Ma was melancholy. Undetectable to anyone else but obvious to me. This time, I knew, she was even more certain that the Rock that looked over us as we crossed the harbour waters would be lost to her for ever when the ship sailed.

There were sailors, cheerful young men, to help us up on to the deck of SS *Brittany*, and down again into the hold, smelling now of nothing worse than a tang of oil and the slight staleness of air trapped between metal walls. The hold had been divided up with flimsy partitions that gave an illusion of privacy, though even our allotted space was not private. We were with people from our neighbourhood, who were familiar to us. Mrs Echado from the basement of our building, grieving for her dog, left behind in the doubtful care of Luis Gutierrez; and the Molinary family, who lived in the building next door: Lydia and Lydia's children, Maribel and Horace. I would not have chosen this family as travelling companions. Lydia was loud and argumentative; I found Maribel, who was a little younger than me, very dull, and Horace, a schoolboy, rather sullen. As it turned out, though, we were lucky to have Lydia at our side. I had thought her good for nothing except shouting insults from her doorstep, but she proved to be, in these new circumstances a long way from her doorstep, both capable and energetic.

While it was calm, the children were able to go out on deck. Lydia took our soiled clothes – mired with spilt food and the little accidents the children could not avoid – and washed them in the tubs provided, found places on deck where she could fix them to dry in the wind. She offered to do washing for the sailors, who had to dodge the unexpected skirts and nappies hung up in their path, and soon had an efficient laundry service in operation, with a band of helpers, mostly young girls who wanted the opportunity to talk to the sailors, as well as to escape their mothers and younger siblings. They sang, in their improvised laundry room, and the tunes were cheerful, reminded us of home but blended with the constant thrumming of a ship at sea.

As we rounded the top of Spain and entered the Bay of Biscay, the waves began to rise. I knew where we were on this journey thanks to Lydia's son, Horace, who turned out not to be sullen as much as studious. He had got himself a map before departure, and asked each day for an indication of where we were on the big blank area of sea, plotting the points the sailors showed him. They may have been making it up to rid themselves of a tedious child, but this was the point at which we had been warned there was a risk of bad weather. Over the smells of several hundred people living, eating and sleeping in a confined space, the sharp scent of vomit became a constant companion.

A woman went into labour, the cries beginning in the middle of the night when even those hitherto convinced they were dying from seasickness had finally fallen asleep. There was no doctor on board, but a sailor with first-aid training was sent to help. The women, with Lydia in the forefront wearing a sheet like a toga to protect her clothes, told him to go back to bed.

'We'll let you know if we need you,' she said. Her daughter translated this into English and the sailor, a young man whose head and face were both red, looked relieved.

For the rest of the night I could hear the woman panting and crying out, sometimes in my dreams as I slept despite myself, more often through long, wakeful hours. Conchita rolled herself closer to me in her cocoon of blankets.

'What are you thinking, sister-in-law?' she whispered. 'That you're well out of it, this messy business of giving birth, or wishing that was you with a baby coming?'

'I'm glad it's not me, at this very moment,' I said. 'There must be more comfortable places to give birth.'

'It is never comfortable,' she said, a sneer in her voice.

'More private, then,' I said. 'You must be glad your baby isn't due until after we arrive.'

'I just want it done with,' she said. 'All of it. The travelling and the baby and the not knowing where exactly we are going or how we are going to live.'

Conchita's moods had been fluctuating during the time on board. She was still excited about going to London, but as the other pretty girls had been enjoying themselves flirting with the sailors, her swollen belly had begun to aggravate her and resentment had made her fractious.

'We managed well in Casablanca,' I said.

'That doesn't mean anything,' she said. 'We were lucky once. So what? It doesn't follow that we'll be lucky again.'

Which, it struck me, was something Ma might have said, in response to the kind of meaningless phrase I had used, and was obviously true. I turned my head towards where Ma slept on a mattress on the other side of me. She appeared to be asleep. I thought of all the times she had been through this pain and effort with no baby to care for at the end of it, and crossed my fingers under the blanket, wishing for this not to be the fate of the mother labouring so noisily behind her screen of attendant women. How bad an omen would that seem, to a ship full of the displaced. And the superstitious.

Just after daybreak (which we only knew had arrived, in our windowless hold, because we had become familiar with the clanging of bells), there was a moment of stillness. Then the thin, sharp sound of a baby taking its first breath and letting the world know of its disappointment at this brutal change of circumstances, and throughout the hold, throughout the ship, I suspect, everyone smiled and breathed more easily.

Wanting air, and relief from the noisy and evil-smelling hold, I climbed the ladder to experience the deck of a ship at sea in rough weather. The noise below was as nothing to the howl of the wind and the thump of the waves against the ship's side. I held on to the gantry supporting a lifeboat, a little way from the railing over which spray broke, dampening my skirt, my hair, my face, limiting my view of the water to a pattern of grey foam and mist. When it cleared, all I could see was sea. I turned round and looked across to the other side of the ship. Dimly, amid the waves, I could see other ships in the convoy, but no land. This was the reality of a sailor's life, I thought, as I waited for another wave to break and fall back so I could see again the edgeless expanse of water on which we were nothing more significant than driftwood.

A passing sailor paused in the shelter of the lifeboat beside me.

'All right, my lover?' he said.

'What a strange life you must lead,' I said. 'Out here, day after day.'

He laughed. 'Aye, it seems strange, at the start of a voyage, then it seems normal. Then Bristol seems strange, when you get back to it, till it becomes normal again. Nothing to look at that's not far away, then hardly a glimpse of the sky for buildings. We get used to anything, in the end.'

'Is that where you're from, Bristol?'

'That's home,' he said.

He took a quick look around, then shuffled closer, feeling in his pockets. He brought out a packet of cigarettes and offered me one. I shook my head. I rarely smoke, and even if I had had the habit, it felt an absurd thing to be doing in the salty bluster of the wind.

'You speak good English,' he said. He was a little shorter than me, and burly.

'My father's family was Scottish, originally,' I said. 'We've always spoken it at home.'

He squinted at me through the smoke of his cigarette.

'Unusual cargo, you Gibraltarians,' he said.

'Unusual how?'

'Don't puff yourself up, Miss Speaks-English-at-Home. I only meant we've usually got a hold full of crates or lengths of timber, not people. Especially not girls, not women.'

'It must be easier looking after crates,' I said. 'They don't move.'

'No good for a chat, though, and not so much fun to look at.' He winked at me, flipped his cigarette end over the railing and went about whatever business he had interrupted to talk to me.

When he had gone I stood watching the water curving away from the side of the ship, swelling and sliding at the whim of the wind and the hidden forces that control it, rising to peaks and falling back, and the immensity of it began to overwhelm me. The lifeboat I stood beside looked bulky and substantial, from my position on the deck. When I imagined it loosed from its gantry, tossed into the water below, it seemed impossible it could stay afloat. I tried to picture it in the sea, full of the twenty people a notice stencilled on the side indicated was its capacity, and could not imagine it. It was only as I made my cautious way back to the hatch that I realized I could see only three other lifeboats. Twenty times four. There must have been twenty times forty people in the hold. I could hear Sonia's dear, familiar voice in my head: 'You think too much.'

The baby was named Juan Brittany Gomez. When the weather improved as we passed the north-west tip of France, we climbed the ladders up to the deck so that Father Garrigo, travelling with us for our spiritual, or his physical safety – I'm not sure which – could speak over this wailing scrap the words that would shield him from the fires of hell if he failed to survive. As he, and the rest of us, might not have done.

8

Arrival

The ship berthed in Liverpool. The port had the aspect of a mouth from which teeth had been randomly pulled or broken off. Bomb damage, the whisper went round the deck, where we were lined up with our rolls of bedding and bags of personal belongings.

'I thought we'd come here to escape German bombs,' Conchita said.

'If bombs fall,' said Ma, 'we will be safer here than we would be at home.'

'Why?'

'Because there is more room, and therefore more opportunities to provide shelter.'

'But maybe there won't be any bombs on the Rock,' said Conchita. 'We haven't had anything as bad as this yet. It might never happen.'

'It's possible, of course,' said Ma, 'but it's also possible we would be in the way, bombs or not. And it's possible that none of us will be safe, wherever we are, until the war is over. And maybe not even then.'

Conchita moved her hand over her stomach in the familiar gesture.

'You shouldn't talk to me like that,' she said.

We were taken to a reception centre. I have no idea what the building was before the arrival of displaced persons required it to be turned into such a thing, but it was rather like a hospital, with rooms full of beds, and smaller rooms where men who were dressed like doctors spoke to us confidentially, and bathrooms where women dressed as nurses scrubbed us down and inspected us for lice. The nurses were peremptory in the orders they gave us, and being forced to have my hair combed while someone I had never met before scrutinized each strand created a relationship between us that was uncomfortably intimate. But, at the same time, there was comfort in the certainty and efficiency. We had to do nothing except obey, and the process cleaned us up and delivered us to a table where plates full of food were put in front of us – better food than we had endured for the last ten days, since the fresh ingredients we had carried with us on board had run out.

There was no evidence of what I had heard one of the sailors on SS *Brittany* describe as 'uppitiness', which had prevailed between incidents of seasickness on board. Even the children were quiet, overawed by the building and the brilliant whiteness of the doctors' coats and the nurses' aprons.

I began a letter to Peter Povedano on the train to London which started with the words 'We are on a train going to London', and had to stop and look from the paper to the pen in my hand and then out of the window to confirm the truth of what was on the page, what my hand had written. As we had stood on the platform waiting, I had thought about the scene in *Dombey and Son* when the odious Mr Carker falls on to the track, and the arrival of the train was just as dramatic, mysterious and threatening as this episode had led me to expect.

The engine was powerful and menacing in a way nothing else I had come across in my life had been. It puffed steam at us, as it came to rest beside us, like a muscular man blowing smoke in the eyes of children.

I wish I had that letter now, to remind me of everything I thought and felt at the time, assuming it wasn't all taken out by the censor. The land was so green; not the uniform dark green of conifer forests but bright green, a green symphony with high notes and low notes, light and cheerful, strong and stern, heavy and dark. Doll's houses, I thought, as the villages and towns flashed past outside the train window. I remembered the doll's house that Sonia's charges had in their nursery, the perfect replica of a fantasy home. I had wanted to pick up the dolls that fitted that house and move them from room to room, adult though I was, so enchanting an idea had it been that I could have control over spaces clearly marked with boundaries. When the train slowed on the outskirts of a town, I pointed to the street we were passing and asked Alf:

'Would you like to live in one of those houses?'

'Yes!' he shouted. 'That one! With the red door.'

Then the train picked up speed again and the house with the red door became just one more thing along the way that I had lost without ever having known it.

We had no idea where we were; none of the stations we slowed down to pass through had names on them, but these would not have helped us even if they had still been labelled. We stopped outside one, a neat-roofed rectangle of a building aligned with the platform, a wooden bridge going up and over and down to the opposite platform, a strip of garden full of roses against the fence that defined where the station ended and the village street beyond began. From the carriage window, we had a view of the back of a cottage beside the station, a stretch of green space behind the red brick of the house.

A woman came out of the door with a basket full of washing in her arms. She put it down and began to peg things out on a line that stretched between two poles. Everyone in our carriage – Conchita, Ma, Lydia, Maribel, Horace, Alf, Freddo and I – clustered at the window with a view of the woman and her work, watching through the glass this domestic routine being carried out in such different surroundings. A child toddled out of the open back door and stood staring at the train. Lydia waved. The child stumbled to the safety of his mother's legs, hung on to her skirt. She looked round and saw Lydia and, by now, Alf and Freddo waving. She waved back. Lifted the child in her arms and raised his little fist, encouraging him to do the same.

With a final wave, she went back through the door. I followed her in my imagination into the kitchen; saw her fill the kettle and place it on the hob, open the larder and take out a jug of cold milk and a biscuit to set before the little one on the wooden tabletop; imagined her turning to the sheets she had soaking, ready to be thumped on the washboard, run through the mangle, then deciding there was time enough for that before her husband came home, and sitting down beside her child, lighting a cigarette, looking at the flowers in a milk bottle on the windowsill and thinking she should throw them out, pick some more from the brightly coloured beds beside the fence – her beds, her fence, her flowers. For as long as the train sat there, I was that woman, with the freedom to do this now, that later, or nothing at all while the kettle came to the boil.

'Women's work,' said Lydia, turning away from the window as the train started to move again. 'The same everywhere.'

If I'd been amazed at the open spaces and the green fields, London, when we reached it, was just as breathtaking. There was so much of it, so many miles of houses, factories, churches, schools before we reached the station, such quantities of rails stretched gleaming in parallel curved and straight rows. Our carriage had become light-hearted and cheerful after we had finished exclaiming over everything we saw. We had eaten the sandwiches we had been given and played games with the little ones, setting them to guess whether the next field would have horses, sheep or cows in it, telling them to look out for anything red. But as the end of the journey approached, it occurred to us all, again, that we had no idea where we were going, what would be happening to us next in this alien land, and we sank into silence.

The bus that drove us through the streets was a double-decker, and the children were too thrilled, fighting their way up the steps to the top deck, to worry about where it would stop. This time, I had no thought of a hotel. I expected we would be going to some shed, hastily made habitable for us; that we would be treated again as the debris that had been cleared out of a part of the British Empire which had been reclaimed for its proper purpose. This sounds bitter, as I write it. You will not criticize me for that, but I think I am displaying an understanding I did not have at the time. I do know my expectations of where we were going were low because I remember so clearly my amazement when we arrived in Kensington.

The place to which we were delivered was called the Royal Palace Hotel. Ma and I were on the wrong side of the bus and had a view, as we drew up outside it, only of the wet pavements opposite, and the scurry of legs and umbrellas obscuring the shopfronts. But we were alerted by the gasps from those able to see our destination clearly that it was something unexpected.

'Do the King and Queen live here?' asked a child's voice. Because, at home, so bold and big a construction could not have been meant for any but the highest of all the high authorities who moved in a layer of atmosphere far above us.

We stood on its polished tiled floor, afraid to put our cases down, afraid to let the rain drip off our clothing in case we should be told we had no business here, had been guilty of some moral, social or legal infringement in insinuating ourselves beneath the elegant plasterwork of the ceiling and the sparkle of the chandeliers. At least, so I felt. I am guilty, I know, of projecting what I felt on to the crowded mass of equally displaced people around me, with their drips and their cases.

There were queues for tables where forms were consulted or stamped or filled in, and this much at least had become familiar. I looked around for a seat for Ma; there were several upholstered benches, all of them occupied. I went up to one where two women – one elderly, one young – and a child were sitting.

'Can my mother sit down, please?' I said, looking at the child but meaning my words for the mother, who responded at once.

'Of course, of course,' she said. 'Come, Juan, move yourself.'

Shamed by her ready acceptance of a request I had convinced myself she would refuse, I asked if someone was queuing for her, if there was anything I could do.

'No, no,' she said, smiling. 'My sister-in-law is up there, somewhere. She'll be a match for them.'

I went back into the crowd and found Conchita and the boys. She had set her suitcase down and was balancing herself on top of it, looking, as only Conchita could manage to look, exhausted and uncomfortable but also beautiful and tragic. I directed her to the bench where I had left Ma, took the papers that served to identify us, and joined a queue.

At the head of it was a well-dressed young man supported by an even better-dressed older woman, allocating rooms. All the rooms, I heard him say to the couple in front of me, were in the building we were standing in. He said this wearily, as if every second person had demanded to know where we were being sent off to next, not believing we would be allowed to take advantage of the luxury in which we currently found ourselves. I presented my sheaf of papers and the woman ran her finger down a list of rooms and gave the man a number which he wrote in a book in front of him.

'Room four-two-eight,' he said to me, filling in our names, all five of us, on a sheet of paper, putting this number at the top.

'Could you tell me, is it upstairs?' I asked.

The woman lifted her head and looked at me, curiously, as if it had just occurred to her I was not merely a number.

'Fourth floor,' said the man. Weariness appeared to be his default expression.

'Why do you ask?' said the woman.

I looked at her, noticed her for the first time, as someone who was more than just a perfect twinset over a good-quality linen skirt. She was grey-haired, with a face that looked pursed up, the mouth and the cheeks sucked in, the eyes heavy-lidded as if she was expecting to hear or see evil in the world and was preparing herself to respond to the shock. But that impression was fleeting, because as she waited for the answer to her question, she smiled at me, and the lines that had looked reproving eddied outwards and framed an expression of pure benevolence.

'My mother's disabled,' I said. 'She can't climb stairs. Not easily. Not four flights.'

'Oh!' The woman's eyes and hands flew upwards. 'Why could they not have given us this information? So awkward for you, my dear,' she added, in a confidential tone, 'to have to keep *telling* everyone you need extra help when extra help should have been made available *at once*.'

'There's a lift,' the young man said, still not looking at me. 'Strictly for those authorized to use it.'

The woman ignored him. She began to hum, on a single note, while she turned the pages in front of her. The young man, who had dandruff sprinkled like salt on the collar of his dark suit jacket, looked to have gone beyond weariness to comatose. Behind me, the next family in the queue shuffled forward to peer round me, whispering to each other, in Spanish, 'What is going on?' The man was unmoved by the impatience of the queue. The woman was not.

'My dear.' She looked down at the documents in front of her. 'My dear Rose, is it, or Rosa?'

'Rose,' I said.

'Well, Rose, it will take me a while to sort this out, but I will, I promise, make arrangements for your family to be on the ground floor. Can I ask you to wait until I do that?' She looked at me appealingly, though it was obvious to me that there was nothing else I could do. She told me her name was

Mrs Almondsbury. 'Moira,' she added, smiling ever more sweetly. I imagined myself saying: 'No, Moira, this is not good enough. I will not wait. I demand a room at once,' and I smiled back at her, tickled by the thought.

By the time I returned to the bench, there was space for Conchita and me to sit alongside Ma. Freddo and Alf were too wound up by the day to sit at all; there was a magnificent staircase that started with shallow steps then split in two to lead up to a gallery above us. The first steps were wide and low, and the two boys, with a number of other children, were hopping up these, running round the semicircle of them and hopping down again. The noise in the hall had subsided as families left to find their rooms and the waiting was no hardship, for me. But the bench, having no back, was painful for Ma to stay on for any time, and Conchita, who had been thrilled at the realization we would be staying in a building so grand, so redolent of a life she imagined she would love to lead, had become restless. The longer we sat there, the more convinced she became that all the good rooms were being taken by the people leaving the hall before us. That her chance to make the most of this opportunity had been snatched from her by my inability to insist on my right to have the best of what was available.

At last I saw Mrs Almondsbury, who was bulkier but shorter than she had looked sitting down, coming through the thinned-out crowd towards us. I stood up, ready to intercept her because for all I knew, she had told any number of people that her name was Moira and she would sort them out later if they would agree to wait. But I was wrong. She was aiming for us, all amiability.

'Rose,' she said, with something like pleasure in her voice. Then, looking past me at Ma and Conchita on the bench, 'Oh, my goodness, my goodness. Why, I see, you, my dear' – to Conchita – 'are as much a special case as your mother-in-law. Mrs Dunbar' – to Ma – 'I hope you can forgive us for keeping you sitting here so long.'

'It is not comfortable,' said Ma. 'But you must do your job and I accept you are doing it as efficiently as you can.'

'I hope so,' Moira Almondsbury said, 'though not as efficiently as I would like. Now, Mrs Dunbar junior' – turning to Conchita again – 'please round up your children and follow me.'

She led us out of the hall to a long corridor with doors on either side. My heart sank at the sight of it; I didn't know if Ma, even with my arm to lean on, could make it to the end. But we stopped by only the second door, number 122, which opened on to a room larger than any we had occupied at home. It held two single beds, two camp beds and a cot, all made up with sheets and blankets. There was a wardrobe, a small table and one armchair. There were curtains at the window, deep-crimson velvet, and a carpet on the floor of a similar shade. Outside the window was a view of heads bobbing past on the pavement and the shopfronts opposite; the sun had come out and it was flashing off the windows of passing cars and buses. The room was as much as I could have hoped for; I wanted to be alone with Ma in that room, just long enough to settle her in comfort, and unwind the sense of responsibility that had kept me upright and rigid all day, sink back into my usual reflective detachment. But it was already full of Conchita and the boys.

The bathroom was two doors away, Mrs Almondsbury explained. The dining room, where a meal would be served in an hour, was on this same floor. Everything would be well, she seemed to be saying. I went with her to the door of the room, when she left, and she shook my hand.

'Good girl, Rose,' she said. 'Good girl.'

I thought, when the door to Room 122 opened, that we had at last reached a haven where it would be possible to live in a degree of comfort I had not imagined. I was looking forward to the next day, when I could go out and explore. After all, this was not Morocco. There would be no hostility towards us and we spoke (or I did) the same language. So that night, although the meal we had been given sat heavily in my stomach, I was hopeful, and happy. We had been instructed on the use of the blackout which had been stowed under our beds ready for use when it grew dark. The velvet curtains were not enough; we had to hoist solid squares of dense material into position to prevent even a chink of light escaping. We did as we were told, though the idea of war, as represented by planes, bombs, explosions, fires, bullets, damage, destruction and death, was no more obviously present in the Royal Palace Hotel at the end of Kensington High Street than it had been in MacPhail's Passage in Gibraltar.

I slept on one of the camp beds beside Ma. I woke in the pitch black, unable to tell if it was still night or if dawn had broken, but sure, somehow, it was still time for the world to be asleep. Conchita was snoring lightly; one of the boys was snuffling. Ma was silent. I reached out a hand to reassure myself she was still there. My fingers touched her hand, warm and knobbed, and her fingers curled round mine. When I was woken by Freddo wailing for his mother, my hand still trailed on the floor beside me, and Ma, when I turned the light on, was turned away from me.

*

The hotel was noisy, in the morning. It was a shock to realize, as I guided Ma towards the bathroom, how repressed we had all been on SS *Brittany*. It had been easier to go through the business of preparing myself and my mother for the day in those primitive conditions than it was now that the natural exuberance of my fellow Gibraltarians had been released. Any reticence about finding ourselves in so grand a building was wearing off, beginning with the youngest, who were stampeding up and down staircases. The mothers were going in and out of each other's rooms, discussing the furniture, the decoration, the beds, the bedding. The few men who had accompanied their wives or daughters, being judged to be of no use on the Rock, gathered in the entrance hall and sat smoking on the benches, exchanging remarks that appeared to be made more for the benefit of the speaker than for the purpose of being heard. It was like a Sunday on Main Street. Everyone released from the toils of a working day, free to roam about and gossip, while the children made the most of hours without school or chores to exercise their lungs and their imaginations.

Alf and Freddo were among the children playing racing, rolling, jumping games in the corridor, beguiled by the softness of the carpeted floor. As we left our room, Ma and I, dressed and ready for breakfast, we found an attempt being made by a couple of women in uniforms to control the tumbling mess of tiny bodies.

'Children!' bellowed one. 'Children! Will you go to your rooms, now! Now.' Her accent was Scottish. My father loved the sound of the Scottish voice; it made him feel privileged, I think. Rang in his ear like an echo linking him to his ancestors, making him something greater and grander than a dockyard worker in Gibraltar. Whenever Scottish performers visited the Rock, he would be sure to go, to take me and Jamie, even when the performance was a concert where he could not be sure words would be spoken. I missed my father with a sharpness that was painful, as this overlarge and unattractive female shouted at the children.

'They're like puppies,' said a voice (an English voice) beside me. 'Not house-trained.' It was Moira Almondsbury, wearing a frock this morning. Tailored and belted.

'They are not animals,' Ma said. 'They are not under control, that is true, but they have knowledge of manners and clean habits.'

'Mrs Dunbar,' said Mrs Almondsbury. 'Forgive me. I was speaking idly and without purpose.'

'They're not used to carpet,' I said. 'They've never seen it close up before.'

'Then I can see it would be unnatural for them to behave in any other way.'

A tiny, agile little girl with a mop of dark curls completed a somersault that brought her up against Mrs Almondsbury's neat ankles and polished shoes, with her skirt flipped over her head and a pair of not-exactly-white knickers pointing upwards towards Mrs Almondsbury's face. Ma spoke to the girl in Spanish.

'Stand up, child, and take care you do not disturb the adults.'

The girl did as she was told, gazing thoughtfully at Ma then sticking her thumb in her mouth and walking away.

'I know what we should do,' said Mrs Almondsbury. 'We should take them all into the park and let them run around outside. It's a beautiful day. Shall we do that?' She seemed to be asking me.

'It's a good idea,' said Conchita, who had finally finished dressing and come out to join us.

'It will happen,' declared Mrs Almondsbury, and strode off down the corridor. The women in uniforms, which I now saw were the uniforms of hotel staff, had managed to stop the children having fun and the noise and congestion had retreated. To another corridor, I suspect, where there were no women trying to prevent them from touching the walls or banging against doors.

The outing to the park took place; I went with the boys. It was a lovely day, warm enough to go out without a cardigan, which had not been a possibility in my preconceived idea of England. The park was green and full of growth; trees and plants I could not dream of putting a name to, then. I saw them as shapes, domes and spikes, arrows and cushions. There were birds, too, small birds and, on the water of the enormous lake, ducks and geese. I picked up a long, arching feather, white at the tip, black fading to grey at the base. I wondered if Ma could walk this far.

The children were loud and boisterous as they had been in the hotel but, out here, it made people smile rather than frown.

'They look happy,' I heard one woman walking past say to the one beside her.

'Refugees, I imagine,' said the second woman. 'Lucky to have escaped, I shouldn't wonder.'

Freddo fell over and I picked him up and cuddled him. He was only just beyond babyhood, and needed to be cuddled. Always a happy child, he was beginning to be fractious, to whine in a way he hadn't before, as Conchita's belly grew larger and she pushed him away more and more. We sat on a bench, his legs curled up on my lap and his chin tucked under mine. I watched Alf playing with the other children. I wondered how much of this experience he would remember. I was still thinking, then, that this would be over before any of us was much older. That we would return to Gibraltar and file away this time in our lives as something to look back upon and relish the memories. I could not have imagined that we would stay long enough to form not just memories but new ideas about how we might live our lives when all this was over.

Mrs Almondsbury came and sat beside me. She smoothed Freddo's hair; he was almost asleep. I could tell by the heavy stillness of him. A woman with a collection of bags – one over her shoulder, one in each hand – paused as she passed.

'Hello, Winifred,' Mrs Almondsbury said.

'Here's a happy bunch of children,' the woman said. 'Where are they from?'

'Gibraltar.'

'I see a lot of refugees at the Shelter,' the woman called Winifred said, 'but none as cheerful as these.'

'We're not refugees,' I said. 'We're evacuees.' I hadn't had the courage to challenge the two women I'd overheard earlier, but this was not a passer-by but a friend, so it seemed, of Mrs Almondsbury. She was quite young, and untidy; even without the bags she would have looked like someone in a rush to be somewhere else, with more important things to do than brush her hair or sort out her wardrobe.

'Sorry,' she said. 'I thought you were one of Moira's helpers. I didn't mean to be rude.'

'We haven't run away from the war,' I said. 'We were told to leave.'

'That's right, I suppose,' said Mrs Almondsbury, 'but you must expect most people won't understand the difference.'

'We should, though,' said Winifred, putting all her bags down and searching through her pockets. 'We don't call the children we've sent out of London to the countryside refugees, do we? I think you're quite right to correct me.' She found a handkerchief, finally, in one of her pockets and bent over to wipe Freddo's face. His nose had been running and I hadn't noticed. 'There, now. I must go.' She picked up her bags and set off across the park, weaving her way in and out of the children's games.

'She works for a charity that helps refugees and the homeless,' Mrs Almondsbury said, when she had gone. 'We're most of us doing something. Which is fulfilling, of course.' She stretched out her rather chunky legs in stockings so fine I could not imagine what it would be like to wear them. 'My children are grown up, now, and I suppose I must have filled the days somehow, before the war, but it's hard to remember how. But there' – she patted my arm, wrapped round Freddo's sleeping bulk – 'I don't suppose you've ever known idleness.'

'No,' I said. 'I would fill my time with reading, if I had any spare.'

'Even reading is not enough to fill all the time in the day. I don't expect you to believe me, but it's true. Doing anything is better than doing nothing, but doing the same thing, day after day and hour after hour, is almost as bad.'

I appreciated the way she spoke to me, as if I was a woman of her class with whom she was happy to share confidences. At the same time, I felt uneasy that I would reveal myself to be someone other than the person she thought me. I was worried she had singled me out as more of an equal than the other women chasing round collecting toddlers about to fall in the pond or sitting gossiping together. As if she understood my thoughts from my expression, she said: 'You remind me of my daughter, so you'll have to forgive me if I chat away to you as if I knew you. You don't exactly look like Martha, but you have the same way of holding yourself slightly aloof, and your voice – I was taken aback when I first heard your voice. You speak English so perfectly and you sound just like her. I hope you don't mind if I seem to be making a bit of a pal of you.'

'Where is your daughter?' I asked. 'Is she working with refugees, too?'

'No, she's in the Wrens. She's down on the south coast learning all about ships and naval warfare. Or so I assume. I don't know what you need to know to be a Wren. It's only just over a year ago that she was going to dances and playing tennis and planning to go to university, and now she is off where I can't visit her, leading a life I have no way of imagining. I know we were told again and again that war was almost inevitable, but it is still a shock to find it has changed everything quite so completely. My son is away training somewhere, too. Scotland, I think. He's joined the army, but I always expected he would go off into a life I didn't understand. I thought I would be able to watch Martha having fun, without a war going on.'

'Is she enjoying it?' I asked. I was wondering, would I enjoy it?

'She's loving it,' said Mrs Almondsbury. She looked at her watch and stood up. 'Time to go back for lunch, I think.'

On the way back, she walked with me, holding Alf's hand because Freddo refused to walk and I had to carry him.

'I know you've probably more than enough to do with

your mother and the children,' she said, 'but if ever you do have time to spare, do let me know.'

I had been idle, for much of the time, on the ship, but it had been a fractured, uneasy idleness, without regular occupation but also without liberty and freedom. Now we were settled – if we were settled – there was a blank space ahead of me I would need to fill, and this was exciting. What might I find to do? Who might I meet?

'Where will I find you?' I said.

'I'll find you,' said Mrs Almondsbury.

9

A Sort of Safety

The unfamiliar takes so little time to become the ordinary. What is unthinkable so suddenly tips over into the banal. I know this because I can say with certainty on what date one memorable event happened, and on what other date something else occurred. We arrived on 15 August. On 30 September, my niece, Mercy, was born. I know how little time there is between the two, and yet I had already absorbed what was shockingly alien, at the start, into my view of what passed for normal.

We had arrived as enemy planes began to appear in the sky above London. Two weeks later, the raids began. We were finishing our supper the first time the unearthly wail of the siren silenced the room. Eyes turned upwards, as if the menace the siren warned us of would be visible through the floors and the roof above us. We had been given instructions about what to do in an air raid, which was to go down to the cellar, with our gas masks. This sounded easy and orderly. It was not easy, or orderly. Not everyone had brought their gas mask into the dining room with them, and so some people, thinking this the more important of the two instructions, ran upwards rather than downwards. Others, who had their masks and had

96

made the same assumption, were reluctant to move while there was still bottled fruit and custard in front of them waiting to be eaten. Those who thought the cellar, not the mask, was the better source of safety, rushed to the doors leading to the kitchen, the only access to the stairs down, and crowded together in the narrow gap, impeding each other.

'Like so many sacks of rubbish in a chute,' Ma said.

Ma and I waited until the way was clear, then I helped her down the stone steps to the dimly lit, cold, vaulted cellar. There was a corner taken up with stores – tins and bottles and sacks of dried goods – but most of the space was empty, swept clean. There were bunks installed round the walls, but for most of us it was either stand up or sit on the floor. As we were among the last down, we stopped at the bottom step and sat on that, an easier manoeuvre for Ma to achieve than folding herself up on to the stones.

'We should be better prepared,' I said. 'I should have a bag ready, with cushions and blankets.'

'Perhaps,' Ma said. 'Or we should accept that there is no such thing as safety, and stay where we are comfortable.'

It would have been impossible to maintain the pitch of terror of that first time. When the raids were in daylight, people would come in from the street and report that there was nothing to be seen, no planes overhead, which must mean the raid was not close enough to us for fear to be necessary. Or there were one or two planes and in all the vastness of the sky above us it was easy to believe they would not drop bombs precisely on the block that was the Royal Palace Hotel. And the gap between the warning and the all-clear, during the day, was frequently so short it was almost, so it seemed, not worth the bother of moving. It took longer to begin to feel irritated rather than terrified by the raids at night. The noise of the anti-aircraft guns in the park next door, muted though it was, was enough.

It depended where we were, when the sirens went, whether we put comfort ahead of safety or safety ahead of comfort. If we were not in our room, I would help Ma down the steps and make her as comfortable as possible with the blankets and pillows that were piled up on the bunks. We would sit among others in the near darkness, watching women knit; men, and some women, play cards. There would often be singing. Less often, squabbles. Once, an actual fight. But mostly it was peaceful. There was nothing to do but accept that there was nothing to do. Few bombs fell close enough to create a sense of real danger and I would not have minded being in the cellar if it had been possible to sleep.

If Ma was in bed, and as comfortable as she could ever make herself, she refused to move in response to the sirens. I could still have sought safety below stairs, but I knew that I would fret, knowing Ma was alone when she might need me. I imagined the windows in our room shattering and Ma needing help to move away from the broken glass, handkerchiefs to wipe away the blood from scratches. Anything more extreme, I did not picture. At times I felt oppressed by the weight of floors above us, but I believed that, if the hotel were hit, they would protect us. It would crumble from the top, I thought, the rooms above folding in and crushing anyone foolish enough still to be in them, but our lair right at the bottom of this monumental structure would remain intact. How could anything man-made destroy this building so completely? More often than not, when the siren went, we stayed where we were.

We became used to it. In the letters I wrote to home, to Peter, Jamie and my father, I only mentioned the raids when they did not happen, or happened with less intensity. 'A quiet week,' I would say. The new normality was the nightly bombardment of the city we were living in by squadrons of German bombers being targeted by gun emplacements in the park beside us and pursued across the sky by our own fighter planes, and the knowledge that there might come a time when one or more of these bombs, striking the earth, killed or injured us. When this did not happen, it was worth remarking, as any dramatic change in, for example, the weather would be.

The hotel became less luxurious, almost at once. Not just because we had grown accustomed to it. The carpets stayed, but anything decorative and removable was removed in the first few days – vases and pedestals, drapes framing archways, even the chandeliers. We might have felt we did not deserve these things when we arrived but that did not prevent us resenting others thinking the same, and the workmen carrying out the job suffered some abuse, though as all of it was in Spanish they were unaffected. Then we, the new residents, began to treat the hotel as a living space like the living spaces we had left behind. We spilled out of our rooms and, even though it was not the street outside our doors, we began to behave as if it were. Chairs were dragged into the corridors and clusters of women sat knitting and gossiping; we had been told not to take food into our rooms but we did. The smell of cooked food displaced the odour of polish; stains were beginning to appear on the paintwork, on the carpets. We needed to be taken, or to take ourselves, in hand.

A complicated pattern of organizations had been involved in setting up the systems to cope with us; we were a complex problem. There were men we all understood to be in charge and battalions of women who supplied us with food, with information, with toys and games for the children, with clean sheets and towels. Our responsibilities were not clear, and not all of those working on our behalf understood where the boundaries were, between them and other organizations as well as between them and us. Before long, this confusing mass began to be sorted out, and the first step was the formation of a committee. The word 'committee' was familiar to me; it had been the currency in which the authorities on the Rock dealt. I had said to Sonia once that, despite its familiarity, I had no clear idea of what it meant.

She said: 'A committee is a group of people who agree to talk.'

'Talk about what?'

'Anything that's a problem, or they think is a problem, or anything that they think needs to be done. They talk about it and agree what ought to be done, and then they tell someone else to do it.'

Sonia was always much more knowing than I was. She had her sights fixed on securing a better life for herself than her mother had, and she listened and learned to make sure she had the tools to chip it out for herself. I knew I would have a better life than my mother because I did not have her disease. So I did not have the same urgency to escape as Sonia did, even though, as I realized when Peter Povedano asked me to marry him in the air-raid shelter, I did not want to have the life Mrs Gutierrez, and most of the women I knew, had, either.

So, a committee. To liaise between us and those helping us;

to organize us to help ourselves. To talk, as Sonia had said, about the problem of us and then to tell us what to do about ourselves. I was nothing to do with the committee. I lacked status in all the ways that status was measured: age, sex, wife-hood, motherhood. But I was near the top of the list of those who the committee thought should be doing something rather than talking about what needed doing. All the attributes that made me unfit for authority made me fitter than most to be useful. Maribel Molinary, the daughter of Lydia who had travelled with us on SS *Brittany*, was another in the same young, single, female category. 'I'm going to find a job in a factory,' she told me. 'It can't be worse than working in the kitchen here, and at least I'd be earning some money.'

I was just as determined to avoid the kitchen. I was trapped in the hotel, caring for Ma and, increasingly, the boys, so the option of a job, in a factory or anywhere else, was not open to me. I lay in wait for Mrs Almondsbury. She was in some posi-tion within the Women's Voluntary Services, as were many of the women we saw around the hotel, making things happen. Though Mrs Almondsbury did make things happen, she was closer to the committee level of the octopus that worked on our behalf. She picked things up and carried them to where they needed to go, on occasion, but she never did anything that would make her hands dirty, or wrinkle her clothes. Which sounds like a criticism, but is not. She knew what it was in her power to do well and she stayed within her scope. I told her, boldly, what was within my scope to do, which was more than washing dishes or mopping floors, and she accepted my own assessment of myself and introduced me to Patrick, a man with grey eyes in a grey face, with grey hair and a grey suit, who managed the money. I became his assistant, maintaining records of who was being paid, and how much. It was meticulous and boring work, but Patrick was as close to silent as it was possible for a man to be, and I cherished the time spent in the office, with ledgers where I could slot names into boxes and they could not answer back.

It was easier to work with Patrick than it would have been to be on one of the working parties with other women. Most of them were continuing with the tasks that had filled their days at home, only in a different setting. Although I had cooked and cleaned and done the laundry, this was not where I felt I belonged. I was used to spending days in the still, quiet, book-laden atmosphere of the Garrison Library, where voices were barely raised above a whisper, where movements might be brisk but were never extravagant. In the kitchen of the Royal Palace Hotel, the noise of voices, metal striking metal, boiling liquids, hot fats and jets of water scouring plates was overwhelming. And there was an edge of aggression which the workers appeared to relish.

One of the loudest was Lydia Molinary. I had chided myself, on the voyage, when she had shown such efficiency, for having judged her by what I had seen of her in the streets around MacPhail's Passage, when she was always beginning, ending or in the middle of an argument. On the ship, she overcame difficulties by not seeming to recognize that they were difficulties. Now I saw I had not misjudged her, but had been guilty of assuming that only one judgement could apply – either she was aggressive and foul-mouthed, or she was efficient and helpful. In London, she was both. Being aggressive was her way of being efficient.

I was standing with Mrs Almondsbury in the dining room

one day, when an argument broke out between Lydia and one of the cooks, a man who would have needed a coffin half as big again as Lydia's if they had ended up murdering each other. It sounded as if Lydia was fighting much of the time, so highly pitched and assertive was everything she said, but this time the volume increased as the man shouted back, each of them trying to drown out the other. As we turned towards the noise, Lydia picked up one of the metal trays we used to collect our food from the counter and bashed her opponent on the head with it. It made a satisfyingly loud noise that silenced all the voices in the room but, being light and cheap, did no damage. The cook and Lydia looked at each other in the aftermath, and then Lydia, presumably feeling she could claim victory by tin tray and had no further points to make, turned round and stalked off.

'Oh dear,' said Mrs Almondsbury, her face at its most pinched up. 'What should we be doing to make things calmer?' I told her I thought they should give women like Lydia Molinary more control; over the food in particular, because this was what created the most conflict – what we ate, where we ate, when we ate was dictated to us. We were denied our preferences on every point.

'I thought, when I first met you, that you would be one of the women we could look to to take a lead,' Mrs Almondsbury said. 'I'd rather hand control over to you than to Lydia.'

'You're confusing me with your daughter,' I said. 'I don't have that kind of authority.'

In fact, I was oddly placed, in the Royal Palace. Or felt as if I was. I was often taken for one of the Londoners, by the Londoners themselves and by my fellow residents, those who did not recognize me from home or from the boat. I took after my father, who was taller, with lighter skin and hair, than was usual among Gibraltarians. And when I spoke I sounded English. This meant I had the opportunity to see first-hand how each side irritated the other. I was spoken to by Gibraltarians, thinking me English, as if I was their servant, failing to deliver a service as good as they had a right to expect. More than one of the WVS ladies, thinking me one of them, confided in me her contempt for the sloppy ways and bad manners of those they were trying to help. It seemed to me to be a hopeless task, to maintain complete harmony, even though, for most of the time, most of the women from Gibraltar appreciated the help and most of the women from London were sympathetic and appreciated the willingness of the evacuees to be pleased.

It was a hard time for Ma, too, and she was sharper than usual. No one else would have noticed as she was always so sharp, and those not close to her would not detect that the sharpness had become more cutting. She was saying the same things she would always have said, only using words that hurt. She was being harsh in circumstances I did not think required harshness. Pointing out faults that were no more than good intentions clumsily executed. I noticed this and assumed it was her level of pain increasing. Of course it was, but not her physical pain. I thought her so strong I could not imagine she was suffering from being displaced, as I could see other, lesser women suffering. I had expected Ma to be constant. I believed her to have a fixed outlook, unchanging while everything around her was in flux.

Mrs Almondsbury had procured us a wheeled chair and this allowed me to take Ma to the park. I put her sketchbook in my bag and encouraged her to look at the birds. I was being as naive, in my own way, as Mme Goncourt had been, buying her a bird in a cage in Casablanca. I knew better than to expect her to want to draw a caged bird, but I had expected her to want to draw one from life when they did not fly over but stayed circling near us, waiting for breadcrumbs. She would not.

'I don't need the bird in front of me,' she said. 'I'm not drawing the bird.'

I had taken her sketchbook from my bag and was holding it in my hand, thrust slightly towards her. She lifted an arm in a gesture of repudiation and caught the book with her elbow, knocking it to the ground. It lay splayed open on the path and in picking it up I caught a glimpse of the last drawing she had done. It showed a feather, like the one I had given her after my first visit to the park. She had drawn it diagonally, the pointed end, which would once have attached it to a bird, downwards. The outline and the shape of the markings were done in black ink; the rusty pattern of the original was washed in with the watercolours Ma had begun to use in Morocco. There was nothing in the drawing to signal movement, yet it gave the impression of a moment just after movement had stopped. The point of the feather was buried in the surface of a curved, soft but solid mound; it could have been a duck's breast, or a chicken's thigh, or a woman's hand. The coppery, russet colour was unmistakeably blood, in the drawing, though it had not looked like it on the feather I had picked up, and I don't know how I knew this was what it was in Ma's painting. It pulsed through the black and the white as if the point that dented what could only be skin were drawing out the life force from within the flesh it touched, or injecting into it a jolt of viscous life. It was the most vicious of Ma's drawings I had seen. Much closer to the inspiration for the drawing than most, and yet the most alien. I shut the book and put it back in my bag.

'What are you trying to draw?' I asked.

'What I always draw. Pain.'

'It is worse, then,' I said.

She sighed. 'No. Just harder to bear. The light is fading.'

It was a bright day. It had been warmer than I had imagined it was possible for it to be in England since we had arrived, and the nights were slow in coming, the hours of darkness shorter than they would have been at home, though stretching out longer and longer, week by week. So I knew she did not mean to be taken literally, and I wondered what she would say to me, at that moment, if I was talking of the light fading. If I was giving up hope.

'Do you remember,' I said, 'on the ship, when we left home the first time, you told me not to be weak.'

She said nothing and I did not want to look at her for fear of what I might see in her face. I knew she was not weak. That what she was expressing in her drawings, and in her increased ill humour, was a mournfulness for all she had lost and could not believe she would ever recover. The touch of her husband and son; the sounds and smells of her home, filtered through the walls and windows because she rarely went out, but the sounds and smells she knew, the walls and windows she knew. I let the awareness of her misery wash over me. Thought about how, even though she had little space in her room at home, such as she had was not perpetually full of the unsettling presence of Conchita and the boys. In the silence that followed the remark I had made, which was the one I would have expected her to make to me, I knew I should have said what it came naturally to me to say, at such a time, rather than what came naturally to her.

'Can I do anything?' I said. 'Can I find some way to make it easier for you?'

'It would be weak of me to tell you no one can do anything, least of all you, a woman with no more power than I have. That is, none. I would be sliding into unforgiveable self-pity.'

'I have more physical power,' I said.

'Yes. And I should try to imagine what I would do with physical power if I had it, and ask you to do it for me.'

'I will do whatever you ask,' I said.

'I know.'

I took the handles of her chair and swivelled her round, began pushing her back to the hotel. On the way, we met Winifred, the lady I had first met with Mrs Almondsbury in the park the day after our arrival. I saw the untidiness of the woman walking towards me from a distance, and by the time she reached me, I had recalled who she was, so had a smile ready on my face. I had learned it was important to smile when there was nothing to smile about, in London. It was a sort of currency, passed between passers-by, even when they were unknown to each other. At home, we touched. Here, it was better, I had observed, to restrain from touching. Not all my fellow residents at the Royal Palace Hotel had learned this. Ma had never been ready to touch, except those few who were close to her. And she did not approve of this new social habit of smiling, either. But I smiled as Winifred came up to me. She did not pause in her rushed stride as she passed, but called out that I must come and visit the refuge where she worked.

'Moira will tell you where it is,' she said. 'Can't stop.'

'Why were you smiling at her?' Ma said, when she had gone. 'Had she said something amusing?'

'I wasn't smiling from amusement,' I said. 'Only from courtesy.'

'Then it's meaningless,' Ma said.

I thought everything would be better if I could move Ma out of the Royal Palace, find a way of living where we could be still, and quiet, apart from others even if by just the width of a wall, a flight of stairs. The constant noise, inside and outside the room, was preventing her from slipping into the state of calm acceptance that she had achieved in our rooms in MacPhail's Passage. I wanted to leave for my own sake, too. It was easy and comfortable to live in the hotel but I felt as displaced as I had in the dance hall in Casablanca. We were neither of us good candidates for communal living.

When I mentioned this to Mrs Almondsbury, she pursed herself up and took some time to answer.

'We would prefer you all to stay together,' she said, at last.

I had begun to think of Mrs Almondsbury as someone who was not exactly a friend – that would have been presumptuous – but was, like a distant relative, predisposed to consider herself on my side. When she used the words 'we would prefer', she appeared to be aligning herself with the committee – with the committees, for they were proliferating – when I had assumed that what I wanted was of more interest to her than what 'they' wanted.

'Why?' I said.

She looked uncomfortable for a moment, then the pursed lines vanished and her face relaxed. She, too, I think, had known a moment's hesitation over which side of the line she stood, and had come to a decision to step over to my side.

'Because it will be easier to ship you back, if you stay where you were put.'

'Is there talk of shipping us back?' I asked. I was momentarily relieved and excited that this might be possible and, in the next instant, regretting being delivered back to the life I knew when I had not yet explored a different life, here in London.

'Well, when we've won the war,' said Mrs Almondsbury, 'of course, you will go back. But just now, there is a plan to send you to Jamaica. It is being discussed, I should say. Not a plan. Not yet a plan.'

'Jamaica?'

'You see, it isn't safe for you in London and there isn't anywhere outside London – at least, no one's come up with anywhere – that you could go. And it is cold in the winter, whereas in Jamaica it would be hot. What you're used to. There is a view it would be better, kinder, to send you all there.'

She was watching me closely as she said all this; I could tell she was striving for a neutral tone of voice. She was capable of being brisk and authoritative; was so, normally. But now she was laying this dish before me with a question mark, inviting me to say whether it was to my taste or not, without letting me know what her own opinion of it was.

'We wouldn't be safe on the voyage,' I said. The very idea of the voyage, so soon after the journey to England, made me feel sick. 'And we belong in Jamaica even less than we belong here.'

Mrs Almondsbury was nodding. 'I know,' she said. 'I agree. It's one of those plans that is convenient for the people making it, dressed up as having the best interests of the people affected by it at heart. You can see why the authorities were hoping to keep you together while they talked about it, though.'

'So they can pick up the parcel they dropped and load it into the hold of another ship.'

'It might not happen. There is resistance, from your own side, in Gibraltar.'

'Would I have the option to stay here, if it did? Ma and me, I mean.'

'I don't know. Of course, if you weren't actually in the hotel any more, you'd be harder to sweep up, if it wasn't what you wanted.'

It wasn't what I wanted, but moving out of the Royal Palace to avoid it happening was only a dream. Ma would not go and leave Conchita still pregnant.

10

Labour

On the night of 29 September, Ma and I were standing up, ready to leave the dining room, when the sirens started, so we turned round and were among the first to reach the cellar. I settled Ma on a bunk at the back of the room and stood looking around for Conchita and the boys. They were quite wild, in those days. At home, they would never have been out of their mother's sight for so long. And if they were, there would have been other adults who knew them and kept them from harm. Inside the hotel, Conchita believed they were safe wherever they went, or chose to believe it. So when the sirens sounded, unless they were sitting at a table or tucked up in bed, she had difficulty finding them. Unlike Ma and me, she was convinced the cellar was the only place to be safe and was desperate to be down the steps and pegging out her piece of floor; rounding up the boys was a torture for her.

That night we were so early I was at once hemmed in by other people pouring down the steps and jostling for positions, struggling to reach other members of their family or their friends. The cellar was not big enough for everyone in the hotel; if we had all stood, shoulder to shoulder, maybe we could have fitted ourselves in, but as it was the cellar was used mainly by those with children or elderly relatives; the younger, unencumbered residents stayed in the dining room or went to other shelters. I had seen girls I recognized in the queues forming in the street in the middle of the day for the Underground station, including Lydia Molinary's daughter, Maribel. I had stopped to ask her, once, why they chose to do this. She told me it was fun, in the shelter set up in the station. I asked what sort of fun, and the girls laughed, tossed their hair and looked at me as if I were an old unmarried aunt who had no idea about boys, or flirting, or sex.

But even so, the cellar was crowded and I could not see Conchita, nor could I reach the stairs to go back up and find her. The sirens had died away when she came down the steps, a child grasped in either hand. She looked around for me and Ma, but it was too crowded; she could not reach us, so had no choice but to settle down where she was. Because she was so near to giving birth, and because she always remembered to scatter smiles and charm when it cost her nothing to do so, she was much cossetted by the other women in the hotel, even though she was no use to them at all. She was the part of the Dunbar family that fitted into the pattern, the one who could accommodate herself to interlock with others. So Conchita was petted and given a share of the blankets and pillows.

Over nights and nights of raids, I had become used to sleeping whenever and wherever I could. An unbroken night was a dream from a past life and there was no point waiting for the dream to become a reality again. So I slept, only to be woken by a woman yelling in pain. I looked at Ma, who was awake and looking beyond me towards the steps.

'Conchita,' she said. 'Go to her.'

I was not the person who would be either helpful or wanted, but I went, because Ma had asked me. I took a while to find spaces to put my feet without treading on outspread limbs, but the whole cellar was awake by this time, and everyone hunched up to give me room. Conchita was walking back and forth. Lydia Molinary had hold of her arm and was whispering words of encouragement.

'What can I do?' I asked.

'Take the children away,' said Lydia.

I looked round and saw Alf and Freddo huddled together, pressed up against the wall, watching their mother as if terrified that to look away might result in disaster. The lights that were left on at the top of the stairs showed up the tears on Freddo's cheeks. A woman kneeling beside them was trying to comfort them but she made way for me, with relief.

'Come with me,' I said, scooping up Freddo and holding out a hand to Alf. 'Grandma wants you.'

They came willingly enough, and I was less cautious about where I put my feet on the way back, but no one complained. I put Freddo down on the bunk where Ma was lying, and she reached out and pulled him towards her, holding him close against her chest, which was an uncommon gesture for her, and must have caused her pain. I sat on the floor beside her, and let Alf crawl on to my lap.

'Is Mama dying?' Freddo asked.

'No,' said Ma. 'Mama is making a big noise to help her give birth to the baby.'

'Like Angela?' said Alf. Angela was the name of the woman who had given birth on SS *Brittany*, with less drama, as far as I could remember, than Conchita was bringing to the business.

'Just like Angela,' I said. 'You'll have a little brother or sister soon. We'll wait here together, you, me, Freddo and Grandma, until the new baby arrives.'

'God willing,' said Ma, under her breath, and I thought again of all the babies she had lost.

The door at the top of the cellar steps opened and closed again and again as women went up and down in search of whatever they thought was needed or would help – towels, more blankets, cups of tea. One of Lydia's helpers came over and asked me if I could persuade my sister-in-law to go up to the floor above, where there were rooms set aside for the sick.

'She says she knows she'll be killed by a bomb if she goes up the stairs,' the woman explained, 'but, honestly, it's hard to do anything for her down here, and it's upsetting everyone else.'

'Tell her to go,' Ma said to me. 'And if she won't, tell her I will come and speak to her.'

I worked my way back across the room. During the raids, we could hear little in the cellar. When Ma and I stayed in our room, it was noisy, with the gunfire from the park, the thump of an impact, whistles and cracks and alarm bells, which we had come to interpret as an animal might, scenting danger on the wind, recognizing when that danger was far away, alert for it coming closer. But in the cellar it was only possible to make out, when everyone was quiet, the thudding of the guns. As I made my way across to Conchita there was a boom, loud enough to provoke a gasp of fear from this cellar full of people, all of them, thanks to Conchita, awake. Seconds later, the building shook. Fine particles of dust dislodged from the bricks and hung in the air, misting the faint light from the stairway. Everyone in the room, including Conchita, was momentarily still. Then the children began to wail. I turned back, to be with Ma; I was suddenly terrified, had lost all confidence that the building would stand up and protect us, and if we were to be buried in the rubble, I wanted to be close enough to hold her hand while we waited for rescue, or death.

But then Conchita's shouts rose above the hubbub and that convinced me, for no logical reason, that we were not going to be destroyed as we lay or crouched in the cellar. It was too ridiculous; for all the drama she wrapped round herself, Conchita was not born to tragedy. I kept moving towards her and gripped her arm.

'It's safer upstairs,' I said, as if I knew it, or believed it, and Conchita, whose skin felt clammy when I touched it, did not resist. Between us, Lydia and I half pushed, half pulled her up the stone steps and out into the corridor. The dust in the air was thicker here but there was no sign of any damage, no cracks in the walls.

We went through the dining room, the tables still laden with the dirty dishes no one had had time to clear away, to the rooms beyond where the doctors came every week to check on the sick. Conchita paused every few steps as the pains hit her, but she was not screaming now, just uttering moans that were almost more terrifying. Such restraint, I thought, must mean she was too lost in the agony to remember to perform.

In the room, Lydia and a couple of the other women who had come up the steps with us persuaded Conchita on to the bed and began to strip off her underclothes. I backed away but waited, unsure what I should be most frightened of: the raid, or Conchita's condition, or Ma's situation, left with the boys in the cellar. When Conchita was naked from the waist down, Lydia began to feel her stomach, running her hands over the mountain of belly that Conchita had been caressing for so many months. She spoke, quietly, to the other women then turned to me.

'You speak English. Call the doctor.'

'Why?' I asked. 'What shall I say?'

'Say it looks like a breech birth,' she said. 'If you know what that is in English.'

I didn't, but I understood what it meant, and the woman who answered the emergency number told me the phrase, when I explained that the baby was coming buttocks first. I now knew how to describe what was happening, or what was preventing the birth from happening, in two languages, but I had no idea what it signified. How serious it was. I wanted to ask Lydia but it did not seem right to do so in Conchita's presence, even if she gave no sign of being aware of anything except her own labours. I escaped from the room where I was definitely not needed, but stayed outside the door. I could not go back to Ma and tell her the doctor had been called without being able to tell her also what the doctor had said.

One of Lydia's helpers, a woman called Vera Lopez, came out and lit a cigarette.

'Bet you're thinking "Glad it's not me", eh?' she said, indicating the room behind her with a jerk of her head. 'You've got all this to come, mind. But don't despair, you're a big girl; they'll slip out easily, as likely as not, for you.'

'Is a breech birth serious?' I asked. She was an older woman, older than Ma, and she must have had children herself, though none were with her in the hotel.

'Can be,' she said. 'The baby can get wedged, you know . . .' She bent her legs apart and gestured with the hand holding the cigarette towards her crotch. 'But don't you worry. The doctor will deal with it.' Conchita began to wail again and Vera rolled her eyes skywards. She lifted her foot and stubbed out her cigarette on the sole of her shoe, then went back inside the room.

I went out into the lobby, waiting for the doctor. The door and windows were covered with blackout material, but there were no lights on, so I lifted it aside. The sky was beginning to lighten and I could see the outline of the other buildings in the street. They were all still standing. There was nothing to show a bomb had fallen close enough to shake the walls of the cellar. No damage that I could see at all. An ambulance came past, bells ringing, but it could have come from anywhere.

The nightwatchman came out of his cubbyhole and stood beside me. He was a Black man with one arm, called Jonas, and when Ma and I stayed in Room 122 during raids, he would come to check on us and stay to play tunes on his mouth organ, or tell us stories of the marvels he had seen. He had a capacity, which I envied, for seeing marvels. His stories could as easily be about the ingenuity of a child he had observed trying to extract a gobstopper from a jar with a lid barely wider than the sweet, as about the flying fish he had seen at night, reflecting the moonlight off their scales, which was a sight he had witnessed when he was a sailor. When he still had two arms. His voice alone was soothing, with a lilt that was like the deepest notes he played on the mouth organ. For now, though, he was silent, as I was.

An ambulance drew up outside the door and Conchita, on a stretcher, was loaded into it. Lydia stood beside me on the step as it drew away. She looked defeated.

'They'll deliver the baby at the hospital,' she said. 'Caesarean section.' She lifted her shoulders, let them drop. 'It's a shame, but there it is. She'll be all right.'

'And the baby?'

'Still breathing,' Lydia said. She turned to go back into the hotel. 'Hey!' she said. 'These things happen. It's no fun being a woman, haven't I told you that before? Get rid of the long face.'

The all-clear sounded as I went back down the cellar steps and there was a chaos of waking bodies struggling upright from their comfortless resting places on the floor.

'Go to the hospital,' Ma said. 'Come back and tell me when my grandchild has been born.'

I walked to the hospital but ran back.

Some workmen clearing rubble whistled at me as I went.

'Where's the fire?' one of them shouted, and I laughed and shook my head. Kept running.

Ma was alone in the room. The curtains had not been drawn back fully and it was barely light enough to see her face on the pillow, turned towards me.

'Tell me,' she said.

'Baby girl,' I panted. 'Six pounds ten ounces. Caesarean section.'

'A girl,' my mother whispered. 'Praise be.'

When she married my father in 1916, my mother must have expected to have a house full of children. Although we rarely went to church, we were Roman Catholics, and she would not have tried to limit her family. It might not have been the one thing she had wished for, as Mme Goncourt had, but she must have looked forward to having her own babies, watching them grow. But year after year had robbed her of the hope for more than my brother, until I arrived. I had not understood until I saw how she reacted to her granddaughter's birth, that day and in the weeks that followed, how much of her sadness was for her lost children.

I put my arms round her, resting them lightly on her shoulders, giving her my shoulder to lean against, and she folded into me, all the tension leaving her body. So we stayed, for just a minute or two, then she pulled away from me.

'Better get some sleep,' she said. 'The hard work starts now.'

11

Mercy

The weeks after the baby was born were the hardest since we had left Gibraltar. Conchita, who had been a good enough mother to Alf and had managed with Freddo, an easier baby, was not ready to be any sort of mother to the child that had, literally, ripped her apart. Left her with a scar that was so much smaller than I had guessed it would be, but so much of an affront to the body she had cherished. She had missed the moment when the child emerges into the world. I don't know if that was significant, but it may have added to the distance between her and her child, a distance she could not bridge.

We named the child Mercedes and called her Mercy. It might not have been Conchita's choice, but she could not be persuaded to make one, so I chose the name. I arranged the baptism, in the chapel in the hotel. Although little Mercy was a healthy baby, she came weighted with the drama of her birth, which left the sense that she was a miracle and that her long-term survival could not be counted as certain. So the women around us and the priest who looked after our spiritual well-being were anxious that this important ceremony took place without delay. We did not delay. Conchita and Mercy came out of the hospital, and the next day we dressed ourselves up and gathered in the chapel, which was no more than an ordinary room into which the trappings of religion had been introduced, and Mercy, yelling her little self scarlet, was cleansed of all the sins for which she had inadvertently become responsible in the womb.

She could not cleanse herself of the sin of having caused Conchita so much fear and pain, though, for having caused her to be cut open, and, as a result, Conchita did almost nothing for the child. She was an invalid and needed looking after herself. She had come back to us with her features newly expressive of a buried fury and she set herself up to resist and demand.

We were all still in the one room. There were other, larger families than ours living as we did, but for Ma and me, it was now almost unbearable. The boys were not interested in Mercy, except as a curiosity. They wanted their mother to pay attention to them, but the harder they tried – through pleading and tantrums, climbing into her lap or holding on to her skirts and howling – the more irritated she became. The nights were growing longer; the attacks on London went on, day and night, almost without pause, and often, now, near enough to the hotel for us to feel the shocks.

Mercy needed feeding every few hours and Conchita would not (could not, she said) breastfeed, so bottles had to be sterilized and warmed up in the kitchen because we had no way of doing this in the room. Conchita would, I think, have refused to do even this task, if she could, but was not bold enough, with Ma's watchfulness, to go so far. But whenever she could, she left it to me. Only two things eased the burden of those first few weeks of Mercy's life. Ma was brighter than she had been since we had sailed from Gibraltar in August; despite the constant noise and chaos, she achieved an unexpected level of contentment in watching her grandchildren, even when the boys were badly behaved, as they were more often than not. But chiefly her pleasure came from Mercy, who was my other source of happiness. She stopped me falling into despair through lack of sleep, unrelenting demands on my time, numbing and repetitive chores. She was a little nugget of perfection, nestled in the cot that had been provided. When she was asleep, I envied Ma the opportunity just to lie still and look at her breathing.

Freddo was still in nappies when we arrived in London and, before Mercy was born, Conchita had been training him to use the toilet. He was dry, most of the time, before Mercy. Afterwards, he began to have accidents. I was carrying him to the bathroom, after one of these incidents. He had to be carried because he would not leave the room otherwise, and I could feel the urine on his trousers soaking into my skirt as I went. I had had no more than three hours' sleep the night before and, quite probably, the night before that, too. I don't know if my arms were numb with exhaustion, or if Freddo's struggles made me lose my grip, or if, in some deep recess of my unconscious mind, I thought 'enough', and let go. But he fell. We were in the bathroom by this time, and he caught the side of his face on the lid of a metal bin and hit the hard floor with a terrifying thud. He lay, howling, with a smear of blood on his cheek. I slid down the wall to join him on the floor and took him in my arms, crying almost as hard as he was, though this is not something I do easily. It was Freddo who stopped first, setting his hot little hand on my wet cheek.

'No crying, Rose. Rose, Rose, no crying.'

'No crying, Freddo,' I said, and took out a handkerchief to wipe his face. He took it from me and wiped mine. Then we both stood up and I washed and changed him. By the time we got back to the room, there was a bruise developing on his cheek, as well as the angry red slash of the scratch.

'Look, Mama,' he said, pulling at Conchita's sleeve. 'Rose dropped me.'

'Oh, my poor precious,' she said, idly, hardly glancing up from the magazine she was reading.

I changed my skirt and went to Patrick's office.

'Can you find out where a Mrs Eugenia Gatt is staying?' I asked.

He looked up over his glasses, his grey eyes empty of interest, but also of speculation or judgement. I sometimes felt this office was the oasis Peter Povedano had spoken of, where I could believe everything was over and the world back in control.

'Gibraltarian?'

'Yes.'

'Come back in an hour.'

When I went back there was a note on my desk saying Eugenia was at St Katherine's College in White Hart Lane.

Next day, after consulting with Jonas, who knew everything about bus routes, I caught a bus to Stoke Newington and another to Tottenham, where I walked past a football ground to the address I had been given. It was an adventure, to be out alone, so far from the places within walking distance of the hotel that I had come to know well. From the top of the bus I could see down into the piles of rubble that were all that remained of houses and shops which had received direct hits, and into the windows of the upper floors of houses where the walls had been left standing but what had made the buildings useful, as homes or businesses, had been burned or bombed into nothingness. Yet most of London still stood. It had been hard to believe, when we first arrived, that any city could withstand the number of air raids we had experienced and be anything but a shell. Now we knew the damage was only ever local. Sometimes so local as to pick out one house in a terrace, leaving untouched the others to right and left. But if noise could kill, we would all have been laid out along the street, rows of corpses.

A group of women climbed the stairs of the bus and sat in the seats around me. They seemed to have finished a night shift and were on their way home, elated by the excitements of the night. These had included an incendiary falling in the yard of the place where they worked, which one of them had been involved in extinguishing with water pumped from a bath filled and ready for the purpose. They were all young, though I did not want to stare at them so I couldn't say how young. I did want to stare at them, of course, but did not want it to become obvious to them, in case they stopped their idle, intimate chatter.

It seemed that fire-watching duties were carried out in pairs and the young woman with a starring role in the night's adventure had been watching with Eric. He might have been called some other, similar name beginning with an 'H' that the speakers did not bother to pronounce, but it sounded like Eric. He was the object of more interest than the bomb. There was much speculation about whether the female fire-watcher – who had unnaturally blonde hair, with a flimsy scarf laid over it and hanging loose, in contrast to the more sober, tightly tied headwear of the others – had taken advantage of the darkness and Eric's proximity to indulge in what they called 'hanky-panky' and 'canoodling' and 'fun and games'. The blonde was happy to play along with this, denying it but implying with shrugs and knowing giggles that it might nevertheless have been so.

'Have you seen the length of his fingernails?' she said. 'Would you let them near you?'

'It's not the length of his *fingernails* that matters,' said another, and they hooted and squealed with delight.

All that the girls wanted to know about the business of putting out the fire caused by the incendiary was: how useful was Eric?

'About as useful as a wet rag,' said the blonde, and the others had plenty of suggestions for how useful a wet rag might be, in intimate and domestic situations.

'You could always have thrown him on the fire to smother it.'

I was thinking, while they talked, how I would never be able to fit in as one of such a group, happy to laugh at, if not make, jokes about subjects I would be embarrassed to discuss with anyone (except, perhaps, Sonia). But when they stood up and clattered past me down the stairs, I saw that they were not all of a type. One of them, a small, brown woman with a coat that was too big for her, turned her head and lifted the corners of her mouth in the hint of a smile as she passed me. Perhaps she had not laughed with the others, and wanted to make a connection with the only other person on the top deck who hadn't laughed. Seeking a companion in her condemnation of their vulgarity and hilarity. If so, she was wrong to pick me. I didn't condemn them; I envied them. I would have liked to have their easy sense of companionship and their ability to find innocent amusement in the most fearful circumstances.

At last the conductor called up the stairs to let me know we had reached White Hart Lane. I walked up to the doors of the college with the same sense of awe I had had when we first arrived at the Royal Palace Hotel, but for different reasons. Then, I had not believed we could be admitted to a place so redolent of luxury; this time it was a place of too much authority for the likes of me. But inside, it was just a school. Functional and dull. There were women and children passing through the hall and I asked if they knew Eugenia Gatt. No, they said, and directed me to an office where an old man sat reading a newspaper he seemed reluctant to lay aside. He kept one hand on the page he had been studying while flipping through a ledger with the other and, finally, without ever lifting his eyes to my face, gave me a room number. It was up a wide, uncarpeted stair, down a long, uncarpeted corridor (before the Royal Palace I would not even have noticed the lack of carpet, but now it set where we lived apart from this place). I knocked on the door. I could hear a child crying inside, but no one spoke or came to open the door, so I turned the handle and went in.

The room was half the size of the one we had, and there were more beds in it. If there had been carpet on this floor (which there wasn't), it would have been all but invisible. The only people in the room were Eugenia, Anna and the baby. It was Anna who had been crying but she stopped when I came in, and bounced up and down on the bed where she had been sitting beside her mother, calling my name. Eugenia, holding the baby, looked up at me without, at first, appearing to know who I was. She had lost weight since I had seen her last. She had always been a little plump, but now, though not thin, she looked haggard.

'Rose,' she said, at last, and the old, warm, uncomplicated smile made her look like the woman I had come to find. The cheerful, practical, helpful person I needed, when moments before she had looked in need of care rather than able to give it. The next moment, she burst into tears.

I inched round the beds between me and her and sat down, put my arms round her. Anna crawled into my lap and began asking me questions about where was Freddo? Where was Alf?

'Not far away,' I said. 'I'll take you to see them.'

A woman I had never seen before and a teenage boy who looked to be her son came into the room. She didn't say anything but stood with the open door in her hand, making it obvious she expected me to leave, and I couldn't blame her. The room was small enough without extra bodies. Eugenia hoisted the baby on to her hip, took Anna's hand and walked out ahead of me.

'No visitors, remember,' said the newcomer, as we passed.

Downstairs was a room with sofas and chairs, also quite full of people chatting or playing cards or knitting or doing nothing, but we found a space to sit and Eugenia told me what had happened to her since she left Gibraltar for the second time. They had been taken to an ice-skating rink, she said. There was no privacy at all and they had had to sleep on the benches set in tiers round the space the rink would normally occupy. It had been explained to them that this was only temporary, and it was, but not because new accommodation had been found but because the rink was hit by a bomb. They had all been in a shelter at the time, and were unharmed, though she had lost most of her belongings. The bomb was nevertheless a relief, she said, because she had been frightened for the two or three weeks at the rink, not of bombs but of the other families, which included several with delinquent children. There had been no place of safety for her and her children.

After the bomb, they had to be fitted in wherever it was possible, and this is how she had ended up in White Hart Lane, in a room with another family who were neither friendly nor easy to live with, though might have been both if only more space had been available. Eugenia was reluctant to condemn; she set herself high standards of behaviour towards others but would not admit that those who behaved badly towards her in return were therefore less admirable than she was. It was only circumstance that had made them unable to act with the dignity and kindness she felt sure they would normally exhibit. I remembered this aspect of her character from school, when she had, albeit quietly, defended those the rest of us were ready to abuse, often for good reason, and I thought at the time it was a sign of stupidity. Ma would certainly have thought so. My own judgement of the woman I had seen, briefly, in the room with Eugenia was that in any circumstances she would have her elbows out. I admired and was at the same time irritated by Eugenia's tolerance.

It was not difficult, in the circumstances, to persuade her to move to the Royal Palace Hotel. If I could find her a room. The prospect of having Alf and Freddo to look after again, and a baby to deal with, was to her as the offer of a library to work in every day would have been to me.

I don't know how easy it would have been to make this happen without the support of Mrs Almondsbury and Patrick, but I had their support and within a week Eugenia, Anna and the baby – whose name, I found out from the forms, was

Eduardo – were transferred to the Royal Palace. A room was made vacant for them on the same corridor as ours, as one or two families had moved out to stay with relatives or friends already living in England. Mrs Almondsbury suggested that Conchita and her children should move into it, too, leaving Ma and me with space and peace. Conchita, to my surprise, agreed. And so, finally, Ma and I were able to be alone in the room, just as I had imagined on the night we arrived, when I had thought, mistakenly, it was all I wanted.

12

Sonia

I had a letter from Sonia.

'Hola, Rose,' she wrote, 'I just found out where you are so now I can let you know I miss you. Who would have imagined that? You're a dull, sober-faced old grump of a thing and I should be rejoicing – no one to make me feel trivial by just looking at me in that way you have. But the fact is, I do feel trivial when I haven't got you tugging me back over the line between having fun and being ridiculous. I can't see where the line is. I just have this feeling I've crossed it and I need my Rose to take hold of me and lead me to safety. What a state to be in! I don't suppose you miss me, do you? Do you need me to be there, pushing you towards the line between having fun and not living at all? Rose! Rose! I'm a sheet flapping in the wind without you.'

She wrote from an address in Buckinghamshire, where she was living with the family she had worked for in Gibraltar. The father was Bob Thrupp, which was an explosive, monosyllabic name, as I had told Sonia when she first mentioned him.

'Only you, Rose,' she said, 'could use a word like "monosyllabic", just like that.' She snapped her fingers. It tickled her, though, and she shortened his rank, too, calling him 'the Cap' whenever she spoke of him. His wife was Genevieve. 'What's that, then?' Sonia asked. Polysyllabic, I told her, and soft. In name at least, they were incompatible. Though whether they were in fact, I didn't know, as I had never met them, but I had been in their house. I had an image of them from their names. Bob was short and stocky and square; Genevieve was wispy with long arms and legs. Sonia had never described either of them to me, mentioning only their movements or decisions when these affected her. Their children, Dilly and Jane, were bright and funny, according to Sonia, though she did not speak of them much, either. Their house in Gibraltar, its furniture and furnishings, ornaments and cutlery, glassware and plates – I knew all about those.

The Cap was working in London, Sonia said, and Mrs Thrupp, Dilly, Jane and Sonia were all living in what was counted as safety, close enough for the Cap to come home, some nights, if not every night, and every weekend. Far enough away to avoid the bombs. She meant 'to avoid the air raids', because here in central London we were also avoiding the bombs, only in cellars and shelters and Underground stations, rather than the countryside. She could come to London to meet me, she said, on a day off. She would travel down with the Cap. She named a date when she could come and I wrote back at once to agree.

'I miss you, too,' I wrote. 'I need you to remind me that not everything is serious. Fluff me up a bit.'

It was cold, the day she came. It was the end of October and the raids were as intense, the days shorter, the nights longer and darker, and the cold bit into our southern skin.

'Call this cold?' said Jonas when I shivered as I crossed the lobby late one night. 'You wait.'

In anyone else I would have sensed a smacking of the lips behind the few words. Our other helpers, having endured our collective chatter and exuberance, might have been forgiven for some small relish in anticipating the effect temperatures below freezing might have of cutting us down, making us realize what real life was like. But Jonas had told me how much he appreciated the Gibraltarians. They seemed, he said, not to notice the colour of his skin.

I went to Marylebone to meet Sonia off the train. I wore my thickest skirt and coat, and a scarf and gloves in fluffy, ticklish wool, which I had bought from a woman on our corridor who was knitting as if the outcome of the war depended on it. I met Conchita in the lobby as I left and she asked if I was really going out looking like that.

'I hope you're not going to meet anyone important,' she said.

'I'm meeting Sonia Gutierrez.'

'I suppose it doesn't matter, then.'

I was used to Conchita telling me what suited me and what didn't, and although she voiced her remarks as criticism, I was often pleased to take them as advice. But this time I must have looked as if I had got dressed in the dark, and had chosen clothes that did not go with each other, did not even all belong to the same person. Lack of sleep and distaste for the bland dishes served up in the hotel meant I had lost weight, and the hem of my skirt sagged below the coat, which was brown. The skirt was blue. The scarf and gloves were striped in indistinct but bilious shades somewhere between yellow and orange. In Gibraltar, in Casablanca even, I had still had a sense of myself as someone I needed to pay heed to; it had mattered that I considered how I looked. I had not parted company entirely with my younger self who envied Sonia's sleek hair. Now I thought only in terms of lessening hardship. What did it matter how I looked if I could only keep myself warm, find enough time and opportunity to sleep, keep harm from befalling my mother and Conchita's children.

'Sonia is someone important to me,' I said. 'But I don't believe she will mind how I am dressed.'

Nevertheless, as I walked to Marylebone, through the park to Edgware Road, I wished I could have avoided looking quite as comical. I had also forgotten, until the crowd from the train began to spill off the platform into the vast, dirty, cold booking hall where I stood waiting, that she would be with the Cap. The man I had never met but whose image I had fully formed in my head. It would have made no difference to what I wore, but it would have made me more anxious. I did not see the Cap, at first, because I was warm with pleasure from my first glimpse of Sonia's small, trim shape running towards me, and because he was entirely different from the image I had created around the name Bob Thrupp.

Sonia barrelled into me and tugged my face down to hers, kissing me again and again on both cheeks. I became aware, on the periphery of my vision, of a pair of stationary legs in blue uniform trousers rising from highly polished shoes, and when she had finished her assault on my face, Sonia stepped back and said, 'Captain Thrupp,' indicating the trousers and the naval jacket on top. He was tall and lean and, though standing still and smiling, implied movement and severity in the way he stood and the rough-cut planes of his face. He was younger than I had expected, too. I had pictured a man of my father's age, though I knew his eldest child was only six so I should have known he might be no older than my brother.

We went with him to a building in Whitehall, where he wanted Sonia to meet him for the journey home. I did not understand why she could not have met him at the station, but she had obviously agreed to the plan beforehand, so I trotted along at their side, abominably conscious, now, of my ill-fitting, ugly clothes. We walked to Baker Street and went on the Underground. I had passed the Underground stations, walking around Kensington, but the idea of going down the steps had been terrifying. There were queues for overnight places on the platform outside many of them, and this gave me the impression that the space underground would be crowded with desperate people. If I had gone in with the intention of travelling to a given station, I would have had no idea how to reach it. I had an image of trains coming and going in darkness, with no way of distinguishing their destinations.

The Cap and Sonia knew how to navigate below the streets of London, and walked without hesitation up to the ticket window. I thought I should make good use of this experience and learn how to identify where the trains were going; it was easier than I had imagined, and the atmosphere below ground was less threatening. The platform was busy, but with people, like the Cap, who looked as if they were travelling for some serious purpose. Mostly men. Mostly in uniform. I learned that I needed to know which line to travel on, in which direction – north or south, east or west. I was excited by this new knowledge and looked forward to using it in some future venture to places distant from Kensington, until the train arrived. It was, even more than the steam train, like a creature with malice in its heart. Snub-nosed and noisy, pushing the air out of the tunnel ahead of it, snapping its doors open and

shut again, like so many mouths designed to feed on a shoal
of passing plankton – us. Inside, it was both deafening and
silent. No one spoke. We stood beside the Cap, who looked
sideways, slightly upward, for the whole journey. There was
nothing to look at except the other people in the carriage and,
surrounded by so much masculine officialdom, it seemed presumptuous to look at them. So I copied the Cap's withdrawn
stance and endured it till we reached Charing Cross, and
climbed the stairs out into the cold of the street. We parted
from the Cap at the doors of a building with no signs to indicate what went on inside, and whatever it was, it was not for
the likes of us to question. When the polished wood of the
door had swung shut behind him, Sonia grabbed my arm and
began to skip down the pavement, dragging me with her, my
scarf flapping up and down, shedding strands of wool into my
mouth. She had been, after the first greeting, perfectly calm
and quiet, but now I had the real Sonia, my Sonia, back, and
I skipped with her. The only person who could make me want
to skip.

'Where are we going?' I asked, breathless.

'Lyons Corner House,' she shouted. 'You and me, Miss
Rose Dunbar and Miss Sonia Gutierrez. Oh, I'm so pleased to
see you.'

We turned a corner and came to the river. I had not seen
the river in my wanderings, and I was unexpectedly thrilled at
the sudden sight of water. For most of my life I had never
been without a view of it, and though the Thames had none
of the grandeur and movement of the sea, it was still a delight.
The cafe, when we reached it, was crowded, and we sat knee
to knee at a small table wedged between a pillar and a wall.
From where I sat I could see, through the condensation

fogging the huge windows, the ghostly shapes of people walking past. It was warm and I was able to shed my ghastly scarf and coat and feel, with Sonia beside me, like someone I might, myself, be happy to meet.

I could take a good look at Sonia now. Like me, she was a few pounds thinner than she had been last time I had seen her. Her lovely, softly falling dark hair had been cut in a style and artfully curled at the ends. In Gibraltar we had been used to home haircuts. My hair was easily snipped over, and Jamie, Sonia and Conchita had all done what was necessary. Sonia's mother and then her sister had trimmed the ends of hers, but it had always looked perfectly natural; hair as it was meant to be. Now it was less natural, but more stylish; it suited her, but something of the freedom she had always represented for me was gone. She was neatly dressed. I did not recognize the clothes.

'Tell me everything,' she said. 'Start at the beginning and go on to the end. Which is now, the end of the time when I haven't been able to look at your lovely face.'

I tried to tell her a short version – this happened, then this happened – but she kept stopping me, asking for the details, which were just what I would have wanted from her if she had been the one telling the story. What was it like? How did you feel? How did your mother, Conchita, the children react? All the questions that turn a story from something you hear or read about into something you can live through with the person telling it. Sonia lived through the story I told as I told it, and I had not realized until then how lonely it had been, without her. Without anyone with whom to share what I felt at each stage of the journey. (As I am sharing it now, with you.) Her tenderness and sympathy made me cry. Not, as I have said before, something I often do, and Sonia was deeply shocked.

'Don't cry, Rose,' she said. 'You're the strong one.'

'Self-pity,' I said, wiping my eyes, injudiciously, with the fluffy wool of the scarf. 'So demeaning.'

Sonia laughed and laughed until I joined in with her, the table shaking and the empty cups rattling on their saucers.

'Only you, Rose,' she said. 'Demeaning. What a word. What a ridiculous notion. How can you be demeaned by knowing you have had a hard time?'

'I know,' I said. 'I meant, I shouldn't be moved to tears by it, just because I can see that you care, too.'

We walked back to the hotel. Sonia had a little brown book with pages and pages of maps showing all the streets in London, with a fold-out map at the back giving the whole of the centre of the city. The Cap had lent it to her to make sure she did not become lost and could find her way back to the place he had told her to be. We used the larger map to plan a route, up Birdcage Walk, which Sonia thought was a lovely name but which made me think of the caged bird Mme Goncourt had bought for Ma.

'Oh, Rose, my serious friend, I have missed you,' Sonia said, when I told her this.

We went past Buckingham Palace, which did not feel quite real to me, though the bomb damage and defences round it were real enough. The rest of the way was through parkland. Green Park then Hyde Park then Kensington Gardens. Anywhere we walked at home would be nothing but rocks, barely covered with earth, if at all, whereas here the green of the grass, even in the chill of autumn, implied fertility stored up in fathomless depths of soil. The leaves on the deciduous trees, never found in such profusion where we came from, were in shades of burnt orange and amber and pale yellow that made me want to borrow my mother's paints, learn the skills to capture them. I expressed all this to Sonia as we walked, but she tilted her head to the sky and said:

'It's too much. Don't you sometimes wish there wasn't so much . . . room?'

'I don't know,' I said. 'No, I don't think that.'

'Life was much more simple at home, wasn't it?' Sonia said. 'More manageable.'

'I thought I was the one who liked everything orderly,' I said. 'You were the one running around looking for lines to cross.'

'Perhaps it's because you're not with me. I didn't need to be sensible because you were. Come and stay with me for a few days, won't you? The Thrupps have said you can and it would make such a difference.'

'I couldn't, Sonia,' I said. 'Who would look after Ma?'

Ma was in our room, as usual, when we reached the hotel, but not alone. The baby, Mercy, was lying on my bed, on her back, looking, with that fascination of a baby just learning to focus, at nothing in particular, while her hands tried to catch her toes, waving about just beyond her reach. Standing beside the bed was Maribel Molinary. Both Maribel and Ma were watching the child, my mother with a look of the purest pleasure, Maribel with anxiety. Since the night of Mercy's birth, Maribel, who had never carried out her threat to find a job, seemed to feel some responsibility for the Dunbar family, or at least for the baby. Even after Eugenia had arrived, she would appear in the doorway and offer to look after Mercy, to keep

an eye on her, to take her out in the pram that Mrs Almondsbury had found for us. With five children to care for, three of
them in nappies, Eugenia was pleased to accept, even though
Maribel's expression remained sullen, as if she would have
preferred not to make the offer or was hoping it would be
refused. She was only half formed, it seemed to me.

'Sonia,' said Ma, as we came into the room. 'Come and
meet my granddaughter. She is a baby like any other, as you
will observe, but a precious thing to me.'

'She is perfect,' Sonia said. 'I can see that.' She bent over
the child and held out a finger, which the baby gripped, shifting her wandering gaze to this new face in front of her, and
the corners of her mouth lifted, formed a smile.

'Look at that!' said Maribel, crossly. 'I've been waiting for
the first smile and she goes and gives it to just anyone who
comes in the door.'

'You remember Maribel Molinary?' I said to Sonia. And to
Maribel, 'She isn't just anyone, Maribel; she's Sonia Gutierrez
from MacPhail's Passage.'

'All dressed up, then,' said Maribel. 'I wouldn't have known
her if I'd met her on the street.'

'I wouldn't have known you, either,' said Sonia. 'You've
grown into a pretty girl since I saw you last.'

It was true that when she smiled or laughed, Maribel was
pretty. But I only saw her do that when she was with other
girls her own age.

Maribel took the baby away and Sonia sat on my bed
answering the questions Ma asked her, about her family, each
member in turn, and then about herself.

'I'm having an easy life,' Sonia said. 'I'm living in a lovely
house with a room of my own, and all I have to do all day is

look after two well-behaved little girls. Someone else does the cooking and the cleaning and the laundry and the mending. The war is all talk where I am. It's in the newspaper and on the radio but it isn't happening anywhere near Amersham.'

'You shouldn't condemn yourself for being in a fortunate position,' Ma said.

Sonia laughed. 'I should have remembered,' she said, 'that you always understand more than the words I use tell you. You're right, I do feel I've been handed something I don't quite deserve and somehow it reflects badly on me that I've accepted it.'

'Did you have any other choices?'

'Yes, I did, but none that would have made me any more useful, only less comfortable. But now I'm here, I have options. I could go and work in a factory, or join one of the services, or work on the land. Any of the jobs that girls my age who were born here are being forced to do.'

'Doesn't Mrs Thrupp rely on you?' I said.

'Yes,' said Sonia. 'She would be inconvenienced if I left.' We spoke in English. Sonia had understood as a child that fluency in the language spoken by the garrison would be an advantage to her, and she had profited from the time she had spent in my company and the company of my family to improve her ownership of it. Speaking English together had been a way of making ourselves separate from our contemporaries. All of them could speak and understand the language but not well enough to follow what Sonia and I were saying to each other, if we used any but the simplest of vocabularies and sentence constructions. It had encouraged us – or rather Sonia, because I needed no encouragement – to pick out from the books we read and the programmes we heard on the wireless words not in common use on the Rock, and learn how to use them. The word 'inconvenience' as Sonia said it implied she was mimicking her employer's voice.

'You should think carefully,' Ma said. 'When the war is over, or when it is safe to return home, if that is before the end, it will be easier to go back if you are still in the same circumstances as you were when you left.'

This was the point Mrs Almondsbury had made to me when I had asked about moving out of the hotel. I wondered if Ma was also having conversations with Mrs Almondsbury, although I had never seen her do it, or whether she was looking further and deeper into our situation than I was. I had lived one week to another, at first. Now I was living day to day.

Sonia looked thoughtfully at my mother. 'Perhaps I might not want to go back.'

'I can see that's possible,' said Ma.

Conchita and Eugenia and all the children came into the room, to see Sonia, filling it up. Sonia created an impression of excitement over the little ones, hugging them, picking Freddo up and blowing in his ear, pretending not to recognize Alf – 'Who is this handsome young man?' I knew it was an act, but it had the effect of making children respond to her. I wondered whether she managed to maintain the act when she was in the company of Dilly and Jane Thrupp, day after day, or whether she had developed a genuine affection for them that meant acting was not necessary.

'You're very smart,' Conchita said, picking up a corner of the tweed jacket Sonia was wearing and feeling the texture of the fabric, the silkiness of the lining.

'Mrs Thrupp's cast-offs,' Sonia said. 'She's always buying things she doesn't think suit her when she fetches them home.'

Conchita opened her eyes wide and – she probably didn't do this, but in my image of the day she did – licked her lips.

'I wish I had a job like yours,' Conchita said. I suppressed a gasp of astonishment and outrage; Sonia's job was looking after children, and had Conchita been interested in doing that, she could have looked after her own.

'You don't have a job at all,' Ma said.

'No, but I've been thinking of finding one. Jobs in factories are easy enough to get. I might do that.' She tossed her head and looked around at us, challenging us to oppose this. I should not have been surprised. I could see that, lazy and fastidious as she was, such a life might appeal to her. She would fit in with the group of women I had seen on the bus when I went to find Eugenia. She would enjoy their flirtatious attitudes and idle chatter. And though I suspected the idea had been put into her head by Mrs Almondsbury, the great manipulator, Conchita was capable of manipulation, too, albeit without the subtlety and understanding of other people's motivation that Mrs Almondsbury had. If there were an easy option among the tasks to be carried out, Conchita would make sure that was the one allocated to her. She would be the one with the most flamboyant hairstyle and artfully worn clothes who was the centre of attention on the bus. A job in a factory would offer her much of what she missed, separated from her friends and her husband.

Sonia looked at Eugenia. 'You'd be the one left looking after all the children,' she said. 'How do you feel about that?'

Eugenia had been wary of Sonia when we were at school. Many of the girls were. She was sharp and quick and not kind (though not intentionally cruel, at least I think not). She looked wary still.

'I don't mind,' she said.

'Perhaps you should,' said Sonia, and Ma rewarded her with the briefest of smiles.

Before we left to walk back to Whitehall, Sonia told Ma she had invited me to stay with her.

'I don't think I could do that,' I said, though Sonia had not been looking at me for a reaction.

'You should go,' Ma said to me. 'I can see no reason why you could not.'

'What about you?' I said.

'Maribel,' said Ma. 'A girl looking for a purpose in life, as you know.'

The air-raid siren went as we walked back to Westminster, when we were nearing the end of Hyde Park. Everyone within sight stopped and looked upwards, a few dozen people pausing to assess the danger by looking and listening, before deciding on what action to take. Sonia, unused to this, seized my arm and said, 'Quick! Where can we go?', ready to run to any hole in the ground or solid structure to protect us from the bombs which, surely, the wail of the siren suggested, were certain to fall just where we were standing, in the next minute.

'It's all right,' I said. 'I can't hear a plane. But we should find somewhere less exposed than this.'

The other people in the park had come to the same decision, and were now moving briskly to the exits. We came out by a Tube station and Sonia wanted to plunge into its depths in search of safety but, for once, I was the bolder one, and I urged her down the road to Harrods department store.

'We'll be safe here,' I said. 'Don't you want to see inside?'

I wanted to see inside. I had passed a few times, exploring the city I found myself in, but the uniformed men at the doors, and the elegance of the window displays, had robbed me of my courage. With Sonia, it would be an adventure. If we met with scorn, we could, together, reflect it back on whoever chose to project it on us. We were not the only people looking to be off the streets in response to the warning, and we swept through the doors in among others who seemed not to be daunted by the grandeur, so we chose not to be, either. At least outwardly.

The all-clear sounded as we went in, and Sonia lost all sense of impending death in her delight at the extravagances available to buy, and the extravagant way in which these were displayed. At first we touched nothing, fearful of being told we had soiled or spoiled what our grubby fingers had rested on, and must buy it. But Sonia spent so long circling a little tub of a hat in peacock blue, with an artfully placed feather on its brim, perched on a stand in the middle of the floor, that an assistant asked if she would like to try it on. Sonia looked thoughtful, as if weighing up whether this would be a waste of her time, but I knew she would say yes, and she did. The assistant lifted it up and positioned it on Sonia's sleek new hairstyle, standing back to gauge the effect. Sonia lifted her chin and observed herself in a long mirror in which I could also see myself, in my baggy blue skirt and shapeless brown coat and the bilious scarf and gloves. I could, I thought, be taken for Sonia's maid.

'It's a style not everyone can wear,' said the assistant, 'but on you, it is magnificent.'

We neither of us believed the woman's exaggerated praise, but it suited Sonia and I could tell she liked to look at herself wearing it. She turned her head a few times and asked the price. It was more than I had earned in a month at the Garrison Library. Sonia did not blink. She considered herself for a moment or two longer, then sighed and lifted it off her head.

'I love it, but I have nothing, at the moment, to go with it. I'll come back when I've made a decision about a new coat.'

I felt bold and carefree as we walked away.

'She didn't know we were refugees,' I said.

'Refugees! But we're not.'

'No, but if she had known where we came from, she would have thought it, and she would have behaved differently.'

'You've had a tougher time than me,' Sonia said. 'You're tougher than me, too, so I suppose that's only right. But as a reward for your toughness and because I am obviously a kind and caring friend, I shall buy you a cream bun in Harrods' tea room.'

After we had pointed out to each other the intricate delicacy of the china plates and china cups, and of the food on the plates, had picked out which of the outfits worn by the women around us we would choose for ourselves, and had wearied of caressing the napkins and the tablecloth, I asked Sonia to tell me about her life, in the way she had encouraged me to talk about mine. She brushed the question aside.

'There's nothing to tell. I'm doing the same job I did in Gibraltar, in the same family. The only difference is I don't go home at night. So I have no work to do at the beginning and end of the day. And I have my own room with trees outside the window. Only trees. If I want to see another building from the room I sleep in, I have to lean right out and twist to the left and I can make out the chimneys of the next nearest house. Can you imagine that? I couldn't. But I'm used to it now, and, honestly, I'm not sure I like it.'

'What do you do, then, in the hours when you're not working?' I asked.

'You're thinking you'd be reading books, aren't you? You would be, too. There are lots of books in the house, but whenever I pick one up I think of you and then I put it down again because you're not there to tell me why I should read it.'

'You aren't telling me what you do, only what you don't do.'

'I know.' She licked her finger and scooped up a crumb of teacake left behind on her plate. 'I sew. I make clothes for the girls, and for me. And I listen to the wireless with Mrs Thrupp, sometimes, or with Mrs Morton, the housekeeper. She tells me all the scandals of the neighbourhood, going back years and years. I wonder if it's because the houses are more than a hundred years old that the scandals don't get forgotten. I walk into the village with Mrs Morton and she'll point out a window in a cottage we're walking past and start telling me about a woman who was locked up in that room by her husband, and how everyone saw her waving at the window and waved back, but she was actually begging for help, not being friendly. When she started putting her face against the glass and weeping, they thought she was mad. And of course she was, by then, and had to be carted off to a mental hospital. Mrs Morton described it as if it was last year, and I said, surely she could have found some way of communicating, by writing "HELP" on a piece of paper, or on the window, and Mrs Morton said, oh, no, she couldn't write. Not many women in her class could, in the 1860s.'

I would have to go and stay at the Thrupps's house, if I wanted to know what was going on in Sonia's life.

We walked back to Whitehall. It was growing dark and the pavements were crowded with people hurrying home before it became too dark to see where they were putting their feet, and before the Luftwaffe arrived. Sonia told me to leave her to find her own way – she had the map – but I did not want to part with her abruptly, on a street corner. I had stopped believing that we were likely to die, if not today or tonight, then some day or night soon. I knew we could be unlucky, but it was more likely we would not be. Yet the possibility was real that someone you stood beside yesterday might be lost for ever tomorrow, and this meant no parting could be casual, as it would have been when death came only for the old and sick. So I walked with her to the designated meeting place and she did not argue.

We waited in the street outside the building where the Cap spent his days. Sitting on a pile of sandbags in a doorway, Sonia asked if I remembered a night on the Rock when we were walking back from a bay on Europa Point, where we had been swimming. A boy she knew came past on a motorbike. He stopped and offered to give her a ride home. She refused, because it would have meant I had to walk home alone. So he took us, one after the other, on a quick ride up and down the stretch of road we were walking on, to give Sonia an idea of what she had missed. I wasn't sure why she was remembering this. To make herself feel better about accepting my company on the walk across London, or because it was – I remembered it as well as she did – an evening of excitement, promise and happiness that we had shared.

'I remember his jacket smelled of oil,' I said.

'I remember he held on to my leg with his left hand and I could feel it creeping upward. I was glad we weren't going further than the end of the road.'

We didn't notice the Cap until he was right beside us, so dark had it become. He suggested I travel with them as far as Oxford Circus, but I said I knew the way and I would rather walk. We stood for a moment, Sonia and I, with our arms round each other, then I watched her trotting along beside the Cap until I could see them no longer.

I did not walk back through the park; it was hard enough to see where I was going when vehicles passing by had slits of light just enough to let me see where the road lay. The pavement I was walking on was completely dark and I trod carefully, alert for lamp posts or pillar boxes or other pedestrians in my path. When I was nearly back at the hotel, a policeman stopped me to ask what I was doing out after dark.

'Walking home,' I said.

'And where might that be?' He held a torch that had all but the smallest area of light covered over, and he shone this narrow beam in my face.

'The Royal Palace Hotel,' I said. 'It's where we're living; it isn't home really. That's Gibraltar.'

He ran the beam up and down my body as I spoke and I realized, belatedly (Conchita and Sonia would have known at once), that he suspected me of being a prostitute. I smiled to myself at how quickly he would be able to alter this judgement when he caught sight of what I was wearing. He offered to escort me the rest of the way, and I accepted because I was weary and it was easier to walk with his torch giving me an idea of the path ahead. He asked me questions about

Gibraltar as we went, and I was touched by his interest, which I had not met with from anyone else in London.

'Perhaps I'll go there, one day,' he said, when we reached the hotel. 'I'm joining up next month.'

In a city the size of London, such encounters must be commonplace, but I felt, as he vanished into the darkness, deprived of the rest of his story, which I would never know.

13

Hatty and Hetty

I met Mrs Almondsbury in the street. She was talking to Winifred. It is odd that I could not bring myself to call Mrs Almondsbury 'Moira' – in my thoughts, never mind on paper – any more than Mme Goncourt could be Sylvie to me. But Winifred had only been introduced to me by her first name, when I met her in the park, and so she remained. That she was younger, and so much more harum-scarum than Mrs Almondsbury and Mme Goncourt, made it easier. On this day, she was even more burdened with bags than usual. She had set them down on the pavement to talk to Mrs Almondsbury but began to recover them as I came up. I was walking without a purpose, when I met them, for the hour or two before I was needed next, by Patrick, by Ma. I enjoyed these walks but to be without purpose did not suit me. To be aimless made me feel trivial, guilty, so I invented tasks to do as I walked – prepare a description of the houses for my next letter home, make a note of the shops nearby, find a quiet square where I could bring Ma in the wheeled chair on a fine day. Carrying Winifred's bags as I walked was better than any of these strategies for making the walk worthwhile.

'Do you want a hand?' I said.

'Several,' said Winifred. 'Can you imagine having four arms instead of two? How useful would that be?'

'It would be against nature,' said Mrs Almondsbury, pursing her face up.

'Oh, it wouldn't be *right* at all,' said Winifred, laughing. To me she said: 'She doesn't approve of the place where I work, you know.'

'I approve wholeheartedly of what you do,' said Mrs Almondsbury. 'It's the belief system I can't accept. Spiritualism, communing with the dead. You don't believe any of that, though, do you?'

'It brings comfort to people who need it,' said Winifred. 'I don't judge.'

She was right, I found out when I knew her better. She didn't judge. It made her worthy of respect, her refusal to allocate people to categories and assign them characteristics based on those categories.

The place where Winifred worked was a few streets away. As we walked to it, the bags shared out between us, she pointed out all the bomb damage and told me when it had happened, what type of bomb, how many wounded, how many killed.

'We hide, when the raids are on,' I said. 'In the cellar or under the covers with the curtains drawn. I never know what's happening, though we hear the noises, and the hotel shakes, when it's close.'

'Oh, the noise!' she said. 'The whooshes and whistles. I hate that. But this is my home, you see. I want to keep hold of how it used to be and so I have to know what's changed. On my days off, I walk around collecting details for my diary. It seems important, somehow.'

'If I were at home and bombs fell on my streets, I expect I'd do the same,' I said.

I don't know what I expected of the place we were going to, but it was unlike anywhere I had been before. Because of the mention of spiritualism, it would not have surprised me if it had had some of the quiet, scented majesty of a religious building. Because I classed Winifred with Mrs Almondsbury and therefore with authority, I would have assumed there would be order and austerity. It was not majestic, or orderly. It was a large house, in which a large and prosperous family might have lived, but it seemed to have been converted into a depot for random things and random people; things and people were piled in every corner, or travelling in and out of doors, up and down staircases. Winifred was, it appeared, the manifestation of where she worked. Like her, it was overburdened, untidy, welcoming.

It took us some time to cross the hall, which was not large, for the number of people who wanted to ask Winifred a question or give her information, much of which began with, 'Nothing has been done about . . .'

'You can see,' she said, as we finally reached a staircase down to a basement, 'that there is much to do.'

In the basement were bags, boxes and piles of objects too diverse to be understood at first glance. Also in the basement were a very large, very fat woman sitting on a stool and wheezing, audibly, and a very small, very old woman who was standing up leaning on a stick. They looked like two people who had come to the end of something and were wondering what came next, though the disorder in the basement was so great it was hard to see what task could be counted as having been completed.

'Hetty and Hatty,' Winifred said. 'This is Rose.'

'What happens to all this?' I asked, looking round for some clue as to where I should put the bags I held.

Winifred explained that what the basement contained was donations. To be passed on to those in need or to be sold at a Fair (with a capital F, when spoken of by everyone in the Shelter) to raise funds to pass on to these same groups of needy people. They had to be separated into categories, and then the most perfect and polished goods had to be selected for sale. My walk that day, starting out as purposeless, had brought me to this basement where tasks did not need to be invented. Whatever was done here had a purpose and, as far as I could see, no one was doing anything.

'I can stay and help for an hour, if you like.'

'If you don't mind,' Winifred said, already turning to start back up the stairs. 'Hatty and Hetty would be grateful.'

I never did ask which was Hetty and which was Hatty. I arbitrarily bestowed the name Hatty on the fat woman because of the roundness of the vowel, but I took care never to test this and avoided using their names unless in tandem.

I found I had been right in thinking they had recently finished something. They had. A cup of tea. And that they were wondering what to do next. Although I was at least twenty years younger than Hatty and more than forty younger than Hetty, and I had only just arrived, they seemed to expect me to make a suggestion. This was unexpected, and only after a long pause, while I waited for them to tell me what to do and they looked hopefully at me, did I understand they could not tell me what to do because they were overwhelmed with the size of the task. My eye fell on a toy car, lying on its side, which had fallen from a bag on to the floor.

'Shall we start by separating out the toys?' I said.

'Oh, yes,' said Hetty, as if I had offered a plate of biscuits.

'I think we should,' said Hatty. 'Not long till Christmas.'

The problem with the toys, I quickly realized, was that they were mostly small and spread widely among the piles, and I was the only one of us capable of reaching the floor without a struggle. There was a table, covered in boxes, so I lifted these down ('My, you are strong,' said Hetty) and replaced them with armfuls of toys I picked out of the rubble around us. Hatty sat and Hetty stood – I asked if she wanted a chair and Hatty said, 'She never sits down, that one'; 'Never sit down,' echoed Hetty – and sorted them. By the time I left, we had carved out a few square feet of order.

'This is wonderful,' said Winifred, coming back down the stairs with more bags.

'We couldn't have done it without Rose's help,' said Hatty, looking smug.

'So young!' said Hetty. 'So strong!'

I felt, as I walked back to the hotel, some of the same satisfaction I had felt after working at the Garrison Library. Of having connected one thing with another and solved a problem.

After this, I went to the Shelter whenever I could. I reached an understanding with Hatty and Hetty. That is, I came to understand them and they came to accept me. To begin with, Hatty maintained an attitude of being in charge. Whatever approach I suggested, she pursed her lips over before graciously conceding that the idea was acceptable to her. But I soon realized that neither of them was there in the basement, day after day, with the purpose of sorting out donations or giving herself the sense of having helped those less fortunate, or for the pride of doing a job well. They came because they were happier in the basement with each other to talk to, tea and biscuits provided, than they were in their own houses. They could not have cared less about what was done as long as they did not have to put themselves to too much effort in doing it.

Hatty was married to a man who was a drunk and a bully. She was free with the details of his behaviour and I felt sorry for her, and also puzzled as to why she stayed with someone who treated her so badly. Hetty lived alone with a son who was mad. This is the word she used, echoed by Hatty. Mad in what way I did not understand, but he needed looking after and was not grateful for the care Hetty provided. I felt sorry for Hetty, too, but as I sorted and listened, I began to detect a hint of pride in their tales of the hardship they were enduring, a sense of superiority over other women whose husbands and sons had been snatched away from them by the war, and who were left with no one to fill the coal scuttle. Weaker women than they were, with their years of making the best of it.

We fell into a way of working that suited us all. I picked out, sorted and made piles on the table; Hatty and Hetty picked over the piles, exclaiming and discussing, and began to put them into boxes. When the table was full, I diverted to spend time with the books. I had been dividing these into children's, fiction, non-fiction and practical – cookery books, manuals for maintaining engines and so on – without allowing myself to pause and glance inside, doing no more than feeling the cover, fingering the flyleaf. As the chaos slowly reduced, I could allow myself to pause, to read a page or two, slide out of my London basement into other places, other worlds. I began to look forward to my idle hours.

I had no patience for Hatty and Hetty's chatter when I found a book I wanted to read, and I would retreat to a curtained alcove, dark, cold, dirty, but relatively quiet, at the back of the basement. Winifred came across me there, pulling the curtain aside briskly, which I had learned not to do as it released clouds of dust if too sharply handled. She coughed, and I stood up quickly, feeling guilty, as I would have done in the Garrison Library if I had been caught reading when I had work to do.

Winifred said, 'Do you want to take the book with you?'

I could have said I wanted to take all the books with me, but the one I had in my hand was *The Mill on the Floss* and it would have been an almost physical wrench to part with Maggie Tulliver before I had found out what happened to her, so I said yes.

'I'll bring it back,' I promised, 'before the Fair.'

I would have liked to run the bookstall, when the day of the Fair arrived, but Winifred asked me to help her on what she called a White Elephant stall, a phrase I hadn't heard before but which was in general use among the organizers of the Fair. She was selling the best of the ornaments and crockery that had been set aside. As I stood behind the trestle table covered with these things, before the doors opened, I could not imagine anyone would want to pay the prices Winifred had set. Most of what was in front of me was useless (though some of it was lovely) or so commonplace an item (though of superior quality) that surely everyone already owned as many as they needed. Winifred was hopeful, though, and I understood why when the buyers arrived. They were women, and a few men, with more than enough sixpences to be able to indulge a whim. Especially if, by parting with the sixpence and indulging the whim, they could feel they were 'doing their bit'. More than one of them used this phrase, refusing the change from the florin they had offered for a ninepenny cup and saucer. I was just relieved to see the table emptying; fewer items to repack, reallocate to boxes for other purposes.

Ours was the table attracting the most affluent. The clothing and household linens were haggled over; the toys and games needed extra helpers to prevent pilfering. I kept an eye on the bookstall. It was doing well, though not as well as our White Elephants. After it was all over, I went to look at what was left. I had my own few sixpences to spend and I knew what I had wanted from the books we had packed up for the Fair. *Adam Bede*, *Cold Comfort Farm*, *Of Mice and Men* and a book called *Consequences* by E. M. Delafield that I had started to read in the basement and had yet to finish. They were all there except *Cold Comfort Farm*, and I handed over my money. Winifred came up behind me and took it back from the stallholder, returned it to me.

'It's the least we can do,' she said. 'After all your help.'

The King and Queen came to visit us. As ridiculous as if Ratty and Mole from *The Wind in the Willows* had dropped in, all spruced up in knickerbockers, with their hamper full of picnic food. There was enough warning for a chosen child to be groomed in the protocol of presenting the Queen with a bouquet, and for instructions to be issued on how to behave as a happy, cohesive party of British citizens momentarily inconvenienced by the removal of their right to stay at home. But, luckily, not enough time for the fight over the choice of child to lead to violence, or for the worst excesses of cleaning and refurbishing. Or for an orgy of dressmaking which would have seen the majority of the audience for the event turned out like the sort of dolls we sell to visitors on the Rock.

The Dunbar family were in the background, on the day, where Ma and I preferred to be but Conchita did not. The children had been coached to sing a song and Eugenia was part of the group clustered around them, to make sure they behaved themselves or to disguise the effects if they did not, but Conchita was with Ma and me at the back of the family room, under orders to look happy for as long as it took for the royal visitors to walk past. But they didn't, in fact, walk past. They paused and engaged an elderly couple in conversation, so Conchita had time to absorb every detail of the Queen's dress, which is what she had wanted to do.

The visit brought comfort. It gave us status, confirmed our impression of ourselves as displaced British citizens rather than the sweepings of an imperial floor that had ended up in this corner for want of a dustpan. There were journalists and men with cameras ready to record that this had happened, and we knew it would be reported in Gibraltar, too. Even those of us indifferent to being photographed with royalty would have liked to be in the pictures printed on the front page of the *Gibraltar Chronicle*, if only for the pleasure it would bring our relatives left behind to see us there. Also, the food was good. They came at teatime and every conceivable delicacy the royal palate might fancy had been procured or created, and, given they nibbled a biscuit at most, there was plenty left over for us. As we took over more of the responsibility for ourselves, the food had become more to our taste, and the rules around its consumption had been slackened, but it was still central to the experience of being an evacuee.

It was, three times daily, a reminder that this was not home, with its plentiful supply of fresh tomatoes and fish. Hatty and Hetty's favourite topic, apart from their menfolk, was food – shortages, substitutions, the burden of expectation among those being fed that those doing the feeding would continue to supply what they were used to – so maybe we were not alone in seeing a decline in the standard of food as a consequence of war. If worrying about dying becomes too wearisome, then worry about eggs.

After the royal couple had left, we sat down to tuck in. Mrs Almondsbury came to sit with us, bringing a girl in the uniform of a Wren with her. Her daughter, Martha. I looked curiously at this girl in whose image Mrs Almondsbury had re-created me. Physically, we were of a similar type, both tall, angular. And plain? I had never applied this word to myself. I knew I was not pretty, as Sonia was, and Conchita, and Ursula, who had married the man certain to be voted the most gorgeous of our generation, in Gibraltar. I was ordinary, I supposed, but looking at Martha Almondsbury I wondered if I had been thinking myself prettier than I was, because it was the word that sprang to mind. She had such strong features set in such a severe expression and I found her off-putting. I felt as if I should demonstrate friendliness, but surely it was up to her to speak first. She was the daughter of a well-to-do woman who had a position if not exactly of authority over us, then at least of influence where we had none.

It was Ma who spoke first.

'What made you take a decision to join the navy?' she asked.

Martha leaned towards her as if straining to catch the

words, and I was about to repeat them, thinking Ma's accent might have confounded her, when she answered.

'What a curious question,' she said. 'What would you have had me do? Sit at home and knit socks for the troops?'

'You are setting one thing against the other as if there were only two options to discuss,' said Ma. 'I did not ask why you chose to be useful. Only why you chose this way of being useful.'

'I'm sorry,' said Martha. Her face relaxed into a smile which made her look more like her mother, and if not pretty, then pleasant. 'That is a good question and is the one I should have answered straight away, if I had not been cross because I am too hot and also very bored with being a spare face at the feast with no purpose in being here.'

'You came to please your mother,' Ma said. 'That is purpose enough.'

'I did, and I suppose it is,' said Martha, glancing across at Mrs Almondsbury, who was involved in a conversation with some people from the next table and was not listening. 'I joined the navy because I wanted to go to sea. Now I find I am no more likely to go to sea than if I had joined the ATS or become a Land Girl. But the work we are being trained to do is interesting, and will be useful, I hope. I just wish women were allowed as crew on battleships and I could go where the war is being fought, not just endured.'

'It would not be natural,' said Ma. 'Women should not be risked in that way. Especially young women. They are a precious resource for the future and should not be squandered.'

'Shouldn't women have the right to choose if they will take the risk?'

'Men don't,' said Ma. 'They are forced to go where they

might be killed. It is only right that the authorities, who decide on what men should do, should decide on what women should do, also.'

'Why did you ask me about joining the Wrens? Were you just curious or did you think it was a strange choice?'

'I assumed you would be sent to places of danger and I thought it was a strange choice,' said Ma. 'If you had been my daughter, I would have said you did not recognize where your duty lay, in putting yourself at risk.'

'My mother tells me your daughter is very dutiful,' said Martha, 'so I'm sure she would have listened to you.'

'But she knows her own mind,' said Ma, 'so she might not.'

Martha looked at me when she spoke again. 'We've all had to come to terms with having our futures reshaped for us,' she said.

Later, Ma said Martha reminded her of me. I had not told her that Mrs Almondsbury had said that I reminded her of Martha.

'In what way?'

'Thoughtful,' Ma said. 'Serious.'

'I don't mean to be serious,' I said. 'I seem to have fallen into the habit of it without meaning to. Do you think she looks like me?'

'Similar build,' Ma said. 'Not as pretty.'

What those who condemned Ma for her harshness of speech and judgement did not understand was that when she said something that would be an empty compliment spoken by anyone else, it was what she sincerely believed to be true. I loved my mother. Felt cherished by her as the person I truly was.

14

Living and Learning

It was nearly the end of 1940 and, foolishly, I was looking forward to 1941 with some optimism. As if the changing of a date on the calendar could have any impact on the war, and only by making a difference to the war could it impact on us. But, there it was. Optimism. I was not alone in this. There was a perceptible lifting of the collective mood in the Royal Palace Hotel. We set about making our surroundings festive, and I was much in demand, being taller, to pin up the paper chains made by the children and the bunches of holly and mistletoe assembled by their mothers. A Christmas tree was carried into the lobby by two men invisible under its densely needled branches so it seemed to be travelling, head first, without human intervention. The business of decorating this could have been the source of conflict. Should have been, if we had not been bathed in the dying light of a dreadful year with the rising sun of the new one almost in sight. Boxes and boxes of decorations, home-made, bought or donated, were stacked up beneath it and a ladder was unlocked from the maintenance man's store and erected on the marble floor beside it. Warnings were issued about the unimaginable consequences of climbing this ladder, which only the maintenance man, the nightwatchman and one or two of the trustworthy women from the WVS were authorized to do.

On the first day, these worthies took turns to climb the steps (firmly held by one of the others) and accepted the baubles and tinsel handed up to them by the troops below, ignoring or not hearing the shouted instructions about where to put these. The lower branches were a free-for-all, and by the end of that first day, every branch within reach of an average adult was bowed down under the weight of glass balls, knitted balls, wooden balls, clothes pegs dressed in scraps of fabric to represent fairies, and anything else the ingenuity of the hotel residents could devise. The upper branches still had their shape, sparsely sprinkled with the finer offerings passed up to the demigods on the ladder.

Overnight, it all changed. Working parties came and went, stealthily replacing what they could reach and remove with what they had made or found themselves and, for that reason, preferred. The more enterprising of the older children smuggled in a ladder, subsequently found to have been stolen from the premises of the park keepers, but by the time the theft had been discovered and the rightful owners turned up to reclaim their property, the upper branches carried an inharmonious excess, in keeping with the lower branches. Yet no harsh words were spoken, and no one came to blows, on finding a treasured bauble had been discarded between suppertime and breakfast. By lunchtime the trinket removed would be back on display, only to vanish again by teatime in favour of a different decoration, itself displaced from its original position. It became a game; the men started to bet among themselves on which items would be there the next day. No one cared much what was hung on the tree. The fun was in the game.

On the day itself, the children performed a play, the toys that had been supplied for them by the WVS were unwrapped, and quantities of food that was tastier than normal were eaten. We sang songs. Even Ma, who had a sweet voice like a child's, as if it had retained its early purity through lack of use. At the end of the day, I sat on Eugenia's bed with Alf tucked under one arm and Freddo under the other, Anna on my lap, reading the story of Babar the Elephant, one of the gifts they had been given, with just one small lamp lit to illuminate the page. I read quickly through the death of his mother, racing ahead to the story of his exile and his triumphant return as King of the Elephants, but they were too young to draw the parallels I could see with their own situation. When I had finished they were so nearly asleep that I tumbled them into their cots and covered them up with blankets. Eugenia had been sitting on Conchita's bed listening to the story and I went to sit beside her, waiting to make sure the children were safely settled in sleep. Only then did I realize she was crying, silently, in the near darkness.

I took her hand. 'Are you thinking of the Christmas you would have had, if we'd still been at home?' I asked. I had been comparing our own Dunbar family celebrations, which were typically muted and involved no extravagance but had their own sort of peace and happiness, with the noise and splendour of the day we had just passed.

She shuddered. 'No,' she said. 'Christmas was a chore. Humbert's family always put religion before fun. I'm missing Humbert. I wish he could have been here to see the children enjoying themselves, but it doesn't matter what day it is, I miss him all the time. I don't seem to be anyone without him. I'm surprised to see my reflection in the mirror sometimes because I don't feel I exist, unless he's there to make me certain I do.'

I was shocked, and almost angry, that she should count herself of so little worth that she thought she needed a husband to give her shape and substance. I believed Humbert to be a good and honest man, but no better a person than Eugenia. I thought she was confusing the physical strength of masculinity with strength of character. I did not say so; nothing I said would make her see him any differently.

'You do exist, and I'm glad of it,' I said.

The Germans, it seemed, were going to be late arriving, so we all went to bed to sleep off the food and excitement. Only when I woke in the morning did I realize they had never come. Christmas had been a time of peace. In Kensington, at least. It did not last. Before the New Year arrived, the bombers did, in huge numbers. The clock ticked over from 1940 to 1941 while we sat or lay in the cellar, hoping for nothing more from the future than that we would live to experience it.

The children started going to school. Such of them as were of the right age, whose mothers were prepared to accept that it was more important that they should learn, and particularly that they should learn English, than that they should be kept where their families could ensure they were safe. Alf was one of those. The school was in a mews behind the hotel, run by Roman Catholics and half empty because so many children had been evacuated to the country, but even so it must have been difficult for the teachers, who had to cope with teaching and controlling a mass of new pupils who could not be relied on to understand what was said to them. Unsurprisingly, the mothers of the children still living in the district and attending the school did not welcome the mothers or the children from Gibraltar. Eugenia came back in tears, having left Alf, two or three days after they started. A woman much older and larger than she was had stood in front of her as she tried to leave, leaning in and telling her to go back to where she came from.

'We don't want your sort here,' she had said. 'You should have stayed where you were instead of running away, expecting us to feed you and protect you.'

She had spoken slowly and loudly and Eugenia was in no doubt about the sense of what she had said, if not the actual words.

'Her breath smelled,' Eugenia told me, as if this was the ultimate indignity, to be accused of being a parasite by a woman with poor hygiene standards.

Conchita, Eugenia and I took it in turns to go to the school. I was conscious of something stronger than dislike among the parents I saw there, but none of them spoke to me. A teacher came out with Alf one day, to explain how he came to have a scratch on his leg, and told me what a delightful child he was. He was growing fast out of babyhood into a more aware, more thoughtful (though still turbulent) child, and I was pleased at this compliment, made much of it. I was even more pleased to note that he seemed to have no difficulties in mixing with other children, those who lived there as well as those from the hotel. He could speak English well, and this must have helped.

There was an outbreak of nits, which gave the disgruntled mothers of Kensington the chance to point a finger, openly, at the filthy (literally, they felt able to say) foreigners who had arrived in their neighbourhood. There was name-calling among the children, too, and Alf wept as he sat on a chair, on

a newspaper, a towel round his shoulders, with Eugenia comb-
ing eggs out of his wet hair. But the next time he went to
school, he came home cheerfully to tell us that the head
teacher had told the class that nits only liked clean hair, and
those who had escaped the infestation were suddenly the ones
being looked upon as dirty.

If there was one thing I had not anticipated gaining from this
disruption in our lives, it was that I would learn to know my
mother better. We had been so intimate all my life, physically,
that I thought I understood her mind as well as her body. But
I was not prepared for her to champion Eugenia against the
aggressive mothers at the school. She must always have hated
injustice in the way she hated failures to adhere to standards
of moral and social behaviour, the way she hated sloppiness
wherever and however it evidenced itself. But the first time I
understood that wrongs done to an innocent incited her
wrath was when she told Eugenia to push her to the school, in
the wheeled chair Mrs Almondsbury had found for her.

I offered to go, too, to push the chair, if Ma wanted to see
where Alf was spending his days, but she told me I wasn't
needed. She went several times, then stopped. Eugenia could
not tell me what had taken place; in fact she said that, as far
as she could see, nothing had taken place. But the cheerleader
for the schoolyard bullies had been cowed by Ma's visits. I
don't know if it was what she said to them, how she behaved
towards them, or just the quiet dignity in the midst of obvious suffering that she displayed, but the taunting stopped,
and Conchita and I were able to leave it to Eugenia to lead Alf
back and forth each day, which is what we, and Eugenia, but
not Alf, wanted.

15

Mrs Thrupp

I went to stay with Sonia. It was January, and no colder than it had been in October. I began to think I had not been cold then, after all. Only 'chilly', as I had heard people say and had put down to the British talent for understatement. Just as the Blitz was 'a bit noisy'. It had been cold the previous winter, Hatty and Hetty told me, with relish. This winter was nothing to be excited about, and I had come to accept the definition of chilly and to step out of doors without first wrapping myself up in every garment I owned.

I boarded the train looking, I hoped, less like a refugee than the last time Sonia had seen me. I was wearing a coat I had bought from the donations to the Shelter. It was dark blue, and fitted, and was exactly my size. It had failed to sell at the Fair and Winifred, when we were packing the leftover goods away, had pointed out that it was waiting for someone tall and thin.

'Like you,' she said, and held it against me, then told me how much she wanted for it, which was less, I was sure, than she would have told a tall, thin customer at the Fair. Conchita had lent me a close-fitting cloche hat in a dark red she said suited me better than her, and I had shopped among the knitters in the hotel for a pair of mittens that were as close a match for the hat as I could find. I was to stay for three nights and carried what I needed in a little leather suitcase that reminded me of our journeys by sea so forcefully I could almost feel the ground heaving beneath my feet as I stood on the platform at Marylebone. I was relying on the well-fitting hat and coat, the familiar suitcase, to avoid feeling overwhelmed. I was travelling on my own. Not far, it is true. Away from rather than towards danger. But still, an adventure to me.

The train was not crowded. There was one other woman and a boy in my carriage. He kicked his heels against the seat, in an irregular rhythm of hard and soft. She told him to stop. He waited until she was looking out of the window and began again, and she did not notice for a while, but then turned and smacked his leg, hard.

'You'll be annoying this lady,' she said.

I pondered the word 'lady'; whether this was a word, like *señora*, that merely meant 'woman', or whether she intended to imply a level of refinement. Then I, too, started looking out of the window and forgot them both.

Sonia met me at Amersham, the nearest station to the Thrupps's house, and we walked the two miles or so, mostly uphill. Sonia made me walk on the inside, away from the traffic, because she said I wasn't used to the reckless way drivers went round the bends in the countryside. We took turns carrying the suitcase; there was a label on it from the voyage to Liverpool and Sonia told me I must never take it off, because I would want to point it out to my grandchildren in forty years' time, as evidence of what had happened to us. At one point she led me to the opposite side of the road to avoid a malicious dog in one of the houses we passed. It rushed up and down the fence, barking at us, but looked like a dog that would jump up with delight rather than evil intent. She asked me about Mrs Echado from the basement of our building in MacPhail's Passage.

'I can't picture her without her dog,' she said.

I said that Mrs Echado had lost all sense of who she was. She had gone from living with her dog in the basement of a building in Gibraltar to living on the top floor, at the Royal Palace Hotel, in a room with a view over Kensington Gardens, with another old woman and her husband whom I don't believe she knew until we arrived. At first she had talked of the dog, and of home, and of what she would do as soon as she arrived back in her own room. She was dreaming of the moment when she would have her pail and her scrubbing brush beside her as she cleaned the steps. But then the distance between her and those steps became too much for her to bridge, and she stopped talking about home and began to discuss, as if you and she were seeing it for the first time, what was in the view from the window. Last time I had seen her, in the cellar during a raid, she had expressed surprise to see me there.

'Have you come on a visit?' she said.

The Thrupps's house was tucked away at the end of a drive edged with a dense, dark tangle of evergreen shrubs. It looked watchful, when the last of the shrubs was past and it revealed itself, in front of a semicircle of gravel. Its sash windows were like so many unblinking eyes set in a craggy face. Behind it were lawns and flower beds and trees; not trees growing where seeds had fallen and germinated, but trees planted at intervals long ago, now large and elegant.

The watchfulness was inside the house as well as on the

outside. It was quiet when I arrived, as Mrs Thrupp was out for lunch with the children and Mrs Morton was in the kitchen. But even when the family were all there, in the evening, and there was as much noise as that number of people might be expected to make, it felt quiet. There was more space around the bodies in the house than I was used to, but there was also some sort of constraint. This family lived in a section of society far distant from any I had observed closely before, and I wondered if I was just unfamiliar with the good manners that meant words were spoken carefully and physical contact was avoided.

And yet, what I have just written would seem to be incompatible with the impression Genevieve Thrupp made on me. She was, in contrast to my mental picture of her, jolly. She talked, continuously, in whole sentences that travelled between topics without obvious links but also without losing their grammatical structure. She exclaimed and laughed, and she touched.

'It's the nicer friend!' she said, when she came home with the children. 'How I've wanted to meet you! Let me look at you now.' She put both her hands on my shoulders and held me, as if I could not be relied on to stand still without being steadied. 'You've been mentioned so often and I thought Sonia meant you were the nicer of her two friends, but it turned out she meant you were nicer than her, and her only friend, if that could be true of someone so absolutely adorable as Sonia. I have any number of friends and I am not as pleasant a person as she is or, I'm sure, as you are, and I expect Mrs Morton has given you lunch, at least I hope she has, because we were hoping you would both have dinner with us and we have to wait for Bob to arrive home.'

She finally let go of me and stood back, smiling, which gave me a chance to observe her. She was a large woman, from ankle to crown, and had large features, too large for the surface of her face. She might have been drawn by someone who deliberately, or through lack of skill, created a naive effect. The colours she wore – cherry red, bright blue – and her abundant, elaborately waved hair made her look crudely made, though her voice and the quality of her clothes were anything but crude.

The little girls were smart and polite. There was nothing excessive about them and they seemed fond of Sonia. She behaved towards them with good humour and tolerance, and she was capable of quite the opposite, as I knew, so she must have been fond of them. Or at least appreciative of the benefits of the job and prepared to pay the price of holding her temper in check.

When the Cap came home we ate in the dining room with him and Mrs Thrupp. This was a courtesy to me, I understood. Normally Sonia ate with the children. We talked about books. Or the Cap and I talked about books, a topic he introduced as Sonia had told him, so he said, that I was a 'great little reader'. He asked me what I had read recently and I told him, knowing I had nothing to be ashamed of in my choice, but conscious of the narrowness of my knowledge. He was gracious, and invited me to look through the books in the room they called the library. His taste, he said, tended to facts, not fiction. In particular, to historical facts and to those historical facts that related to armed conflict. He said all this deprecatingly, as if he feared I might be repelled by someone who found war fascinating, but I knew he would have been astonished to think I really did find it repellent, and in fact I could have told him that, in this, he was entirely typical of men like him. It was his taste in books that was the core of the collection in the Garrison Library.

Throughout this conversation, Mrs Thrupp chattered to Sonia about the children. She seemed as merry in her talk as she had been earlier in the day, so I could not understand, on the train when I replayed my visit, why it was I was left with the impression of everyone in the house having an ear and an eye open for giving or taking offence. They might each have been given an allotted space and rules on what must be spoken about, and were conscious of these hidden boundaries at all times. Even Mrs Thrupp, who spoke as if she had no thought for what she was about to say until it spilled out of her mouth, and who touched the children, and Sonia and me, while I was there, much as a Gibraltarian mother would. Although not quite like that; Sonia's mother, when she was alive, would hug and push and squeeze and tweak. Mrs Thrupp stroked.

Sonia said almost nothing and looked at me, or the table-cloth. She answered Mrs Thrupp when required. She neither looked at nor spoke to the Cap. I thought she was behaving as if she believed herself to be their inferior and I was glad to escape the room.

'Are you happy here?' I asked, when we were alone.

She shrugged. 'Do I have any choice?' Then she smiled in a way that brought the old, merry Sonia back into the room. 'There's an Italian prisoner of war who helps in the garden, though. It's worth staying just for the sight of him with his shirt off.'

Mrs Thrupp called me into her room the next day to show me a dress she said she could no longer fit into.

'You'd think with rationing, and shortages, I'd be losing weight, wouldn't you? But Mrs Morton is too clever a cook – that's what I blame it on, anyway – and, of course, my mother was a chunky lady, just like me, so Bob must have had an idea what he was marrying at the time, and I've never quite accepted that I'm not as slim as once I was, so I look around for girls like you who might suit the clothes I've bought and never worn.'

Sonia had told me that Mrs Thrupp handed clothes on to her, but she was so much shorter that most of them didn't fit or didn't suit her.

'You're just the right size,' she had said. 'Watch out.'

The dress Mrs Thrupp was holding out to me was wool, with a full skirt, a double row of buttons on the bodice, and a matching belt. It was a beautiful, pale, elegant shade of green.

'I can't accept this, Mrs Thrupp,' I said. 'It is far too expensive for me just to pack it in my suitcase and carry it away.'

'Why?' she said. 'What does how much it cost matter when it will hang in my wardrobe until I have no more space to hang anything else and then I will take it out and cut it up for rags? I might as well cut it up for rags now, this minute, if you say you don't want it.'

'I do want it,' I said, 'but it matters to me how much it cost. I should be prepared to pay for the clothes I wear, and this is worth more than anything I would ever be prepared to pay.'

She came up to me and put her arm round my shoulders, pulling my head towards hers. She rested her forehead on mine.

'Look,' she said, 'we're exactly the same height. If you had money to spare, wouldn't you have brought me a present, coming to stay in my house?'

I had thought so; not at the point I caught the train, when all that was on my mind was seeing Sonia and I imagined the Thrupps would speak to me, if at all, only in passing. But when I sat at their dining table, eating their roast beef with their silver cutlery off their porcelain plates, I thought I would have liked to have some small gift to make in recognition of their kindness. I had wished I was skilful with a needle, or with a pencil and paints. But then I had imagined the embarrassment as Mrs Thrupp looked at whatever I might have brought with an expression of contrived pleasure overlaid on top of revulsion, at worst, puzzlement, at best, and I was glad the idea had not occurred to me in time to do something about it.

'You have been kind to me,' I said, 'and I wish I had something worth giving you, but I do not.'

'You do,' she said. 'You can give me the pleasure of putting the dress on and letting me see you wearing it, and then you can please me even more by taking it home.' I stepped away from her, confused and oppressed by this older, richer, more powerful woman asking me to take from her something I had no right to own. 'Just do this for me,' she said. 'Wear it this afternoon when I have a friend coming for tea. I'm expecting the children, and Sonia, and you, of course, to join us.'

I was wearing my blue skirt with a white blouse and a plum-coloured cardigan; it was not an outfit I was proud of, but it was smart and inoffensive enough not to be noticeable. But maybe it had failed to reach that hurdle, of inoffensiveness, in Mrs Thrupp's eyes. Sonia was better dressed than I was, and the offer of the green dress was, maybe, all about this. Mrs Thrupp wanted the friend of her nursemaid (or lady's maid, or nanny, or whatever other phrase she used to label Sonia) to look as respectable as the nursemaid herself.

'I'll try it on,' I said. 'And if it fits, of course I'll wear it this afternoon.' I was aware as I left the room that she had not moved and I realized she might have wanted me to try it on right there. But if my skirt and blouse fell short of being acceptable, I was sure my underwear would fall shorter still and I was not about to expose it.

Back in Sonia's room, I showed her the dress and repeated the conversation.

'It's lovely,' Sonia said. 'She's treating you like a doll, and you can choose to be huffy about that, but I don't see why you shouldn't just accept it. I do. She's treated me like a doll as long as I've known her. The girls, too. I don't know what she'd have done if she'd had sons instead.'

I tried the dress on and it fitted. Sonia said it made me look elegant.

'I like the inelegant version just as much, though,' she said.

That afternoon, on our way down to join Mrs Thrupp and Miss Everton-Smith for tea, we went into a guest bedroom on the floor below, where Sonia swung open a wardrobe door for me to see myself in the full-length mirror on the inside. Dilly and Jane – dressed, now Sonia had pointed it out, like little dolls in velvet skirts over lacy petticoats – came and stood either side of me, all three of us admiring our reflections. I looked like someone I might not have recognized. I could be anyone I chose, in this dress.

Miss Everton-Smith was not doll-like, unless there is a doll that is more masculine than feminine, more solid than delicate. She sat, teacup in hand, watching us as we trooped into the room. Mrs Thrupp stood up and came over to take my hands.

'There!' she said. 'I knew this was a dress that was just

meant for you, Rose, my dear. Look, Edith' – she turned to Miss Everton-Smith – 'isn't she a lovely girl?'

'She doesn't look very Spanish,' said her friend. I felt like a pony Mrs Thrupp was trying to sell to a reluctant buyer, the one exaggerating the virtues, the other finding fault. I was tempted to bare my teeth for inspection.

'My father's family was originally from Scotland,' I said. Miss Everton-Smith ignored me. She was not about to be impressed by a pony that talked.

The little girls sat, prettily, either side of their mother and were given fancy cakes with pink icing and sugared flowers on top that would have driven Alf and Freddo wild with delight but which the Thrupp children accepted as if they were no more than bread and butter. The two women resumed a conversation they had paused when we entered, about the progress of the war. Miss Everton-Smith had opinions about the members of the Cabinet that she stated as if they were facts, known to everyone and verifiable. I did not follow events closely; none of us did at the Royal Palace – we were too wrapped up in making a life for ourselves and, because we had, hitherto, before the war, paid no attention to British politics, did not feel as close a connection with those in authority as the British did. We kept alert for any mention of Gibraltar, but otherwise, it washed over us. I thought I would ask Winifred, when I saw her next, her opinion of the ministers and the decisions being taken, and I stored up Miss Everton-Smith's opinions – it was mostly she who talked while the ordinarily loquacious Mrs Thrupp sighed and shook her head – to compare with it.

I took the dress back with me. I hardly saw Mrs Thrupp for the remainder of my stay, and could think of no courteous way of returning it. To leave it behind without mentioning it to her would have been churlish; to approach her and insist on handing it back was unthinkable. What would I say? How would I say it? I wrote a note, thanking her, the day after I arrived back in London. I asked Ma's opinion first. She did not find fault with the way I had behaved over the matter.

'If you are uncomfortable,' she said, 'then take it to the Shelter and they can sell it. But there is no need for you to do that, if you like the dress and will wear it.'

I knew that my pleasure in wearing it would be less than it would have been if I had felt I deserved to own it, had worked to earn the money to buy it (though I never would have justified spending so much on anything to wear), or had carried out some service for which this was an appropriate return. Which is not to say it did not give me pleasure, then and now. I am still uncomfortable with the circumstances in which I came to own it, but I am comfortable putting it on, because it is smart and suits me and that is all that matters to me. (What I wear matters not at all to you.)

As the train went past the pleasant houses with land around them, then the smaller houses, then the terraces and, finally, the jumble of buildings, private and public, on the last part of the journey to Marylebone, I tried to think about where in all this I would stop the train, if I had a choice. Which of these villages or suburbs or central London districts would I like to call home? Which could I imagine would ever feel like home? It was not until the train was nearly at the terminus that I had an answer to the second question. This was, now, as close as it came to home. Where the ostentatiously grand stood beside the cramped and mean; where bombed-out properties stood shoulder to shoulder with the untouched walls of their neighbours; where there was no space between one building and another, or acres of parkland. The answer to the first question, I still did not have. If I had been at home (my rightful home) looking at pictures in a book, I would have picked out one of the villages the train whisked past – somewhere neighbourly, with character, with space and beauty around it. Where opening a window gave a view to a far, far horizon. As it would do at home, only this view would change with the seasons, not the weather. The fields and woods turning slowly from one colour to another, unlike the sea, which shifts its shape and runs from dark to light and back again, from minute to minute. I could almost imagine such a village as home, if I pictured Ma in the quaint little cottage with me, Alf, Freddo and Mercy playing in the garden. But they were all in the Royal Palace Hotel, and that, for the moment, though for how much longer no one knew, was where I belonged.

16

Patrick

Most surprisingly, Conchita sorted herself out with a job. Normally, I was the one who made things happen; Conchita played with her hair and waited for what she wanted to fall into her lap. That was not how it was, though. I had made the mistake of judging Conchita, as I had Lydia Molinary, by the patterns of behaviour she demonstrated in Gibraltar. When she had a husband to earn money and babies to look after, why would she go out to work as well? There were no jobs available that would have been better than strolling around the streets chatting to other young women and pleasing her-self, by and large, with how she filled her time. But when she was surrounded by so many possibilities for spending money and the chores of cooking and caring for her children were lifted from her shoulders, she went down to the place she knew she would most like to spend her time, the Selfridges store in Oxford Street, and asked for a job.

They gave her a position in the ladieswear department and she left each morning, neatly dressed in the uniform provided. She came home in the afternoon complaining her feet hurt and her back ached and she was worn out with the effort of listening to the upper-class English accents she was forced to endure. She brought home little presents, though, bought with her staff discount, and made us laugh with her mimicry of the shoppers and the other girls on the section. She was enjoying herself, it was plain. There had been, for as long as I had known her, a sullenness about her, and now that was gone. I feared it would be hard to cram her back into the confines of home and family and repetitive chores, when the time came to return to the Rock.

Maribel Molinary continued to hang about our rooms, and whenever I was out at the Shelter, she would come in and out to see if Ma needed anything. I feared Ma would find her intrusive, but Maribel startled me by saying, as she passed me on my way in one day:

'I like your mother. You know she isn't going to pretend to be nice or pretend to be shocked.'

I listened to their exchanges more carefully, next time I was in the room when Maribel was there. She was no longer the dull, rather sulky girl I had known. Though she had periods of sullen silence, she was more often talkative, telling stories of where she had been, who she had been with, what they had done, and speculating on what she would choose to do, with whom, the next day. She carried on this chatter with Ma, which most girls would have hesitated to do, knowing the sharpness of Ma's judgements. But it seemed to me that Maribel was inviting Ma to condemn her behaviour or her choice of companions. And I thought Ma, though her remarks were as terse and cruel as ever, understood that Maribel wanted a challenge, because her tone was softer, and when she had finished speaking, she would come as close as she ever did to smiling. Maribel, without looking at Ma, would smile, too.

While Conchita was learning how to be useful in a dress

shop, Maribel was trying out new ways of being a young girl in a big city. Her mother was using organizational skills she had never been in a position to show before and was in the centre of a web of women running many parts of the hotel's catering; Maribel's brother, Horace, was learning more than he would have done in a classroom at home and rising to the top through application and ambition. Even Jamie was writing to me about his part in the movement by the men of Gibraltar to make their voices heard, demanding representation on the committees that took decisions and imposed rules they were expected to follow. I was not satisfied with myself, in this comparison.

Nothing changed, for me. The work I was doing was less, not more, demanding than the job I had had at home. Looking after Ma had become more time consuming – and more burdensome, I admit – in this alien way of life where she had no one she could count on except me. I never felt it as a burden, when I was with her, but when I sat in the basement listening to Hatty and Hetty complaining, the one about her husband, the other about her son, I found myself full of bitterness that I, too, though I was younger, fitter and more able in every respect, should also have my life circumscribed by someone else's needs. Ma was not 'someone else' and I loved her, but it was harder to remember both these facts when I was not with her.

As Conchita had looked for somewhere selling clothes to work, I could have looked for somewhere that books were kept: a shop or a library. But I did not feel I had the freedom to commit to a job outside the hotel, so I asked Patrick what else there was that I could do, to take advantage of the time Maribel released for me, and to give myself a challenge. Could

I, I asked him, learn how to work with the figures that occupied so much of his time? No, he said. He didn't want any
help with the figures. When I looked at the account books he
kept so meticulously, columns and rows of numbers, each
written carefully within its allotted box, totalled at the bottom, reconciled with numbers on a page in a different book,
I could see why he wanted to keep this to himself. He was a
man satisfied with his place, and pleased with himself, every
day, for having kept control over something as slippery as the
thousands of small amounts, the pounds, shillings and pence,
he had to make balance precisely to larger amounts, and then
balance again and again to ever larger pots until he reached a
pre-ordained total of money in, money out.

Numbers were Patrick's number one love. Pieces of paper,
preferably with columns, came second. What he shrank from
was people. Which is not to say, though it took me a few
weeks of working with him day after day to understand this,
he did not need or love people. It was only that the category
of those he needed and loved was limited to his daughter, his
grandson, a man called Albert with whom he shared an office
in whatever government building he usually worked in, and
his neighbour with whom he played cribbage on Friday
nights. I knew about this warmth in what everyone else
assumed was his cold, hard nature, because he began to tell
me when he was going to see his family or his friends, sharing
with me what was so obviously the deep pleasure he felt, even
though I still cannot picture him smiling. When he mentioned Albert, it was usually to praise some skill he had, so I
knew, when Patrick looked at my work and told me I had
done it as well as Albert would have done, that the soft heart
of him had accepted me. He might not need me or love me,

but he appreciated and liked me. I appreciated and liked him, too, and was proud of his acceptance of me.

Now Patrick saw the chance to use me to shield him from the mass of people he did not know or want to know. Mrs Almondsbury or one of the other voluntary helpers would come in one day a week to hand out the allowances to the residents, but in between there were queries and requests and no matter how firmly he closed the door, it would keep opening to let in troublesome bodies who wanted something from him. Sometimes it took him a while to find the answer to a question – 'I was getting more in December, I'm sure I was' – and the person asking would drift off instead of waiting and Patrick would have to leave the security of his numbers and seek them out. This, he told me, was what I could do. Answer the queries. Chase round the hotel delivering messages, finding the answers to questions he, Patrick, had that could only be found by talking to someone.

'They won't listen to me,' I said.

'They will.'

If it had been mainly men in the hotel, it might have been a different story, but we were mostly women and the women adapted to my new authority more quickly than I did. I was less austere a figure than Patrick, less intimidating than the lady helpers who gave out the money, so I became the approachable face of the hidden machinery that governed their well-being. I soon found myself stopped in the corridors by women worried about this or that little discrepancy, the business of filling in a form, the matter of an infringement they feared might come back to haunt them. Seeing me passing, they would call out: 'Oh! Miss Dunbar!' My new status was never more clearly signalled than by this formal address.

'Tell them to leave you alone,' said Conchita, when we were held up on our way to the dining room. 'It's not as if you're being paid for this.'

'You should be paid,' said Ma, overhearing her. 'Tell them so.'

I spent a week making a note of the time I spent listening, following up on queries, delivering answers. Then I calculated what those hours represented in terms of money, if I were paid at the rate given to the lowest paid of the kitchen staff. I knew Patrick would respond to figures, not words. I laid the calculation in front of him.

'This is the least it would cost to employ someone to do what I do,' I said, and walked off. Nothing happened for a day or two, then Patrick handed me a contract that paid me a higher sum than I had suggested for each hour of work.

I wrote to Jamie telling him about this small success, and the job I was doing, what I was learning, sitting between those in authority and those the authorities were trying to keep in control, and he wrote back to tell me I should think about what a difference I could make, in Gibraltar, after the war, with this knowledge. He was planning to pursue political office, when the opportunity arose. He believed I could be part of the same adventure, speaking for and influencing the women of the Rock. I was flattered, but I knew I was not so unlike Patrick, happiest in a quiet room with books – only, in my case, books of words.

They were good months, looking back. The early days of 1941 had not brought any change in reality, except worse weather; the raids kept coming, the food was no better, we were still marooned in a building and far apart from the men who had previously been part of our lives. But the period of adjustment was over, and only the disaffected few – or those, like Mrs Echado, whose fragile minds had been splintered by the brutality of their displacement – continued to bemoan the very fact of being in London, and not in Gibraltar. Most of us just 'got on with it', the phrase we had heard used so often when we asked the local people how they coped with the Blitz.

It snowed, which was a delight for the children, who had never seen it before, except on the tops of distant mountains. Here it was piled up on their doorstep, available to them to play with and on. Jonas lent me a pair of gumboots, which I wore on my way about the streets, carrying my indoor shoes in a bag. I felt like a Londoner, those days in the snow. Going about my business no matter what, responding to the ironic comments – 'Cold enough for you?', 'All right for penguins!' – in a way that did not seem to mark me out as different.

Conchita came home with a fur stole round her throat. It looked too expensive an item for her to have come by it honestly, and I didn't find her explanation – that it was a sample that had not been satisfactory and had been sold to her for next to nothing – at all convincing. There was a hard sparkle to Conchita now, not unlike the bright crust on the surface of untrodden snow, and I was hesitant to challenge her, as I might have done in the past when she was an altogether softer and more yielding person. Actually, I mean weaker. She was never soft and yielding, just without the strength to resist or fight back.

Ma said: 'A fur is pretty enough on the animal whose skin it once was. I cannot guess at how much pain has already been caused in its journey to your neck.' Conchita did not respond.

When we were alone, I tried to tell Ma I was worried about Conchita's behaviour, but she stopped me. 'It's not your burden to carry,' she said.

I still helped in the Shelter but my work had moved from the basement, now the Fair was over, upstairs to a huge room with wooden floorboards and a fireplace where coals were heaped up and glowing but failing to live up to the promise of their appearance in the matter of heating the room. There was a large table at which everyone sat, in coats and scarves and fingerless gloves, their ungloved fingers occupied with typing or folding up letters and inserting them into envelopes. An old woman sat by the fire, doing nothing except, quite suddenly, bursting into song. She had the sweetest voice and a store of melodies with sentimental verses, which were obviously well known to many of the other people in the room because they joined in the chorus. Others round the table were refugees, ignorant of the words of the songs. I came to see that I should have rejected the label not because it diminished our status, but because we had no right to claim to sit alongside those who had suffered immense hardship and heartbreak to reach what passed for safety. Up here, the conversation was sporadic, more likely to be about the secret life of the office cat, which I had never seen move from the windowsill, than about the difficulties those around the table had to overcome to keep smiling, keep living. It was a different world to the basement.

17

Outings and Errands

I was surprised, and flattered, when Winifred invited me to tea in the rooms she rented towards Paddington. She had invited one of the refugees who had sat at the table with us, she said, a German Jew called Sigmund Raffberger, who was leaving for America. This made him a lucky man, in the eyes of the office workers, and certainly in the eyes of the other refugees, but he did not behave like a man who recognized himself as one of the lucky ones. He was forlorn, even before news of this escape route arrived, and remained so.

'My aunt will be there,' Winifred said, 'and it would be helpful to have a fourth person to lighten the mix. My aunt is easy enough to entertain, but Mr Raffberger, as you know, is not exactly jolly, and my aunt *is* jolly and I can't help feeling it might be slightly awkward.'

When I arrived, she introduced me to her aunt as a 'young friend of mine'. I had had no idea that I might apply the word 'friend' to my relationship with Winifred. It implied confidences and an intimate knowledge of how the other person thought and felt, and I could not say I wanted to share so much of myself with her. It did suggest, though, that she liked me; that I was more than an extra pair of hands. At home I would have puzzled over her status. She did not behave, or dress, like someone from the class that, for example, the Thrupps belonged to, but she was still a distance from the population of the streets where I lived. I guessed it did not matter to her, in which class she belonged or where other people believed she belonged. Her manner towards me was exactly the same as her manner towards Mrs Almondsbury. She lived without boundaries: she was single, earned her own living, made friends with whomever she chose, whatever their class or nationality. I liked her, too. I could imagine being her.

Winifred's aunt was called Mrs Best, and she looked like Winifred might look if her busy-ness ever deserted her. Winifred gave the impression of being in the middle of a storm that left her hair tangled and her cardigan buttoned up the wrong way. Mrs Best looked as if she had weathered the storm and regained a bit of control, but could never aspire to the neatness other people, who had been spared its fury, could manage. She was plump and exhausted and she talked. She listened, too, but whenever another voice stopped, hers started. She talked about food. She must have talked of other topics than food, but I came away thinking that was all she talked about. How she longed for an orange; what she had done with a cabbage someone had given her; how well last year's preserved plums were lasting; the hint she had been given on how to keep her sponges light and airy without using eggs. I could understand why Winifred had invited me. Mr Raffberger had no interest whatsoever in food. He looked as if he never ate. Mrs Best tried to engage him in speculation on the types, quantities and qualities of food he could expect to find on his plate in America, but this was never going to be a conversation with two sides to it.

Winifred turned to me and said: 'Tell Sigmund what it was like in Morocco.'

I looked at his lined, morose face and could detect no flicker of interest in what I might say.

'It wasn't the same as being here,' I said. 'For one thing, we weren't welcome, and we couldn't speak the language.'

'Ha!' said Mr Raffberger. 'You think that is not the same as my situation here? In what way is it different? No one speaks my language in this country, and when I open my mouth to speak your language I am looked on as the enemy. Before I even open my mouth, they look at me in a way that says, "Oh, yes, we know who you are, you have a bomb in your pocket ready to kill us." You think it was worse to be a refugee from Gibraltar in Morocco than it is to be a German in London?'

'I'm sorry,' I said. 'I see so much sympathy for you at the Shelter. It was silly of me to think everyone would be so kind. And now you are going somewhere else they don't speak German, and you don't know if you will be accepted any better than here. And you go alone, whereas I came in a boatload of people just like me, and we are all still living together, a little Gibraltarian colony in Kensington High Street.'

'I would rather go alone,' Mr Raffberger said. 'I cannot imagine living with so many of my compatriots. No. I will find a way, in America, to make myself a life and go on with my work.'

'You may be able to return to Germany, one day,' Mrs Best said. 'Eat all those sausages again. You have a lot of different sausages in Germany.'

'I will never go back.'

'Don't you think,' Winifred said, 'it is entirely dependent

on what sort of person you are, how much you suffer and how much you gain from life's ups and downs?'

It wasn't clear to whom this was directed.

Patrick asked me to deliver some papers he wanted Mrs Almondsbury to sign and I travelled, following Jonas's advice, by bus to Hampstead Heath, where she lived. The Heath looked boundless, almost foreign to me, after the carefully managed parks of central London. The door was opened by a maid in uniform and everything I saw as she led me through the house was elegant and polished, but Mrs Almondsbury was the same as ever and invited me to stay for lunch. We drank our soup and ate our piece of bread and butter and slice of cake in the dining room, which, if it had had a consciousness, would have been wincing at the informality of the meal and the people eating it, when it was holding itself ready for diners wearing velvet and jewels and drinking wine from cut-glass goblets. There were three of us tucking in at one end of the polished expanse of table, because Mr Almondsbury had joined us. I had pictured him as an older version of the Cap – upright, solid, certain, effortlessly authoritative. He was none of these. He had a disease that caused his limbs to shake, his speech to be slow, his hands and feet to respond clumsily to the commands his brain sent them. He may once have been exactly as I had imagined him, and the person he was once existed still, but hidden inside a block of unresponsive flesh.

Mrs Almondsbury behaved towards him as if she were oblivious to the signs of physical decay, speaking to him naturally and waiting with no hint of impatience for his mouth to frame a response. If he knocked something over, as he frequently did, she would set it upright again and mop up the spillage without interrupting what she was saying, or moving her focus from whoever was talking at the time. Perhaps she had trained herself to do this to avoid distressing him. Or perhaps she did not have to try, because she knew the man inside, and she knew he was still the same person as he had been and required no special treatment. She rarely moved to help him, as he struggled to perform the most basic tasks, but when she did, it was as if she was offering a courtesy; not moving the chair or peeling the orange because he was failing to do it but because she wanted to do it.

I understood, now, the sadness of her face in repose, which had given me my first impression of her as a pinched-up person. She had an enviable life – a beautiful house, money and status. She would have said so herself, I'm sure. Hatty and Hetty used to say to me, almost every time they talked of how hard their lives were: 'It's all right for you, living in luxury, everything done for you.' I had had the same thought about Mrs Almondsbury: 'It's all right for her.' But she was faced day by day with the cruel decline of a man she loved; her children were where she could not see them, and it was possible they would not survive. It was possible she would not survive, either, because beautiful houses, money and status are no sort of defence against bombs.

We walked round her garden and she pointed out to me the trees and shrubs and bulbs coming into leaf or bud or flower. I might never have noticed, if she hadn't pointed them out. I would have seen the snowdrops, hundreds of them, all looking down at the ground around their feet, but I would not have seen the subtle fringe of yellow-green on the fronds of the weeping willow as the leaf buds swelled, or spotted the daffodil flowers beginning to burst through the cowl that surrounded them, or taken note of the explosion of white on the wild cherries in the hedge. I could not believe, once I had looked, that I had never bothered to look before. There must have been such an unfurling of plants in Gibraltar, too, but if so, I had walked past it unheeding.

Eugenia wanted some buttons and thread for a dress she was making for Mercy to wear, in the summer, when the weather was warmer still. Conchita had brought home a piece of fabric from Selfridges for the dress, but had not bothered with the items of scaffolding without which the dress could not be made to hold together. I took a corner of the cloth and set off across Kensington Gardens and Hyde Park to find what Eugenia needed. I could have gone to a shop nearer to us, but wanted the walk, wanted the time in the open, green space, so I went back to Selfridges, where the fabric was sold.

I dawdled as I went, looking at the plants in the gardens, before realizing that the shop would shut before I reached it; the afternoon was already well advanced, so I ran the last part of the way through the park, past Marble Arch, down Oxford Street. Sonia and I used often to run, in Gibraltar. We were always in a hurry to be somewhere, eager to reach the beach or the dance hall, anxious to be home before we were missed or needed. Even without Sonia beside me, I enjoyed running in a London park, and the Selfridges haberdashery department was just as exciting a destination, to me, in its complexity and abundance, as a beach or a dance hall.

I reached the shop slightly out of breath but in time to choose the thread and the little pearly buttons that would work with the flowery cotton to make Mercy a dress suitable for the princess she was to Eugenia and Ma and me. I bought half a yard of ribbon, too. If Eugenia didn't want to trim the dress with it, she could use it to tie bows in Mercy's hair, which was not yet plentiful enough for bows, but soon would be. Altogether, I was happy in the haberdashery department, that late afternoon, with the after-rush of pleasure from running and my imaginings of the new dress and ribbon on Mercy's beloved little body.

As the shop began to shut, I took the nearest exit, which led on to a side street. A stream of shop assistants came past, released after the day's work. The staff entrance was at the back of the shop and I went that way, rather than round the front, thinking I might walk back with Conchita, who was amusing company, these days. As I rounded the corner, I saw her coming through the door, pausing at the top of the steps down to the street to speak to someone following behind her. She was laughing, and so, too, was the man who came out to join her, both of them poised to walk down the steps together, looking – even with the distance of half the length of the building between us, I could tell – like living versions of the smooth-limbed, impossibly beautiful, perfectly clothed dummies in the shop windows.

As they began to descend, I could see Conchita's hand lightly brushing the railing. Her companion's hands were hidden from me, out of sight beyond Conchita, but something about the way both he and she moved and held themselves made me suspect what became obvious when they reached the street and turned away from me in the direction of Marble Arch: that his arm was round her waist, at an angle that allowed his hand to rest on the curve of her buttocks.

I remembered, for no reason except perhaps to displace the image I had just seen with another, a time I had fallen down the steps at the end of MacPhail's Passage, as a very young child, and scraped my knee. Jamie had gone ahead of me down the steps – I probably fell trying to keep up with him – and he came running back at my cries. He borrowed a damp flannel from Mrs Echado and made me sit on one of the steps while he knelt at the bottom, sponging the dirt from the scrape and picking off pieces of grit. All the while he did this I played with his hair, so unexpectedly within my reach. It was quite long and thick and I twisted it into bunches and combed it this way and that with my fingers, causing him, I'm sure, more pain than the fall had caused me. He never said a word. Only finished tending to me and lifted me to my feet, calling me a numpty, a word our father had taught us and one I have not heard any other family use.

I could not believe the be-suited piece of perfection walking along fondling Conchita was capable of such loving care towards a baby sister, making sure she felt safe in a world which could so easily have appeared hostile. And the idea that a woman able to rely on the tenderness of my brother should turn away from it for the sake of the attentions of a man who would play with another man's wife made me so sick I had to lean against the wall to wait for the feeling to pass. They were out of sight when I started walking again.

As I went slowly across the park, I was far away from the mood in which I had run across it less than an hour before. I was too full of disgust and fear to notice anything I walked past. My mind hopped between exaggerating what I had seen and wondering if I had seen anything other than carelessness. I was rounding the end of the Serpentine when the sirens went. I looked up. We had become so accustomed to these raids that the sound of the siren barely interrupted the train of my interminable and fruitless speculation. My instinct was not to run, but to pause, to make a judgement on the degree of urgency. A family walking ahead of me waited, as I did, then they did begin to run. The low rumble of aircraft engines became clearly audible over the dying cadence of the siren. The aircraft were numerous and close. Time to be out of the open. Time to take the thread, buttons and ribbon back to Eugenia. Once again, I ran.

18

The Lights Go Out

I cannot say we were taking the raids so very seriously, by now, inside the Royal Palace Hotel. At the beginning of March there had been a night or two when the walls shook, and for a while after that no one lingered in their room. Those who believed it was safer further underground, or who had found somewhere they liked better than the hotel cellar, left for a local Tube station or neighbourhood shelter at the first wail of the siren; the rest of us went down the steps to the cellar. Then March unfolded with a succession of quiet nights and news reports of victories for Us, or setbacks for Them, and there was more dawdling on the way down the steps, and the cellar was rarely full. There were some who even went outside and stood in the Gardens during the raids, to work out where the bombs were falling, the fires burning in the vast sprawl of London all around us. On this night, though, the ferocity of the raid could not be in doubt, and the meal was being served, early, by the time I arrived.

I had puzzled over whether to take the parcel from Selfridges straight to Eugenia, in the room she shared with the children and Conchita, or whether to give myself time before I had to meet Conchita face to face. I had not decided what, if anything, to say to her, but I knew I would not be able to behave naturally. I need not have worried. In the dining room, Ma was sitting with the children, Eugenia was at the serving hatch and there was no sign of Conchita. I went to help Eugenia with the plates of food.

'Have you seen Conchita?' I asked.

'No. She said this morning she was going to go home with one of the girls she works with. She's getting married, this girl, and she wants Conchita to help her choose designs for the wedding dress and bridesmaids' dresses. She's so good at it, isn't she? Conchita, I mean. She can see at once what looks right.'

I carried the food over to the table but I had difficulty eating it. I realized now I hadn't truly believed this was anything more than a casual flirtation. I had assumed that Conchita was flattered by the attention of the well-dressed, good-looking man and had fallen into an unhealthy but essentially innocent intimacy. Now I knew this was naive. I did not believe it was a friend, a bride-to-be, with whom Conchita was planning to spend the night. I looked up from my plate of earth-coloured sludge and saw Ma watching at me.

'What is it?' she said.

I shook my head. 'I don't know. The food, the noise. Don't you wish we were back at home?'

The dining room was nearly empty as the other diners had rushed their meal and gone to find shelter, and as the chatter subsided the sound of the guns in the park and the drone of aircraft engines was persistent and frightening.

'Always,' Ma said, and began to push herself up, leaning heavily on the table. 'Get the children downstairs, Eugenia. It sounds as if this could be a bad night. Go with her,' she said to me. 'She'll need help, if Conchita isn't coming back.'

'You should come, too,' I said.

'No,' Ma said. 'I'm weary. If the bombs fall on me, so be it. But you need to keep yourself safe. And the children.'

Eugenia already had her bags and bundles with her, ready for the cellar. She was carrying Mercy on one hip and holding her youngest, Eduardo, who had just started walking, by the hand. The older children, Alf, Freddo and Anna, were carrying a favourite toy each, and were too little to be trusted on the stairs with any other burden. I wanted to stay with Ma, but it was plain I had to go down the steps with the children. My hatred for Conchita, as I loaded myself up with the things Eugenia judged necessary, was almost physical, a burden I barely had the strength to carry.

We settled ourselves on our cushions and wrapped the children in the blankets. I read a story from a book I had brought back from the Shelter. It was about a little girl called Milly-Molly-Mandy and I thought it rather silly, but the children loved the sound of the name and turned it into a sort of chant to tease each other. We persuaded them to lie down and I thought they were all asleep, but then, over the murmur of voices and the muffled sounds of the raid, I heard one of them crying, quietly. I lay down beside them and found it was Freddo; the others were, it appeared, asleep.

'What's the matter, my love?' I whispered.

'I don't know where Mama is,' he said.

'I do,' I said. 'She's safe in a friend's house. Just as safe as you are here, with us.'

'I didn't know where she'd gone,' he said, as if his uncertainty on the subject could not so easily be dismissed.

'Now you do,' I said. 'Go to sleep, Freddo.'

Conchita was probably doubly unsafe, wherever she was

spending the night. At risk from the Blitz, for all I knew, and of goodness knows what moral and physical harm at the hands of the smart young man. It might even be better, I could not help thinking, if a direct hit on wherever she was obliterated her from our lives; from Jamie's, Alf's, Freddo's and Mercy's lives. And from mine. As soon as I had allowed this thought into my mind, I had to resist making the sign of the cross, that meaningless, ritual gesture I scorned in others but which was embedded in me as tightly as the impulse to smile in response to a smile. If it happened now that I had imagined it happening, I would be haunted by it as if I had willed it to happen.

I looked over to where Eugenia was holding Mercy, crooning to her gently to persuade her to sleep. The cellar was quiet, now. I touched Eugenia's shoulder to attract her attention.

'I'm going to check on Ma,' I whispered. 'Will you be all right?'

'Of course,' she said, smiling at me over Mercy's head. Eugenia had the sort of prettiness that can be easily equated with stupidity. Her face was round, her nose was snub, she had big eyes and a gap between her two front teeth that we used to tease her about when we were children. Her eyes skittered away from you if the conversation turned to topics she had no interest in, or thought too far above her understanding, but on matters that affected those she loved, she was steady in her concentration. I would have been taken aback if Jamie had chosen her for his wife; I would have felt he deserved better. I understood, now, that happiness was just another word for peace of mind, and Eugenia could have been the clever choice.

We were nearer the steps than the wall but even so it took some time to pick my way between the swaddled bodies on the floor. There was an understanding that, once in the cellar, you stayed in the cellar, and anyone moving was grumbled at, ran the risk of having their ankle swatted with a book or jabbed with a knitting needle. I would not usually leave, having committed to going down there, but usually I was in the same place as Ma. It was only Conchita's absence and the urgency of the warning that had left me stranded below ground while she was alone in Room 122. I could not bear it.

I reached the steps at last and was halfway to the top when the building shook. On previous occasions, there had been a chorus of yelps and groans as sleepers woke suddenly and the nervous suspected their worst fears were being realized. A mist of dust was released into the atmosphere of the cellar, already polluted by the night-time breath of so many people crowded together. This time, the shaking had not subsided by the time everyone had awakened enough to understand the raid was close; it lasted for no more than a few seconds, but still seconds more than previously, while plaster fell from the ceiling. There was a moment of silence when it stopped, everyone's breath held, then there was a crash from overhead, an outburst of wailing, and the lights went out.

I stumbled up the last few steps, tripped at the top and crashed into the door, bruising my shoulder. I fumbled with the handle in the dark, expecting a stampede behind me, but no one else was trying to leave. They were in the safest place left in the hotel. I was the only person fighting to get the door open, desperate to know what was on the other side. What chaos lay behind it.

The dining room was so thick with dust particles, suspended in the air, that I had to bend over, coughing, before I could cross to the lobby. The glass in the doors and windows at the front of the hotel had blown in, and the floor was covered with fragments which caught the passing beams of the searchlights in the park and reflected them like so many jewels. A sparkling carpet covering the marble floor. The air was cold, and the noise of the anti-aircraft guns was loud in the suddenly open space. There was no sign of Jonas.

The corridor was in such a depth of darkness, with the lights out and the doors to the rooms all shut, I had to keep my hand on the wall to avoid blundering into it. I worked my way along, counting doors, to Room 122, where, instead of the door handle I was reaching for, I found emptiness, a gap, an open door.

'Ma!' I said, softly, as if afraid of waking a corridor of peaceful sleepers. 'Ma!'

'All right, Miss Rose,' said Jonas's voice in the darkness. 'Come in, now.'

No matter how familiar I was with where it stood and how much I had moved around this room in darkness night after night, I caught my leg on the end of my own bed before I reached Ma's. It was not completely dark. Where the blackout should have been obscuring the window on to the street, there was a luminous glow, a triangle of not-darkness. Not enough to see by, though. Not sufficient for me to understand what I was groping my way towards. Ma still had not spoken.

'Jonas,' I said, still whispering, the horror of what he might say next robbing me of breath. 'What's happened?'

'The window broke, miss. Come and hold your mother. She won't speak to me but I don't think she's badly hurt. I need to get my torch out of my pocket so we can check.'

At last I saw that he was crouched between the bed and the window, one hip on the mattress, his one arm supporting Ma, who was half in, half out of the bed, tilted towards the floor. I took his place, the warm, heavy, soft feel of Ma so familiar, so comforting. I could hear her breathing, but she did not respond at all to the pressure of my arms around her or my whispers in her ear.

'It'll be all right, Ma. I'm here now. It'll be all right.'

Jonas fumbled in the pockets of his jacket and produced a torch with the usual tape round the outside of the glass to narrow the beam. He played it over Ma's face. Her eyes were shut and her cheek was cut, a trickle of blood running sideways from below her eye towards her ear, as her head rested against my shoulder. Jonas spun the torch away and ran it over the bedside table, where there was usually a jug of water and a glass. The glass was gone but the jug still stood, and Jonas clamped the torch under his chin while he dipped his handkerchief, a huge square of linen so white it was visible in the darkness, into the water and passed it to me. I wiped the cut on Ma's face, still talking to her as if she was awake and alert and just taking her time to respond.

'I'm going to telephone for help now,' Jonas said. 'I'll need the torch.'

'Of course, of course. Are you all right, Jonas? Are you hurt?'

'Oh, no!' His teeth were as white as his handkerchief. 'Just all shook up a moment; you know how it is. We need to get this lady to a doctor. I'll be quick.'

Alone with Ma, I listened to her breathing, felt the beat of her heart against my breast. And beyond the shattered window, I heard the cacophony of an air raid, the sirens of emergency vehicles, the gun salvos, the aircraft, the whistle of heavy objects plunging through the air towards earth, the occasional thump of an explosion. Apart from the guns, none of it seemed particularly close, and I felt particularly isolated from it all, there in the darkness, holding my unconscious mother in my arms.

Jonas came back and, with our three arms, we lifted her and laid her flat on the bed. Jonas ran the torch up and down her body and pointed out other cuts from slivers of glass, and then cuts on my own hands I had not noticed, where I had caught them on the sharp edges of the glass on the blanket or Ma's nightdress or her skin. He explored the floor around his feet and found the batten that had held the blackout against the window, blown into the room by the explosion.

'There you are, miss,' he said, and he sounded jovial, 'just knocked out by a pestilential piece of wood. Nothing to worry about.'

Knocked out by something light enough to be held in one hand. Nothing serious, then. I stayed with Ma, sponging her face and talking to her – mindless chatter, she would have said, if she were only able to speak – while Jonas went back to the lobby. To wait for the ambulance, he said, but it was also his job to prevent looting, in just such a situation as this. He could have been sacked for leaving his post. He had put Ma ahead of duty, knowing her to be alone in the room with the windows likely to be shattered as they had been in the lobby.

There was no looting and no ambulance, but Jonas stopped a crew of firefighters on their way back to their depot, and asked if any of them knew anything about first aid. They teased him about his missing arm, he told me, joking that it was more than first aid he needed, more like a stout needle and thread, but then one of them said he knew a nurse who lived in one of the streets off the High Street, and he went to fetch her. So the first person who came through the door as I crouched beside Ma in my hopeless vigil was a stout lady with her hair in curl papers, wrapped up in a dressing gown, smelling strongly of face cream with an underlying hint of fried food.

There was still no light in the room but the woman, who introduced herself as Mrs Darling, worked away undaunted, feeling Ma's pulse, listening to her heart, massaging her hands and feet. I wanted to stop her doing this as, had she been awake, these ministrations would have caused Ma pain. I said so, to Mrs Darling, who just shook her head and said: 'Poor dear, poor dear.' I don't know if she meant me or Ma. Finally, she produced a torch and lifted Ma's eyelids, then she reached some sort of decision and sent me to find 'that idle lout, Kenneth', the fire-crew member who had fetched her.

Their vehicle was still parked outside and the crew were busy sweeping up the glass from the lobby floor. There was a cheerful willingness to help, in those dark days in London. Perhaps it would have been the same in any city. My impression at the time was that those who were able and honest – so not all but most of the population – kept fear and despair at arm's length with humour and purposeful activity. So I was not surprised to find that a gang of men who had been through gruelling experiences already that night had not carried on with their journey to their depot, a cup of tea and bed, but had found something useful to do while they waited to see if they were needed.

'The ambulance could be a while yet,' Mrs Darling told me, nothing in her tone of voice suggesting any urgency. 'No point hanging around waiting for it.'

The men unfolded a stretcher from among the paraphernalia

in their truck and, as gently as they could manage, but not as gently as I would have wished, they moved Ma on to it and carried her out, loaded her like a sack of coal into the back of the wagon. Mrs Darling wouldn't come with us to the hospital – 'I've only got my slippers on, dear' – but she gave instructions to Kenneth, the idle lout, and they squeezed me into the cab of the truck and took off for St Mary's Hospital in Praed Street, where Mercy had been born six months before.

Ma was taken away from me, at the hospital. I was left on a row of seats occupied by people who were battered and broken, with bloody cloths round a limb or head, and those attending the wounded, who looked just as hopeless as the casualties they were there to support. Ma was assessed too quickly for me to understand what was happening, and the trolley she had been transferred to, from the fire crew's flimsy stretcher, was gone through a door where I could not follow. Kenneth, who was a small man with a smile so fixed I wondered if he had a facial palsy, told me to fill in some forms at the desk, and wait.

I waited, with a curious feeling of calm; whatever I was waiting to find out would be bad – in which case the longer the wait, the better – or good, in which case the waiting would count for nothing. A doctor came and led me to a small room, where we sat facing one another. He was young. Older than me, perhaps, but if so, not much older. His hair was swept back from his forehead and plastered in place on his skull and he looked, in the way he held his clipboard and compressed his lips, as if he wished all of life could so easily be pressed into a shape that was neat, and no bother.

'Miss Dunbar,' he said, not looking at me, 'I understand you speak English?'

'Yes.'

'Your mother' – he looked down at his notes – 'Mrs Mercedes Dunbar, has suffered a stroke.' He lifted his eyes and looked at me for the first time, gauging whether I was going to be troublesome and untidy.

I didn't understand the words he used.

'She was knocked out by a piece of wood,' I said, asking him to confirm this was what he meant.

'Was she? I didn't see any sign of a head injury. I'm afraid it's more serious than that.'

'She's had a stroke.'

'Yes.'

'Tell me what that means.' I did know the words, of course, but they had never mattered to me before.

'It means that the blood supply to her brain has been temporarily disrupted and she is unconscious. If she regains consciousness, you should be aware that there may be lasting damage affecting part of her brain, which will inhibit her ability to speak, or to use some of her limbs.'

The chair I was sitting on had metal arms, one of them with a sharp edge exposed where it had been bent out of shape by some incident in the past. I ran my thumb along this edge, feeling the sharpness of it cutting into my flesh. The ground was shifting, as I sat there, and I could not afford to let myself go, fall to the floor and weep. Ma would not have liked it.

'You say, *if* she regains consciousness,' I said.

'She may not. And you should know that the longer she remains unconscious, the less chance there is that she will recover. Certainly that she will recover back to the woman she was. I'm sorry.'

'Why? Why did she have a stroke?' I wanted to stand up and beat his perfect hair with my fists, demand to know what had brought this upon me. Or upon Ma – but she was peaceful and oblivious, and I was neither.

'It's impossible to say. A weakness in the brain, high blood pressure, an unhealthy lifestyle. Your mother, I see, has suffered from rheumatoid arthritis for a number of years, which would put a strain on her system.'

'Are you saying it was nothing to do with the air raid?' I was looking for something or someone to hate. If it wasn't the innocent wooden batten, then it must have been the Germans.

'No, I'm not saying that. I think the circumstances contributed. But really, Miss Dunbar, we could drive ourselves mad trying to understand exactly what caused an event when we should be concentrating on dealing with its after-effects. In this case, doing our best to keep your mother comfortable and to supply what treatment we can to help her recover.'

When I worked in the Garrison Library, a shelf collapsed, throwing its cargo of books to the floor, damaging the binding and scuffing the covers. Chaos and calamity. My superior, Mrs Mason-Fletcher, was concerned only with the effects of the incident, busy at once with collecting up the fallen volumes, smoothing out their rumpled pages, organizing the repair of the bracket that had failed. Someone higher up the organization saw that dealing with the effect was not enough, in the circumstances, and ordered a survey of all the shelves in the library, identifying several brackets in need of replacement. So I disagreed with the doctor. In principle, it has to be worth understanding the cause, to prevent it happening again. Only in this case, there was no point, because I had only the one mother. What did I care if mothers who were not mine suffered the same fate?

I must have been silent for too long, which gave him time to study me.

'Are you injured, Miss Dunbar? I see you have cuts on your hands.'

'Nothing. They're nothing,' I said.

He held the door open for me and I understood that I had put on a good performance. If only all relatives, his manner managed to imply, were as orderly and controlled as I was. I kept the thumb I had lacerated against my side so he would not see what it took for me to behave this way.

19

At the Hospital

I stayed by Ma's bedside for the rest of the night. The curtains were drawn round her bed and all I could see, apart from her face, which did not change, and the shape of her body under the covers, which did not move, was a light fitting on the end of a thin cord hanging down from the ceiling in the centre of the ward. Each time a door was opened at either end, the light swung to and fro in the draught then settled back into stillness, its oscillations becoming slower and slower. I watched this light as I might have watched a performance in the theatre on the Rock, absorbing every detail of the pattern its bulb made on the floor and the walls, the difference in the pattern according to which door was opened and how hard it was banged shut. I was not aware of being unhappy, only of Ma, so close, so still, so silent, and the swinging light bulb. I was not even impatient for the night to end, but it did end. The nurses pulled the blackout down from the windows and the ward was filled with the wash of morning, trapped between and reflected off the buildings round about. Not the brightness of a day on a sunlit lump of rock in the Mediterranean, but not darkness.

A nurse came and took Ma's temperature, counted the beats of her pulse, made notes.

'No change?' she said. I shook my head. 'Well, nothing to do but wait.' She smiled at me to make it plain her words were meant as encouragement.

An orderly pushed a trolley past and gave me a cup of tea, and I was thinking of asking the ward sister to phone the hotel to let Eugenia know what was happening when Jonas arrived. He was not wearing his uniform and looked smaller and friendlier in the grey trousers, blue pullover and black jacket of an ordinary working man in his leisure hours.

'Oh, Jonas,' I said. 'It wasn't the piece of wood. It's a stroke. She might never wake up.'

'Goddammit,' said Jonas, looking down at the hat he held in his hand. It sounded so incongruous, so unlike what I would expect Jonas to say, that I nearly laughed.

'But she might, Jonas. Let's not lose sight of that.'

He took his handkerchief out to wipe his eyes. It was pink from Ma's blood. We said nothing for a while, just stood beside the bed, sharing the feeling of helplessness. It was good to have someone to share it with.

'I must let Eugenia know where I am,' I said.

'I've done that,' Jonas said. 'They all know. There'll be someone here just as soon as they've got breakfast down their throats. No doubt about that.'

'I'm glad you were there, last night,' I said.

'It was a privilege to be of help to you, miss.'

Lydia and Maribel Molinary were next through the curtains round the bed, which daylight revealed as palest blue with the slightest outline of darker-blue check, long washed away. I tensed all my muscles as they walked up to me, expecting the usual Molinary blast and bluster and not feeling able to withstand it. But they tiptoed, whispered. I told them it

211

was a stroke, and she was still unconscious, and Lydia put an arm round me and pulled me to her chest, which was soft and smelled only fleetingly of grease. It was oddly comforting. Maribel hung back, head down, hair falling forward over her face so I didn't notice at once that she was crying.

'Don't cry,' I said. 'Ma wouldn't expect you to let go so readily.'

She cried harder, more noisily. A woman shuffling past in slippers and a dressing gown stopped and looked towards us, frowned. Lydia hissed at her, in Spanish, to go away and mind her own business, then turned back to me.

'We're here now,' she said. 'Go and get some sleep. If she wakes, I'll send Maribel to fetch you. Maribel can run quicker than anyone I know. She's a champion runner.'

I looked at Maribel, who nodded. I had never seen her move faster than a walk, or even walk fast, so it was a kindness the two of them had invented for me. To make me think I could go without a care to my bed in the Royal Palace, knowing word would reach me in minutes if anything happened. I pretended I believed them because I had no choice. I needed to sleep or I would be no use to Ma when she woke. The front of the hotel was covered in sheets of wood and cardboard from boxes in which deliveries had been made. The lettering, truncated and misaligned, on the fragments announced the contents as Bird's custard powder, Robertson's Golden Shred marmalade and Brown & Polson cornflour. Room 122 had been cleaned up, the floor swept clear of glass, and the square of card covering the broken window came from a box of Spillers Shapes for All Dogs, though I had never seen a dog in the hotel. I went down to Eugenia's room, but it was empty except for a girl called Sylvia who was sitting on a bed reading one of Conchita's magazines.

'I was to tell you,' she said, leaping to her feet, 'that Mrs Gatt has taken Alf to school with all the little ones. She will be back soon.'

'And Conchita?' I said. 'Mrs Dunbar? Do you know where she is?'

Sylvia shook her head. 'I wasn't told anything else,' she said. I felt a Ma-like response rising in my throat – 'You should learn to think and understand, not just wait to be told.' But I smiled at her and went back to my room, undressed, because the clothes I was wearing felt contaminated, and lay down on my bed. I fell asleep even as I was telling myself that I would not be able to do so.

When I woke I thought it was late because the board over the window dimmed the room. I turned my wrist in the direction of what light there was, to read my watch, and realized there was someone sitting on the end of Ma's empty bed. Conchita.

'What time is it?' I said.

'I don't know exactly. Middle of the morning.'

'I must get back to the hospital.' I swung my feet to the floor, turning my back on her.

'I'll come with you,' she said.

I turned to face her. All the fury at her betrayal of Jamie came back to me in a rush, like bile rising. I said, as a child might, because my rage rendered me as incoherent as a child:

'I don't want you anywhere near me.'

I was still not looking at her but I heard the rustle of her clothes and the creak of the bed as she moved position.

'What have I done?' she said. 'I didn't have anything to do with Ma being injured.'

'Where were you?'

'At a friend's house. Didn't Eugenia tell you?'

'She did.' I stood up and turned on the light, so I could see her face. 'But I don't believe the story you told her. Was the "friend" the man I saw you leaving the shop with, yesterday evening?'

Conchita didn't flinch or blush or look shifty or disconcerted, or show any of the other indications of guilt and shame that I would have expected, knowing what my own reaction would have been if I had been caught out in that lie, in that transgression.

'What does it matter to you where I was? It would have made no difference to Ma if I'd been here.'

I knew this was true but I wanted it not to be true. It would have been such a relief to have been able to point at Conchita and say: 'You made this happen.'

'I'd have been with her,' I said. 'I had to go down to the cellar with Eugenia because she couldn't manage all the children alone.'

'I'm sorry,' Conchita said, 'but you have to admit, it would all have turned out just the same.'

I didn't want to admit it, so I picked up my towel and went to the bathroom. Conchita was still there when I got back. She was smoking a cigarette, watching the people on the street through a gap in the board over the window. Eugenia came in while I was dressing, with Mercy and Eduardo, one on each hip.

'Do you want me to come to the hospital?' she said. She looked grey and rumpled and had obviously been crying.

'No,' I said. 'Stay with the children. I'll send you word of how she is.' I put my arm round her shoulder and kissed each of the babies on the head. With her arms full of infant, she could not hug me in return, for which I was grateful. I did not need any more emotion.

I put my shoes on and left, without looking again at Conchita, ready to be disgusted by whatever she did, whether she followed me or not. She followed. We walked side by side. I retained enough self-respect not to try to outpace her or deliberately hang back, but I was not going to talk to her. She talked to me, though.

'I know what you think of me,' she said, walking at my side. I am taller than she is but not tall enough to see over her head, so I had to keep my face turned slightly away to avoid seeing hers. 'But I don't think you understand what it is like to be me. I've only been given one thing to help me make the most of my life, and that's, whatever you want to call it, prettiness, or sex appeal. And the point is, it doesn't last, does it? Not like your cleverness and your confidence and your ability to always do the right thing. You have lots of ways to make your life better and better and you won't lose any of that as you get older. You'll always have more chances coming your way. And I won't. You shouldn't blame me if I'm tempted to use what I've got, while I can.'

I stopped and turned to face her. She was breathing heavily. I had been walking quickly.

'You climbed out of your own family into mine,' I said. 'Now you're saying that was only the first step in making the most of your life. And the next step is finding someone more exciting than Jamie? Someone with more money? And you expect me to agree with you that this is only natural because you won't stay lovely for long? What is wrong with what you have?'

I was shouting. We had this conversation in English.

Conchita's English had improved during our months in London. She was taking her chance to polish up a skill that might be useful to her one day. I saw the curious glances the passers-by in the street – whichever one it was we were walking down in the neighbourhood of Paddington – gave us, two women standing face to face, one of them shouting at the other. I turned away from her and kept walking. Conchita fell into step beside me once again.

'You don't understand,' she said. 'I knew you wouldn't. I know I'm lucky to be married to Jamie. I love him, I truly do. Only, when I'm old, when I'm sitting in the sun on my doorstep and gossiping, because I suppose it must come to that in the end, I want to have had some . . . oh, I don't know . . . adventures, to give me a feeling that life wasn't all about nothing. I want to have had fun.' I walked faster. Conchita kept up with me. 'You won't tell Jamie, will you?' she said, panting.

'Don't ask me,' I said. 'I can't think about it yet. I can hardly bear to speak to you when Ma might . . .' I stopped talking. So did she.

Maribel was sitting by the nurses' desk, showing the nurse on duty there the colour of her fingernails. I found it a reassuring sight. Maribel would hardly have been talking about nail varnish if Ma had died. She jumped up, though, in confusion at being caught out relaxing.

'There's no change,' she said, quickly. 'No change at all.'

I could hear Lydia's voice as we walked down the ward. She was talking, not to Ma, who was still unconscious, but to a large woman in the next bed. Lydia was sitting behind the curtains still surrounding Ma, but had her head tucked through the corner where two curtains met, and was improving her

English by exploring every ailment the other woman was suffering from or had ever suffered from in her life.

'In-grow-ing toe-nail,' Lydia was repeating, carefully. The woman had her foot thrust out of the bed and was pointing at the big toe, making a curving motion with her hands. 'Ah! *Uña encarnada*!' Lydia said, triumphantly, and they both laughed. Like Maribel and the nurse, they were enjoying themselves.

'No change,' Lydia said. 'What can you do except wait and hope and talk? I don't know if Mercedes can hear us, but it's worth a try.' It would irritate Ma, I thought, if she could hear, being trapped listening to Lydia chattering on about diseases and disabilities as if these were to be relished. Which might in fact be helpful.

Lydia and Maribel said goodbye to their new friends, leaving Conchita and me perched in silence, one either side of the bed. Conchita's hand reached out and smoothed a wisp of hair from Ma's forehead, then rested lightly on her arm where it lay, unmoving, on top of the blankets. I wanted to slap her hand away and she read the thought in my face.

'You think I don't care about her,' she said. When she had been talking to me on the way to the hospital I had been disgusted by what she said, but I had believed her to be genuine. Now I was facing her, all my usual mistrust came back to me, and for all her touch on Ma's arm was gentle, I did not believe her.

'Stop telling me you know what I think,' I said. 'You don't. And you don't need to stay. I'll be here.'

She did stay, and I began to long to be rid of her and decided to answer the question she had left with me, on the walk.

'I won't tell Jamie about your little adventure,' I said. 'It would only hurt him. I accept that you don't want to do that.'

'I don't,' she said.

She hesitated as if she wanted to add a caveat to this; I sensed a 'but' that would have pitched us into a repeat of the conversation we had had on the way and we neither of us wanted that. Not in front of Ma. And she might, as Lydia had suggested, be able to hear us. In which case, I realized after Conchita had gone, she would have understood my remark about a little adventure. I hoped she had. Then I would not have to make a decision about whether to share it with her when she woke up.

I had not provided myself with anything to occupy me, in my rush to escape the hotel and Conchita. I had no book, no sewing, no paper to write a letter on. I wished I had thought, before I left the hotel, to write to my father. He would be at home, putting on his overalls, going to work with his lunch in a tin box, knowing nothing of what was happening to his wife, in another country.

The woman in the next bed called to me, softly.

'Are you the daughter, dear?'

Her name was Mrs Hampton – she said 'Ampton' and it was only when a passing nurse spoke to her that I discovered it began with an 'H' – and her mother had had a stroke. She told me about it, but with kindness and sensitivity, without any drama. The long wait for returning consciousness; the long struggle to return to a manageable level of disability; the second stroke, a couple of years later, from which she did not wake up. Mrs Hampton was filling in the gaps in what the doctor had said. She was answering the question: 'What does this mean?' Not by describing the disease but by describing the experience of living through it.

We were interrupted by the arrival of Mrs Almondsbury. Mrs Hampton cut herself off in mid-flow.

'Never mind me, dear. You want to talk to your friend, now, don't you?'

We went to the ground floor of the hospital, where the WVS had a counter dispensing tea, and Mrs Almondsbury bought me a bun. She had already arranged for a cable to be sent to my father and had notified whoever it was she thought could arrange passage for him on a ship. I was pleased, yet fearful of what lay behind this kindness. Inexplicably, I found myself talking not about Ma, but about Conchita.

Mrs Almondsbury's face fell into its pursed-up expression as she listened, but I had learned not to take this as a sign of disapproval. She was concentrating on what I was saying. She asked me about Conchita's childhood, what sort of family background she had.

'Chaotic,' I said. 'Her mother was no more than sixteen when Conchita was born, and I don't think she ever named the father. She married later but the man she married was a bad lot and there were more babies, no money. Conchita always says her mother blamed her, could never forgive her for being born, messing up her mother's chances of finding a decent husband, just by existing.'

Mrs Almondsbury nodded. 'She was right to say you had advantages she didn't, then. You had a strong loving family behind you. All the standards you have, your understanding of what matters, you will have learned from them. Conchita only learned it was every woman for herself, and that success meant finding a good prospect in the marriage market.'

'But she did,' I said. 'She found Jamie.'

'The problem with ambition,' Mrs Almondsbury said, 'is recognizing when it has been satisfied. Let's say you always wanted to be a dressmaker – would you be happy when you ended up owning your own little shop in a quiet street, or would you never be satisfied until you were based in Savile Row, making clothes for the Queen? Or, if you were a man, would you reach the rank of colonel, say, in the army, and think: "Good, this is what I wanted to achieve and I neither want nor expect to be a general one day"? I don't expect you to understand, necessarily, because you are young, and I don't know if you even know what your dreams are, yet. But, believe me, it is a happy person who can say: "Enough – I am satisfied." I suspect that Conchita's ambition never looked beyond marrying a man who earned enough money and who was not, as you describe her stepfather, a "bad lot". But, having achieved that, she finds she is restless. Is ambitious for more, or for something else.'

'She wouldn't feel like that if she loved Jamie as she should,' I said.

'I'm not sure I agree. You're suggesting that once married to a man you love, you would feel your every need had been met. You would cease looking beyond your husband and your home, suppress all curiosity and desire to see and do and experience more. I happen to think women shouldn't limit their lives in that way.'

'I still can't forgive her,' I said.

'I didn't expect you to.'

'I don't know what my ambitions are, either.'

'I didn't think you did,' said Mrs Almondsbury, smiling, all the tension in her face relaxed. 'I hope they go beyond marriage, though.'

20

Mercedes Dunbar

It was quiet, in the middle of the afternoon, the sun hitting the white wall opposite the bed, painting a rectangle of brightness on to its blank surface. We were in the separate room Mrs Almondsbury had arranged for us. Mrs Hampton had squeezed my hand as the orderlies pushed the trolley out of the ward where Ma had been before.

'Let me know,' she whispered. 'Come and talk to me. Any time.'

Ma was still unconscious. I was holding a book called *South Riding* by Winifred Holtby, which Mrs Almondsbury had left with me, although she had not finished reading it; a bookmark of fine linen with a border of ivy leaves and a central panel of roses, exquisitely embroidered, marked a page less than halfway through. It was the only book she had with her. She had taken it out of her bag and handed it to me.

'You need something to read,' she said.

It was a kindness only another lover of books would appreciate fully. To give away a book half read. But I had not been reading it.

Eugenia had come to visit, with Mercy.

'I thought, maybe just the one little one, until she's able to cope,' Eugenia said, averting her eyes from the bed as if not looking at Ma meant she could remain in ignorance of her condition. I lay on the bed beside Ma, cradling Mercy, half asleep, between us, hoping she would know we were there, feel the touch of our skin against hers, the healthy daughter she had finally given birth to, the granddaughter she had been so moved to meet. When Mercy became restless, I gave her back to Eugenia and told her to go.

Now I was alone with Ma, *South Riding* open on my knee, watching the slow shift of the oblong of brightness along the wall as the sun moved round. A nurse came in and took the usual readings, entered the results on a chart at the end of the bed. She made what felt like an unnecessary amount of noise doing this. Her shoes clicked on the floor, her voice filled the room and, when she was not speaking, she hummed to herself, not letting the silence settle for a moment. When she had gone, I held Ma's hand and let the peacefulness float over me, like the gossamer-thin veil of lace she had worn at her wedding, and lent to Conchita for hers.

Ma opened her eyes. She looked at me, though I could not be sure she was seeing me. Even though she held my gaze, she seemed further from me than when her eyes had been shut.

'Ma,' I said. Her eyes did not move, nor did her expression change, but she uttered a sound, a deep, ugly, guttural noise that was terrifying.

I ran to the door and called for a nurse who in turn fetched a doctor. The same doctor as I had seen before. He sat on the side of Ma's bed and spoke to her as if she was any other patient. As if she was Mrs Hampton, ready and willing to articulate every symptom. Could she feel this? Would she lift her left hand? Her right hand? Follow his finger with her eyes? I liked him for behaving in this way, and for the soothing statements interspersed through the questions – 'You're doing well, Mrs Dunbar'; 'It's a lovely day out there, you can see the sun is shining'; 'Your daughter is here with you'; 'It will be all right'. How Ma would have snapped at him, had she been able! I had gone to stand by the window when the doctor came in, so I could not be sure, but I didn't think Ma responded to the questions. The doctor came over and joined me and we looked together out of the window, down to a yard where a couple of men were sitting on the back of a truck, smoking.

'There's a long way to go,' he said. 'As I expect you realize.'

I nodded. 'I don't expect you can tell me if she has any chance of recovery?'

'I'm afraid I can't.' One of the men on the truck had made the other one laugh. I couldn't hear the laughter but I could see it, the delight of the one hearing the joke, the delight of the one telling it at having provoked laughter. 'If she recovers at all, it will be a long, long process. And I am not hopeful that she will.'

I walked out of the room, unable to bear it.

I found a door and ended up where the ambulances were parked. I sat on a low wall that ran down one side of the yard, and rocked back and forth, back and forth. An ambulance crew came out, one of them whistling, and headed for their vehicle. They caught sight of me and hesitated and I was afraid that if they spoke to me I would scream, but they glanced at one another and then opened the doors of the ambulance and climbed in. The bell was clanging as they turned on to the street. Someone else, somewhere, was confronting the dislocation, the misery, the realization that their world had been squeezed like a bar of wet soap into a shape they did not recognize, without hope of ever being returned to its original form. Or maybe not. The ambulance could be travelling towards someone who had tripped on a piece of rubble and broken a bone that needed setting, and the most serious implication as she sat on the ground in pain was who would cook the meat she had in her bag for the evening meal.

I needed to breathe, in and out, in and out. I needed to take hold of myself, as Ma had told me to on the way to Casablanca.

'I do not expect you to be weak,' she had said, when she thought I was crying by the slick, salty rail of the *Mohammed Ali el-Kebir.*

'I won't be,' I had answered her. And I wouldn't be now.

I stood up and walked back into the hospital, found a lavatory where I washed my face and drank some water from the tap. Then I went back to Ma. She was lying with her eyes closed but she opened them as I walked in. I sat beside her and took her hand. I began to talk to her about the children. I told her what would become of them, what would happen in their lives because they chose to make it happen or by accident, as if I knew. As I created and unfolded these stories to lay before her, they began to seem not like speculation, or even a prediction, but like the actual truth. The truth that existed thirty years in the future, when I might have accepted sitting by Ma's bed as she slipped away from me, reminding her of the success her grandchildren had made of their lives. Alf, I said, was an engineer; he was an expert in the mechanics of bridge-building and travelled the world, bringing home with him, from a trip to Africa, a girl who was taller than he was, with a noble face and an acceptance of life that made her, as a companion, like a drink of cold water on a hot day. Freddo – of course, she knew this – had become a diplomat, had been to the Palace once already to receive an honour for his services, and was expected to go back one day soon, to be given a title. Sir Frederick Dunbar. He had married a girl from the next street, whose pigtails he had pulled in primary school, and she, this urchin from the Rock in hand-me-down dresses, would soon be Lady Dunbar. And Mercy. I faltered here. The details of Alf's and Freddo's magical futures had come easily to me. But to imagine what Mercy might become – would that not be a version of what I wanted for myself? Would I be describing what I hoped for for her, or for me? So I modelled Mercy's future on Mrs Almondsbury. I gave her an influential husband, a capacity for helping those less fortunate, tirelessly working in the slums of London. Mercy had never been to the Rock and it was easier to anchor her somewhere far away from it. I could not so readily detach Alf and Freddo. As I neared the end of this, the might-be Mercy's might-be future, I allowed myself to think, what if that were me? Would I be satisfied? I could not be sure I would.

Ma's hand rested in mine, still. I watched the oblong of sunlight as I talked, shifted so far it had almost vanished, running out of wall to shine on. I could think of nothing else to say. Silence fell. Then Ma lifted her chin, uttered a sound that was like a sigh, like a gentle giving-up, and I knew, without calling the nurse to confirm it, that she had died. She had waited to hear the end of the children's stories. She had gone without having had to live with a level of physical and mental disability beyond my ability to bear. I began to cry, in my last moments alone with her, but it was not only the sorrow of her loss, which would be painful for a long time yet to come; it was relief at all she had been spared.

21

Endings

I had allowed myself half an hour with Ma, after she died, before I called the nurse; stepped from one side of the line, where Ma still lived, to the other, where the whole business of her dying had to be managed through talking, listening, doing. While the doctor filled in the paperwork (since leaving Gibraltar we had been kept afloat by pieces of paper), I went to see Mrs Hampton. Another woman was in the bed that had been Ma's, asleep, so I knelt by Mrs Hampton's bedside and whispered: 'She died.'

Mrs Hampton lifted a hand and placed it over mine. Her knuckles looked like the skulls of tiny creatures, knobbed and creviced.

'When my mother couldn't speak,' she said, 'and she was writing down what she wanted, she kept writing "Let me go", and I kept asking, "Go where, Mum? Where do you want to go?" and she got more and more het up. She didn't want to write the word "die", but that's what she meant. "Let me die." She couldn't face living, the way she was.'

'Did you help her?' I asked.

'No. Too much of a coward; you know how it is. I wish I'd been able to do something, but I couldn't.'

I was thankful it was not a choice I had had to face. Because I think I am too much of a coward, too, and would have let Ma down, at the end.

I went to see Mrs Echado, when I got back to the hotel. It was a compulsion I did not understand, though if we had been at home, and Ma had died, as it seemed she could have done, in just this way, I would have knocked on the door of Mrs Echado's rooms to tell her the news. She was part of the fabric of our lives. She was sitting, as she always was these days, back turned to the door, looking through the window, though from where she sat she could have seen nothing except clouds and sky.

All of us had been overturned in the last few months, tumbled from the familiar to the foreign, but I noticed, even more forcefully than before, how extreme Mrs Echado's translation must have been. From the basement of a building to the top, from a room with a view of nothing but a corner of the yard and a slice of passageway, to a window full of sky. In her room in MacPhail's Passage there had been a cloth on the table and a blanket over the bed. In this room, there was carpet on the floor, curtains at the window, cushions on the chairs. Mrs Echado had travelled not just the miles by sea and land but from the hard, dark depths, upwards to light and softness. Which sounds like a happy ending, but Mrs Echado had been happy before and now she was troubled, unable to understand what had happened to her.

I reminded her who I was, as I sat down beside her and took her hand.

'Little Milagros,' she said, acknowledging that she knew exactly who I was.

'I've come to tell you my mother has died,' I said. She turned her face from the window and looked closely at mine.

'You don't look like her,' she said. 'More like the man she married.' She folded her lips in and out. 'Duncan Dunbar. Married Mercedes Gonzalez. I was there.'

I squeezed her hand. 'Now she's gone,' I said. 'We've lost her.'

'Mercedes Dunbar.' Mrs Echado closed her eyes then opened them again. 'Dead, is it? She was younger than me. That's another one I've outlived.' I waited to see if she could find anything to say about Ma except her name and the fact of her marriage, and, after a moment, she did. 'She had a tongue on her, that one. No one's fool.'

In all the talking and weeping in the next few weeks, I held on to this. Keeping the essence of Ma alive as Mrs Echado had described it. I could imagine Ma smiling at that and nodding. Satisfied.

Mrs Echado's triumph over outliving Ma was short-lived. She died herself, peacefully in her sleep, just days later. Her funeral did not have to wait for the arrival of family because she had none. The church was full, though. There were plenty of people in the hotel who, if they had not known her before, recognized her now as one of them, whose passing should not go unnoticed.

'She missed her dog, you know,' said someone beside me at the ceremony. Mrs Echado might have been pleased at this epitaph, too.

My father and Jamie both came to London for Ma's funeral. I thought, when they left, when the business of the funeral was over, I would be able to face whatever future it was that lay open to me now. I would be able to grieve in the private, quiet way I had not managed while there was still a flurry and noise over the death. But the day they went home, the raids stopped and there was another reason to hold my breath, wait for something to happen. In fact, the Blitz had ended. It was impossible to believe at first. We listened to the silence, or what sounded like silence without the drone of aircraft engines, the thump of artillery, the wail of the sirens. Night after night we wondered how far away tonight's raid was that we could not hear it. Only gradually did it become clear that the Germans were pursuing other targets. They no longer had any interest in destroying London and everyone in it, or they no longer had the ability to do it, though this idea was not one it was acceptable to voice. The mood of the moment was not so optimistic. If the Londoners had been stoical and humorous while the worst was happening, their reaction to a release from constant fear was to be cynical and peevish.

Jonas spent much of his shift outside the hotel, on the pavement, looking upwards.

'I can't abide sneakiness,' he told me. 'All right, so come out and hit us and see how that doesn't work, but don't go hiding in the clouds, waiting till we're feeling cheerful, then come at us again.'

'They say it's something to do with Russia,' I said. 'Having to divert to fighting in the East.'

'They say, they say,' said Jonas. 'How can we know? You can't believe what the papers say because it's what they're told to say.'

So the ending of the Blitz was not like the lifting of a cloud, darkness and damp replaced with warmth and sunshine. It was a long time before we understood we no longer had to prepare ourselves for disaster, could unbutton our coats and put away our umbrellas. But with the long, hot days of summer, it began to be obvious. We were no longer under attack.

I had continued doing my job keeping the people away from Patrick, and the paperwork tidy and up to date in the hotel, and helping Winifred in the basement or at the Shelter. I moved into a room with Maribel Molinary and a sulky girl called Aida who had fallen out with her mother, because I had no one else to share with who needed me. I was free, all of a sudden. It paralysed me. For week after week I observed myself going about the hotel, doing this, doing that, and I judged myself to be useless. A useless mouth, as we had all been labelled by the authorities in Gibraltar, a pair of useless hands, a person of no consequence or relevance. I had fallen into a trough of self-pity that would have angered Ma, if she had still been alive.

I went with Winifred to an outpost of the Shelter somewhere south of the Thames. I didn't pay any attention to where I was going. Winifred pointed out to me, on the bus, all the churches that had, or had not, been damaged by the Blitz and it was hard to concentrate because this was not my city. What did it matter to me if a stained-glass window had been lost or a wall painting survived? We arrived with our boxes and Winifred was at once caught up in conversations, surrounded by the helpers and the helpless. I went outside and sat down on the step, waiting for her to finish. When she came to find me, I said:

'I can't do this any more.'

'No,' she said. 'I know. You need peace and quiet.'

'Do I?'

'For a time, I would say so. I have a proposition for you.'

Her proposition was that I should help a distant relative of hers who lived in the country and who was writing a book.

'Don't ask me what sort of book because I don't know, but it's something historical, a memoir, probably, or a family history.'

He lived in a village which sounded like one of those I had seen from the train from Amersham and had imagined myself living in. With Ma. The job involved, Winifred said, typing and organizing the manuscript, as far as it existed, but also research for the parts that did not.

'It would be working with books, only with the contents of books, not books as objects.'

'There's something you're not saying,' I said. Winifred was always direct and cheerful but also careful, anxious not to give offence or say what might lead someone to reject the help being offered, or to decide not to offer the help she was asking them to give. I wasn't sure which she was doing, in this case, but I suspected this man must be, in some way she was not spelling out, a monster. He must be so rude or fussy he was impossible to work with, or to like. 'What happened to his last assistant?'

'He was a German-speaking refugee and he found translation work. Major Inchbold didn't drive him out, if that's what you're thinking. What I haven't mentioned is that the Major is blind.'

I understood at once why she had avoided slipping in this information at the start. Released from caring for one person, I was being offered the chance to plunge into caring for another.

'So I would be responsible for him,' I said.

She laughed. 'He is responsible for himself. He needs

secretarial help. He might want you to walk with him, for exercise. That's all.'

'I'll think about it,' I said.

I said yes. I was finding it so hard to wake up each morning, plod through each day, that I was beginning to frighten myself. Something had to change, and if I accepted Winifred's proposal, everything would. When I left, I appreciated how very far from useless the people around me believed me to be. The children shed tears, but I had expected that. I was surprised how hard Patrick pleaded with me to stay, and how the women I had helped wailed in despair at the thought of losing me. Hatty and Hetty became thoroughly grumpy, as if I were letting them down, just as everyone else, and life itself, let them down.

I boarded a train for Oxford, as I had boarded the ship to Morocco and the ship to England, not knowing if what I was going to was better or worse than what I was leaving. Not knowing if life was about to let me down.

Part Three

Easterbrook

22

Major Inchbold

The house I went to was called Pool House, in the village of Easterbrook, close to the town of Witney, where blankets were made in mills with tall chimneys that, on certain days in certain weather, spread the smell of blanket-making across the town and as far as the nearest villages. It was a wet, hot smell. The house faced an open green space beside a church and was solid, respectable. It had a front door painted gloss black and a door knocker in the shape of a dolphin, though we were so far from the sea. I stood outside this, with my suitcase, knowing nothing about the man whose house it was except his name, that he was writing a book, and that he was sightless. His name was Major Edward St. John Inchbold. The middle name was pronounced 'Sinjon'; I hoped the Major did not expect me to use it, but had memorized the way Winifred pronounced it, just in case. His sightlessness was the result of an injury sustained in the last war, which I anticipated would be the subject of the book I would be helping him to complete. I banged the dolphin against its metal plate and waited.

The man who opened the door stood a little way back from it, in the dimness of the hallway, and looked nothing like my image of Major Inchbold. Also, he did not appear to be blind. He looked straight at me and said:

'Miss Dunbar?'

I nodded. When he neither responded nor moved aside to let me in, I looked more closely at him and saw his eyes were unfocussed.

'Yes,' I said, 'I'm Rose.'

'Lesson one, in dealing with the blind,' he said. 'I can't see you nod, which is what I'm assuming you just did.'

'I'm sorry, Major Inchbold,' I said. 'You didn't appear to be blind.'

'I've had practice at not appearing to be blind, and please call me Inchbold. The rest is just empty syllables we can do without.'

The physical body in front of me did not appear to go with the string of names I had been given. I had expected someone tall, upright, polished, full of certainty. The man I was looking at was no taller than me, and unsettled. His hair was unruly and his clothes slightly baggy. He had the look of someone waiting to board a bus while those in front of him in the queue wasted his time, dawdling over the business of stepping on board.

He led me through the narrow hall to a room at the back of the house which looked out over a garden. The French windows were open and it was full of the heat of the sun and the scent of the roses in full bloom in the borders. There was little furniture. No lamps. No ornaments. I can remember almost nothing of what we talked about, sitting in the only two chairs in the room. It has merged with all the conversations we have had since. But I remember noticing, as I sat facing Inchbold, that he had mud on his shoes, and a relaxation came over me, an unwinding, as if the clothes I had been wearing were too small, and I had been released from them.

There were four of us living in and around Pool House. Myself and Inchbold, and Greta Seccombe and her son, Amos. They lived in a cottage at the back, separate but within the high walls that surrounded the property. Greta did the cooking and the cleaning and behaved as if she saw herself simultaneously as of no account and yet entitled. Her son had one leg shorter than the other and had been spared military service because of this. He looked after the garden and worked on a farm in Easterbrook.

I wrote to everyone describing the situation I found myself in. In my letter to Pa and Jamie, I described the elegance of the house I was living in, of the library, of my own bedroom, on the top floor with two windows, one set in the roof which looked over the churchyard, and one set so low in the wall at the back I could only see through it when I sat down at the desk where I wrote these letters. Through this window, I had a view over the garden. One of the walls sloped inwards to accommodate the slope of the roof, and the floor, of polished boards, sloped also, from back to front, so anything I dropped from my desk by the low window rattled across to the further side. I had one of Ma's last drawings, framed for me by someone Jonas knew, on the wall by the bed, where the light from one window or the other picked it out as the hours of the day went by. It was more representative of a real bird than most of her drawings. It had one wing stretched out and its head twisted round and hidden below the other, as if it was ready to move, but was thinking things through before it did so.

I wrote to Peter Povedano with a description of the garden,

its vegetable beds and orchard. I described the beetroot and carrots freshly dug from the ground by Amos, cooked by Greta within an hour of leaving the soil. I wrote of the plums dropping from the trees and the early apples I was allowed to pick whenever I passed by, authorized by Amos, who had spoken to me only to name types and varieties of fruit and vegetables, and to tell me what was ready to pick and what would be better in a week or two. Peter had spent his life buying, fetching, delivering and selling the fruit and vegetables that grew over the border in Spain. I felt closest to him when I wandered round the Pool House grounds with Amos, though Amos could not grow the aubergines and peppers I missed so much.

I told Conchita about the clothes the women wore, here in Oxfordshire. There was nothing exciting to say about this, but it was the topic I thought would interest her most. The streets of the town and the village were dull in comparison with London, where there was always someone dressed in clothes of a strange design or in vibrant colours or made from exotic materials. I found it soothing, but I described it as if I was disappointed with the lack of style, like Conchita would have been.

All this – the house, the food, the surroundings – however great an impact it made on me at the time, is of little moment in comparison to what I wrote about in my letters to Sonia and Mrs Almondsbury. These were about Inchbold, and how I filled my days.

I soon discovered that Inchbold was an angry man. It was mostly inward anger; he raged against himself and his circumstances. I was taken aback, the first time I saw him in a temper, but I had had no experience of rage and was not frightened, only uneasy. I learned, soon enough, to keep still and quiet until it passed, like a sneezing fit that interrupts a conversation. It lasted no longer than that. Underneath, though, I began to recognize that the anger was always there, some times worse than others. He had no quarrel with individuals, and so the anger was not apparent, day to day, in the dealings he had with other people. It was the burden he lived with, as much as his blindness was. When he exploded into fury because, as happened often, something had been moved from its place, he would not abuse whoever was responsible or whoever was at hand to blame, as a lesser man might have done, but the object itself. Greta, who had known him far longer than I had, never understood that there was nothing personal in his rage.

'I don't know how he can expect me to remember which side of the hat stand to put his stick,' she would say. Or: 'I hope he doesn't think I was the one who moved the boot scraper. It was probably the window cleaner. Why doesn't he shout at him?'

She had never noticed that Inchbold was not shouting at her. Had never, from what I could see, shouted at her. She chose to think herself persecuted in this as in many other ways, and she was not entirely wrong, because she was, by birth, German. She had escaped internment because Inchbold spoke up for her, but not everyone was large enough to overlook her wholly inadvertent and unwanted link to the enemy. She remained frightened of him, which had the benefit of preventing her from irritating him, as she otherwise would certainly have done, with her monologues on the reasons why she was owed respect and the reasons why she didn't receive it.

There was a pattern to the days and it went like this. We ate the breakfast Greta prepared at the table by the French windows. Then we went for a walk. The walks could be long, out of Easterbrook, along footpaths over farmland, climbing up gentle hills to stand at the top; or short, round the village, or even just the garden and orchard. We spent the rest of the morning in the library, where Inchbold worked on his book and I helped, by finding and reading out to him the sources he wanted to use, or by taking notes while he talked. After lunch, he went to the music room on the first floor and played the piano, or listened to music on the wireless or gramophone, and I helped Greta with her work. At teatime, I read to him. *Our Mutual Friend* by Charles Dickens, broken up, for variety, by translations of Latin texts, books from the Bible, essays by men whose names I did not know. Apart from the Dickens, these texts were hard for me to understand and often a challenge to my ability to read written English. All of them – including, though not usually, the Dickens – fed Inchbold's inner anger and he would occasionally interrupt me to express his fury at the injustices he saw in what I was reading. His rage at the vengeful attitude of God as described in the Book of Genesis broke out after almost every verse. When I read God's curse on Eve, that 'thy desire shall be to thy husband, and he shall rule over thee', Inchbold said:

'So any man, however mean or weak, can claim to be the master of any woman who is persuaded to marry him? It's rubbish.'

'That's so wrong,' he said, about an essay by Francis Bacon titled 'Of Deformity'. 'He's saying the physical defect defines the man who has it. When all it does is define how other people see him. I'm the person I was before. Not better. Not worse. The same.' I wished I knew if that were true.

After supper, Inchbold became restless. This could mean he went back to the music room and I was free to do as I pleased. But he could not always bear to stay in the house and I had to go out when he did, because even if the land and streets around Pool House were familiar to him, he could not be certain there were no obstacles in his way, nothing left lying about to trip him, and it was hard for him to steer a path if he went somewhere without boundaries he could touch, as he often did. So I went too. Not with him, as I did on our morning walks, at his side, in conversation, but in attendance, touching his arm to stop him if he was veering towards danger, turning him towards home when he had lost all idea of where he was. I took a torch, to make sure that at least one of us could see the potholes on the road before we fell into them, but even so, I was unsettled by these night-time rambles. Both the silence and the sounds of the countryside were strange to me, and if we went any distance from the village, I was overwhelmed by the emptiness of the landscape with no one's footsteps but ours, and no voices. He did not want to need me, in his evening mood, and preferred it if he could forget I was there.

On Saturdays, Greta had a day off and left food out for me to prepare and serve, and on Sundays we went to church in the morning. I described all this in my letters to Sonia and Mrs Almondsbury, but the words I wrote on the page could not begin to express the way this new life had taken hold of me. Every moment of every day had a significance. Each day I learned more, understood more, experienced more. It was a banquet of a life and I gorged on it.

Inchbold's book was not about the war in which he had lost his sight.

'I want it out of my head,' he said. 'I'd like to take a shovel to it. Get rid of it, one way or another. I'm not going to write about it. That would fix it for ever.'

Instead, he was writing a history of the Inchbold family, who had lived in Pool House for two hundred years. But the path back through the generations had forks and crossroads and he could not bring himself to pass these by without taking a diversion of a few steps, or even a few miles. Sometimes these paths led to members of the family not central to the story – the childless wives, illegitimate children, children born to younger daughters, who had had no role to play in keeping the tree growing steadily from generation to generation, but who turned out to have had interesting lives. More often it was a topic that he stumbled across because it had a bearing on his ancestors' happiness or prosperity – their politics, their ways of making money, their religious beliefs. These were the longer diversions, because once his interest had been hooked on, for example, the Gordon Riots of the eighteenth century, he had difficulty pulling himself away while there was still more to find out. And it didn't matter. This history was not bounded by anything other than the hours left in Inchbold's life. He didn't want to finish it.

Greta told me I was being exploited.

'When do you have a moment to yourself?' she said. 'You should be having fun, at your age, not stuck with a grumpy old man all day, every day.'

But it was this that saved me from the abyss of grief that yawned at my feet when I allowed myself to contemplate Ma's absence. In the Royal Palace Hotel I had had to walk through the same doors and remember I did not have to hold them open for her. I had had to walk down corridors with an empty space in front of me where her wheeled chair should have been. I had had to eat my meals at a table she no longer shared with me. Here, I could avoid being crippled by loss for most of the day. Only last thing at night and first thing in the morning, when I turned in my bed to look, first and last, at Ma's drawing, would I let myself acknowledge how much I missed her.

I said to Greta: 'I'm not being exploited. If I say I want time off, I'm sure Inchbold would let me take it.'

'You're a strange one,' she said.

The first Sunday we went to church, I had anticipated the turning of heads to take in this stranger, but not how strange I would feel myself to be. I had chosen the wrong head covering. The end of my shawl came loose as we walked and brushed against the brim of a hat at the end of a pew further back than the Inchbold family's. It was the sort of hat I should have worn, and hadn't. The woman wearing it lifted a hand to brush my shawl away and I checked, turned to apologize, confusing Inchbold.

'What is it?' he said.

I had my mouth open to apologize to the woman but then I would have had to explain to Inchbold what the apology was for, and there was a hushed expectancy among the congregation for what this flagrantly foreign woman would do or say that made me want to shout at them that I was a Catholic, had never before been in a Protestant church, had no idea what to wear or how to behave. I wanted to tell the woman staring at me that she would look as out of place, in her olive-brown hat, her tweed coat, her tightly laced brogues, in the church on Main Street as I did here. Only the whiskers on her chin and the troubled expression on her face reminded me of Mrs Echado, so I smiled at her and said:

'Nothing.'

She was, I found out later, a friend of Greta's whose rather lovely name was Annabel, and she often reminded me, as she sat drinking tea in the kitchen at Pool House, of this brief encounter.

'Strutting down the aisle like a cock pheasant,' she'd say. 'Didn't know what to make of you. I didn't think you could be a nice girl, when I first saw you, but I know better now. She's a nice girl, isn't she, Greta?'

And Greta would grunt, not wanting to agree.

I followed Inchbold's lead on when to stand, when to sit, when to kneel, but my awkwardness could not have gone unnoticed. I did not know the responses or the words to the hymns and prayers, and Inchbold, of course, did not have any books for me to follow. As we settled back in our pew for the sermon, I heard a whisper of the word 'Spanish' being passed along the row behind us. This, I knew from the reactions we had seen in London when anyone recognized the language we were speaking among ourselves, was little better than 'German'. Though Spain had not joined the war, this was not a time when neutrality was a state anyone was ready to recognize. If not with us, then against us. And Spain was not with us.

When we walked out into the sunshine again, the vicar was shaking hands with his parishioners as they left. He stepped forward to make sure we did not pass him by.

'Inchbold!' he said, in a hearty, man-to-man voice. He was not hearty to look at; rather pink, rather moist. I judged his age to be around forty, so Inchbold, who had been blind for twenty-four years, would never have seen this man's face and would not realize that it was disconnected from the person his voice proclaimed him to be. 'And this is . . .?'

'Miss Dunbar.' Inchbold spoke louder than normal. 'My new assistant.'

'Miss . . . ah! . . . Dunbar,' the vicar said, discomforted. 'I'm delighted to meet you. You must come to tea. Yes, indeed, you must. My wife will arrange it.'

As we walked back to Pool House, Inchbold grew angry.

'How incredibly stupid of me. You're a Catholic, aren't you? I should have known that. How could I expect you to sit through all the dreary nonsense of a Church of England matins with the whispering classes putting you in a place you don't belong? Which is worse, them or me? Nothing to choose between us.' And so on. I held on to his arm, which I might ordinarily have released when we were clear of the church and only yards from his gate, and let the anger flow out of him. When he stopped, I said:

'I'm not a child. I knew it was not a Catholic church. I just hadn't appreciated how different it would be.'

'Was it?' said Inchbold, instantly interested, instantly recovered. 'You must tell me. It will be relevant to the History.' The Inchbolds had remained Catholic for longer than it was politic to do so, and there was a branch that had never converted.

23

Tea at the Vicarage

The invitation to tea at the vicarage arrived in the form of a white card with the address embossed at the top and mannered lettering appointing a day and time for a 'small tea party'. I went for a walk by myself that evening, when Inchbold was assaulting the piano, tramped up fields and through a wooded dell leading to a ridge. From here, the village and the valley were visible but distant in daylight; in the dusk, the buildings and roofs were dark angles and shapes among the less angular, lighter fields and hedgerows. As I walked I thought about who I had become. It was barely a year since I had been living in what would look like squalor to the people I was now living among. Small, dark, crowded rooms, however clean, tidy and well-kept they were. I had been at a lower level, socially. At home I might have spoken to some whose position was solidly based on the might of the garrison and the government. I would never have been invited, as a guest, into the house of a senior figure in the Church. In Easterbrook, the layers were less sharply separated than they were on the Rock, where there were places only those authorized to do so could go. Here, those with money and status came into frequent contact with those with neither, but Greta, for example, would probably not be sent a crisp, white card, handwritten, inviting her to tea at the vicarage.

Now, it seemed, I was the same person with the same education, the same accent, the same manners as I had always had, yet I was being invited in where I did not fit. Was this good, or bad? An invitation to take advantage of opportunities that might lead to a future forever lived above where my birth had placed me, or an invitation to make a fool of myself, make me think myself more important than I was, setting me up to fall? What would Ma say? I knew the answer to this. She would say I should hold on to an understanding of who and what I was, but to think myself inferior to no one unless I could see in what way they were superior to me. That superiority did not lie in dress and accent but in thoughts and deeds. This is what she had brought me up to believe, but believing it was easier than acting as if I believed it.

Apart from the items of knitwear and the second-hand coat from the Shelter, I had bought no new clothes. I had the green dress Mrs Thrupp had given me, or the skirts and blouses and dresses I had brought from home. To dress as the women I would meet and the women in church dressed would not be pretending to be one of them, I told myself, it would be avoiding making myself conspicuous by being so obviously alien. I told Inchbold I would like to go to Witney, to buy some clothes. I could catch a bus, but the buses were not frequent and I would be gone for at least three hours.

'Take the car,' he said. Inchbold had a car that Amos drove, when something needed fetching from a distance.

'I can't drive,' I said.

'No, of course not, why would you? Let Amos take you. Or take a bicycle. Can you ride a bicycle?'

'I've never learned to do that, either.'

'I know so little about you,' he said. 'You give so little away.'

'I don't keep things from you. I'll answer any questions.'

'No, I'm not criticizing you. I like the way you don't rush to create an impression of yourself. Only I have a rule not to keep asking questions. After I came out of hospital, I was asking questions all the time, like a five-year-old. "What day is it? Is the sun shining? What colour is the jumper I'm wearing? What food is on the plate?" And I couldn't bear to hear my own voice, needing someone else to tell me what I couldn't see for myself, so I decided to stop. Work things out for myself in any way I could, without being able to see them. It's become a sort of game, almost, something I'm proud of, but I don't have many chances to feel pleased with myself, so I forgive myself this one.

'Before you came, I didn't know a thing about you. I was told your name and that you were young, that you had been evacuated from Gibraltar, and I stopped them telling me anything else because I wanted my judgement to be unclouded by what other people had to say. I wanted to have the fun of discovering you. When I opened the door to you, you could have been short or tall, fat or thin, plain or beautiful, healthy or unhealthy, cheerful or morose. I have found out most of this now, and because you don't chatter on about how you feel and what you're thinking, it's been more fun for me. I had to listen to your breathing the first time we climbed a hill together, to see if I could hear you labouring to catch your breath, so I would know how fit you were. I've had to listen carefully to everything you've said, to determine whether you have a positive or a negative view of the world. Whether you are looking for things to grumble about or things to make you happy. I've lingered in the hall – I admit it – to overhear you talking to Greta, or opened the window so I can listen to you chatting to Amos in the garden. I'm pleased you didn't make it easy for me to know you all at once.'

'And what have you concluded about me?' I asked.

'I conclude that you are not easily summed up. That you are thoughtful. And sensible. And there is still much I don't know. Including, of course, the things I should have known if I hadn't set off on this little-by-little way of finding out about you. I'd have known, if I'd asked, that you were brought up a Catholic, that you can't drive a car or ride a bicycle.' He hesitated a moment. 'And though I've worked out how tall you are, and how fit, I don't know what you look like. I know your voice is beautiful. I don't know about your face. I wonder. Would you mind if I touched it?'

'I don't mind,' I said.

He had soft fingers. He had no work to do to roughen them. He cupped my face in his palms then ran his thumb around my jawline, traced my eyes and nose and mouth with his index fingers. Then he smiled.

'I see,' he said.

'What do you see?'

'I see that you have a strong face. Am I right? And that you are an attractive girl.'

'I can't tell if you're right or not,' I said. 'I'm not the best judge of my own appearance. And I knew nothing about you, either, when I knocked on your door. Only your name and your disability. I'm pleased to have found out about you, too, without having someone else's opinion first.'

He lifted his hands to his own face, as if reacquainting himself with it.

'One day, you must tell me what you have found out.'

Amos drove me to Witney but, after that, I asked him to teach me to ride a bicycle. The car was old, noisy and uncomfortable, and I was conscious of keeping Amos waiting in the town to drive me home, though he did not seem to mind.

'Things to do,' he said, and walked away. As it happened, clothes rationing had just been introduced and I could only buy one dress, one hat and one pair of shoes, which took less than an hour. I wished I had Conchita with me in the dress shop, but the choice was limited and I was looking to be inconspicuously ordinary, not striking. Still, she would have been able to see which colours and styles suited me best, better than I could.

The idea of riding a bicycle appealed to me, for the added independence and because I could explore further on two wheels than I could on foot. Amos was a patient and willing teacher. We wheeled the machine to a quiet lane behind the church and he made me sit on it and balance, without moving, until I understood the feel of a bicycle about to fall, and how to distinguish it from one that is under control. Then I pedalled, slowly, while he held the saddle. He began to let go, for short bursts, and, after a few stumbles and falls, I suddenly found I could be at ease, on a bicycle. To know I was not going to fall and therefore not to fall. Amos was proud of me.

'You're a natural,' he said. 'You're a sight better than the wet rag he had helping him before you came.'

This was a rare reference to Wilhelm, the Austrian refugee who had preceded me. He seemed to have made little impression on anyone though he had worked for Inchbold for more than a year, doing what I now did, sleeping in my room. No one spoke of him much; I had been told no stories about him, which meant he was no problem, he irritated no one, but no one particularly liked him, either. I had been curious, at first, because I wanted to be sure I was at least meeting the same standard, and that Inchbold was not constantly wishing he had Wilhelm back again, but I had no such uncertainty by this time.

'Did you try to teach Wilhelm to ride a bicycle?' I asked.

Amos snorted. 'He didn't ask. I didn't offer.'

I rode back to Pool House with Amos running beside and then behind me, his awkward gait preventing him reaching even the moderate speed I was now able to achieve. He arrived, breathless from the run, as I was putting the bicycle away in the outbuilding where it was kept.

'There's a dance in the church hall on Saturday night, if you want to come,' he said.

'Your mother told me I should be going out and having fun,' I said. I was unsure what his words meant. Was he asking if I wanted to be his partner for the dance, or whether I wanted to walk down to it with him? He seemed to understand my answer that was no answer, because he said:

'You wouldn't have to spend the evening dancing with a cripple. There'll be others there you might like to meet.'

'Thank you,' I said. 'I'd like to go.'

For the vicarage tea I wore Mrs Thrupp's green dress, in the end. It was a lovely afternoon. It was a whole season of lovely afternoons, and I often looked up at the empty blue of the sky as I walked around outside or sat beside my window and made myself notice the absence of planes. I did so as I walked to the vicarage, which was on the further side of the church, more or less concealed behind a high wall and immaculate hedges. I could hear voices as I went up the path and a maid in a black-and-white uniform directed me round the corner of the house to a lawn where a table and chairs were set out in the shade of a walnut tree. I tried to remember, as I crossed over the soft grass towards the ladies (they were definitely ladies, not mere women) clinking their teaspoons on their china cups, which book I had read in which just such a scene was described. More than one, I felt sure.

It was not all women, I realized when I reached them. The vicar was there, and another man, old, grey, wearing a suit and waistcoat though the day was gloriously warm. The women were the vicar's wife, whom I had met at church and who was reassuringly dull and dowdy, however grand the garden in which she sat and the stone façade of the house behind her; three others, older, carefully dressed; and one younger, no less perfectly turned out. Their names were familiar to me. I had heard them spoken in church, seen them on tombstones and memorial plaques, caught mentions of them in Greta's rambles through village gossip. Armstrong, Netherwood, Whitchurch, Field. The upper reaches of Easterbrook society.

'Don't be taken in by them,' Inchbold had said when I told him where I was going. 'Don't let them bully you. Their curiosity is of the idle sort.'

They were certainly curious about me. They did nothing as vulgar as asking direct questions, at first. They invited me to share my story with them by expressing sympathy or admiration, or speculating and then pausing for me to confirm or correct what they had said.

'It must have been terrible for you, to leave your home, so suddenly. And to arrive in this country where I imagine you knew no one, all alone. You seem to be managing admirably.' And so on.

I corrected the worst of their errors. No, it had not been sudden. We had known for a long time that, in the event of war, the Rock would be needed for military purposes and the civilian population would be at risk if we stayed. I had not come alone. We had travelled together, in family groups, and been accommodated together. We had been looked after. This was how the authorities who had planned and carried out the evacuation would have described what happened, what the reports they wrote would have said. Not how it felt to us. Not our real experience, with its hardships, physical and emotional. The ladies' curiosity, I could tell, was as Inchbold had said: idle. They wanted an explanation that was not disturbing, did not cause the sugar tongs to falter as they lifted a cube from the bowl and dropped it in their cup.

I had arrived with my mother, my sister-in-law and my nephews, I said, but my mother had died and this was why I was here on my own. This was the only information I gave them without being prompted and only to avoid questions about Ma, not having understood the hunger of the older generation for details on illness and causes of mortality – I should have remembered Mrs Hampton, but she was, in all other respects, so unlike the guests at the vicarage tea party that I had not expected them to agree on any topic. The youngest woman there, Isabel Field, came to my rescue when she saw the questions were upsetting me.

'Oh, I'm sure you don't want to dwell on it. Just accept our sympathy.'

I was clearly not found to be a rewarding guest and I was satisfied with that. The talk veered away from my personal circumstances on to the topic of evacuees generally. Most of these women had taken in children from London; some of them had returned home, but Mrs Whitchurch, for example, was still caring for two small girls who had arrived like parcels, labelled and inadequately wrapped, at the end of 1939. She was, her tone and everything she said implied, an expert on evacuees. She understood exactly how they should be treated, the extent to which they were better off here than at home, the need – imperative, this – to manage their expectations.

'They can't be taught to assume their lives will always be as easy and pleasant as they are at Glebe House,' she said. 'It would be a big mistake to lead them to think they belong in a higher station than the one they were born into.'

I kept my face as expressionless as I could manage, but no one was looking at me. It had not occurred to them that I was also above my station, sitting on the vicarage lawn. Because I was not a child, I was clean and well dressed, I spoke with grammatical correctness and my accent was not one they recognized as being working class, only foreign. I felt deeply sorry for the children passing part of their childhood at Glebe House in the care of Mrs Whitchurch. If she had been treating them as she would her own children, I could see that they would find it difficult to adjust to the life of hard work and relative poverty that waited for them at home. If she was making sure they did not imagine they deserved to be in the same circumstances as her children, then their lives would surely be a misery now and blighted by a sense of inferiority later.

I mentioned Mrs Whitchurch and the evacuees to Greta when I got back to Pool House.

'She hardly sees them,' she said. 'The chauffeur's wife cares for them. Mrs Hoity-Toity Whitchurch just makes sure she is getting all the credit for good deeds.'

At church the next Sunday, Isabel Field asked me if I would care to give her a hand at a bring-and-buy sale in the church hall on Friday. Of course I had not been invited to tea because they thought I might be one of them. They had wanted to assess my usefulness. I was comfortable with that. I understood it. I said yes.

24

The Dance

I went to the dance with Amos. That is, we walked down the road together to the building attached to the church, which was a huge, empty space with high windows round three sides, too high to see anything through except sky, and that distorted by the warped panes of yellow glass set in metal latticework. On the fourth side, the front, the windows were lower and gave a view of the street outside. All these windows were masked with blackout, for the dance, which would go on after dark. Though they did not live in fear of bombs in the village, they still were subject to the same rules and were even more precise and self-righteous about their observation than the population of London. I wore my new dress, and fitted in, as I'd hoped I would. The other girls were wearing just the same sort of dress. Conchita would have made an effort – successfully – to stand out from the crowd. I was pleased to find I did not.

There were more women than men, and they danced together when no man had asked them, which meant there was almost no one sitting out round the edges of the hall, and, though I had imagined myself, and even hoped to be, an observer not a participant for much of the time, I would have been conspicuous. So I accepted every invitation. Because I was new, and a curiosity, when word spread who I was, I was not short of these.

I danced with Billy, the son of the farmer Amos worked for. He smelled of fresh air and animals and was taller and broader than any man I had danced with before, at home. He had blond hair, too. In Gibraltar, I stood out as being the tall one, the light-haired one, and I wanted Sonia to be there to see this strange spectacle of me dwarfed and outshone by the bulky fairness of this man. I wished Sonia were there from the first moment I stepped through the door to be confronted by a dance floor on which I knew no one. I was almost more unsettled by this than I had been on finding myself on the vicarage lawn. That had been so unreal I could treat it like a stage set on to which I was walking to play a minor role, before vanishing again into the wings. This hall was somewhere I should have belonged, at a social event with young people around my own age, but they were the wrong young people because I did not know them and they did not know me.

'You're quite posh, then, are you?' said Billy, one large hand clasping mine, the other on my waist.

'I'm not,' I said. 'My father works on the docks and my brother is a clerk in a tailor's shop.'

'Amos says you don't seem bothered by all the bookwork you have to do for Inchbold.'

'No. I was working in a library before I left Gibraltar. That doesn't make me posh.'

'Brainy, then.'

'Brainy enough for the job, anyway.'

I had the impression that Billy was the king of the village

youth. Like Eligio Montez, who had married my friend Ursula while we waited to leave the second time, he was the pinnacle of all the girls' ambitions and he knew it. He had stepped in to claim me first so he could make a judgement on me, and the others would be waiting to hear what it was.

I danced with Amos, who was an awkward partner because of his disability, and with two young men in uniform, home on leave, who I think were pushed forward by their girlfriends, anxious to know more about me. I danced with a blacksmith's apprentice who was shorter than me and spent the entire time we were on the floor together explaining why he was not in uniform (tuberculosis) and what he would love to be doing to Fritz if only he had the chance (imaginatively unpleasant and unlikely). Most of my partners expressed an interest in Gibraltar which, in the case of a youth waiting for his call-up papers to arrive when he turned eighteen the next month, appeared genuine. This boy smelled of some form of soap and whatever he used to smooth his hair; the men in uniform smelled of polish and dusty wool, the blacksmith of metal and unwashed flesh. Amos had an earthy smell I liked. I absorbed their smells because it was too hard, in the noise and the crush, to remember their names, or to hear and understand much of what they said.

It became hot, in the hall, with the doors shut and any breeze through the few windows that opened stifled by blackout. When there was a break in the dancing, for the band of three rather old but competent fiddlers to have a drink, they announced they would turn the lights off for ten minutes, so the doors could be opened. There were cheers. Several of the couples hooked hands and made for the exit, others turned towards each other to exchange more passionate embraces than they would have done with the lights on. I left the hall and walked a little way away from it, towards the church. I went to the further side of a high stone tomb with a rounded top, and leaned against it, feeling the coolness of the stone through my dress, looking up at the still, starlit sky.

Someone came out of the darkness and pushed me hard against the side of the tomb. One of his hands held me pinned there while the other began to fumble with the buttons down the front of my dress. I knew at once who it was. Sometimes it is better to know a person's smell than his name, but I wished I also knew his name so I could use it.

'Stop it,' I said. I tried to wriggle free of his grasp and was surprised to find – because I am a strong woman – I could not shift his arm. He brought his mouth to mine and stopped whatever I might have said next. I rammed my knee into his crotch with as much force as I could manage, and he loosened his grip for an instant. I used both my arms to break his hold and tried to duck out of the reach of his hands. He held me back, grabbing my wrist and swinging me round towards him, catching my other wrist to stop me fighting back.

'Come on!' he said. 'I'm off to fight next month – don't you want to give me a good time before I go?'

Another figure came round the end of the tomb and lifted the boy away from me, spun him round and set him down again, facing in the opposite direction. I already knew it was Amos before he spoke, because of the peculiarity of his gait.

'Get out of it,' he said to the boy. 'Make yourself scarce and pray I won't tell your mother.'

The boy was holding a hand to his face, which Amos must have cuffed in pulling him away.

'I thought . . .'

'I know what you thought. You thought Rose was foreign, and foreign girls are fair game. Well, she isn't. Either foreign or fair game. So get going.'

'Thank you,' I said, when he had gone. I hoped Amos wouldn't touch me, because I was surprised to find I was shaking and I didn't want him to know that.

'He won't have the nerve to go back to the dance,' he said. 'But it would be best if you came back. If you both leave, he might be tempted to claim he was successful. We don't want that.'

'We don't,' I said. 'Let's go back.'

The girls had not approached me before but when the lights came on, a group of three came up to talk. It was a relief; I'm not sure I would have been happy to be touched by any of the men, just then. The girls invited me to agree with them on a number of topics – how boring it was in Easterbrook, how difficult it was to cope with clothes rationing, how good-looking Billy was. They asked me about the people of Pool House. What did I think of Amos? A very kind man, I said. He was, wasn't he? they said. Wasn't Inchbold odd? Certainly not ordinary, I said. But he treated me well and I liked the work I did for him. They were less satisfied with this answer. Didn't Greta make the best, honestly *the best* cakes? I didn't know that, I said. I loved her cakes; I just hadn't realized other women's weren't as good.

They couldn't ask me about where I was from, what it felt like to be evacuated, because they couldn't phrase the question. Their understanding didn't stretch as far as to know what exactly to ask.

'I hope you don't wish you hadn't gone,' Amos said on the walk home.

'No, I'm glad I did.'

'They're all right, most of them,' he said.

'Did you enjoy yourself?' Inchbold asked, the next day. He turned his head towards me whenever he spoke to me, but often missed the precise alignment of his face with mine; he looked past me to right or left, which made no difference but mattered to me and would, I think, have mattered to him had he known of it. I had to resist the temptation to move so that our faces were lined up as those of two sighted persons might be. When he asked this question (which I had not anticipated because he asked so few) he looked even less than usual as if he were asking it of me rather than of someone standing off to one side of me, an impression enhanced by the tone, which was challenging.

'It was full of people I did not know,' I said. 'But I danced. I talked to girls my own age.'

'Young people can be cruel,' he said. 'To strangers.'

'Yes, but these young people weren't cruel.'

He was silent, his fingers moving over the embossed sheets his Braille-writer produced. He read with his fingers and I could not be sure when he was reading and when his hand just happened to be lying across a page of symbols.

'And Amos looked out for you?'

'He did.'

'Will you go again?' He lifted his head sharply from the page under his hand and, for once, fixed the position of his eyes so that he appeared to be looking straight at me.

'I'm not sure.' I had asked myself the same question during the night, when I had had difficulty sleeping, the hot press of the soon-to-be soldier's body against me, the mass of foreign faces circulating before me in time with music that was also foreign still too present in my mind.

I thought back, as the light that had faded from the sky only a few hours before began to creep back into it, to a girl who had arrived in our school as a stranger when we were fourteen or so. She had been eager in her quest for friendship, wanting to know all of us, intimately, as quickly as she could. Her energy was drawn from others and without those others around her, she did not know what to do, how to behave, how to be herself. I was not like her. I had Inchbold, Amos and Greta in this place. That was enough.

The boy in the churchyard did not occupy my thoughts for long. I had already taken this incident and framed it, with a caption that read 'irrelevant'. Filed it away where it need not intrude on me.

Inchbold seemed satisfied that I had said everything he needed to know about the previous evening, or had said everything I was going to say, and so we started work.

25

Braille

Our work was made difficult because I could not read what Inchbold wrote and he could not see what I had written. Sometimes he dictated to me and I typed, on a conventional machine. Then I would read it back to him and he would ponder changes, becoming angry when he could not find a form of words that adequately described what he wanted to say, or distracted when he thought some topic needed more facts. I enjoyed the distractions, which would let me haul books off the shelves and read out sections while Inchbold became introspective or excited, became more like the man I detected he might have been before 1917. The editing, the searching for words and phrases, was frustrating, and he could not trust his own memory sufficiently so would ask me to read out the vexed passage again and again. When he was unable to make a decision, in the grip of his temper, we would reverse roles and I would dictate his own words back for him to transcribe on the Braille-writer. He would play around with the words himself and read them back to me so I could correct the version I had typed.

This fractured process not only meant more work, but it prevented the manuscript from having a shape in which connecting threads could be seen to be linking the whole together. It was like a chest of drawers, with each drawer containing fragments of the whole. If the drawers were labelled by the method used to produce the sheets inside, there would be one for what Inchbold had written himself, without the help of a sighted assistant, accessible only to him. There would be another for what he had dictated to me or my predecessors; Inchbold's words, but only accessible to him through the eyes of another. There would be a drawer for what existed in type-script duplicated elsewhere in Braille, and one for Braille duplicated elsewhere in typescript, which only the two of us working together could hope to check for consistency. I thought the frustration of this was greater for a sighted person – for me – than for Inchbold, because he had the ability to read what he had written and could command the reading of what others had written at his dictation. The pattern of the whole was wholly hidden from me.

So I asked if it was hard to learn how to read and to write Braille.

'No one who didn't have to would try,' Inchbold said.

'I think I do have to try if I ever want to see this book finished,' I said.

Inchbold said: 'What?' I began to repeat myself but he interrupted me. 'No, no. I heard you.'

Then he stood up and began to walk round the room. Whenever he moved about indoors, he did it to the sound of a percussion of taps, using a cane to know where he was. There was no hesitation in the way he moved; no delay, however slight, to allow the information the cane taps gave him to be absorbed and understood. At home, he saw with his cane as well as I did with my eyes.

So he walked freely round the library where we worked, tapping the legs of the furniture, the skirting boards, the waste-paper basket, round his desk to the window, back past my little table which sat at right angles to his desk, to the bookcases, to the door. It was behaviour I had seen before, when he tried to manage his anger, and I wondered what it was that had angered him this time. While I could see, though she could not, that he never lost his temper with Greta, would make every allowance for the flaws that would have caused irritation in a lesser man, I was never so confident on my own behalf. I continued to believe that there would be something I might do or say that would go beyond what he could tolerate. Part of me wanted this to happen, to know where the threshold lay; I was not frightened of him. But I was anxious not to cause him pain, as his anger seemed to do, so I watched him walking and worried about why he was doing it.

At last he sat down again at his desk and said:

'You don't want to do this. You can't. It would be perverse of you to pretend it would be anything but a chore.'

'The question is,' I said, 'how much of a chore? Because I wasn't expecting to enjoy learning it. But I would like to be able to read it.'

He reached out his hand to me. My desk was close enough to his that I could have taken his hand, but I was not sure that was what he intended. I hesitated to interpret the gesture as meaning he wanted to touch me. He stood up, then, and took a step sideways to complete the action he had in mind. His palm fell on my upper arm. I moved quickly to put my hand in his and he squeezed it.

'Thank you,' he said.

*

Inchbold was good at teaching but not always a good teacher. He had the skills, but his personality interfered with his ability to use them. At some distance, now, from my days in the classroom, I can see that the same could be said for many of the women who taught me. Inchbold's problem was not an impatience for me to learn – on the contrary, he took delight in my every small step towards understanding – but with his own limitations, which would, inevitably, lead to outbreaks of rage, tap-tap-tapping circuits of the library and, finally, a retreat to the music room and the solace of the piano. So it took longer for me to learn Braille than if he had accepted his own shortcomings as easily as he accepted mine. Once I had understood the principles, I practised on my own and eventually reached a point where I could read the raised dots Inchbold created on his Braille-writer, and transpose them on to a page on my typewriter, without having to wait for him to read it to me. I learned to read the dots by eye. I did not tell him this. He only knew how to make sense of them by touch and the lessons had involved passing the alphabet cards on which he had learned from hand to hand, his fingers running over a letter then guiding mine to run over it in the same way, until I could pick out that one from all the others without hesitation. He seemed to forget that I could see his fingers and mine as they worked, and I could also see the pattern the dots made. I was better at seeing the pattern than feeling it; if I closed my eyes to read Braille, I went slowly through the process of working out the shape, converting the shape to a visual, then translating the visual to a letter. With my eyes open, I was soon quick enough to provoke a transport of delight in Inchbold.

He went out to the top of the stairs and shouted for Greta,

who came up to the half-landing and asked what was the matter, her tone already defensive.

'There is nothing at all the matter, my good woman,' said Inchbold. 'What are you doing, lurking down there? Come here! Come here!'

She followed him into the room, looking suspiciously at me, seated at my little table, as ignorant as she was of what was in Inchbold's mind. I tried to indicate this with a smile and a shrug but Greta was permanently at odds with me by now. I had joined the ranks of those who despised her, as she supposed, because my lessons with Inchbold had appeared as intimacy, to her. She felt excluded. The lessons and the extra work had left me no time to help her as I had done when I first arrived and this, too, she took personally. What Inchbold had to say only confirmed her view that I had moved into the camp of her enemies.

'I want to have a party, Greta,' he said. 'A small party, of course. Just a few people who I can talk to about the work Rose and I are doing. A celebration. Yes! That's it! A celebration. What do you think?'

What Greta thought, I could tell, was that no one ever suggested a party to celebrate the work she and Amos did, and I had sympathy for her. So it was at home, I wanted to tell her. The pageants laid on to trumpet an anniversary of a national triumph or the departure of a dignitary, a new dignitary arriving, were partly for our benefit, but to impress us, not congratulate us. No one thought to organize such a display to reward us for the work we did daily.

Inchbold's party was small enough, as a social event, though Greta resented it no less, nor did her resentment diminish when I abandoned my work on the book for the two days beforehand to help her cook and clean and polish silver that looked to me in no need of polishing. Inchbold invited a man called Sebastian who was a cleric and an academic, a dry-skinned man with wet lips, hollow cheeks and hair that was thinly spread across his scalp but plentiful in respect of length. He wore glasses and gave the impression of finding them a hindrance rather than a help, looking over them or turning his head to peer round the edges. There was mutual respect between him and Inchbold. I understood immediately, as he stood in the hall, water dripping off the ferrule of his umbrella – for it rained, the night of the party – that he had no interest whatsoever in anyone else present.

The drawing room looked lovely. Greta was a diligent and expert cleaner and polisher, and Amos had provided lupins, roses and delphiniums that glowed more brightly, certainly with more depth of colour, than the silver. None of the people in the room were as colourful or glowing as the setting. I include myself, though I wore Mrs Thrupp's green dress. I felt appropriate; at least, as appropriate as the only other woman, Mrs Carlyle, accompanying her husband, who owned a book-shop in Oxford. They had been Inchbold's friends for so long they no longer worried about causing offence, which meant they were relaxed guests, but also seemed to prefer to listen rather than talk and to notice rather than be noticed.

The final member of the party was Sir William Bland, who was younger than the others and who did, I guessed, want to talk and to be noticed, but despite the title, which overawed me easily enough, and a position of authority as a magistrate, he was diffident, and the only one there who responded with enthusiasm to Inchbold's story of the difference it made to him that I had learned Braille. The others were interested, but muted. That was the mood of this event, which I had looked forward to with more pleasure than I had the tea at the vicarage, but with much greater trepidation. It mattered to me that Inchbold should not realize the distance that existed between his learning and my ignorance, his cultural level and mine. I valued his respect for me too greatly to feel easy about exposing myself in front of people whose opinions were important to him. I wasn't concerned I might say or do something awkward, as I had resolved to say and do little, but I could not help fearing that Inchbold's more acute, sighted friends would see through me as he could not, and that he would catch their uneasiness at the unworthiness of his protégée and his absolute faith in me would be shaken.

The focus (I should have foreseen this) was so much on Inchbold, so little on me. He wanted them to acknowledge I had done something that was not easy and was important to him. They acknowledged it, but at once passed on; even Sir William, who said, 'Oh, I say! Well done, you!' as if he genuinely admired me, wanted only to talk about the book itself, the content, not the process by which it was being created. Quite right too, I thought, as I handed round the glasses of sherry and the plates of cheese straws, squares of toast spread with meat paste and tiny sausages, skewered on sticks, that Greta had conjured up. Had Inchbold invited them for the purpose of expressing their admiration for Greta's ability to create such food at a time of rationing and shortages, they would have been more appreciative of her efforts than of mine. They responded enthusiastically to the food, but only to each other, and though I tried to commit their remarks to memory to repeat to Greta, I knew she would still feel overlooked.

In describing to his friends the book he was writing,

Inchbold gave a much clearer account than he had ever bothered to give me (but I had not asked) and I felt the party was worthwhile for this alone. He was telling the story of his family, he said, through individuals around whom other members of the Inchbold family swarmed, as they would in every generation, but whose history he was suppressing.

'I see the family as a pond,' he said. 'I can't begin to describe every molecule, so I'm creating a set of stepping stones across the surface to give a view of the whole. I can give a much better idea of the part of the pond each of them lived in this way, than I could if I stuffed the pages with the basic facts of all of them.'

'You could limit yourself to the male line,' Sir William said, and Inchbold frowned.

'Why would I do that? The women are usually the more interesting characters.'

'Are you going to finish with yourself?' asked Mrs Carlyle. 'With your own experiences?'

'No.'

'Isn't it important to bear witness to the horrors of war?' she said.

'Do you imagine it will all be forgotten if I don't bother to commit my own memories to paper, my dear Lucy? It will never be forgotten, and telling the same story again and again and again would only diminish the horror of it. No. This war, now. This war is different. There are so many stories unfolding, so many different triumphs and tragedies. Rose's story, for instance.'

They all looked at me as if they had, until that moment, failed to perceive that I was someone whose experience was not limited to this drawing room on this evening. Inchbold had told them, when he introduced me, that I came from Gibraltar, and had he told them I had stepped out of one of the books on his shelves, they would have shown as little interest in me.

'And what is your story?' asked Mrs Carlyle.

I was momentarily robbed of words. To answer the question would have meant using more than one or two sentences, could have led to whole paragraphs, and I could see them unfolding ahead of me with no end in sight. Better not to start. Mr Carlyle, tired of waiting for my answer, laughed.

'Let us guess,' he said. 'Dunbar is an interesting name. She is, we could imagine, descended from a branch of an old Scottish family. Let's say her grandfather travelled to Spain in the last decades of the nineteenth century, pursuing an interest in, I don't know, Moorish architecture? He married the granddaughter of the crabbed old custodian of an ancient palace in Toledo and together they travelled south – on donkeys, I think. Yes, definitely on donkeys, drinking wine and making love until they reached the very tip of the peninsula, across the water from Morocco, where their son was born. Rose's grandfather left his wife to cross the sea in search of more buildings he could sketch and weave dreams around, and he never came back. In time, the child grew up and married and Rose was born, and now she needs to trace her origins back to their beginning in Scotland to understand who she really is.'

'I know who I am,' I said. 'I'm the daughter of a dockyard worker who was born in Gibraltar, as my mother was, as my grandparents were and their parents before them.'

I was angry. Not with Inchbold's pure, blind fury but with frustration, a petulant form of anger I struggled to keep from showing itself in either words or tears. The implication of what Mr Carlyle had said was that, without a connection back to a landowning family in Great Britain, I was no one. Unless Moorish architecture and donkeys featured in it, my story was not worth telling.

Inchbold said: 'It's not her ancestors that are interesting. It's Rose herself.' He turned until he was looking towards the space I occupied. 'You should record what has happened to you,' he said. 'And not just what has happened. You don't reveal enough of yourself to me. I want to know what you think, what you feel.'

('You should record what has happened to you,' you said, for this was the moment when the idea became real to you and you set yourself from then on the task of making it real to me, too. I will continue referring to you in the third person because this account is mine, not yours, but before I do, perhaps now is the time to consider whether I have met the standards I set myself when I started. Have I avoided exaggeration, pettiness and self-righteousness? Looking back, I can see that I have given myself insights I did not have at the time. I have allowed my confidence with words to make me sound bold, when, so often, I am not. But I am well enough pleased with what I have written. Is it petty to say so? But, in any case, it is done now.)

After the party, after Inchbold had begun to accept it was quite natural for me to read Braille, we sank back into a pattern of working days, all four of us – Greta, Amos, Inchbold, me. Inchbold pressed me in the following weeks to take the suggestion of writing my story seriously, but I told him it was not over and I would not start until it was.

'When will it be over?' he asked. 'When you are an old woman looking over the heads of your grandchildren to a past that you will no longer remember clearly?'

'No,' I said. 'When I return to Gibraltar.'

'Who knows when that will be,' he said. And, later: 'Remember you are writing this for me, so if we are to go in separate directions when the war is over, you must write it before that happens.'

No one knew, as Inchbold said, how long it would be before I could go home. I had stopped thinking that it would be soon. I had also stopped thinking it would be the same.

26

Correspondence

I put my hand in the pocket of a cardigan I had not worn for a week or so, looking for a handkerchief, but what I pulled out was a letter from Peter Povedano. Unopened. I had meant to read it later, and then forgotten about it. Inchbold, ever alert to sounds that I do not realize I am making, asked: 'Is anything the matter?'

We were sitting, as we always did, he at his desk, I at mine, set at right angles. Touching at the corners.

'I've just found a letter I've forgotten to read.'

'If it was important, you would have read it.'

It was unimportant. Nothing Peter wrote in his letters to me, or that I wrote in mine to him, had any significance. He told me about the people he had seen who we both knew. Only that: he had seen them and they looked 'well' or 'cheerful'. And that he was 'well' and 'happy enough'. At first I had written him descriptions of London, but once I came to Pool House, all I ever spoke of in my letters was the vegetables and fruit in Amos's garden.

'No,' I said. 'Not important. But I should have remembered to read it.'

I opened it and spread the single, flimsy sheet out on the desk, began reading.

'You notice,' Inchbold said, 'that I have not asked you who it is from.'

'I remember you said you do not like to ask questions.'

'In this instance, I would like to ask the question but would not like you to feel you have to answer.'

'It's from a man called Peter Povedano. He asked me to marry him before I left Gibraltar and I said no.'

He was silent and I continued reading Peter's letter, which, suddenly and shockingly, was about something other than the people passing in the street. A man he knew, someone he had gone to school with and whose name I recognized and could almost put a face to, had walked off the end of the landing strip, now extended into the bay, without a pause. Just one step then another until there was no ground beneath his foot, only rocks and the sea. He had not survived. Peter described this in plain language and I could see it plainly in my mind. The solitary figure walking forward, the moment when all hope of keeping contact with the earth was lost, the moment-ary cessation of forward movement before the plunge.

'He was there one minute,' Peter wrote, 'and the next, just gone. I don't know what he was thinking. I can't stop thinking about it.'

I read this part of the letter – all of the letter, really, because the endearments at the beginning and end were the only other words in it – to Inchbold.

'War has a way of detaching us from ourselves,' he said.

I wrote back to Peter sympathetically, I hope, but the idea of detachment had lodged in my mind.

The loss of Ma was still an ache that had been eased by the move to this place, where she had never been, but also made worse by the lack of anyone to whom I could speak of her. There were moments when I was struck, in the course of putting one foot in front of the other, with the impossibility of her loss. At first these moments occurred almost daily; over time, such sorrow caught me less often, though it never left me and never will. (Writing the book, this book, has helped, as I thought it might.)

As well as Ma, I missed the children, but they at least were where I could still visit them. I went twice, in the first few weeks in Easterbrook, back to London to stay a couple of nights in the room which Maribel Molinary was still sharing with Aida, the sulky teenager, who had remained as sulky as she was when I left. Freddo was ecstatic when he saw me.

'You've come back,' he said, again and again, trying to climb up into my arms, his rather grubby sandals scratching my legs and leaving streaks of dust on my skirt. I was filled with grief on his behalf, this poor little scrap who had seen his father every day of his life until, suddenly, his father had gone, then his grandmother and his aunt, familiar presences, were missing and he did not know where any of them were, because none of the explanations made sense to him. That I had returned must have looked to him like a promise that all he had lost would be restored to him. On my own behalf, I felt guilt. I had chosen to leave, unlike his father and grandmother, who had been given no choice in the matter.

Eugenia, still caring for Conchita's children when she could, said I should not worry about this.

'They live in the moment, at this age. One moment happy, next moment sad, one moment cross, next moment loving.'

When I held the baby, Mercy, I felt grief on my own behalf that I no longer saw her every day, bathed her, cuddled her, played with her. She was so curious, so solemn one minute, so giggly the next. But she was well cared for and well loved. She had no need of a stray aunt who was not the most expert at engaging her attention or making her laugh. I had imagined I was the best at loving her; no one else, now Ma had gone and Jamie was still over the seas at home, could feel as deeply as I could. But when Conchita came home from work and the baby crowed with delight and Conchita, immaculate as always, picked her up and nuzzled her tummy, blew on her lips, crooning a litany of endearments in her ear, I felt relieved of this burden, too. The trauma of the birth, the unwelcome curtailment of Conchita's freedom, all forgotten. I was not needed there. Had I stayed, I would have been just a spare, unmarried woman.

There was a change in Conchita apart from the late awakening of love for her daughter. She was happier than I had ever known her to be. I had never really known her happy except on her wedding day, when all eyes were on her and she looked magnificent. Playing with her children – when they were well behaved, at least (which they usually were) – then she had seemed content. But, otherwise, she was sullen with dissatisfaction and because I could not comprehend what right she had to feel dissatisfied, I had disliked her for it. Now she was not. Which worried me. There was a new, quiet confidence about her, too, which I told myself was a result of doing a job she liked and being praised for doing it well. Maybe she was finding her looks were not her only asset, that she could command respect for her skills. This new Conchita would make Jamie a much better wife than the old one had done. But I could not avoid suspecting she had found someone who worshipped her in a way that was not Jamie's. Not quietly, soberly, but extravagantly.

'Conchita seems happier,' I said to Eugenia.

'Oh, she does, doesn't she? It makes her much easier to be with, don't you think?'

Live in the moment, Eugenia, I thought, like the children. I should try to do that, too.

My second visit to London, I went to have lunch with Mrs Almondsbury, her daughter, Martha, and Winifred. During lunch we talked about Inchbold and the book he was writing. Winifred tried to explain what the relationship was, between herself and Inchbold, but became tangled up in names and degrees of kinship. I recognized some of the names she mentioned as they occurred in the pages I had typed. Although the process of writing appeared to be endlessly disrupted by side alleys and cul-de-sacs, what ended up on the page was orderly and, listening to Winifred, I was silently admiring of Inchbold's skill in ignoring so much that would have made the story unwieldy, as Winifred's was, while having a coherent thread through the generations.

Martha said almost nothing at lunch, but when we rose from the table she asked me to walk round the garden with her.

'It seems possible I'll be going abroad, after all,' she said. 'To Gibraltar. They want some of us to be based there, decoding signals. I probably shouldn't be telling you this, but, honestly, I don't see that the enemy would have anything to gain from knowing where I go, and I'm sure you won't be bumping into any agents in Oxfordshire who might winkle it out of you.'

'I'm pleased for you,' I said, although I felt a jolt of bitterness that this privileged girl would be shipped back to walk along Main Street and watch the sunset.

'Tell me what it's like,' she said. 'I can't imagine it.'

'I don't think I can describe it. It's home, to me. It's like nowhere else.'

'Do you want me to look up your family? Your father is still there, Mummy says, and your brother.'

The idea of Martha in her twinset and pearls, or in the pristine uniform she was wearing that day, climbing the hill behind Main Street, finding her way up the steps and along the passageways to reach the door of the house where my father and Jamie lived, was unthinkable. She would be disgusted with the lack of order in everything, in the layout of the streets and the behaviour of the people, sitting on their doorsteps, sharing their lives with whoever passed, before she reached the staircase up to the darkness of the floor where we lived.

'That's kind of you, but they are working men and I don't think you will come into contact with them. You will be busy with parties at the Governor's House when you are not on duty.'

'I've upset you,' she said. 'How foolish of me. Of course, you want to go home and see the people you love, and here am I, all excited because I am going where you can't.'

'I'll tell Jamie, my brother, to look out for you,' I said. 'He works in an office at the port. I'm pleased for you that you have this chance. Truthfully.'

'When I get back,' she said, 'if nothing has changed for you in the meantime, I'll talk to you again about Gibraltar, when we have common ground, as it were.'

'Yes, I'd like that,' I said.

My letters from Sonia made me think that she, like the man Peter had written to me about, was at risk of becoming detached. She sounded like someone walking forward without caring whether there would be ground beneath her feet on the next step, or not. She continued to say I was an anchor she was missing but when I invited her, with Inch-bold's agreement, to visit me at Pool House, there were always reasons why she could not. She wrote in excitable language about the Italian prisoner of war who worked in the garden. She told me his name – Guido – but, otherwise, too much about the colour of his eyes and skin, the shape of his muscles and his mouth for me to feel comfortable. She had said Mrs Thrupp treated her daughters, and Sonia herself, like dolls, and I was afraid Sonia was doing the same thing with Guido, choosing a toy to play with to take her mind off her unhappiness. Because that was the one thing I became sure of, reading her letters: she was unhappy.

I wrote back reminding her of some of the boys we had gone to dances and to the beach with in Gibraltar. Did she remember how witty one of them was, how another was a complete idiot but very kind, a third arrogant yet full of interesting ideas? Her obsession with Guido was too extreme; I wanted her to put him in perspective. She did not respond to any of this. When I asked, outright, if she was happy, she wrote back:

'You ask if I am happy – well, are you? Isn't it hard, being here instead of at home, speaking English all the time, but never feeling English? Not being able to see the sea? Being surrounded by greenery instead of by rock? Not knowing what is going to happen to us next? I suppose you're going to say you can bury yourself in a book and forget all about how uncertain everything is. I can't do that, but I can find reasons to be cheerful. I'm the cheery one, remember? You're the solemn one. Trust me to find something to be cheerful about. Stop worrying about me.'

I didn't stop worrying about her but she did make me realize what I had not acknowledged to myself: that I was happy. I had, on top of the reasons she mentioned, the loss of Ma to justify feeling sorrowful, but from the moment I stepped into Pool House, I had the sense that I had found what I was looking for, without ever knowing what it was.

27

Martha

Inchbold lay back on the grass, his ruined eyes closed against the sun which glistened on the scars from the shrapnel that had severed his optic nerve, like so many snail trails of lighter skin.

'When I was a boy,' he said, 'there was a hole in the wall between the room my brother and I slept in and the bathroom next door. No one but us used that bathroom unless we had visitors with children who were put up on the third floor with us. We had a cousin, Julia, who was two or three years older than us, and when she came, we took turns to watch her through the hole. At first we were just being naughty. We thought nakedness was funny. But it stopped being funny as we grew older, and so did she, and became exciting instead. We also knew by then it was something worse than naughtiness and we stopped giggling about it. We stopped talking about it at all, but we didn't stop taking turns to watch Julia undressing. She was a pretty girl and probably still is an attractive woman, though she is married to a farmer and has six children, so I suspect that I wouldn't find it exciting any more, seeing her lift her dress up over her head.'

I knew he was talking about the attics where I slept, where

the hole almost certainly still existed in the wall of the bathroom, and I shivered at the thought, though there was no
man in the house capable of using it. That Inchbold would
have done, as a boy, did not surprise or even shock me. If I
imagined Jamie or Peter Povedano being given the chance to
see a girl undressing, without her knowledge, I was not sure
either of them would look away.

'It was one of the first things I thought of when I began to
realize I would never recover my sight. I was tormented by the
idea that the Fates were punishing me for looking when I
should not have looked, by robbing me of the chance ever to
see a pretty girl stepping out of her clothes again.'

'You don't still think that?'

'No.' He smiled, his eyes flickering open for a second then
closing. 'It drove me mad, for a while, that I could not go
back and undo this misuse of the gift of sight. But then, I
thought that if the Fates were punishing me for peeping at
Julia, what crime had my brother committed that was so
much greater he deserved to suffocate to death in the mud?
And sanity, on this matter at least, was restored to me. Now I
think it's a good thing I took the chance to see a girl naked
while I could, because I have few enough such memories
stored up and cannot hope to make more.'

I sat watching his face, the slight smile on his lips, and
thought he looked younger than I had taken him to be when
he opened the door to me six months before.

'Have I shocked you?'

'No.'

'Are you studying my face?'

'How did you know?'

'Because I have learned to detect movement, however

slight, and I know that you have not turned your head away, yet you are not speaking to me. What are you thinking, Rose Dunbar?'

'I was thinking you looked younger, lying in the sun like this, than you usually do.'

'Is that the truth?'

'I don't find it easy to lie.'

'I'm forty-three,' he said. 'I don't feel old, but I am a long, long way from youth.'

At the end of the walk, as Inchbold unlatched the gate into the garden, he turned to me and said, smiling, 'Home!' I knew he meant this to apply to both of us, but I have resisted using the word 'home' for Pool House or, before that, the Royal Palace Hotel, because it seemed presumptuous and, also, a betrayal. Gibraltar was my home, MacPhail's Passage. I had to keep hold of where I belonged or it might slip away from me, leaving me belonging nowhere.

Greta came out of the kitchen when she heard us at the door.

'Ah, Greta,' said Inchbold. 'Tea. Tea would be pleasant.'

'You've had a phone call,' Greta said. 'From a Miss Hobson.' She was looking at me, and when I didn't react she said, 'A Miss Winifred Hobson.'

'Winifred?' I said. 'What did she say?'

'I know who Winifred Hobson is,' said Inchbold. 'She's the daughter of my second cousin . . . let me see . . . how many times removed? She recommended you, didn't she, Rose? I'm disposed to think I like her.'

'She said' – Greta pulled a piece of paper from the pocket of her apron – 'to let you know the ship taking the Wrens to

Gibraltar has been sunk.' She articulated each word carefully, as if she knew she had to say this correctly but had no idea what it meant. Nor, for a moment, did I.

'What does that mean, Rose?' asked Inchbold, reaching out a hand to me, but I was too far away for him to touch me.

'I think it means Mrs Almondsbury has lost her daughter.'

'Tea!' said Inchbold, briskly. 'Please, Greta.'

As I explained to Inchbold how I knew what the message meant, it sounded as if it should have been of little importance to me. The mother was one of those who had come forward to help out when boatloads of displaced citizens of the British Empire arrived in London at the start of the Blitz. Her daughter was a girl I barely knew and was not sure I liked, but her death touched me. It came too close. I had wondered what it would be like to be her, and it was as if a version of me had died. But what made the tears come was the thought of Mrs Almondsbury's loss; I knew that my grief at losing Ma was nothing to what she would have felt if it had been me, drowned off the coast of Spain.

I was full of uneasiness about what I should do with the news. But Inchbold had no such uncertainty. It turned out he knew who Mrs Almondsbury was, had met her and her husband at some time, and the way forward was perfectly clear to him. First, he said, we should telephone Winifred to make sure that 'sunk' meant all on board were lost, then he would dictate to me a letter of condolence to the Almondsburys. Whether I also wrote on my own behalf, or rang Mrs Almondsbury up, or even travelled to London to visit her, Inchbold said, we would leave to Winifred's judgement.

The ship, SS *Aguila*, had been torpedoed by a U-boat in the darkest hours after the passengers had gone to bed, elated (this detail emerged later from the testimony of some of the crew who survived) from an impromptu sing-song that had taken place after dinner in reaction to the relief of having repelled an earlier attack from the sky. It took just ninety seconds from the time it was hit to the moment it sank. I tried holding my breath for ninety seconds, when I had all these facts, and it was a long, long time to be struggling without being able to breathe. And who knew when, during the attack and the wreckage, Martha Almondsbury had been able to give up the struggle.

The women were on a merchant ship, Winifred said on the telephone that evening. Because it was not deemed suitable to transport them on naval vessels, being female and not, in the eyes of the Admiralty, members of the naval establishment. None of the armed escort vessels were sunk in this attack.

I did not telephone Mrs Almondsbury, following Winifred's advice, but wrote her a letter to which she answered:

'I don't know if I ever want to see you again, because I am afraid I would hate you for reminding me of Martha while not being Martha. Yet, sometimes, I feel as if I want you to come and live with me here, so I can have a constant, breathing presence that has some flavour of Martha about it. Forgive me for being so frank and so selfish.'

I wrote back to her, saying I would come or stay away, as she preferred, and we continued to write to each other for more than a year. Then, in the summer of 1942, Winifred came to see us and she brought Mrs Almondsbury with her. I had, with Inchbold's agreement, invited Winifred several times, but she had never before accepted, and when she did, I realized this was because she was in awe of Inchbold. She appeared so breezy and capable among the people she knew in

London that I had not expected her to be hesitant with someone who was, after all, no more challenging or damaged, or cleverer than many of the refugees she dealt with daily. Over lunch she and Inchbold talked about family connections, how this man was linked to this one, through which marriages and blood ties in earlier generations. Listening to them, I thought Inchbold, for whom this was the least interesting part of his family studies, was humouring Winifred, for whom this tangle of knots turned out to be important. And whatever Inchbold's position in it was, she saw him as central, an authority, a figure to be approached with humility.

Mrs Almondsbury had shrunk since last I had seen her. I used to apply the word 'stout' to her when I first met her, before she became so familiar to me that I ceased to notice what she looked like. She did not convey stoutness now. Her face was set in its pinched-up, tucked-in expression, which I had also stopped noticing, but which was now so marked that had I been seeing her for the first time, in the queue to be allocated a room at the Royal Palace Hotel, I would have looked around for a different queue to join.

After lunch, in an echo of the last time I had met Martha, we went for a walk in the garden. We sat on a stone bench by a small stone circle surrounded by roses in bloom, with a pond in the middle and a fountain, now silenced because it seemed the right thing to do, in the circumstances, to step aside from such frivolities.

'Now I see you again,' Mrs Almondsbury said, 'I find you don't remind me of Martha at all. You are simply you.'

'I hope that's not a disappointment.'

'I find I am holding Martha in my mind as a much younger girl than you are. She is only fifteen or sixteen, when

I think of her. I can remember her at that age better than as her twenty-four-year-old self. I can't picture you at fifteen at all.'

'It's been lucky for me that you saw us as similar,' I said. 'I owe a lot to the kindness you showed me because of it.'

'I don't know if it was kindness, Rose. It was selfishness, in a way, though I suppose the outcome is the same, whatever the motivation. But I was looking for a project to occupy myself when my children were not mine to manage any more. I told myself the evacuees would be a project as a group, but I suspect I was always looking for the individual I could adopt, and you were it. You were a rewarding choice. So I should be thanking you for having filled a void before the void became too deep to fill.'

I knew from her letters that she had cut herself off from any involvement with the evacuees and was spending her time caring for her husband, whose physical condition had deteriorated. I wanted to tell her that she could do more, that whatever the motivation, she could be helpful and she should find other projects. Ma would have said something like this but I lacked the courage. I was not sure I could find the words that would make this sound, as it was meant to be, a compliment. And, after all, what business had I, a poorly educated girl from a poor district in an isolated colony, to give advice to someone with power and authority? So I said nothing and she patted my hand and we walked back to the house, where Greta, with a face grimmer than Mrs Almondsbury's, had once again conjured up a spread of cakes and scones, using ingenuity and, for all I knew, the black market to circumvent shortages.

I continued to write to Mrs Almondsbury, but our letters

became less frequent and almost domestic; she told me of the books she had read and the failure of the beetroot crop through lack of rain. I told her of the progress of Inchbold's manuscript and passed on tips from Greta and Amos for producing the most, and the most palatable, food while the war lasted.

28

Christmas at Easterbrook

My life in the village, in Pool House, has spread across years by the time I am writing this, and while at the beginning of this story I was conscious of having to record every week, if not every day, then every month if not every week, now I find myself at the end of a period of time that has been punctuated by events but not at weekly or even monthly intervals.

My first Christmas at Pool House, Conchita and the children came to stay. I had Greta to thank for this. She caught Inchbold on his way to the music room to beat out his frustrations on the piano, and told him the Christmas season only made sense if you had children in the house. Otherwise, it was so much empty ritual and she was not prepared to put the effort into making it special unless children could be procured. Inchbold repeated this conversation to me later. It had delighted him, as he could admire Greta in combative mood; it was the endless grumpiness he found hard.

'I don't know any children,' he had said to her.

'Rose has nephews, and a niece. They should be invited.'

'Then they shall be.' As she stomped back down the stairs, he called after her. 'Of course, Christmas makes sense if you believe in the virgin birth and the divinity of the Christ child.'

Her reply was inaudible but might have been, he thought, 'Poppycock.'

I was not sure if Conchita would want to leave the comfort of the hotel where the boys had friends, and activities laid on for them, and where Eugenia was always on hand to help with Mercy. But she did.

The attics where I slept were made up of a series of rooms of which only mine was clean and properly furnished. The others had become home to the debris of lives lived in the recent and distant past, and in preparation for Conchita's visit, Greta and Amos and I set about preparing spaces for her and the children to sleep. It proved beyond us to empty, clean and furnish more than one other room in the time we had, and even this was at the expense of my work with Inchbold, who was neglected for the week it took. He stood at the bottom of the attic steps calling my name, and I would go down, covered in cobwebs, with splinters in my fingers, smudges on my face, and try to sound calm as I reassured him that soon I would be able to return to the library. In the room up the stairs behind me Amos would be standing holding up one end of a chest of drawers, waiting for me to pick up the other end. He was a patient man and in this he reminded me of my father. I had become fond of him. We were friends.

There had been moments, when he was teaching me to ride the bike, walking to and from the dances, which I was beginning to enjoy, when I had sensed he was wondering whether to make a move that would have gone beyond friendship. I was grateful he had not. I knew if I relaxed, let him kiss me and hold my hand, it would have been because it would be easier; easier to avoid incidents like the one in the churchyard at the first dance, easier to be friends with Greta, of whom I had also grown fond. But I set Amos alongside Peter Povedano and I could see that they were similar: diligent, patient, thoughtful men. But Peter was the more physically attractive and I shared a history with him, a store of jokes and memories it would take me years to build up with Amos. When I had rejected Peter's proposal of marriage, I had done so because he was not quite enough; I wanted something more than marriage to him would have given me. So if I had turned towards Amos rather than away from him at the critical moments when all that we might be to one another hung in the balance, it would have been a weakness, and one I was sure I would come to regret.

If this makes me sound calculating, it is because I was. I had no idea where I would be in five years' time, nor how much more I would live through before then. Maybe rejecting the immediate prospect to give the future time to reveal itself was a mature decision.

Inchbold was not a patient man and, at the end of a week, we had to abandon the task, with one room and two beds for the boys, and an ancient cot and second bed in my room for Mercy and Conchita. We had shared a room at the Royal Palace and could do so again.

I went with Amos in the old car to the station to collect them. Conchita walked down the platform like a vision of motherhood, Mercy in her arms, holding one of Freddo's hands, Alf holding the other. It was a sunny day and the sun picked out all the bright spots on her costume and her hair so she seemed to shimmer as she walked towards us. Heads turned, and she knew it. A porter followed her with suitcases and there was a moment's stand-off between him and Amos, the one reluctant to surrender his connection with such perfection, the other eager to take over.

'You're looking well, Rose,' she said, relinquishing Mercy to my arms. Like her clothes, her accent had taken on a sophistication it had previously lacked. To an Englishman, she would still have sounded foreign, but at home she would have been accused of aping a British accent. Mercy looked up at me from under a fringe with a hint of the curliness of my own hair, and said, loudly, 'Down!' Alf and Freddo were already clamouring round my skirts, shouting their news, wanting me to pay attention to them. Now! Now! By the time we reached the car Conchita, with a handbag over her shoulder, unencumbered by children or suitcases, looked like a woman of substance, Amos and I her lackeys.

In bed, in the dark, which was darker here in the country than it had been in London, despite the blackout in the streets there, Conchita and I talked to each other as we had not done when last we shared a room. Now we were alone except for the sleeping form of Mercy. In the absence of Ma. In these sightless conversations Conchita was more open with me than she had ever been. And, listening to her, I came close to accepting that she and I were sisters, because some of what she shared with me about her feelings, I could have shared with her about mine. She had been excited, she said, when we first came to London. She had wanted to have more fun than she had had at home. She had wanted to be something other than a wife and a mother for a short time, to remind herself how that felt, before she went back to the security of the life she had left. All that was delayed by her pregnancy and Mercy's birth and she had had a sense of urgency when she recovered, to pluck as much as she could from whatever time she had left in England. She had gone too fast and (she did not say this but

I heard it) too far, in the time between Mercy's birth at the end of September and Ma's death in April. She wanted to try to explain her feelings about Ma, she said.

'But you might not like what I say.'

'That shouldn't stop you saying it.'

'It won't. I'm not worried about upsetting you. I've actually tried to do that in the past and it hasn't worked.'

She told me she had never felt, for one solitary, single minute, that she came close to meeting the standard needed for Ma's approval. She knew, she said, that few people did, but most of these could shrug off the feeling of not being as worthwhile as they wanted to be, because they were not defined by her. Conchita, though, was no one's daughter; an unknown father and a mother no one would want to claim. She had wanted so badly to be someone's wife, part of someone else's family.

'I was happier than you can possibly imagine on the day I married Jamie.'

I could imagine it. I had seen it, but I had attributed it to the pleasure she took in her loveliness, in being the centre of attention.

Marrying into the Dunbar family had felt like moving out of a packing case into a solidly built house. She knew Ma did not think she was a suitable wife for Jamie, but what mothers did think the girls their sons married were worthy of the honour? And once inside, so she calculated, she would be able to win her round. She thought she only had to be charming, and obliging, in addition to being beautiful, and Ma would be seduced into loving her. It had worked in the past. But it foundered on the rock that was Ma's sense of decency and dignity.

'I do like to be liked, Rose. I like to be loved. I know that sounds feeble to you. You and Ma never set being liked above telling the truth.'

I had the idea she might be crying, quietly, in the darkness. Perhaps I should have left my bed and crawled into hers, cuddled up, as sisters might. But I didn't.

She gave up trying to make Ma love her and worked, instead, at not caring. Then Ma died – and I braced myself, at this stage of the confessional, to hear that Conchita was relieved at the removal of someone who reminded her she was worthless. I would have understood the reaction but I didn't want to hear it.

'I realized I had to care. Without her there to remind me all the time of the ways in which I wasn't a good person, what was going to stop me becoming utterly despicable? Becoming my own mother?'

She told me she hadn't slept with the man I saw her leaving the shop with on the night when Ma had her stroke.

'I think I meant to, when I agreed to go home with him, but then it seemed so wicked a thing to do I couldn't believe I'd ever thought of agreeing to it. He didn't like me much, after that.'

I haven't used all Conchita's words to describe this conversation, which went on over a few nights, but she used words more freely than I would have expected. I could not entirely rid myself of the suspicion that, with Ma gone and under cover of darkness, she was using her tricks on me, manipulating me, playing her games to make me love her, as I had seen her do often with others. With those, I would have said, who didn't know her as well as I did. When she told me about her attack of virtue at the point of giving in to seduction, I was cynical. But then, on Christmas Day, she was genuinely shocked at the suggestion she should go with me to the Protestant church in the village. It frightened her, that she might be committing a sin for which God would never forgive her.

I did, desperately, want to believe her when she talked about her plans for when she went back to Gibraltar. She was hoping to find a way to set up her own shop selling clothes never before available on the Rock, starting with a market stall, perhaps, growing to a business she and Jamie could run together.

'This isn't as short-term as we thought, is it?' she said. 'But it isn't permanent, either.'

She had certainties I was lacking.

Conchita and the children delighted the entire household. If she had been granted a house full of children to care for, Greta might have been a happier woman. I had worried that her never-completely-buried resentment would be brought to the surface by Conchita's beauty and her careless ways, but Conchita made an effort and this was good enough for Greta to decide she was charming. Amos was dazzled by her, but was mostly, like his mother, captivated by the children. We kept them away from Inchbold, nevertheless; Greta advised that he 'didn't like children'. Inchbold could not see Conchita so had no idea of how beautiful she was, and she had no idea, in the absence of beauty as a power, how to charm him. We ate dinner the first night in the dining room together, but it was an uncomfortable occasion and we left Inchbold to eat alone the following nights.

But then, on about the third day, I heard voices as I approached the library: Inchbold in conversation with Alf. If it did not sound like a misplaced word, I would describe Alf at this age as more sober. He did not swing from temper to sorrow to glee as readily as he had. He had developed a capacity for listening, and there was much he wanted to know. He was puzzled but not embarrassed by Inchbold's blindness, and was thus able to ask questions an adult would not dream of asking.

'Don't you ever put your pullover on back to front? Because *I* do and *I* can see which way round it should be.'

'How do you know you've eaten every last crumb on your plate if you can't see it? I'd leave the cabbage and say I didn't know it was there.'

'Can you still imagine yellow? And blue?'

Inchbold liked the questions. Although he had told me he was a long, long way from youth, he had been a young man, younger than I was by then, when he lost his sight, and he had a close connection to his childhood self as a result. It was the last time he had been able to see, and remembering what things looked like made that time more immediate to him than it might have been for a sighted person whose visual memories were being perpetually overlaid with later images. He responded to Alf's curiosity with childlike candour. He made Alf close his eyes and took his hand to guide him through the feel of things, the difference in the pattern of the knife handle and the fork handle, the feel of the label sewn into the back of a garment, the difference in weight of a full against an empty glass, the sound of a spoon scraping an empty bowl in contrast to the noise it made when a coating of custard remained.

What captivated Alf the most was the Braille. Being able to read with your fingers seemed to him so much better an accomplishment than having to use your eyes. I taught him a few simple words – he could read well, for his age, but he was only six – and he carried the sheets I had created for him from adult to adult, showing off or, in Inchbold's case, demanding to be tested on his ability to pick out 'cat' and 'dog' using just his hands.

The only time I ever felt truly sorry for Inchbold was when I looked at Mercy, her pudgy little arms and legs, her lopsided, wide-eyed smiles, her curiosity over everything that came within her reach – a leaf, a pebble, the tassel on a curtain, her own foot. Although I loved to cuddle her, which Inchbold did not attempt to do, the deepest pleasure was just to watch her going about the serious business of being one and a quarter years old, and that Inchbold could not do.

We ate our Christmas dinner in the kitchen, which was hot and full of hot, sticky, meaty smells. English smells. Inchbold went to the vicarage for his lunch. I took him down there after church and left him. He had seemed surprised I had not also been invited but, by this time, Mrs Uppingham, the vicar's wife, had me – correctly, I would say – in the category of 'educated help'. I was in the position that the governesses in the books I read from Inchbold's library – to myself and to him – always were. Not servants. Not of their class. I was relieved when, through all the little interactions around church, jumble sales and fêtes, I realized she and the other women I had met at the tea party had ceased to regard me as an equal. I had felt an imposter in the position. Not because I did not know myself to be their equal in all the respects that mattered to me – integrity, the ability to love, the pursuit of knowledge and understanding – but because I knew they would know I was not, once they understood me better, in all the aspects that mattered to them – family, upbringing, knowledge of manners and social norms.

When we walked into the vicarage drawing room, I saw Sir William Bland was one of the company and he, seeing me enter, stood up and shook my hand. I could see Mrs Uppingham wondering how best to convey to him that this was unnecessary courtesy, and her dilemma amused me, as I walked back to where the children were waiting for me before filling themselves up with the food Greta had prepared for them.

After we had eaten, we played games. Greta produced two trays of random objects – a thimble, a feather, a walnut, a matchbox, a teaspoon – each different. We divided into two teams and had ten seconds to memorize the contents, then ten minutes to remember as many as we could. The other team won because it had Amos on it and he proved to have an excellent visual memory.

'Inchbold wouldn't be able to play this game,' Alf said.

'He would,' I said. 'He'd probably win. Only he'd have to have a little longer at the start to feel all the objects.'

It was dark when I walked back to the vicarage to collect Inchbold, and icy. I had yet to become familiar with the ice. It had taken me by surprise the first winter and the cold was even more intense this year, in the village with open countryside all around us. The frost and frozen puddles were manifestations of a malign and vicious god, to me. I walked carefully and was glad to have Inchbold to cling on to on the way back, which made me feel safer even though it only meant that if one of us had fallen, we both would have done so.

He had a fit of rage on the way home, after I told him of the games we had played that afternoon.

'Look what I've done,' he shouted, suddenly standing still. 'Stupid! Stupid! Stupid!'

'I don't see what you've done,' I said, glancing at his clothes to see if he had ripped them or spilled food on them, which he rarely did.

'No, of course, how would you, when I can't even express myself clearly? But what does it matter now, it's too late.'

We carried on our slow way home and he eventually calmed down enough to explain. He should have agreed to take evacuees when the bombing started. He had refused Greta's request to sign them up for a couple of children because he could only imagine the risk. That they would be where he did not expect them to be and he would fall over them. That they would be so noisy he would be unable to work. That they would break things that were precious to him. He had never thought, he said, of what it would mean to Greta to have children in the house. Look how much happier she had been this week! And he had never imagined there could be anything positive for him – selfish, selfish Inchbold!

'You would have liked to have evacuees here, too.'

'I wasn't here at the time, though, so you can't be blamed for not having taken my feelings into consideration.'

'I can blame myself for anything, Rose. You should know that by now.'

Conchita and her children came twice a year to stay at Pool House. A fortnight in the summer and a week at Christmas. Between these visits I would go back to the Royal Palace for a day or two, and I knew that at Pool House they were on their best behaviour. Not only the children, who had their share of tantrums at the place they now called home but none in Easterbrook, but also Conchita. She was calm and gracious when she stayed with us. In London she was sometimes more lively than Ma would have found seemly, sometimes sulky. Eugenia would brush either mood aside, telling me it was only because of praise or slights she had received at work, and of no more moment than the children's little triumphs and tragedies. She still had more, and better, clothes and bags, bracelets and scarves than I could quite believe she had come by honestly. Yet throughout she talked about her plans for what she intended to do back home.

29

Sonia

I realized, once I had mastered Braille and had the whole of Inchbold's book available to me, that its progress towards completion was much like our walk on the icy road on Christmas Day. Slow, subject to sudden stops and slides. But, like that walk, it had an end in sight. Inchbold had always had the shape of it in his head and knew where the end was. I also realized that progress had become faster and more sure-footed since I had come. Inchbold was reluctant to throw out drafts but meticulously dated them, and the number of false starts and revisions on chapters one to five each filled several of the apple crates Amos provided for storage. Chapter Six was only one crateful. Chapter Seven, less than that. Chapter Eight, by which time we had arrived at the best way of working together and the days slid past in an even rhythm, was rewritten only twice, the second time for the purposes of perfection, not to revisit the structure and content.

There would be twelve chapters, each dealing with a character selected from the vast tree of family members towering above Inchbold, its branches burdened with multiple marriages and children from which more marriages and children grew, spreading ever wider as the tree built up (or down, for the earliest ancestors were at the top) from generation to generation. This tree existed only in Braille, because Inchbold had researched and created it after the war, so I only understood how the pattern of his work fitted the family picture when I could redraw it in a form I could see, rather than read.

It had puzzled me, until then, that there were so many names in Inchbold's family history and none living now who were close to him. But when I had it before me in all its complexity, I could see clearly the dead end that had Inchbold's name at the bottom. His father had been an only child and married late in life to a woman who was the only offspring of a second marriage. They were in their late thirties when the marriage took place and his mother was already forty when Inchbold, the second of her two sons, was born. His father did not long survive the loss of his eldest son, but his mother was still alive when the second war was declared in 1939, dying before hostilities started. There was a portrait of her in the drawing room, a slight, pretty, bland face which revealed nothing.

I asked Greta about her and was brushed aside with sniffs and facial expressions I understood to indicate disapproval, and some enigmatic remarks. Eventually, over time, the remarks became less impenetrable and I disentangled them to make a story I found both sad and inspiring. Evelyn Inchbold had spent the greater part of her life – before and during marriage, as well as in widowhood – living with a woman called Thomasina, known as Tom. Tom had lived with Mr and Mrs Inchbold at Pool House; then, after Mr Inchbold had died and their youngest son had come home from the war, she had moved with Evelyn to a house in the village. They had died within two weeks of one another. I was sorry for Inchbold's father, for the lack of intimacy and love which he might have had if he had been, as he must have hoped to be, the most important person in his wife's life. But I admired the late Mrs Inchbold for having lived a life, if not exactly as she might have wished, then with as little compromise as was possible.

I never mentioned any of this to Inchbold. I did mention his isolation at the end of his particular network of branches, when I had the tree drawn up in front of me.

'Lucky, eh?' he said. 'If I'd had family close enough to meddle in my life, just think how much explaining and justification I'd have had to do for every page of writing.' Then, when I didn't reply, he said: 'You're very hard for me to read, Rose. Most people respond verbally, or else I can tell by the movements they make if they're shocked or irritated or sympathetic. You don't speak and you don't move.'

'I don't like to speak unless I have something worth saying.'

'And thank the Lord for that. A rare gift, my dear, and one I would never criticize because it makes you the perfect assistant. But do remember – I think I pointed this out to you the day you came – I can't judge your reactions unless you speak.'

'If you're worried about what I'm thinking, it must be because you've said something you believe to be provocative.'

'Not entirely true. I'm always interested in what you think. I've learned to value your opinions. But I acknowledge a hit in this instance. I expected you to argue with me, to tell me you would never trade the closeness of your bond with your brother for the freedom to write whatever you chose about your family without interference. You'd have been right, too. I would say the same if my brother were still alive.'

'That is what I was thinking, when you were wondering what I was thinking.'

'You thought: "Pathetic old fool, he's trying to convince himself he's happier without close family."'

'Were you?'

'No. I don't know if I can explain it to you. I would give anything to have my brother back. But he is lost, and now I am living a life without him I have to question myself from inside that life, and I am, truly, grateful not to be besieged by the likes of your friend Miss Hobson, for example, feeling they have a close enough connection to intrude into it.'

'I'm sorry,' I said.

'I won't ask what you mean by that. To work!'

The book took shape through 1942 and by the middle of 1943 I could see that the end was in sight, and so could Inchbold, though we did not speak of it. Neither cf us wanted it to be finished. I was fearful that I would no longer be needed and would be sent back to the Royal Palace to work with Patrick and help Winifred in the Shelter. Not the worst prospect, but I was involved in Inchbold's story in a way I could never be with Hatty and Hetty in the Shelter's basement. Also, it was quiet, in Pool House; I had never before known what it felt like to live without noise and I did not want to give it up. Inchbold, I suspected, had no idea what he would find to do with the time the book had taken up and was terrified at the prospect. He became tetchy. This wasn't a word I knew until I heard Greta use it to describe Inchbold's mooc when nothing was quite right, and I liked it.

His friends from Oxford, Sebastian and the Carlyles, were the only people other than me who were allowed glimpses of the book, and whose guidance and reassurance Inchbold wanted. He was interested in Sebastian's opinions on matters of history and doctrine – several of his chosen subjects had had lives directed, or distorted, by religion. Each time I typed up a letter from Inchbold to Sebastian or read the reply out loud, I was aware of the gulf between us. I could learn the facts around, for example, Tractarianism in the nineteenth century, but it was beyond me to follow, never mind engage in, the analysis the two men delighted in, twisting the facts about to understand how they related to other aspects of society at the time, what they could be manipulated to reveal, whether they were actual facts or misinterpretations. It was not just that they were cleverer than me; they had been schooled in philosophy and philosophical debate and I had not. I did not go to Oxford with Inchbold, or stay in the room when Sebastian visited, and Inchbold never asked me to.

The Carlyles were engaged with the book on a more practical level. Mr Carlyle was in discussions with publishers. These had been going on before I arrived, when there were only random boxes of pages and ideas in note form to talk about. Inchbold had been quite excited by every sign of progress, back then, when it was no more than conversations over dinner tables. He would ask me to reread the sentences in Carlyle's letters that spoke of reactions from the publishers he had met.

'What did he say the man said about the book? That it sounded as if it had . . . "intellectual promise", was it?'

' "It holds the promise of intellectual satisfaction for the reader." '

But as the number of publishers showing polite interest had narrowed down to two who were seriously considering it, Inchbold had become tetchy. By this time, we were sending the first two chapters out for them to read. The responses came to Carlyle and he provided a summary of the contents, not the letters themselves. I suspected he was editing them to prevent Inchbold becoming so irritated he rejected any offer made, but, even so, Inchbold would find reasons why he couldn't listen to Carlyle's letters just at this moment, and the letters back went through several drafts, the first angry, the second querulous (another new word for me, learned from Inchbold) and the final one tart but civil.

Offers were made by both publishers and Carlyle wanted Inchbold to spend time meeting them, discussing the deal, and invited him to Oxford for a week during which all of this would be talked through. By now, Inchbold was not trying, at least with me, to disguise his reluctance to reach a conclusion. On any of it: the writing or the publishing.

'There's no rush,' he said. 'There's no paper, for one thing. Wait until the war's over. I'm thinking I should revisit the chapter on Violet Inchbold, anyway. I don't think I've captured the domestic side of her life well enough.'

But Carlyle was implacable. This was the right moment to seal a deal, he said. The publishers were looking ahead to a post-war world when the recent past would be the last thing readers wanted, and the more distant past could fill the gap.

Inchbold went to Oxford. I was not invited. The Carlyle house had no room for me, Inchbold said, and I said, truthfully, that I had not expected to be included. As it happened, his trip coincided with a visit that Sonia had finally agreed to make to Pool House. She had written to say she would come in a few days' time – 'Definitely, definitely, dear Rose.'

I went by bus to meet her from the train and she overwhelmed me with the excitement of being together again. I could not quite take her in, so lively was she, so quick to jump from topic to topic, to laugh and exclaim and put her arms round me for yet another hug. I went along with it. Knowing something was, indeed, wrong. Willing to wait to find out what it was until we were somewhere quiet and private.

There were two other attic bedrooms cleaned up and furnished now: one for Conchita, one for the children. But I had kept the extra bed in mine and I took Sonia up there and offered her the choice of a room to herself or sharing with me.

'Share with you,' she said. 'Didn't we always share everything?'

'Are you going to share your troubles with me? Don't tell me nothing is wrong, because I can tell that something is.'

A stiffness came over her and she kept her eyes on my face as she began, button by button, to undo the coat she was wearing. She shrugged it off her shoulders and let it fall to the floor, but even before that, I had noticed what had been hidden from me on the journey: the slight but unmistakeable swell of her belly.

'Oh, Sonia,' I said, and took her in my arms, holding her tightly but without the fierceness of the embraces we had exchanged before.

I went to the kitchen to make us a cup of tea before asking for the story.

'Your friend's in trouble,' said Greta, rolling out pastry on a marble slab.

She could only have seen Sonia for a moment as we passed through on our way upstairs.

'I didn't know,' I said. 'She's just told me.'

Greta didn't say anything else, but she put two slices of cake on a plate to add to my tray. An indication of sympathy, of not making judgements, which was unexpected and comforting. Only later did it occur to me that there may never have been a Mr Seccombe, and that part of Greta's sense of difference and isolation within the community might have arisen from just such a circumstance as Sonia now faced.

In the time it took to fetch the tea, I had travelled through all the ways in which I might react when Sonia explained how this had happened. From anger that she had been so stupid, to sympathy that she had been so unlucky, to despair at the ruin of her life. The story she told me at last raised all of these emotions. But, in addition, guilt. Guilt that I hadn't understood, in our two meetings and constant exchange of letters, what she was going through. It is the duty of a friend to be present in times of trouble. In my defence, none of what she told me now had she so much as hinted at before. But I should have guessed, or at least kept asking questions until I found the right one.

The Cap, that upright, authoritative man in his polished brogues, had cared more for his own sexual satisfaction than for his position of trust or for her well-being. From the time they had settled in Amersham, out of the press of society where eyes might see and others might judge, he had begun to touch her, to speak to her in ways that were inappropriate but, apparently, meant to be harmless, amusing; so she had not reacted, she admitted, as strongly as she should have done. As she would have done if she had realized he was not joking but serious. He had intended, from the start, to have sex with her, and by the time she realized this, she had put herself in the position where outrage no longer seemed appropriate.

She was further distracted from taking the Cap seriously by the behaviour of Mrs Thrupp. She had always known the

Cap's wife to be slightly odd, rather lonely, but when there were few people around her, she had revealed a need to be loved that, if not overtly sexual, had had its measure, too, of touching, of stepping over boundaries. This, I should have known. The memory of the gift of the green dress came back to me.

It was the attentions of Mrs Thrupp that Sonia had initially found most oppressive, and this had led her to have sympathy with the Cap. Who wouldn't be starved of affection, married to so strange and perverted (this was Sonia's word) a wife? This, in turn, made the situation with the Cap worse, as she softened towards him and he took advantage of her softness. To the extent that her sympathies swung the other way. What woman would not look for affection from her own sex, she thought, married to a predator like the Cap? There was no one in the house she could turn to, who could rescue her from the one or the other, when those who should have protected her were bouncing her back and forth between them like a toy they both wanted to play with.

'You could have turned to me,' I said.

'You know when you have something precious to you?' she said. 'A special dress or a pair of shoes. Or a book, I suppose, if you're Rose Dunbar. You take every care to make sure nothing touches it that is going to make it less perfect. No dirt or stickiness. You don't even want to wear it – this is Sonia Gutierrez speaking now – to somewhere that is not quite as good as the dress or shoes deserve, in case you take a little of the shine off it. That's how I felt about you. I so nearly told you everything so many times, and then I couldn't bear you to be touched by the grubbiness of it all.'

'I'm touched now,' I said. 'When it's too late.'

Instead of turning to me she had turned to Guido. She might have fallen for any young man who was normal, whose interest in her felt wholesome, natural and real. But Guido was not just any young man. He could be – she had thought he was – the love of her life. She thought that still.

'You can't know that until you have met him in normal circumstances,' I said.

'You can't know that because you have never been in love,' she said.

Whenever the Cap came home from London, she knew to expect him to turn up in her bedroom, after the rest of the household was in bed. He would have fortified himself with a few glasses of whisky; and the more glasses, the better able she was to resist. But it was not always possible. He knew he was forcing her, but he kept up the pretence that they wanted each other. He needed the whisky to be able to do this.

During the day, she and Guido would find time to talk, then cuddle, then kiss and finally to love each other, in the hidden depths of the Thrupps's garden.

She had no idea which of the two men was the father of the baby. Neither of them knew about her relationship with the other. She was protecting Guido, in keeping this secret. If the Cap came to know of it, he had the power to send Guido away. If Guido found out, he had no resources except the use of physical violence. The outcome would be the same, from her point of view. She would lose Guido. Though she enjoyed imagining the sort of damage Guido might inflict on the Cap, she could not afford to let these fantasies be played out. She had told neither of them she was pregnant, either. When it was about to become impossible to conceal it, then she had come to me.

'I had nowhere else to turn. In the end, I had to bring all my dirtiness to you.'

'Good,' I said.

I had no idea what to do, though, which didn't matter, at first. Sonia was full of her own suggestions, all of them dramatic and drastic. She would go back to Amersham and confront the Cap, tell him it was his baby and he had to take care of her, and the infant. She would go to London and find an abortionist who would rid her of the foetus and, quite probably, her own life. She would go back to Guido and persuade him to abscond from the camp and run away with her to Scotland. She had the idea that Scotland was so big, empty and far away no one would ever find them and they could live in a cottage by the sea, fishing and growing vegetables. All of which meant she could not picture a future. A blind had come down, hiding her view of where she might be in a year's time. Further than that, we were none of us picturing too clearly, in those days.

For as long as Inchbold was away I was happy to let Sonia talk, in the hopes that at last she would talk herself to a plan. On the third day, though, Inchbold was due to come home and I could not keep Sonia in the attic with me, eating his food, without explaining why I was doing it. I didn't know what his attitude would be, so, at the end of the second day, with Sonia still ricocheting between the romantic, the captive and the dead ends to her story, I telephoned Winifred.

I could picture her at the Shelter as we spoke, surrounded by piles of paper, bags of clothes, the gas fire pop-popping in the background and the cat curled up on the windowsill.

'Poor girl,' Winifred said. 'We must sort this out for her. I think the best thing would be if she came to me here. We have space for her in the Shelter and I assume she'd be prepared to make herself useful, as long as she can. That will give her time to work out whether she wants to keep the baby or give it up for adoption.'

After two days of listening to Sonia, I could almost have cried with relief at Winifred's assumption that a solution existed and could be made to work, so easily that it was as if the problem was of no matter.

'I don't think she's got so far as to worry about what happens to the baby.'

'It's the only important question, dear.'

I didn't know if Winifred meant the baby was more important than the mother, or whether she was still thinking of Sonia, and what her life would be in future if she kept the child. I thought she was right, though. What happened to the baby mattered.

Sonia, though relieved, could not let go of the unsolved (and unsolvable) elements – whose baby was it? What would her future be without Guido in it? Was there any hope for a future with Guido in it? Why should the Cap be allowed to escape punishment? She could not fill the gap left by having a solution to the immediate problem – where she would go until the baby was born – with more positive thoughts.

Amos went to Oxford to fetch Inchbold, and I could tell by the fidgeting in the hall when he arrived back, by the way he opened and closed doors, his very tread on the stairs, that he was not happy. I had fallen into the habit of listening for the audible signals Inchbold himself used to tell him what people felt, and there was no mistaking it. I had to talk to him about Sonia, and I trusted him. Whatever his personal anguish, he never let it influence the way he treated others.

I took Sonia to meet him and he held out his hand to shake hers. When she gave it to him, he folded his other hand over it and held it for a moment.

'Now I see you are smaller than Rose,' he said. 'I don't have any way to judge what you look like, but I do have an impression you take up less space than she does.'

Sonia laughed, a happy echo of the Sonia I had known and loved.

'Rose isn't fat, though. She's just taller than me. She has longer arms and legs.'

'And bigger hands and feet,' I said.

This little exchange seemed to have exhausted their capacity for being light-hearted and I could see that Inchbold could think of nothing to say to Sonia and she was oppressed by his otherness. So I indicated she should leave and shut the door behind her.

'Inchbold,' I said, 'I have something to tell you.'

'What?' He sounded angry.

'It's not about me. It's about Sonia.'

I told him her story. The behaviour of the Thrupps; her ill-judged (to my mind) affair with Guido. The outcome. Then, without pausing to allow him to comment, the solution proposed by Winifred.

'I need to go to London tomorrow with Sonia, to settle her at the Shelter. Is that all right? Can I do that?'

'I don't understand the man,' Inchbold said. 'How could he behave in such a way?'

'You mean Captain Thrupp?'

'Of course. This young woman was entrusted to his care.'

'I suppose he couldn't control himself,' I said. I could think of no one more controlled than the Cap and could have said he was too selfish, too sure of his own importance, to care whether he injured others or not, but I wanted to spare Inchbold distress.

'Most of us do, don't we? Men. Or can you tell me that it isn't so, because sometimes I feel as if I'm washed up on the shores of an island and out there in the bay everyone is sailing to and fro, and I imagine them sailing the boats I sailed, as a boy, and doing the same as I did, thinking the same way. But I can't know, can I? Because I'm marooned on the shore. Out of touch.'

'Most men control themselves.'

'You've met him, haven't you? Could you tell he was this sort of man, the sort he's shown himself to be?'

'His shoes were always very shiny,' I said.

'Are mine?'

'They're as shiny as they need to be.'

'You can go with her to London. But don't stay too long. I seem to have accepted an offer from a publisher. We have work to do.'

30

Captain Thrupp

Winifred was the only truly selfless person I had ever met. She had no concern for herself; she had no image for herself she had created and needed to put effort into maintaining; she did not worry about what impression she was making on others; she had no expectation of personal pleasure from helping others (though it did please her, I'm sure; she just never paused to consider that). She was only influenced to do one thing or another by the needs of the person she was helping, never by her own interests. It made her curiously remote, as a personality. It perhaps accounted for why she was still single. Though, of course, this might have been from choice. But becoming close friends means that each of you understands what it is that pleases the other, and tries to provide it. It was not possible to spot what would please Winifred, in the absence of refugees, the needy and the unexpectedly pregnant, and she was therefore hard to become close to.

I could see Sonia relaxing into the girl I had known before all her certainties, all her grasp of the ways of the world (always clearer to her than to me) were swept away by isolation and exploitation. When she had said, in the first letter she wrote to me from Amersham, that she was incomplete without me,

I should have understood what she meant. That although she appeared grounded, when she needed help to find the ground I was the one she thought would help her.

Sonia and I went down to the basement at the Shelter, looking for Hetty and Hatty. Only one of them was there, surrounded by the same jumble; not in fact, but in essence. It was the younger one, whom I had chosen to identify as Hatty. There was a sullen youth with her who either spoke no English or didn't speak at all. Hatty looked delighted to see me.

'Are you coming back? I could do with the company.'

I couldn't ask where Hetty was as it was only a fifty-fifty chance it was Hetty who was missing.

'Where's your fellow worker, then? Aren't you a team any more?'

She shook her head. 'Gone,' she said.

'Gone?'

Hatty heaved a sigh so deep it fluttered a scarf resting on the top of the unsorted pile in front of her.

'To Tottenham.' It was only my long-ago trip to fetch Eugenia that allowed me to recognize she was referring to a place rather than using a euphemism for a state of mind or body.

'That's a long way.'

'She's got a sister.' Hatty managed to imply this was an affliction.

'I'm not coming back,' I said, 'but I've brought a friend to stay here. She might be able to give you a hand, if Winifred hasn't found too many other jobs for her to do.'

Sonia stepped out of the shadows behind me.

'Are you Hetty?' she asked. 'Or Hatty?'

'I'm Hetty,' said the woman I had until then assumed was Hatty.

'I'm Sonia,' Sonia said. 'Why don't you tell me what needs to be done?'

Hetty and the silent youth became, in that instant, the children Sonia would be looking after. She would not be as efficient or effective as I had been, but she would be better, for them. Make them happier, by making them feel better about themselves.

When she fled their house, Sonia had told the Thrupps that I was ill and needed her. She had repeated this when Mrs Thrupp had telephoned to see if a date could be set for her return.

'You'll have to tell them something, soon,' I said.

But Sonia could not frame what she might say. If she told Mrs Thrupp she was pregnant, without naming the father, then she might suspect Guido, and protecting Guido was the most important thing. I had never known Sonia treat any of the young men who chased after her in Gibraltar, with whom she was happy to have fun, with anything other than amused tolerance. I still could not tell if the change was because she no longer felt safe and needed a haven, or because she was truly in love with him. It seemed to me the answer was to tell Mrs Thrupp the baby was definitely the Cap's and let him do the explaining. But Sonia foresaw that Mrs Thrupp would not easily abandon the blind eye she had been turning all her married life to the true nature of the man she had married, and she would, again, blame Guido.

She finally wrote to the Thrupps the day we left for London. She told me so much, but not what she had said in the letter. It became clear the day after I returned to Pool House what she had not said. She had not told them where she was going or even, possibly, that she had gone, because the Cap arrived at the door. He was wearing his uniform; a staff car with a young woman, also in uniform, behind the wheel was sitting by the kerb, advertising to the village that Inchbold had a visitor of rank and, therefore, of importance.

Greta opened the door. I was on my way from the dining room with a tray of breakfast dishes. Inchbold had gone up to the library with some bee of a notion about the reason his grandfather's sister, Henrietta Inchbold, had converted to Catholicism buzzing around in his head, making him restless. I paused in the dining-room doorway, hearing the voice of British authority, clipped and clear, telling Greta it wished to see Major Inchbold. I could see Greta's back from where I stood, her hands reaching behind her to tighten her apron strings and make herself as neat as possible.

'He's in his study, sir.' She turned to lead the way to the stairs but he pushed past her.

'Up here, is it?'

I drew back into the dining room but he would not have registered I was there even if I had stayed where I was. A young woman holding a tray of dishes. The corners of the world he lived in would be full of such figures, no more worthy of remark than the curtains or the door handles.

I hurried to the kitchen then started up the stairs after him, but paused on the half-landing, to listen to what was said before going in.

'Perhaps you can tell me,' the Cap was saying, 'where I may find her?' His first question, before I arrived, had presumably been whether Sonia was still staying at Pool House.

There was the creak of a chair and the sound of a book being set down on the desk.

'You're her employer, am I right?' said Inchbold.

'I am, and I have a responsibility for her well-being. I understood she had come to stay with her friend, who works for you, I believe. But now I have had the most extraordinary letter from her to say she is not planning to return to her post. Which is, frankly, unacceptable.'

'I have no responsibility for Miss Gutierrez,' Inchbold said. 'You should perhaps be asking Miss Dunbar where her friend is, rather than me.'

The Cap's footsteps travelled across the library floor to the window.

'I will, of course,' he said, with less arrogance in his voice than he had had at first, 'but I was hoping you could help me sort this out without too much fuss.' A chair creaked again. The Cap, I guessed, had sat down. 'Women, as I'm sure you know, become so emotional.'

'It seems to me that in the circumstances emotion is merited, and sorting this out is very far from straightforward.'

'I'm not sure I catch your meaning.'

'Did the girl not tell you she was pregnant?'

'Ah!' said the Cap. 'She did, in her letter. I wasn't sure you were aware of it.'

'Miss Dunbar explained the situation to me.'

'Did she?' said the Cap, almost under his breath. 'Then you must understand how important it is that I make sure she is being properly cared for. Even though she has behaved badly and her actions have had disastrous consequences, she was under my roof at the time and I feel it is my duty to take charge of her welfare. So if you know where she has gone, I would like you to tell me.'

'I don't know precisely,' Inchbold said. 'And if I did, I would ask the young woman's permission to pass the address on to you, which I assume, as she did not inform you of it, would be refused.'

'Do I understand you correctly?' said the Cap. 'You seem to be saying you would allow an uneducated girl, who has given ample evidence of a lack of judgement, to dictate whether she will return to the protection of those to whom she owes respect and loyalty, or remain in whatever place of squalor – danger, even – she has chosen for herself.'

'I told you that Rose explained the situation to me,' Inchbold said. 'The girl believes she has good reason to escape from your house.'

I could hear the hiss of the Cap's uniform-trousered legs as they changed position, crossed or uncrossed.

'What possible reason could she have?'

'If you were responsible for the condition she finds herself in, would that not be reason enough?'

I was in the same position, temporarily, as Inchbold is permanently, as I leaned on the banister on the half-landing. I could hear the words spoken but none of the visual clues to the mood of either of the parties involved in the discussion were available to me. I imagined Inchbold's expression was neutral. I could only wait, as he was doing, to hear what the Cap said next: whether he would continue the condescending, high-handed tone he had adopted so far, keep up the man-to-man approach, or become, for once, honest. Inchbold spoke again before the Cap had replied.

'You would say it is none of my business, as indeed it isn't. But if you believe you are responsible, I agree you should do something to help her. If you were to write a letter proposing what you will do, I am sure Rose would see it was delivered.'

'It isn't any of your business and I have no idea what you think I should propose, supposing the chit's accusation were true.'

The Cap's tone was aggressive but Inchbold's reply was calm.

'If it were me, I would propose marriage, but I understand you are already married and this must put you in the awkward position of having to let down one woman or another.'

Inchbold had finally shocked the Cap into an honest reaction. He laughed; genuinely, I felt.

'Marry her? That's ridiculous! You know the sort of girls these are.'

'No. Tell me.'

'Let's just say they're not the sort of wife to have for a man in my position. Or yours, come to that. They don't have the right background; they wouldn't know how to behave. They're' – he gave another little laugh – 'what we call Rock Scorpions.'

There was a sudden crash and I had started up the stairs towards the library by the time Inchbold shouted. The day was dull and the library unlit; I had not been up there before the Cap came and Inchbold would not have thought to turn the lights on. In the gloom, I could make out the Cap, standing by a chair he had just left, and Inchbold, also standing, gripping the desk, his chair overturned behind him. He was shouting not just my name, but Greta's and Amos's. Summoning us all. Amos must have been in the kitchen because he arrived almost at once, with Greta puffing up the stairs behind him.

'Get this man out of the house,' Inchbold said.

I turned the switch and the room lit up. The Cap, now I had a clear sight of him, looked less comfortable, less controlled than his voice would have suggested. But even as I thought this, I could see him sizing us all up. A blind man, a cripple, an overweight cook, an insignificant girl.

'I have no wish to stay,' he said, and pushed past Greta, still in the doorway. She followed him downstairs, Amos behind her. I heard the bolts on the front door being shot into their sockets as it closed behind the Cap.

'Rose?' said Inchbold. 'Are you still here?'

'Yes,' I said, walking round him to put his chair upright.

'Please go. I need to calm down. I'm better alone.'

He spent the day alone. In the library and then in the music room. Greta delivered his lunch to him and I didn't see him until dinner, when he came down to the dining room and asked me to join him.

'I want you to write to Sonia,' he said, 'and tell her Captain Thrupp has been here and I find him to be a person with no sense of what is right. If she can tell you what she wants from him, I will try to see she gets it.'

'I'm sorry I seem to have involved you in such trouble,' I said.

'I wonder if I would like the world, today, if I could see it and go about in it and mix with other men. Or if I had never been shut away, as I have been, with books and a handful of acquaintances, would I have become the sort of man who fits in the world Thrupp lives in, and happy to be part of it.'

'Not all men are like Captain Thrupp, and you could never

become like him.' I said this with confidence because Inchbold looked so sad, and I was as certain as I could be that the
last part was true.

'You're trying to comfort me,' Inchbold said. 'Thank you.'

'You know he never admitted to you the baby could be
his,' I said, 'and you have chosen to believe Sonia rather than
a man of your own class.'

'You believed her.'

'I know her.'

'And I know you.'

31

Guido

Sonia's baby was due in April 1944 and I concentrated on this date, in looking to the future, and, in the present, on preparing Inchbold's book for publication. The war went on, remotely. An enemy plane landed in a field a few miles away and caused a sensation locally. Everyone had a story of where they were, what they saw, what had happened. The nights in London with bombs falling all around were already impossibly distant.

We, Inchbold and I, worked like house-builders on the book. We were disciplined and orderly; we took regular stock of progress, adjusted our plans for the next week accordingly. The joy had gone out of it, though. I had not noticed at the time how joyful it was, to be chasing obscure facts, throwing out sections of a life that was turning out to be dull, finding that someone else who had appeared to be in the shadows had a story much more worth telling. Now all that was over and we only had to make sure the structure was safe, to check every bolt and fixing.

Inchbold became obsessed with the way the war was going. He had been less interested than I was, when I first arrived. Perhaps, having suffered and lost so much in one war, he could not bring himself to take the next too seriously. He said to me once that the worst thing about the current conflict was that it put Greta in an ill temper, and his life was easier if she was in a good mood.

But as the newspaper headlines became less cautious, more triumphant, and I began to worry less, Inchbold started to listen to the news and demand that I read aloud to him from the papers, rather than our usual classic novels. We had exhausted Dickens by this time, but there was still plenty of Trollope I would have preferred to the repetitive, teasingly detail-less reports in the press. And Inchbold appeared to take no pleasure from hearing the news or the journalists' speculation, though the former was often good, and the latter optimistic. He seemed to be waiting for disaster, or at least for an enduring gloom.

'This will go on for ever,' he said. 'I've reconciled myself to that.'

At Christmas, Conchita brought rumours of how soon the repatriation to Gibraltar would begin. The 'theatre of operations', she said, as if this was a phrase she had long been familiar with, had moved away from the Mediterranean and any risk to a civilian population was small. The problem was housing, which was a problem we had lived with and read about in the *Gibraltar Chronicle* and *El Calpense* for so long it was part of the fabric of our lives. It wouldn't affect her, Conchita said; she could move in with Jamie and my father in the two rooms they occupied in our old building in MacPhail's Passage.

'Won't you miss London?' Inchbold asked. 'All the shops and whatever else it is in London that young women are supposed to find so exciting.'

Conchita had remained awkward with Inchbold and (because?) he had remained oblivious to her charms. So she answered carefully.

'It has been fun to live in London but I want to have my own home again.'

'I thought you said you'd only have two rooms. Between six of you.'

'My rooms,' said Conchita.

She had always felt like a fancifully coloured bird which would fly off to seek adoration somewhere else if there was a hint of hard work or hardship. I had overlooked her essential ordinariness. That however much she appeared to want more than she had, there were limits to her ambition. I had no closer connection to her than I had had before: we had nothing in common. I liked her better, though. She had come to understand that not all of life's fulfilment came from the men she attracted, and this could only mean she would be a better wife to Jamie, once she was back in Gibraltar.

By then Inchbold, as well as Greta and Amos, had become so fond of the children he was doubtful if Conchita was right to take them back to Gibraltar. It was a place Alf and Freddo could hardly remember and somewhere Mercy had never been.

'Will they get a proper education there, Rose? Tell me honestly. Will they have all the same opportunities they might have here?'

'They'll have a home,' I said. 'They'll have a family. A mother and a father and a grandfather. And an aunt, when I go back.'

But you weren't yet ready for me to talk of going back, so the conversation ended.

*

I went down to London to see Sonia when Inchbold was visiting the Carlyles. She had become Sonia again. The personality I had known and loved, which had been punched out of her as if it were air and she a balloon, had been pumped back in by the move from Amersham to Kensington. It was not only that she was free of the Thrupps. As I walked with her up to the little room at the top of the Shelter which she shared with a Polish girl, I could see how much better suited she was to living among a crowd than living quietly. We had grown up in the same building, but leaving it had created a void, for Sonia, a longing for a house that was full. Leaving it had made me realize how much I liked space around me.

Her roommate was an unattractive, gloomy girl but even this did nothing to reduce Sonia's enthusiasm for the Shelter. Every person we met on the stairs paused to greet her, for every one she had a smile, the sort of smile she would have given to the neighbours on the steps or in the alleyways around MacPhail's Passage. She had fitted herself in and was happy. No one judged her for the condition she was in. They were either, like Winifred, committed to helping others without making judgements, or were the victims of such misfortunes that they could only imagine misfortune had befallen Sonia and she was not to blame.

It was another story at the Royal Palace Hotel, where the disapproval was strong enough to touch. Sonia still visited Conchita and the children, but it took courage, which she had never before lacked and seemed to have found again. Conchita, Sonia told me, was sympathetic and did not judge. The same was true of Patrick, when Sonia approached him to ask if she could move into the hotel after the birth. Many of the people who had previously supported us had drifted away – in Mrs Almondsbury's case for obvious reasons, but mainly because they were no longer necessary – which left Patrick as the acknowledged voice of authority. He made a note of when the room might be needed and then said:

'Can you please tell Miss Dunbar that I would greatly appreciate it if she would also return.' Sonia did a convincing imitation of his dry, emotionless manner when she repeated this.

Italy had declared war on Germany in October 1943, and I had assumed that Guido would be released from the camp where he had been held prisoner and Sonia's dream of a future for the two of them together might no longer be as unrealistic as it had seemed a month earlier, but his situation still seemed ambiguous. He had not been released from the camp, but the rules under which he had previously lived had relaxed and he was able to make occasional trips to London to visit Sonia. Even then, he pretended he was going to see a cousin in the East End. A liaison with a girl who was British, even if not a resident of Britain, would not have been encouraged. One of these trips occurred when I was visiting. We went together to meet him from the train and walked to a cafe within sight of the hospital where Ma had died. Through the misted window I could see the cold grey stone of its walls.

Guido was short – shorter than me – but the shortness was confined to his arms and legs; his torso was large and solid, filling the canvas jacket he wore to bursting point, though the ends of the sleeves half covered his hands. He was dark, as dark as Sonia, with a face that made me think of Puck in *A Midsummer Night's Dream*. I had never seen the play but I had a notion of what the character should look like – mischievous, cheerful, determined – and this is what Guido's features seemed designed to make him appear. Only his expression, when we met and throughout the awkwardness of the three of us finding seats at a table and ordering food, was melancholy.

Although they wrote to each other, their letters were opened by the authorities at the camp and so Sonia had waited until his first visit to tell him about the pregnancy, and the possibility that the baby was not his. His reaction, she wrote to tell me at the time, had been extreme, in all the ways she might have wished. Extreme excitement at the idea of the baby, extreme anger at the Cap's behaviour. She had had to walk round and round the pond in Kensington Palace Gardens, talking him down from his first intention of stealing a kitchen knife and exacting revenge with its blade. He had allowed himself to be persuaded and requested a transfer to another job, to avoid the risk that his passion would break out into violence if he met the man coming round the hedge when he, Guido, was trimming it with a pair of newly sharpened shears.

I had come with the expectation that I would know, by the time Guido had to catch a train back to Buckinghamshire, whether he was the right person for Sonia to love, and whether she did, truly, love him. It was not easy to make either judgement. There was an easiness in the way Sonia greeted him and spoke to him, but I could not tell if this was more than friendship. The only certainty about him, obvious from the first moments, was that he loved her. Neither of them spoke much. The eggs on toast and tea we had ordered had been delivered to the table and the only conversation had been about Guido's journey and his new job. We could have been three people forced into meeting with nothing at all in common. As we picked up our knives and forks I said:

'Could you leave the camp? Take any job, live where you like?'

'It is not so simple,' he said. 'No one has said I must not, but where I live now, I have food and I am safe. And the job I do, the farmer does not pay the same as he pays the local men, so maybe there is no job if I ask for enough money to live outside the camp.'

'You could ask all the people still living in the Royal Palace the same question,' Sonia said. 'Why haven't they left and found themselves somewhere else to live?'

'I suppose they're waiting to go home.'

'This is right,' said Guido. 'So are we all.'

Sonia looked down at the tablecloth and smoothed out a crease. Guido put his hand over hers, holding it still.

'First,' he said, 'we must wait for the baby.'

I looked at Sonia's downcast face.

'Will the decisions you need to make be any easier when the baby has been born?' I asked.

'Of course!' said Sonia, fiercely. 'Nothing is certain until she has been born.'

'Or until he has,' said Guido, and Sonia smiled at him in a way I had never seen her smile at the men who she had allowed to kiss her in the past.

'Or until he has been born. Until then, we won't know if we have a healthy child to care for or not. Then we must decide how to live until the war is over. Then where to live.'

If she had already made the decision to keep the baby, I thought she must also have made the decision to stay with Guido. There seemed only one question left to ask.

'When do you intend to get married?'

'Ah!' Guido threw his hands in the air and looked more

like Puck than ever. 'Tell her! You are her friend. It should be tomorrow. Today!'

'It can't be today or tomorrow,' Sonia said, 'because Guido has to have permission from the authorities and I don't want him to decide to do this until after the birth.'

'So you will make our son a bastard.' Guido said this a little too loudly. I noticed a couple of heads in neat felt hats twitch in our direction.

'I don't care, as long as our daughter has two parents who love her to bring her up.' Sonia was laughing, now.

'She thinks,' Guido said to me, 'that if God does not let our child live, I will wish I had not got myself a wife who is not Italian. She thinks it is better to wait because she thinks I will love an Italian girl better than her. I tell her, I will love no one better than her.' This, too, was a little loud and I was pleased to think he was happy for the whole steamy cafe full of strangers to hear it. 'You tell her, Rose.'

'She makes up her own mind,' I said. And I could see it was made up. 'But perhaps she doesn't want to be pregnant on her wedding day.'

Sonia made a face at me. 'It would be more fun, afterwards,' she said. 'We could appoint Rose as baby-holder-in-chief. I could dress up in something smaller than a tent.'

'Whatever you want, my darling, I will give you,' said Guido. He said it in Italian but the sense of it was entirely clear.

When I was back at Pool House, I wrote to Peter Povedano and told him I did not believe we would suit each other. That however much we might appreciate each other's good points, we did not have enough connections to make a future together that would be anything other than ordinary. He wrote back to say he had always known I would, at some time, say this; it was what he had expected and what he had predicted, that night in the tunnel in the Rock. He would settle for ordinary. He could see that I would not.

32

Birth and Marriage

In April a page turned over on the calendar, so it felt. Sonia's baby, Marco, was born and the first ship went back to Gibraltar with evacuees on it. Among them, Conchita, Alf, Freddo and Mercy. That Conchita had gone was a relief; the return of the children left me abandoned. They had sailed away from me and so, it seemed, had Sonia. Marco was so much the centre of her world that the space left round the edges was not enough for me to feel as if I was important to her, as I had once been. I had, as Inchbold requested, asked her what she wanted from the Cap in recognition that Marco might be his son. Her philosophy of waiting until the baby was born meant she refused to answer me. I asked again when I went to see her, after Marco's birth. She had moved out of the Shelter and into the Royal Palace, where the disapproval could not touch her now. She needed no one except the child in her arms. She declared with absolute certainty that this was Guido's son and she wanted nothing from the Cap. I was relieved. It meant Inchbold did not have to approach the man on her behalf, which I knew he would hate doing.

I don't believe she lifted her head from the boy to look at me while we talked of this. So completely had her world contracted to his pudgy little face and curling fingers. It was not possible to tell whose son he was. The Cap and Guido were both dark. Their features were more or less regular, though Guido had a snub nose and the Cap a lean one, but so did Sonia. And all babies have snub noses. Time would tell if Marco had inherited Guido's ratio of arm to leg, or the Cap's, but I felt sure that, by then, the answer would not matter.

I went back to the village and told Inchbold that Sonia wanted nothing.

'She's convinced the baby isn't his.'

'That makes no difference. He should be made to pay for abusing his position.'

'You can't say he's ruined her life. I've never seen her so happy.'

'Aren't all mothers with a newborn happy, and does it always last?'

'With a first newborn, perhaps. But if you mean it's too early to tell if she has ruined her life, it probably is.'

When I was a child, Jamie used to make me kites with the pieces of fabric Mr Mifsud had cast aside in the cutting-out of suits and shirts. He sewed these together into a kite shape and Ma drew a bird's eye or a bird's wing or a feather on to the patches of white fabric in black ink, so the finished kite had the appearance of a suit jacket with parts of a bird peeping out through the opening. The kites never lasted long but there was always another being fashioned by lamplight in the dark, idle evenings to replace the one we would shortly lose to the wind or the rocks and bushes, or to the apes. Nineteen forty-four was like standing on top of the Rock again, watching one of these precious, fragile constructions soar and swoop and promise to hold aloft all the hope and love that had gone into making it, only for the wind to veer and drop and what had for one moment seemed to be the embodiment of a dream to reveal itself to be no more than a tangle of sticks and torn scraps.

In April, my spirits soared with the joy of knowing that Sonia and her baby were safe and well, that Conchita and the children were home, that the war, whatever Inchbold said, was edging towards an end. If I felt, at the same time, abandoned, this was just a downward dip in the prevailing, upward current of warm air. Then, in June, a new sort of bomb began to fall on London. By July, the Royal Palace Hotel, where Sonia and Marco had found a room, had been emptied. The people with power over us in London had declared the capital was no longer safe; the people with power over us in Gibraltar had declared there was no room for us there. The result, with almost no notice, was that the population of a place that had held a community of my friends and neighbours had been packed into ships and sent to camps in Northern Ireland. Among them, Eugenia, her two children and the unborn child conceived when Humbert had taken advantage of a scheme to allow men from the Rock to visit their wives.

Eugenia wrote to me from County Antrim in despair. The camp was brutal, after the hotel in London. She was again sharing a tiny space with another family she did not know well, and the lovely park where the children had played had been replaced by an empty field. I could not reach out to her, this time, as I had in Morocco and in London, to offer her a better alternative. There was no better alternative; her best chance of being able to return home was to be part of the pot from which the authorities would draw up lists of names as places to live and ways to reach them became available. I wrote to Mrs Almondsbury instead. Was there anything she could do to lift Eugenia's name to the top of these lists, so her unborn child could be born in Gibraltar? I felt guilty asking this; I was using such influence as I had to manipulate a better outcome for Eugenia at the expense, perhaps, of another family, equally deserving. I was asking for what might be an injustice to be visited on one person because I had chosen to help another. But Mrs Almondsbury wrote back to say she had enquired and Eugenia's name was already near the top of the list. In time, I had a letter from Eugenia announcing the birth of Brenda Gatt, in Gibraltar.

Sonia was not on any list as an evacuee, and the machinery that swiftly scooped up the other residents of the hotel and spat them out in Northern Ireland did not detect her presence. It passed over her and left her homeless, the doors of the hotel shut behind her. She telephoned Pool House. Inchbold showed no hesitation in agreeing to help. Once again I met her at the station, her old suitcase at her feet. Only this time she also had Marco, asleep in a shawl tied round her chest, and Amos was waiting with the car to take us back to the village. Even now, she was happy. She had only to look down for her world to narrow to the scope of Marco's dark lashes lying on his flushed cheek, and nothing else mattered.

It was bad timing, for Inchbold and me. Our painstaking work on the book was nearly over, but not complete. The last few hurdles to jump were the most tedious: check every date, every spelling of every name, make a final decision on whether to leave a word, a sentence or a paragraph in, or take it out. There was nothing creative in this. We had instructions from the publisher to add nothing. It made Inchbold angry to find he could not remould his creation, only polish it. I had to cope with both the tedium of the task and the lack of companionship in carrying it out. We both knew we had to keep pushing on, or the whole enterprise, and we with it, would slide into a pit of inertia from which we and it might never be able to climb out. Sonia was a distraction we did not need.

We were rescued by Sir William Bland. He had proved a good friend to Inchbold during these months. He had ridden over once a week, claiming the horse needed the exercise and he had nowhere else to go that was as peaceful as Pool House. He would drink a cup of tea and talk about every topic except the book, disagreeing with Inchbold on almost everything – how long the war would last, the government's handling of rationing, the need for continuing the blackout, the usefulness of the Home Guard, even the best alternative to bacon. I appreciated Sir William's kindness in drawing Inchbold into arguments on topics which neither of them knew anything about, beyond what they read in the newspapers, and which, with the exception of the first, mattered to them very little.

He came when Sonia had been staying with us for two or three days and I was pegging out the quantities of laundry that she and Marco created.

'Here's our young friend!' he said, walking past me on the way from the yard where he left the horse. 'Good morning!'

He never used my name and rarely a pronoun when speaking to or about me. I was always 'our young friend'. He gave the impression of having stumbled, in the recent past, and being anxious to avoid obstacles that might trip him up again.

Inchbold brought him down to meet Sonia, later. We were sitting on a bench with Greta, outside the kitchen door. Sonia was singing songs to Marco, the songs her mother had sung to her. He was at the age when his eyes could focus and hold on to what was close to him, and his smiles were bountiful. All three of us sat smiling fondly back at him. Greta was embarrassed to have been caught in idleness and stood up at once, whisked through the open door. Sonia straightened her clothing, tugged her skirt over her knees.

'Sir William wants to meet you,' Inchbold said.

'Yes,' said Sir William, tasting the word to see if it was fit for purpose.

We walked round the orchard; I held Inchbold's arm, as I was in the habit of doing when we walked, though he knew the position of all the trees. Sir William and Sonia walked together and he asked her questions about Marco, first, then about herself and Guido. Sonia soon relaxed, with her baby in her arms and the sun on her bare legs and a diffident stranger showing interest in her, and she sparkled. I hoped Inchbold noticed the sparkle. I wanted him to understand why I loved her.

Sir William had a need, or had been persuaded by Inchbold that he had a need, for a man to help in the stables and grounds. His mother, who lived with him and was not well, would enjoy the occasional company of a young woman to sit with her and read to her. There were rooms they could have to live in. This was not all agreed that first afternoon, but within a few days the decision had been made. It was another two weeks before everything was in place. Sir William was a godly man and, while he would not condemn Sonia for having an illegitimate child, he could not allow her to live with a man who was not her husband, on his property. The authorities responsible for Guido had to approve his release from their care and sanction his marriage. The marriage had to take place.

Sonia's wedding was in London, at the church where Marco was christened, and where her friends from the Shelter and any Gibraltarians left behind in the capital could join her. Which they did. The church was full and there was dancing, afterwards, in the hall at the Shelter where the jumble sales were held, the tables and any bags and boxes left over from the last event pushed to the side to make room. A fiddler from Czechoslovakia played the tunes he knew and the wedding guests adapted the dance steps they knew to the unfamiliar music. Marco was passed from lap to lap and made much of, until he wearied of the variety and became fractious and Sonia stopped dancing mid-step and scooped him up, caught Guido's eye, and the three of them slipped away to the room Winifred had set aside for them for the night.

Inchbold's wedding present was the dress Sonia wore, pale-green silk embroidered with pink rosebuds. He had offered whatever we could find in the trunks in the attic and this dress had been Sonia's choice. He had fingered the hem with its raised stitchwork and said he remembered it. It was his mother's. It was a dress she had worn for occasions of celebration, and they had never been a family with many such occasions, so he had seen it only two or three times but had retained an image of it, and her in it.

'I'm glad you chose this dress,' he said.

He did not come to the wedding. I described it to him when I got back and he said:

'I might have enjoyed the dancing. It's a long time since I danced.'

We were sitting in the music room, where I had come to find him.

'There's room to dance here,' I said. 'I'll wind the gramophone.'

I put on a waltz tune and touched his arm. He stood up

slowly and held my hands without moving until the music, or the silence beneath the music, reminded him he knew how to do this, and he put his arms round me, and we waltzed.

At first he moved stiffly, not sure how soon, in this unfamiliar motion, he would come up to the nearest wall or piece of furniture. And I was stiff, too, noticing how our bodies fitted together, how different was the sensation of closeness – the smell, the texture of him – when we were face to face instead of arm in arm. Then we both relaxed into the movement of the dance. We both danced well. We danced well together.

The ending of the war was like its beginning, not in doubt but not yet happening. At the start of 1940 we were officially at war but the war had not begun. At the end of 1944 the war was won but not yet over. But the book was finished. On the morning after it had been sent off in its final form, I woke up unsure what the pattern of the day would be. What was there to do? It was early September and the days were still warm, and I thought I would ask Greta for a picnic and suggest to Inchbold that we went out for the day, walking further than we usually did, or going just as far as usual but sitting on the riverbank with our sandwiches and ginger beer, doing nothing in particular.

When I went downstairs, Inchbold had already gone out.

'Don't ask me where,' Greta said. 'Took his stick and said he'd be back when he was tired.'

I thought about going after him, but I didn't know which way he had gone. And he did not want me. He never went beyond the edges of Easterbrook without me, so if he had set off alone, it was a deliberate decision. I was a little hurt; this first day of life without the book in it belonged to us both. Then, as the day wore on, I became worried. He was well known in the neighbourhood and anyone seeing him far from home would offer to guide him back. But he could have wandered far from home and ended up in a place where there were no passers-by to notice him.

After lunch I took the bicycle and pedalled along all the lanes and tracks he might have taken. I asked everyone I met if they had seen him and no one had. Some of the comments they made were hurtful, when I took them out and examined them later ('Done a runner, eh?'; 'Got away from you, has he?'), but at the time I was thinking only of Inchbold and I did not care if I was giving the village food for gossip. I looked in the church and the graveyard in case he had gone only so far and then sat down in a hidden place, thinking, while the clock ticked on. I set off a second time up and down the same lanes and tracks and I almost missed him in my desperate rush to go as far, as fast as I could. He was sitting on a bank with his feet in a ditch, obscured by the beech trees overhead, his tweedy jacket merging with the moss and ferns at his back. I dropped the bike and ran over to him.

'Rose,' he said. Not a question.

He was smeared with mud: face, hands, clothes. His trousers were torn and a scratch on his cheek had bled down into his shirt collar. He looked exhausted.

'Are you tired yet?'

'What?'

'You told Greta you'd come back when you were tired.'

'You're angry with me,' he said, and smiled.

'I have wasted a lot of energy cycling about looking for you.'

'It wasn't wasted, though, was it, because you found me. I needed you to find me. I don't know where I am. And I am tired.'

I helped him up and we walked the three miles back to the village, each holding one side of the bike's handlebars.

The next morning he was sitting at his desk in the library as usual. He had one of the crates of papers in front of him.

'We have to have a programme of work, Rose, or we will run mad. Or I will run mad and you will run after me, like the good girl you are, and we will tumble over the cliff together.'

'I agree. What should we do?'

'I am going to sort through everything in this room that is written in Braille and do something with it. Throw it away, or label and file it, or see if it leads me to another story I want to tell.'

'And I will go through everything not in Braille and you will tell me which of those categories to put it in.'

I was excited at the idea. Having grown up in cramped spaces, it distressed me to think how much of the floor of this room was rendered unusable by boxes and files, even though there was no pressing alternative use to which it could be put. I had also been full of fear that the outcome of the thinking he did on that long, exhausting walk was a realization that he had no further use for me.

'Yes,' he said, 'but that is less important than the work you should be doing. Writing the story of your journey here. You must start that now.'

'I am to write while you shuffle papers?'

'What's wrong with that? I want to read your story.'

'Why?'

'To find out what the end is.'

I am near the end of the story now and I still do not know the answer to that.

33

Correspondence

There were a few days when Inchbold became frustrated with the tedium of his task. One day he became, for the first time, angry with me. I had begun writing and the clatter of the typewriter, he said, drove him to distraction. I will stop, I said. I don't want you to, he said. He would leave me to it and go out for a walk alone. I don't want you to, I said. And he began to shout at me. Life was hard enough without the interference of a woman who had no business interfering. He insisted on doing what he wanted to do, today or any other day. He was not my responsibility any more than I was his. If he chose to go out and die in a ditch, then, God help him, he would. Heaven only knew how often he had thought there was no better solution to the horror that was living as he did.

He picked up his stick and went out, taking his hat and coat from the stand in the hall and slamming the door behind him. I followed, of course, and he knew I would, because after an hour he stopped, felt around with his stick for somewhere to sit down and, finding nothing, leaned on a gate waiting for me to come up to him.

'Everything I said to you was false,' he said.

'Including the desire to die in a ditch?'

'That as well, though it is all I deserve.'

Greta had heard him shouting and was ready to express her outrage on my behalf, but I refused to acknowledge any hurt.

'Have it your own way,' she said; then, under her breath, 'you always do.'

The next day I found him stroking the Braille label on the outside of a polished wooden box with brass corners and a pretty brass inlay round the lock. I had never seen it before.

'My mother's letters,' he said. 'At least, I believe so, I was told so, and I labelled the box and put it away in my room because I did not want anyone to read them.'

'Do you want to read them?'

'I'm not sure. She never really belonged to us, my brother, my father and me. It would seem particularly intrusive.'

'If she didn't destroy them, perhaps she hoped you would read them, after she was gone.'

'She gave me the box, and told me what it was, and she didn't ask me to destroy them. So perhaps she did. Or perhaps she wanted to die knowing they still existed, so she gave them to the one person who would never be able to read them.'

'Shall I catalogue them? Make you a list of what is there, who they are from and to, and the dates. I can do that without reading them.'

The box was packed with envelopes of several different colours and sizes, tied up into bundles. Most of the bundles were of one colour but one of the smallest was a mixture of blue, buff, white and brown. I started with this one, and it was letters to his mother from Inchbold's father, from Inchbold himself and from his brother. I read out one or two of his own and his brother's letters and he laughed at the childish obsessions they revealed. He remembered writing some of them, and had an idea of what the response had been, but the replies were all lost. Schoolboys have no notion that they may one day wish to reread the letters their mother sends promising a certain cake for when they come home, or letting them know the cat has had eight kittens, all black.

The smallest bundle was letters from her parents to Evelyn Inchbold, written after her marriage and spread out, one a month or less. Inchbold asked me to read a few of those, too, and I stumbled over some of the words her parents had used – 'propriety', 'acquiesce' – not only because they were unfamiliar but because they seemed, from what I could gather of the meaning, harsh words for parents to use to a child, at whatever age.

'I never met my grandparents,' Inchbold said. 'It sounds as if I should be grateful for that.'

Most of the letters, tied in larger bundles, were both sides of a correspondence between Evelyn and her lover, Tom. These covered almost the whole of Evelyn's adult life, even though they had rarely been apart. Many were single sheets, with only a sentence or two on them. Notes. As if, when they were out of earshot of each other for an hour, they could not bear to stop talking.

'Do you want to read these?' I said.

'How can I tell without reading them? But if Mother left the letters on purpose, it must have been these she meant me to read.'

'I'll type them up in Braille. I'll try my best not to read them as I do it.'

So we ended up in a new rhythm, as the war, like a beached whale, kept causing damage when the outcome was in no possible doubt. In the afternoons, when Inchbold was in the music room, playing the piano or listening to the gramophone and reading, I would type up his mother's correspondence on the Braille-writer. I tried to do this one word at a time, avoiding stringing them together into sentences, not letting their meaning register. But I hoped to be able to revisit them one day and absorb everything these women had said to each other over the years. There was boundless tenderness in it, and wisdom, and wit.

In the mornings, Inchbold read those letters and began to take notes, for a project he had not yet defined. I worked on the words that have turned into this book. We worked alongside each other without interruption until eleven o'clock, when we had a break, signalled by the chiming of the clock in the library and its echo from those in the hall and the dining room. Then I would go down to fetch a pot of tea, biscuits, and the post, and Inchbold would raise all the queries he had saved up. Could I check I had transcribed this phrase correctly? Could I look up this word in the dictionary?

It was a cold, cold winter and the work involved in carrying coals up to both the music room and the library was too much, Inchbold declared, so we began to spend all our days together, snug in the library, the typewriter or the Braille-writer chattering away, with breaks when Inchbold was reading and I was using paper and pencil to order my thoughts. Then the only sound was the coal cracking in the grate, the whisper of Inchbold's fingers moving over the dots on the page, the rub of our clothing as we shifted. I would sometimes sit and watch Inchbold during these lulls; he did not know I was doing this and I knew it was a form of deception, that I was letting him believe I was concentrating on my work when I was concentrating on him. I am confessing it here. By watching him, I came to know him. He ceased to be alien, to be Major Edward St. John Inchbold, an educated, wealthy blind man, a different species to me, and became simply Inchbold, friend, colleague and someone dear to me.

The letters I brought up with the tea and biscuits were mostly for Inchbold, from friends and relatives but also business correspondence. I opened all this and read it to him and wrote back, to his dictation, when this was required. He was mildly interested in, or indifferent to, the letters he received; none of it mattered to him very much and he did not care when the snow fell or a train was derailed and there was a gap of a few days before the post reached us. My correspondence was from friends and relatives and I looked forward to it all, treasured it, worried when it was interrupted, was cast down or buoyed up by the news from home or from London. But I never received business letters, so when a brown envelope arrived as winter faded into spring, I assumed it was for Inchbold and opened it without checking the name that came before the address. I had started reading it aloud before I realized my mistake.

It was from the Colonial Office and I had said as much by the time I reached the phrase: 'Dear Miss Dunbar'.

'Oh!' I said. 'I think this is for me.' But it was too late to avoid telling Inchbold what it said.

It was asking whether I wished to continue to be considered an evacuee, or if I had made permanent arrangements to stay in Britain. If I wanted to return to Gibraltar, I should complete the form attached and send it back to them so my name could be added to those eligible for transportation. The room had never before been so silent. Even the coal in the grate seemed to be holding its breath.

I had always known this would come to an end. The book was finished and with it my role in the house, and in Inchbold's life. We were pretending it was not so, inventing tasks for ourselves, but it was over. The time in Pool House had been fulfilling in a way I had never been able to picture when I was rejecting Peter Povedano's offer of marriage in favour of a future that was in some indefinable way better. I had found that future, but I had known it would not be permanent. The letter in my hand was the full stop; the instruction, as I read it, to pack up and go home had come.

At last Inchbold said: 'Would you have told me of this letter if you hadn't let it slip by mistake?'

'Maybe. Maybe not.'

'I can't bear it that you can keep secrets from me but I can have no secrets from you.'

He was working himself up into a fury and I did not think that would help us.

'Inchbold,' I said. 'Stop it. You can't know what I would have done because I don't know. I want to go home and I don't want to leave. Now apply your logic to that and tell me how I can arrive at a decision.'

'Come here,' he said. 'Come here where I can hold you and touch your face so I will know what you are feeling as we talk. We need to talk.'

We talked. You and I. Through the afternoon and during the days that followed. You said, with all the tenderness of your mother talking to her lover, that you wanted to keep me with you always, as more than a secretary, or whatever I had been, because secretary was too harsh and ugly a word for the place I had occupied in your life, and though amanuensis was a softer, prettier word, it still didn't sound as good as the Anglo-Saxon monosyllable: wife.

We argued this with one another as we abandoned our industry in favour of long walks and endless hours sitting close together by the fire. Because I wanted you to understand what an extraordinary offer you were making, I pointed out how far outside your own class of society this would put you, quoted the Cap's nasty words and the gossipy sneers the village was already bandying about. And because you were quite sure what you wanted, you said that you were well placed to ignore the view of others, and could not care less. You would trade the whole airy cattle shed of the county for a chicken coop with just the two of us inside it.

Then, because you are a fair man, you pointed out that you are nearly twenty years older than I am and it would be wrong for me to confine myself to a coop in which I would have to live, alone, for two decades after your death. Because I knew what was entirely irrelevant in making the decision, I reminded you your mother had been close to eighty when she died. Mine had gone when she was not yet sixty. Date of birth did not necessarily predict date of death, and to allow one's choices to be dictated by the assumption of this date would be to waste the years before it occurred.

Then you said, 'And I am blind.' And I laughed. I told you about the conversation I had had with Peter Povedano, when he had withdrawn his suggestion of immediate or committed future marriage on the basis that he might be crippled in the fighting and I would have tied myself to a lifetime of care. I could imagine what a burden a man like Peter – a man who lived to work and would be unable to find anything to replace it, if he could do it no longer – would be if he were disabled.

Your disability, like the age gap, was part of the man I knew and it did not occur to me to link the word 'burden' to it.

Because I knew what it felt like to live somewhere I did not belong, I said I was concerned with the way society would view me, if we decided to take this step, even if you were not concerned with how it would view you. I could picture the awkwardness of the Uppinghams and the other families who had thought they understood my position. The level of condescension they would show, if they decided to recognize me as Mrs Inchbold, would be hard to bear. But I would have to bear it, or drop out of village life entirely, because the class I belonged to, the young men I danced with in the village hall and the girls who let me into their conversations about which shop had supplies of silk stockings, would no longer admit me. I knew, also, that the men of Easterbrook, the society women's husbands, would look at me and wonder whether they might have had a chance, if they had been bold enough, because surely I would not have expected marriage? And I would see this thought in the way they looked at me, if not in what they said. This last point I did not say to you at the time, knowing it would make you angry to imagine men you could not see behaving in this way. I am putting it in here because I know you like to know everything. (That is why the book took so long to finish.) So I am making it available to you to read.

'We could move,' you said, and I could see the pain it cost you even to utter such a thought aloud. You could not move because Pool House was your home, as Gibraltar was mine. One of us would have to accept a future in a foreign land. And I knew that would be me. I would have to go back, to measure what I would be giving up against what I would be gaining.

So we agreed. I wrote back to the Colonial Office saying I did not want to be repatriated in the immediate future, and I understood that, in saying this, I was accepting that if I wanted to return later, I would need to pay my own passage. I wrote to my family saying I was committed to a project I was working on with you, but would return for a visit when peace was declared. In the meantime, as the days became warmer and war lurched towards the finish line, we carried on as before. More or less. Greta and Amos knew what had changed between us. No one else.

Now. It is September. It is warm, up here at Princess Caroline's Battery, where I am sitting on a rock looking out over the bay at Algeciras in the distance; in the foreground, construction work, building homes for returning families. I am writing these last pages with a pencil as I have no typewriter here. When I have spent enough time with the people whose love and happiness are important to me, and have visited all the places on the Rock that hold memories I treasure, I will book a passage on a ship – I can see one now, leaving the harbour, heading west towards Cádiz and the Bay of Biscay – and go back to Easterbrook, where I will re-create these words, from the first to the last, in Braille. I will give them to you to read. Then, I believe, I will know the ending. And so will you.

Author's Note

I am indebted to the BBC's 'WW2 People's War' online archive
(www.bbc.co.uk/history/ww2peopleswar/) for the inspiration
for this novel. I was looking for ideas for short stories when I
came across a reference to Gibraltar, and a story too big to be
told in a few pages: the evacuation of the entire civilian population. I looked for other sources and found that the experience
these families – mainly women and children – went through
was extraordinary. All those involved faced challenges to their
understanding of where they belonged, geographically and cul-
turally. It is an enormous credit to the spirit and resilience of
the people of Gibraltar that they retained and strengthened
their sense of identity, and made sure the record of what happened to them was not lost. It is recorded through first-hand
accounts in *We Thank God and England* by Joe Gingell, and
through the meticulous historical research of T. J. Finlayson in
The Fortress Came First. I have used both of these to ensure the
details of Rose's journey, the dates, transport and accommodation, are accurate. This is a work of fiction; I have created Rose
and her family and the people she travels with and meets along
the way as a means of exploring the impact of the displacement
and alienation, the disruption and alternative choices for the

future that the evacuees faced. I have made Rose an oddity, someone who does not fit, and I hope this will excuse the ways in which a Gibraltarian reader would find her alien.

Gibraltar played an important part in the Second World War, and this is well documented. I relied on *Defending the Rock* by Nicholas Rankin to provide the background. *Convoy Commodore* by Rear Admiral Sir Kenneth Creighton gives a detailed account of the deportation from Morocco. I am also grateful to Dr Jennifer Ballantine Pereira and Chris Tavares of the Garrison Library in Gibraltar for access to their newspaper archive. For a background to London in the Blitz, I owe a debt of gratitude to the wonderful Persephone Books, who have reissued *London War Notes* by Mollie Panter-Downes, and *Few Eggs and No Oranges: The Diaries of Vere Hodgson, 1940–45*. I have included a character based on Miss Hodgson as a tribute. The incident with the sinking of the SS *Aguila* is covered in *A Game of Birds and Wolves* by Simon Parkin.

I am privileged to have met and talked to Mrs Marie de Lourdes Ollive, who lived through this experience and retold it with humour and the sharpest of observations. I am sorry she did not live to see my version of it published.

I am, as always, thankful to have a team of professionals on my side in bringing the book to market, in particular Judith Murray, Kate Rizzo, Jane Lawson, Alison Barrow, Hayley Barnes and Kate Samano. My early readers, Fiona Clarke, Rebecca Mackay and Felicity Zeigler, were encouraging but also immensely helpful.

Anne Youngson's debut novel *Meet Me at the Museum* was shortlisted for the Costa Best First Novel Award and won the inaugural Paul Torday Memorial Prize for debut fiction by writers over sixty. Her second novel, *Three Women and a Boat*, was a BBC Radio 2 Book Club pick. *A Complicated Matter* is her first historical novel and was inspired by an episode of *From the Archives* on BBC Radio 4. She has had a successful career in product development with Land Rover before turning her hand to a writing career. She lives in Oxfordshire and is married with two children and four grandchildren.

MEET ME AT THE MUSEUM
Anne Youngson

When Tina Hopgood, housewife and mother, writes a letter of regret to a man she has never met, she doesn't expect a reply.

When Anders Larsen, a lonely museum curator, answers it, neither does he.

Tina and Anders are searching for something – they just don't know it yet.

As they bare their souls to each other, stories of joy, anguish and discovery pour out of them. Suddenly Tina stops writing, and Anders is thrown into despair.

Can their unexpected friendship survive?

In this deep and luminous novel of self-discovery and second chances, Anne Youngson polishes the everyday until it gleams.

'Full of grace and humanity' *SUNDAY TIMES*

'Gentle and joyous' *GUARDIAN*

'A beautiful novel of late love' NINA STIBBE

THREE WOMEN AND A BOAT
Anne Youngson

Meet **Eve**, who has departed from her thirty-year career to become a Free Spirit; **Sally**, who has waved goodbye to her indifferent husband and two grown-up children; and **Anastasia**: defiantly independent narrowboat-dweller, suddenly vulnerable as she awaits a life-saving operation.

Inexperienced and ill-equipped, Sally and Eve embark upon a journey through the canals of England, guided by the remote and unsympathetic Anastasia. As they glide gently – and not so gently – through the countryside, the eccentricities and challenges of canalboat life draw them inexorably together.

Disarmingly truthful and narrated with a rare wit, THREE WOMEN AND A BOAT is a journey through the glorious waterways of England and into the unfathomable depths of the human heart.

'A meander down England's waterways. Bittersweet and charming' *MAIL ON SUNDAY*

'A tender story of friendship' *WOMAN'S WEEKLY*

THE SIX WHO CAME TO DINNER
Anne Youngson

Six short stories full of colourful suspects and complicated motives by the winner of the Paul Torday Memorial Prize for debut authors over sixty – perfect for fans of grisly mysteries set in the English countryside.

The village cleaning lady who holds everyone's house-keys opens a boot to find some unexpected baggage; a vengeful dinner-party host serves more than just a roast to her six guests; driven to distraction by his young new wife, a man resorts to two grisly acts, in a gripping reimagining of a famous Irish ballad.

Ripping away the polite façade of small communities, these tales of love, lies and revenge reveal the roiling emotions and frustrations that can drive seemingly good people to do bad things. Rich in compassion, pathos and delicious humour, Anne Youngson's dark take on human foibles is utterly unputdownable.

'An extraordinary new writer' NINA STIBBE